LINKAG

The Narrows of Ti

Book 1

Written By Jay J. Falconer
www.JayFalconer.com

Published 2011, 2014, 2016 by BookBreeze.com LLC
ISBN-13: 978-0-9840011-8-7
ISBN-10: 0-9840011-8-2

April 17, 2016 Edition

This is a work of fiction. Names, characters, places, and incidents are the product of the author's imagination or are used fictitiously. Any resemblance to actual persons living or dead, or business establishments or organizations, actual events or locales is entirely coincidental.

BOOKS BY JAY J. FALCONER

Frozen World Series
Silo: Summer's End
Silo: Hope's Return
Silo: Nomad's Revenge

American Prepper Series
Lethal Rain Book 1
Lethal Rain Book 2
Lethal Rain Book 3 (Coming Soon)
(previously published as *REDFALL*)

Mission Critical Series
Bunker: Born to Fight
Bunker: Dogs of War
Bunker: Code of Honor
Bunker: Lock and Load
Bunker: Zero Hour

Narrows of Time Series
Linkage
Incursion
Reversion

Time Jumper Series
Shadow Games
Shadow Prey
Shadow Justice
(previously published as *GLASSFORD GIRL*)

1
Friday, December 21
Tucson, Arizona

"Reckless. Undisciplined. Arrogant," were the words Dr. Green posted to describe Lucas Ramsay's thesis in the online science magazine called *Astrophysics Today*.

Lucas couldn't help but stare at those twenty-nine letters filling the screen space on his aging laptop. The display was covered in lingering dust, with scratches spreading across its surface. Every time he opened the unit, it seemed like they were multiplying in the dark.

The screen looked like he felt—tired and worn out from years of abuse. But regardless, the marred surface didn't obscure the words making his stomach ache and churn. He wanted to close the laptop and forget he ever saw the article, but he couldn't. His career was now circling the black hole of ruin and he knew there'd be no escape.

He sat on the edge of his bed in the apartment he shared with his foster brother Drew, wondering if life could get any worse. He ran his bare feet across the tile floor, letting the coldness penetrate the skin. The drab green Army surplus blanket scratched at his thighs, so he tossed it aside, making a clear path for the chilly Tucson air to surround him. The burn of his senses was welcomed; he figured it would help etch this moment in his mind for all of eternity.

Life was about to take a wicked turn south now that his public disgrace was official. He needed to remember how he got here and why—the exact moment when history changed and swallowed him alive.

He looked down at the laptop, seeing Dr. Green's summary staring back at him with vicious intent. He closed his eyes and took a deep breath, hoping the words would magically disappear when he brought his attention back to the screen.

Lucas counted to ten, then opened his eyes.

They were still there—bold and harsh, not like any words he'd read before. Sure, he'd enjoyed plenty of scathing reviews of scientific papers before, but never one aimed squarely at him.

Dr. Green had a knack for tearing theories apart with a few choice phrases. The man's reputation as a self-righteous prima donna was legendary. So was his literary temper. The retired eighty-year-old physicist was revered as a god in the realm of theoretical physics. His words alone could spark endless research grants and guarantee immortality in the annals of science. Or they could be used to kill a career.

Like mine, Lucas thought, knowing his humiliation had gone global, coursing through cyberspace like a malevolent force hell-bent on global annihilation.

Until a minute ago, Lucas had been proud of his thesis titled "The Laws of Physics Are Merely a Suggestion." He thought it was a brilliant take on inter-dimensional connectivity theory. True, his paper on quantum linkage stretched the envelope a bit, challenging mainstream science at every turn, but the work was sound and he could prove it. All he wanted was a chance to be part of the conversation.

Of course, now that the senior editor had shit all over it, no respected scientist on the planet would consider it, not without reaping the whirlwind that was Dr. Green.

Lucas' heart sank. The glimmer of respect he'd worked painstakingly to build during his first two years as a physicist was now being swallowed by an ever-expanding digital black hole. A gnawing sensation was building in the pit of his stomach, somewhere between nausea and hunger.

There was simply no way to recover from a debacle of this magnitude. Not after the world's most famous physicist called your theories "pure speculation founded on nothing more than adolescent fantasy," and then blasted it across the Internet for all to see.

He closed his eyes again for another ten count, trying to untangle the knot swelling in his gut. It was useless. The knot grew unchecked. The only way to change things would be to travel back in time and stop himself from pressing that damned SEND button on the keyboard. All it took was one snap decision made in the wee hours of a brisk December morning to ruin everything. What the hell had he been thinking? He wasn't ready. Neither were his theories. He should've known this would happen.

He groaned, chastising himself for being impulsive and undisciplined. His foolish arrogance would now harm not only him, but his family, too.

He let out a slow exhale, then shut the laptop quietly, trying not to wake his foster brother sleeping in the bed across from him. It seemed to work. There was no sign of movement from under the pile of covers. Just the usual rumble of disjointed snoring.

Drew was a noisy sleeper but Lucas had gotten used to it over the years. Others might complain or walk away, but he didn't. He had no choice, really—you never give up on family. Or maybe it was that he didn't want to have a choice, since Drew was one of the few good things in his life. Lucas would never walk away from the one person he trusted above all others. The one person who always had his back, no matter what came gunning for them.

Sometimes in the middle of the night, he'd lie in bed and just listen. The rhythm of Drew's night sounds was comforting, finding its way across the room and landing softly on the petals of his heart. The snoring had become a soothing reassurance in an otherwise chaotic world. Knowing his brother was nestled safely in the bed across the room was a constant reminder that all would be right again in the morning, as long as the two of them stuck together.

Lucas unplugged the laptop from the wall socket and put the thin-profile device on the floor next to the bed. He slid his body under the edge of the covers, hoping to catch another ten minutes of shuteye. Maybe his stomach pain would subside if he lay still enough and let the thoughts of disgrace melt away against the backdrop of Drew's breathing.

A split second later, he felt something crawl across his shin and down the inside of his right calf. "Holy shit!" he screamed, tossing off the covers.

A brown scorpion the size of a hockey puck sat on the sheet, with its venomous stinger arched high above its back. It had crawled into his bed, searching for prey.

Lucas grabbed one of the sneakers from the nightstand between the twin double beds and smashed the creature with such force that he jammed his right wrist, but the four-inch beast was still alive and coming his way.

"Die, you bastard!" he shouted, whacking the invader three more times, until its front claws, stinger, and eight legs stopped moving. He hated the stealthy night crawlers almost as much as his adoptive father did, and would've gladly used a bazooka to kill it.

"Geeze, Lucas. Did he owe you money or something?" Drew asked, sitting up in his bed. He used the tip of his index finger to pry the sleeper crust from the corners of his watery Italian eyes. His curly hair was flat on one side after pressing against the pillow all night. Some of it had fallen forward, covering his forehead and one eye. His olive skin was usually perfectly smooth, but right now it was covered in temporary wrinkles, matching the creases in the pillowcase.

"Sorry, bro. I didn't mean to wake you up."

"You didn't. I was awake already," Drew said, yawning and stretching, which showed off his stout chest and thickly muscled arms. If it weren't for the car accident that crushed his legs, he could've easily passed for a collegiate athlete, or maybe even a pro.

"Anyway, sorry about that. Not like I had much of a choice. Look at the size of this thing," Lucas said, using the cardboard backing from one of his notebooks to scoop the carcass into a plastic cup. "You'd think we'd be safe on the third floor."

"Not with the way those things can climb. They're relentless."

"I'd give anything to have a few of Dad's sonic pads to spread around. Those things worked perfectly," Lucas said, thinking about his father and the device he'd designed specifically to deal with scorpions. "If it wasn't for the damn EPA, every house in Arizona would have them by now. And we'd probably be rich."

"Yeah, all he needed was another chance."

Lucas carried the remains to the bathroom and dumped the creature into the bottom of the toilet and gave it a middle-finger salute. He saw a two-inch black cockroach lying on its back next to the tub, with one set of legs still kicking. It crunched louder than he expected when he stepped on it with the heel of his left foot. He used a Kleenex to pick it up and toss it into the toilet and used the same sheet of tissue to wipe the creature's runny blood and guts from his foot.

"And we wouldn't be living in this dump either. We'd have a big house with plenty of room for Mom," he said loud enough for Drew to hear in the next room.

"Still, you can't beat the price."

"Maybe so, but that's beside the point. We wouldn't need free rent if they hadn't killed his invention," Lucas yelled, flushing the john to send the pair of mangled carcasses swirling around the bowl and into the sewer. He emptied the toilet a second time for good measure before returning to the bedroom.

He took a seat on his bed across from Drew and continued, "He could've solved the problem with the dogs. But no . . . all it took was one scathing report from the EPA and the investors go running for the hills. Don't they know science is all about trial and error? Bunch of wimps. All Dad needed was a little more time. He would've worked out the bugs. No pun intended."

Drew nodded. "Sometimes, all someone needs is a second chance."

"You got that right, brother," Lucas said, moving Drew's wheelchair closer to the bed. He waited for him to slide his frail legs over the edge and onto the floor. "Need any help?" he asked, already knowing the answer.

"No, I got it. Just give me a minute."

Drew used a handlebar hanging from the ceiling to prop himself up against the side of the raised bed. He was able to stand for short periods, but couldn't walk, at least not without assistance. He turned around and sat in the wheelchair, then looked at the floor. "What were you doing with the laptop?"

Lucas paused, taking a moment to think. "Nothing. I woke up early and couldn't sleep, so I was just reading Dr. Green's blog. Checking out the new submissions and his reviews, You know, to kill some time."

"Anything interesting today?" Drew asked, bending down to get the computer.

Lucas grabbed it, holding it out of reach. "Just the usual half-baked theories submitted by wannabe scientists. Nothing nearly as cool as what we're working on in our lab."

Drew sat upright in his chair. "Maybe someday we'll publish one of our theories on that website. Then we'll be as famous as Dr. Green."

"No thanks. It's better to stay off the grid. Remain anonymous. Prehistoric dinosaurs like Green steal people's ideas all the time and cash in. The shitty thing is, people like us can't do a thing about it. After all, it would be his word against ours, and who are we? Right now, we're nobodies. You don't even have your doctorate yet, and I'm just starting my career."

"I never thought of it that way," Drew said with a perplexed look on his unshaven face.

Lucas tossed the laptop to the farthest corner of his bed, making sure Drew couldn't reach it easily. "Trust me. You don't want to be famous. It's not all it's cracked up to be. If you ask me, it's best to be the brains behind the scenes, and not the person out front in the limelight."

A shiver ran down Lucas' spine and he wrapped his arms around his rail-thin, nude body—a stark contrast to his foster brother's handsome Mediterranean looks and muscular upper body. Lucas hated his red hair and freckles, but at least he had blue eyes. One redeeming feature at least. Well, that and his prominent dimples, something his adoptive mother cherished. However, they didn't do much for his confidence, not with the prominent cheek scars nearby.

He shivered again, inwardly cursing the ancient heating system in their apartment. Most people didn't realize that even in the desert, the nights turned chilly. He walked four steps to the end of the room, where the in-wall HVAC system was installed, and rubbed his hands over the rattling output vents. "Hardly anything coming out of this piece of crap."

"What'd you expect? That thing's probably older than Sputnik."

"Even so, you'd think Kleezebee's Super could find a way to keep this thing working. We could hang meat in here."

Lucas returned and slipped on a pair of navy blue boxers and a long-sleeved faded red t-shirt with ARIZONA printed on the front of it.

Drew pulled out a neatly rolled pair of socks from a custom-built dresser compartment under the bed and tossed it to Lucas. They had raised their mattresses four feet off the ground, using 4x4 redwood posts and birch plywood from their dad's workshop. Storage space was at a premium in their five-hundred-square-foot apartment.

Lucas walked to the study desk to see what yesterday's mail had brought them. Three envelopes were sitting on top of the last pile, face up, with fresh postmarks and no doubt, a swatch of Drew's fingerprints. All three were from someone in the medical field.

"More bills for Mom? Are you kidding me?"

"They keep multiplying," Drew answered, his brow furrowed.

Lucas opened the first envelope and almost puked when his eyes locked onto the invoice's grand total. "Twenty-two grand for three days in urgent care?"

Drew rolled next to Lucas in his wheelchair. "Good thing you had them send the bills here. If Mom finds out, she'll have another heart attack. I doubt she'd survive another one."

Lucas opened a second bill—it was even more. He slammed it onto the pile, face down.

Drew snatched the invoice and looked at it with eyes wide. He gasped. "Fifty-two thousand?"

Lucas gritted his teeth and shook his head. "This day just keeps on getting better. It just never ends."

"You can bet if Mom knew the insurance company was going to deny her claims, she would've just told the attending physician to pull the plug. End it right then and there. How are we gonna pay for all this?"

Lucas sighed as he put his elbows on the desk, resting his face in his hands. He didn't know how much they owed in total, but the figure had to be staggering. He wished he'd told his family the truth—that he'd forgotten to mail the check for his mother's insurance premium, which was why the claims department denied the coverage. But at this point, he was too embarrassed to come clean. He already felt bad enough, and it wouldn't change anything, anyway. It was his problem and he needed to solve it.

His original plan was to pay off the medical bills after he proved one of his revolutionary theories and sold the rights to a defense contractor or to NASA. He hoped submitting his paper to Green would've been the first step toward funding a project of his own. But after Dr. Green's harsh public criticism, he knew nothing short of a miracle could help them now.

"I don't know. We'll think of something."

"We could ask Professor Kleezebee."

"Borrow money from my boss?"

"Why not? He's loaded. Besides, he might just give us the money."

"No. We're not gonna take handouts. Not if I have anything to say about it. We'll figure it out on our own."

Just then, his mind played a vision of him walking into a crowded grocery store with a black ski mask, gun, and brown paper sack, only to be shot dead before he reached the cash register by some Weight Watcher flunky in a wrinkled security guard uniform.

A minute later, Lucas looked at the clock. "Damn, it's almost nine. We'll have to bust nuts if we're going to make breakfast with Trevor."

"Uh, yeah, it's Friday. Knowing Trevor, he's probably already in the cafeteria, waiting for us."

"Which means we're late—again."

"He'll understand. He always does."

"That man has more patience than me," Lucas said.

"Yeah, there's a shock."

Lucas ignored the dig. "I hope he fixed the computer glitch in his code. I want to run a few more system checks tonight in the lab, while we still can. I'm guessing you're not going to do your workout today?"

"No, I'll do my push-ups tomorrow. Besides, I'm pretty sure I'm at DEFCON 1 already. Right Guard only covers up so much."

Lucas' sour mood made it easy to hold back a chuckle, now standing in front of his brother's side of the closet. "What shirt do you want?"

"Come on, that was funny," Drew said, giving Lucas a playful shove.

"Yeah, it was. I'm laughing on the inside; can't you tell?"

"Everything ok, bro?"

Lucas wanted to tell Drew what had happened with Green and the insurance premium check, but he couldn't find the courage to come clean. His brother counted on him to handle everything, and he didn't want to shatter his confidence. "Yeah, I'm fine. Didn't sleep well last night. So, I ask again, what shirt do you want?"

"It doesn't matter. You know, something with long sleeves, as long as it's—"

"Blue. Yep, it's Friday. I should've known," Lucas said, retrieving a pullover shirt from a hanger. He removed it from the red hanger and gave it to his brother. He was careful to put the hanger back in the closet precisely where it had been, exactly two fingers away from the hangers on either side of it.

Drew slipped the shirt over his head.

Lucas handed Drew the wallet-sized leather pouch on the nightstand next to the bed. "Don't forget this."

"No. Never." Drew opened the straps and put them around his head and neck. He tied them together and tucked the pouch inside the front of the collared shirt.

* * *

Lucas and Drew were headed east along one of the sidewalks bordering the landscaped student mall. The entrance to the University of Arizona's Student Union was now only a half a block away, meaning their morning trek was almost complete.

The low angle of the brilliant sunlight cut through the shade trees lining their path, casting a wide array of shapes across the concrete sidewalk. When the gentle breeze rustled the leaves, the changing shadows reminded Lucas of the calculations he and Drew had been working on in the lab all week. For the uninitiated, the endless fractal patterns could've been used as a rudimentary demonstration of subatomic space-time turbulence, also known as quantum foam.

"You can always tell when Christmas break hits. The place empties out the minute finals are over," Lucas said, missing the abundance of stunning eye candy that typically blanketed the mall. Seeing all the girls running around in their skimpy outfits was his favorite part of the day.

"I like it this way," Drew said. "I hate it when I have to dodge everyone on the mall. Those Ultimate Frisbee players always find a way to hit me when I'm crossing."

"That's because you cut right across in the middle of their game."

"That's where the sidewalk is. Why should I have to go all the way around?"

Lucas stood behind Drew as he effortlessly wheeled himself up the steep incline to the building's main entrance. When Drew reached to open the glass entrance door, a tall, gorgeous blond co-ed beat him to it. She was on the inside and held the door open for him, giving Drew a friendly, rainbow smile as he rolled past her.

Lucas couldn't see her eyes through her sunglasses, but the woman's body language suggested she knew his brother, or possibly was attracted to him. She wore a short dark miniskirt and tight t-shirt, despite the cool morning temperature. She had legs for days and a toned figure that could only be the result of plenty of gym time. Sometimes he was jealous of his little brother. It was common for women to be intrigued by Drew's boyishly handsome good looks. If it weren't for a car accident that mangled his legs, Drew surely would've been a world-famous Italian underwear model instead of a PhD candidate.

But on the other hand, Lucas thought, if not for the accident, they never would've met in the orphanage and been adopted together by the Ramsay family. The universe works in mysterious ways. The *multiverse*, he corrected himself.

Before she looked his way, Lucas checked that his shirt was tucked in and his fly was zipped. He rubbed his tongue across the front of his teeth to make sure nothing foreign was attached.

The girl glanced his way and her smile faded. Lucas wasn't surprised. Women didn't always go for the jagged scars on his face. He thought they made him look ruggedly handsome, but that obviously wasn't the case with this chick. Years of living in state-run facilities had taken their toll, leaving him looking more like an Irish gangster than a nerdy scientist.

Despite her reaction, he gave her his best smile and said, "Thanks for your help. It's much appreciated."

The cafeteria line extended outside the entrance and past a pair of vending machines in the hall. Two dozen students were waiting in line before the buffet closed its doors until lunchtime. Most were chatting with each other, but a few were rocking on their heels, listening to headphones.

Lucas recognized the elderly woman walking toward him with a cane and swollen ankles. "Would you like to go ahead of us, Professor Atkins?" he asked her.

She smiled, but her saggy, spotted skin camouflaged most of the grin. "Why, thank you, young man."

Lucas moved his brother aside to let the woman waddle past. It took her a good thirty seconds, giving Lucas plenty of time to sample her aroma: a powerful combination of hairspray and Ben Gay. All she was missing was blue hair and support hose.

Lucas waited for her to move ahead before whispering into Drew's ear, "I wonder if she knew Columbus?"

Drew smiled through a partially held-back laugh, then said, "Maybe one of us should go find Trevor and let him know we're stuck in line."

"I'm assuming that someone is *me*?"

"Wow, that's awfully nice of you, brother. I'll stay here and keep our place in line."

Lucas found their Swedish lab assistant sitting at a table in the back of the dining area, his weightlifting belt and workout clothes still damp with perspiration and clinging to his well-defined physique.

Everyone on campus knew who the imposing blonde figure was—Trevor Johansson, former Olympic wrestler turned scientist, a giant who could block out the sun at six foot seven inches tall. His enormous size rivaled that of a defensive lineman in the NFL—not an old school defensive lineman who was nothing but big and oafish, but one of the freakishly athletic new breed of linemen filling the broadcast screen on Sundays around America. Even his appetite was huge, with four plates sitting in front of him, overflowing with a pile of fruits and vegetables.

"Having a little snack, are we?" Lucas said, using humor to disguise his trepidation around the giant.

Trevor responded, his Swedish accent thick. "*Ja*, hungry. *Vawnt some?*"

"No, thanks. I'm not a big fan of fruit. I'll grab something else."

Each time Trevor put the fork to his mouth, his biceps came alive as the twisted cords of muscle and vein stretched the skin to the point of eruption. Drew was the only other person Lucas knew with arms close to that size.

It wasn't only his arms, though. Everything about Trevor was cut—even his jaw muscles bulged when he chewed. The guy could probably chew rocks.

Trevor opened an issue of *Olympic Coach* magazine and turned to the table of contents. His meaty fingers struggled with the periodical's flimsy paper.

"You're not thinking of leaving us, are you?" Lucas asked, trying to gauge his friend's interest in the sports magazine.

"No. I stay here," Trevor said, flipping to an article with photos of two male wrestlers.

"Are any of your old friends still on the team?"

"*Ja*. They do *vell*. Two gold medals and a silver."

"Do you miss it?"

"*Ja*, very much."

"Did they ever apologize for botching your drug tests?"

Trevor stopped chewing in an instant, then his eyes glazed over and his face went blank. He looked down at his food in silence, not moving a muscle.

Lucas knew he'd just upset his mammoth assistant, putting his foot in his mouth. He'd obviously crossed the line from professional colleague to nosy friend. He scrambled to change the subject. "Uh, did you order your tickets yet for the twenty-fifteen games in Orlando?"

Life returned to Trevor's face. "Tampa Bay. *Ja*, tickets ordered."

"Sorry, my bad. Shows you how much I know about the Olympics. I might have to actually watch some of the events this time, since our country's hosting it."

Trevor only grunted before scooping up another spoonful of mixed fruit.

Lucas had known Trevor for almost two years and had eaten with him countless times. He knew it was pointless to try to carry on a meaningful conversation with his lab assistant once the brute started replenishing his calories. Trevor was on the other side of thirty, but there certainly wasn't anything wrong with his appetite—a byproduct, no doubt, of his over-charged metabolism.

Trevor had started his academic career late but held twin doctorates in physics and computer engineering. Lucas was intimidated by his friend's sheer size and would take odds that Trevor was probably the largest scientist on the planet.

Even though Trevor was assigned to their team as his underling, Lucas never really felt comfortable about it. Trevor was almost nine years older than he was, and he often wondered how his Swedish friend felt about working for—as some of the other researchers called him—a grubby-faced youngster. Trevor never gave him any indication there was an issue, but Lucas was cautious nonetheless.

"Okay, then. I guess I should get back to Drew. I just wanted to let you know we're here, but it may take a few minutes to get through the line."

Lucas returned to the cafeteria door and saw Drew in trouble. A bespectacled, lanky student was standing between Drew and three burly students wearing red and blue rugby uniforms. The athletes were all tall, tan, and clearly spent far more time working on their muscles in the gym and lounging in the sun than they did studying in the library. Rugby wasn't an official Pac-12 NCAA sport, but the members of the rugby club were every bit the arrogant jocks as the guys on the football team. They walked around campus like they owned the place and were notorious for getting drunk and picking on anyone they determined to be a geek.

His eyes took in the facts, instantly realizing what was happening across the room: his disabled brother was being picked on, and the underweight kid with glasses was sticking up for him. Lucas couldn't make out what Drew's protector was saying, but it was obvious the skinny guy was arguing with the rugby jocks.

Great, Lucas thought. *Just what we need today. More bullshit.* He took off for his brother.

The tallest stranger, who sported a Mohawk-style haircut, grabbed the skinny kid and shoved him hard, sending him across the polished tile floor. He landed in an awkward sprawl.

Then the burly jock took the handles on the back of Drew's wheelchair and shoved it with force toward the back of the line. The chair wobbled to the right as it shot across the floor, sending the upper half of Drew's body over the left armrest.

2

Lucas made it to Drew, glancing back at the rugby players to check their position. They weren't close.

"Are you okay?" he asked Drew.

Drew nodded, though it wasn't convincing.

"What the hell's going on here?"

The skinny kid with the glasses stood up and came over to Lucas, looking more than a little agitated. He pointed at the rugby players. "Those assholes were trying to cut in front of your brother."

"Thanks for sticking up for him," Lucas said, trying to remember where he knew this kid from. "I know you, right?"

The young man nodded. "I'm Stephen Carr. I work in the Geophysics Lab, two buildings down from you guys. The three of us had a class together a couple of semesters ago. You guys are the Ramsay brothers, right?"

Lucas gave him a quick, respectful nod. "Thanks Stephen. You didn't have to do that."

"Yeah, I did. Guys like that think they can do anything. I'm sick of it."

"You ain't the only one," Lucas said, looking back at the miscreants, who were laughing with each other.

Just then the tallest of the rugby players shouted with a confident smile on his face, "Look guys, another nerd joined the herd. They're everywhere, like goddamn cockroaches."

Another of the players spoke. "You got that right, Zack. A bunch of spineless, limp-dick cockroaches."

Lucas pushed Drew back in line, then looked at Stephen. "Will you stay here with Drew?"

"Sure. Why?"

"Time to put a stop to this, once and for all."

"Lucas, no. They'll kill you!" Drew snapped, grabbing Lucas by the arm.

"I'll be right back," he said, pulling out of his brother's one-handed grip.

Lucas walked over to the tallest rugby player, taking position in directly front of him. The skin across his forehead tightened as a warm sensation swelled within his cheeks. "Keep your goddamn hands off my brother!"

The rugby player moved a step closer, flared his eyes, and then raised his chin. "Oh, yeah, what are *you* gonna do about it?"

Lucas pushed out his chest and stood toe-to-toe with the stout man. He leaned in close to his face and looked him dead in the eye. "Go ahead, asshole. Take your best shot. I'm not afraid of you."

A slender, redheaded security officer appeared from around the corner and pulled Lucas away from the rugby player. He stood between the two would-be combatants with a hand pressed against both of their chests. "Someone care to explain?"

"These assholes cut in line," Lucas answered, fixing his shirt collar. The officer looked vaguely familiar, but Lucas couldn't place him. He figured he must've seen the older man around campus somewhere.

Two British students waiting in line behind them agreed. "Yes, they jumped the line in front of all of us."

The security guard turned to Stephen. "What did you see?"

"Same thing. They cut the line then started getting physical with me and the kid in the wheelchair," Stephen added.

The officer went to the rugby players, who were no longer laughing or smiling. In fact, they looked concerned.

"Time for you boys to leave," the officer said, his face stiff and flushing with red. "I don't want to see you here for the rest of the day.

And next time, wait in line like everyone else. If this happens again, I'll drag your ass in and have you expelled. Am I making myself clear?"

The brutes complained to the officer before finally leaving the cafeteria and walking upstairs. They maintained eye contact with Lucas the entire way up the steps. The player with the Mohawk mouthed the words, "Your ass is mine, punk," on his way out, then flipped Lucas the bird.

Lucas crossed his arms and put his trembling hands under his sweat-soaked armpits.

The officer spoke to Lucas. "Just because they cut in front of you is no reason to get physical."

"You're absolutely right, Officer. I'm sorry. I overreacted, but really—picking on a guy in a wheelchair? That's crossing the line. Somebody had to stand up to them."

"He's right," Stephen said, butting into the conversation. "Enough is enough."

"I understand. And frankly, I might've done the same thing if I'd been in your shoes. But regardless, next time, just ignore them and let the situation deescalate on its own. A few extra minutes in line aren't worth a fight or a trip to the medical center."

"Yes, sir. Won't happen again." Lucas waited for the officer to disappear around the corner before asking Drew, "Did you see the size of those guys? They would've kicked my ass six ways from Sunday."

Drew nodded. "Maybe we should eat someplace else tomorrow."

"No. We eat here, same as usual. You can't let guys like that push you around, because if you back down once, they own your ass. Just like back when we lived in the orphanage. Gotta show strength."

"But those guys—" Drew said.

Lucas wasn't going to let his brother cave. "No, Drew. We stand our ground. Nobody puts their hands on a Ramsay and gets away with it. And I mean nobody."

Drew nodded, letting his eyes run soft.

Lucas followed his brother through the buffet line, waiting for his temper to cool as he dished up two trays of food and slid along the display counter. His pulse rate was still in overdrive, but he knew once the adrenaline eased, so would his shaking hands. He finished the load out and carried both of their trays to Trevor's table in the back and put them down. He removed one of the chairs to allow Drew to scoot his wheelchair under the table. Lucas sat between Drew and Trevor.

"Sorry we're late again," Lucas told Trevor. "We got delayed by a bunch of soccer hooligans."

"They were rugby players," Drew said.

"Rugby, soccer—same difference. Jerks are jerks."

Trevor glanced at both of them but did not respond. He was busy eating a large cluster of seedless grapes. One of the grapes squirted its juice across Lucas' tray.

"You ready for lab tonight, Trevor? Did you fix the programming bug?" Lucas asked, watching Drew rearrange his chow in alphabetical order, carefully spacing each food group a precise distance from the others.

"*Ja*. No more system crash."

"Good thing, because they're taking down the mainframe tomorrow for maintenance. After tonight, we won't have computer access again until late Sunday."

"Isn't tonight when the new lab tech arrives?" Drew asked.

Lucas loathed the documentation requirements of their research. "I hope so. We could use the help. You know me and paperwork. I'd rather have my toenails pulled out."

"It's too bad Gracie graduated. I really liked her. She was nice."

A smile grew on Trevor's lips as he shoveled in another spoonful.

Lucas had been glad to see Gracie leave. She was always staring at his scars, making him even more self-conscious about them than he already was. She was a quirky young woman who seemed to twitch and prance when she got nervous, but he had to admit she was an excellent assistant, and kept their paperwork in perfect order. "Let's hope the E-121 material gets here soon. If we have to keep running simulations, I'm going to go Bundy on somebody."

Trevor nodded, then put his hand on Lucas' shoulder and squeezed gently. It was clear Lucas wasn't the only one tired of waiting for the Navy to deliver the power cores.

Lucas saw an abandoned newspaper sitting on a neighboring table. "Drew, could you hand me that paper over there? I want to see if the Board of Regents voted to increase the tuition again—only one more semester to go, brother."

"You're lucky you're done. I've still got a full load to get through, plus exams," Drew said, handing the paper to Lucas.

"Don't sweat it. You'll ace them; you always do. I was the one who had to study my ass off."

"At least you're getting a steady paycheck. I'm still working for free."

"How about I trade you my puny paycheck for your eidetic memory?"

"Fine by me. I'd rather work in the lab than study, anytime."

Lucas opened the paper and scanned through the articles while they finished breakfast. His mind quickly wandered, dreaming about Drew's graduation day, when Drew would receive his PhD and could join their anti-gravity project as a paid physicist.

He smiled, thinking about his mother sitting in the audience, watching Drew roll up to the podium after hearing his name announced by the university president. She'd cried at Lucas' graduation ceremony and he figured she'd do the same for Drew. Too bad Dad hadn't lived long enough to see it. If there was a heaven, Lucas figured his old man was looking down right about now and watching with a grin on his face.

Both of his adoptive parents put everything they had into making a better future for the two of them, and he was thankful. Drew's life in the wheelchair would've been much different if they hadn't been adopted out of the orphanage together.

Drew owed the Ramsays big time, and so did Lucas. More than either of them could ever repay. It was the most compelling reason Lucas was committed to doing everything possible to make them proud. PhDs were just the first step—both he and Drew were going to make something of themselves. Then they'd make their mark in the scientific community.

At least that was the plan before his paper submittal to Dr. Green went completely off the rails.

Shit.

He still didn't know how he was going to break the news to his wide-eyed little brother.

* * *

That evening, Lucas and Drew cut across the street just west of the Student Union, headed to the John Koehn Memorial Science Lab for their nightly shift.

The Tucson sun had just disappeared below the horizon in the west, setting the edge of the sky ablaze with color. Red, orange and purple hues stretched across the fading sky in random patterns, giving way to the first twinkle of stars. Nighttime viewing was about to begin, making all those waiting astronomers giddy with anticipation. Soon the heavens would open their folds and reveal more of their precious secrets.

The science lab's exterior was boring and drab, like its neighboring buildings: red bricked and shaped like an oversized chalkboard eraser. Each floor was outlined by a protracted series of evenly spaced, metal-grated windows, giving it a 1950s industrial look.

The complete lack of imagination that went into the exterior design of the science buildings on campus always baffled Lucas. He couldn't think of anything less conducive to inspiration and creative thought, two essential ingredients in the advancement of science. He'd always thought the buildings on campus looked more like Soviet tractor factories than university laboratories, which just so happened to be located in the heart of the desert southwest.

He could hear the grind of motorized gears overhead while walking through the building's courtyard. Above him was an 8.4-meter binocular telescope being repositioned along the building's roofline. The $136 million telescope was the pride of the Astronomy Department. His boss, Dr. D.L. Kleezebee, Dean of the Astrophysics Department, had labored for years to raise the funds needed for its construction.

"Looks like they finally got that thing operational. Kleezebee must be pleased," Lucas said, letting a thin smile grow on his lips.

"Speaking of Kleezebee, there he is," Drew said, pushing his wheelchair forward with both hands.

"Where? I don't see him."

"You don't have to. Just follow your nose."

Lucas caught a whiff of acrid cigar smoke in the air. He'd never understood why Kleezebee, who was loaded with money, chose to smoke the cheapest cigars on the planet. "Ah, yes. You're right. He's close—I smell him, but I still don't see him."

"He's to the right, behind the flower bed."

Lucas leaned to his right to see beyond the rose bushes blocking his view. His mentor was wearing his usual attire, blue coveralls and an orange-colored flannel shirt, standing bent over with one foot resting on the top of a short, cement wall.

As they moved closer, Lucas realized Kleezebee was talking on his cell phone. It was partially hidden by a gray beard that stretched down to the middle of his chest. His trademark cigar smoldered between the index and middle fingers of his other hand, dangling precariously close to the flammable hairs of his frazzled beard.

"Damn, that thing is disgusting. I can't believe he smokes them."

"I can't believe he gets away with it," Drew replied.

"Seriously, who's going to stop him? Certainly not us."

"Still, it's against the law."

"Never gonna happen, little brother. In the world of UofA Astrophysics, D.L. Kleezebee is the law. And let's be honest, the powers that be would rather look the other way than give up all the money he raises."

Lucas intended to stop and ask his boss about their new lab tech, but changed his mind when he overheard Kleezebee's side of the heated conversation. Some poor, unfortunate soul was on the other end of the line, getting an earful. He knew firsthand not to stand in the way of Kleezebee, once that flannel-covered tornado got rolling.

Kleezebee's voice was sharp and charged with anger. "Look, I don't give a rat's ass what you think. You don't know the first thing about it. Show me your degree in experimental physics, and I'll listen to what you have to say. Until then, you have to trust me. I'm the expert, and this is what the university hired me to do. You need to let me do my damn job, and quit sticking your nose in where it doesn't belong. I've been at this for more years than I can count and I guarantee you the project is perfectly safe. Besides that, it's a done deal. The committee already signed off on it . . ."

"Let's talk to him later," Lucas said, grabbing hold of Drew's wheelchair and pushing him to the entrance of the science lab. The ancient revolving door screeched on its bearings as they made their way inside the apparatus together. Space was at a premium, so Lucas tilted the wheelchair back to raise up the footrests before pushing them against the thick Plexiglas. He'd learned through years of trial and error that this was the best method to fit them both inside at the same time—far easier than the backwards dance they had to perform on most regular doors.

The brothers were waiting in line to check in through the lab's front desk security when Kleezebee approached them from behind, gently grabbing Lucas by the shoulders.

"How're my two favorite scientists doing today?" he asked, massaging Lucas' neck with finger squeezes.

Lucas slid out of Kleezebee's grasp and turned around. The professor's keen, dark eyes were intense and probing, set deep in his face under a crop of thick, gray eyebrows.

Lucas always had the sense his boss was hiding a myriad of secrets behind those eyes, making him wonder if he was about to become the punch line of a cosmic joke. It was a strange feeling, and difficult to explain—a feeling he figured was due to lingering paranoia from his younger days, when he struggled to survive in a state-run orphanage.

"We're good, boss," Lucas said as his nose was hit with a waft of cigar smoke from Kleezebee's wrinkled clothes. The odor nearly knocked Lucas off his feet, smelling as though the professor just walked through a rubber fire. "What's the latest on the new lab tech?"

"She starts tonight. I think you'll like her—she's brilliant. I just have to arrange her security pass, and then I'll send her down with Trevor. Do your best to bring her up to speed quickly, all right?"

"Will do," Lucas replied, praying the new girl wasn't as high-maintenance as their last assistant.

"How's your mom doing after her surgery?" Kleezebee asked with a genuine tone in his voice.

Lucas appreciated the man's concern. "She's getting around okay. The neighbor lady's keeping an eye on her."

"Are you guys planning to go home for the holiday?"

"No, we've got way too much work to do here."

"You know, if you like, I can send Bruno to Phoenix to pick her up for you. I'd be more than happy to let her stay in one of my vacant apartments. I hate to think she'll be spending Christmas alone."

"Thanks, Professor. It's really nice of you to offer. I'll ask her but I doubt she'll take you up on it. She hates to be a bother to anyone."

"It's no bother at all. It's the least I can do, since she always takes care of me with her delicious care packages," Kleezebee said, smiling. "Dorothy should really open a bakery. She'd make a killing."

"Everyone tells her that, but she likes teaching at the college too much. I don't think she'll ever leave that place."

"I know how she feels. I don't know what I'd do if I couldn't work here every day," Kleezebee said, patting Drew on the back. "I'm having Bruno and his guys over for a poker party at my apartment on Christmas Eve, if you're interested."

Lucas wasn't sure how to respond. He didn't want to disappoint his boss by saying no, but he and Drew didn't play poker. He knew they'd be the suckers at the table. "We appreciate the invite, but we really don't know much about poker."

"I think it sounds like fun," Drew said to Lucas. "Come on, let's give it a shot. How hard can it be? It's all about numbers and probabilities, right? We're good at those, remember?"

Lucas nodded but didn't give an answer.

"I'll make sure there's plenty of grape soda and nachos for you two," Kleezebee said.

"How much money would we need to bring?" Lucas asked, considering the idea. It would need to be a super cheap buy-in; otherwise, they couldn't afford the play. Not with Mom's medical bills piling up.

"We don't play for money. We play for vacation days," the professor said in a confident voice.

That was exactly what Lucas needed to hear. "Okay, then, if that's the case, we're in. What time should we show up?"

"The game starts promptly at eight; don't be late."

"Anything else you need, Professor?" Lucas asked, remembering Kleezebee's heated phone call outside the building. He pushed Drew's wheelchair to the front of the screening line, wondering what bombshell was about to explode.

"Yeah, there's one more thing I need to talk to you about. One of those goddamn suits from Legal is on his way over here. It's that frickin' a-hole of a prick, Larson. God, I hate that pompous bastard. He says he wants to see firsthand what you two are working on. I hope you don't mind the intrusion, but I need to give him the nickel tour."

"No problem," Lucas replied, trying to hide his nervousness. The last thing he needed was some bureaucrat poking his nose around their lab. He didn't want the scrutiny—not ever and certainly not today. He was worried that the paper he'd submitted online and the subsequent criticism from Dr. Green had sparked the inspection. If Kleezebee found out, he was fucked. All because of one mistake—something he did on impulse—something he wished he could take back. "Any idea what it's about?"

"I have no idea what his true agenda is. You'd think even a suck-ass weasel like him would have something better to do on a Friday night, but apparently not. I think he really gets off on being a total pain in my ass."

Lucas nodded in support as Kleezebee continued. "The man is a real piece of work, always pretending the rules don't apply to him. He doesn't think I know what he does at lunchtime, but I do. Sneaking off like that behind his wife's back. He should be ashamed of himself."

"What does he do?" Lucas asked, wondering if he might be able to use the juicy secret as leverage against the man if he ever needed it.

"It doesn't matter. Let's just say it's not the type of behavior you'd expect from a former gunnery sergeant in the Marines. It's a wonder he still has a job around here."

Lucas was disappointed Kleezebee didn't cough up the secret, but he wasn't surprised. "When are you coming by, Professor?"

"In about thirty minutes. Don't worry, I'll run interference and handle the prick."

"Okay, no problem. Whatever we can do to help. You know my motto. The project—"

"—always comes first. That's one of the main reasons I hired you, Lucas. I know you've got your priorities straight and you'll never let me down."

A stabbing pressure hit the middle of Lucas' chest when he heard those words.

Shit. That'll all change if he catches wind of the Dr. Green debacle. What the hell was I thinking?

Kleezebee turned to walk toward the building's entrance door. Then he stopped. "Hey, I almost forgot to tell you . . . your material finally arrived."

"Really? When?" Lucas said, celebrating with a huge grin.

"A short while ago," Kleezebee answered, returning his grin. "You look like a kid on Christmas."

"Yeah, I'm psyched. Never thought we'd ever get that stuff."

"Well, we have it now. Which means this is a big night for us. I need you to have everything ready to run, okay?"

"Don't worry, Professor. We're on it," Lucas answered, thinking about the unbelievable timing of this delivery. They'd been waiting for this material for months and months, and had he known it would arrive today, he never would've sent his paper to Dr. Green. He should've waited. Damn it, he couldn't believe his luck. A few more days and he never would've been humiliated in front of the entire scientific community. It was almost like time and history were conspiring to twist his life into a knot with circumstances and coincidences meant to torment him, then sit back and see how'd he'd react.

"I'll see you in a bit," Kleezebee said before walking back outside the building.

Lucas swung his eyes around, focusing them on the three armed security officers monitoring the security checkpoint. He emptied his pockets, as did Drew, preparing for the usual inspection of their possessions before they'd be allowed to walk through the x-ray scanner and weapons detector.

As the lead officer came toward them, Lucas leaned in close to his brother's ear and spoke in a whisper. "Here comes Bruno. Remember, don't mention Mom, okay?"

Drew nodded. "Yeah, got it."

Drew's disability required a member of the security staff to carry him through the scanners. The task was usually handled by Bruno

Benner, a twenty-year veteran of the campus security force. Bruno was easy to recognize even from a distance, given his hefty size, shaved head, and neatly groomed goatee.

Bruno removed his duty belt and all the metal objects from his pockets before asking Drew, "Hey, Chief, you ready for a lift?"

Drew smiled and nodded. "Taxi!" he joked.

"Where to, mister?" Bruno replied.

"Uptown," Drew said. "The Ritz."

"Yes, sir."

Bruno lifted Drew from his wheelchair and used his keg-sized gut to prop up and carry Drew to the security equipment. Both of the guard's powerful forearms were covered with orange and black-colored tattoos of ferocious-looking creatures, which came alive whenever his muscles were active.

The tattoos reminded Lucas of sinister comic book creatures, complete with big heads, pincher claws, and sweeping, long tails. He'd never asked his friend about the amazing artwork, even though he was curious to know why Bruno chose them over something more common. The guard was a talkative guy and Lucas figured Bruno would someday tell him the story behind the tattoos, and the expensive-looking digital watch he wore on his right wrist. It was a unique timepiece with a five-sided shape, much like the Pentagon building, and featured a series of tiny orange push buttons around its perimeter.

Just before entering the first screening device, Bruno told one of his colleagues to fetch the backpack from the back of Drew's wheelchair and bring it through the inspection station. A second wheelchair was waiting for Drew on the other side of security.

"How's that project of yours coming along, Dr. Lucas? Did you hear Dr. Kleezebee found a replacement for Ms. Gracie?" Bruno asked.

"Yes, DL just told us. Trevor's supposed to bring her by shortly. I don't know about Drew, but I'm pretty excited. Always nice to have some new blood in the fire."

"New blood in the fire, huh? That's an interesting way to put it."

"Yeah, you know, anything to get out of all that damn paperwork. Gracie was much better at it than me. If the new chick is half as good, we'll be golden," Lucas said, thinking about remaining behind for a few minutes to witness the new lab tech's first encounter with Bruno.

The guard had an uncanny knack for putting people at ease with very few words. His ability was truly remarkable, and it seemed to work on everyone he met. Bruno could probe someone's background and gather details about their life and family with just a couple of choice phrases, while revealing very little about himself.

Lucas knew about it firsthand because it had happened to him the first time he'd met the friendly soul. Within seconds, he began sharing private information with Bruno—information he thought he'd never tell anyone outside his immediate circle of trust, much less a total stranger.

Whenever he needed the inside scoop on someone, he'd ask Bruno. The man was a walking, talking information station and seemed to have the lowdown on everyone. The CIA and NSA had nothing on this dude.

Once through screening, Bruno deposited the younger Ramsay into the wheelchair waiting on the other side. "There you go, Chief, safe and sound. The uptown Ritz, as promised."

"Thank you, sir," Drew said, giving Bruno a firm fist bump. "Don't know what I'd do without you."

Drew turned around in the seat to make sure his backpack was in its proper place, hanging over the handles on the back of the wheelchair. Drew was obsessive about his pack and tended to freak out if it wasn't exactly where he expected it to be at all times.

Bruno adjusted the spin of his belt and raised it up along his waistline before leaning back and rubbing his oversized belly. "Now that I've had my exercise for the day, I think I might take a break to get my chocolate fix. Obviously, I need it to maintain my girlish figure."

Lucas laughed at the man's worn-out gag even though he'd heard it a dozen times. He liked Bruno and accepted the heavyset man for who he was, but it still didn't stop him from worrying Bruno would develop diabetes. All his friend seemed to eat was mounds of sugar from the vending machines in the security team's breakroom, only a short fifteen feet inside the checkpoint. Candy bars seemed to be Bruno's order of choice, though he did see him munching on a sleeve of Oreo cookies a few times. Regardless of the snack food, a can of Pepsi was sure to follow it down the hatch. And there was no chance it would ever be a can of diet.

Bruno started down the hallway for the breakroom, then stopped and turned back. "Dr. Lucas, I forgot to ask . . . How's your dear, sweet mother doing these days?"

Lucas had to bite his lip, stopping the urge to release too much personal information. Bruno was a one-man intelligence gathering agency, after all, and he didn't want everyone in the lab to know his family business. Not that he didn't trust Bruno; he just thought it best to keep most of the family matters private. Especially the medical bills and the stupid decision to submit his paper to Dr. Green.

He locked eyes with Bruno and faked a thin smile. "Pretty good, considering everything she's been through. The doc says she can go back to work in January, thank God. I think she's starting to go a little stir-crazy without work to keep her busy."

"That's great news. I'd be tired of being cooped up in that house, too. It's always better to have something to do other than just sit around all day and stare at the wall."

"Yeah, no lie."

Bruno gave him a quick hand wave. "Be sure to tell her I said hi, and that I'm looking forward to more of her delicious fudge bars."

Lucas responded with a quick nod and said, "Will do."

He turned and grabbed the handles on the wheelchair, pushing Drew down the hallway toward their lab.

Their assigned workspace was located at the far end of the science lab, through a maze of interconnecting corridors five hundred feet away. Along the way, they passed two dozen lab doors, many without windows, plus a scattering of restrooms, storage rooms, and utility closets. A security card-reader controlled access to each lab and was installed a few inches above the project number next to the doors.

The hallways between the security checkpoint and the entrance to their lab were a curious mix of odors: old, musty, moldy smells were strong in some places, while bleach and cleaning products dominated others.

The same contrast was true with the paint and lighting fixtures. Some hallways were bright, shiny, and clean, while others were downright dilapidated, with paint cracking and ancient fluorescent lights buzzing and blinking sporadically.

Lucas assumed the disparity was tied to the amount of funding each of the individual projects received from the University. He was thankful his section of the building was in the well-kept category: it smelled clean, the lights worked perfectly, and while the paint in the hallway outside his lab wasn't exactly new, it wasn't peeling, either.

When he pushed Drew around the final corner, he saw three silver-colored boxes the size of microwave ovens sitting outside the double automatic swing doors of their lab. The containers were labeled with block lettering that read U.S. DEPARTMENT OF DEFENSE and wrapped with three evenly spaced strips of yellow security tape.

Lucas wanted to let out an excited *whoop* and give Drew a high-five when he saw the delivery, but thought better of it when he noticed two imposing Marines guarding the precious cargo. They were standing at attention with shoulder-slung rifles and unyielding attitudes.

The taller man, a first lieutenant by his insignia, was holding a red briefcase and fussing with the handcuff fastened around his left wrist.

3

Lucas wondered how the Marines were able to pass through security with their weapons in hand. Bruno's scanning systems must've lit up like a Christmas tree the second they got close to the equipment. Then again, Kleezebee may have cleared the way since he seemed to have pull with almost everyone. The professor was the man in charge of the Science Lab after all, so who would've questioned his decision to send them through?

"Which of you is Dr. Ramsay?" the lieutenant asked.

Lucas raised his hand. "That'd be me," he said. He held up his ID for the Marine to check. The lieutenant nodded once and then removed a written manifest from the briefcase. He gave it to Lucas.

"Project AG-356-12," Lucas said in a matter of fact tone, scanning the paperwork. He checked the items against the boxes sitting on the floor. "Yes, that's correct. Looks like it's all here. Do I need to sign for it?"

"Yes, sir. Just sign the form on the line at the bottom."

Lucas pulled a pen from his shirt pocket and signed it. The Marine took the document, put it in his briefcase, and the two marched in unison the opposite way down the hall toward the newly-completed NASA annex. Their movements were measured, precise, and efficient, without a single misstep the entire way.

"Drew, did you see where they went? That's weird."

"Yeah. Kleezebee didn't say this stuff was from NASA, did he?"

"Not that I remember. But I guess it doesn't really matter where it came from. I'm just glad it's here. We finally get to move ahead. We've been in a holding pattern for way too long."

Drew snatched the manifest from his brother and looked at it. "Me too. I'm tired of running simulations. We needed this stuff months ago."

Lucas bent over and tested the weight of the closest box. "These modules are much heavier than they look." He wondered how the two Marines managed to carry the containers. They were both taller and stronger than he was, but still, they must've had help. "Hang on a minute while I find a dolly. There has to be one around here somewhere."

"I think there's one in Dr. Davies' lab. He usually works all night on Fridays and should still be there."

Lucas whirled around and stared at the door to Dr. Griffith Davies' lab with trepidation—the lab of a world-renowned astrobiologist who specialized in the origin and evolution of life in the universe. The man held a slew of PhDs in chemistry, molecular biology, physics, and astronomy. From what Lucas had heard from Bruno, Dr. Davies was the go-to guy for Dr. Kleezebee whenever something unexplained landed on his desk.

Davies was beyond brilliant and well-respected by his peers, but had a few personality quirks that jumped off the page. He was an odd duck to be sure, but then again, most would say the same thing about any of the accomplished scientists working in the Science Lab. Intelligence and polished social skills didn't always go hand in hand for the members of the genius guild.

"That guy drives me crazy. He never shuts up and is always trying to ingratiate himself," Lucas said.

"That's because he has a little man-crush on you."

Lucas ignored the imagery swirling around his head. "Thanks, just what I needed."

"I think he wants you as his boy-toy."

"Knock it off. That's not even funny. The guy's not gay. You've seen his wife—she's a total knockout."

"Yes, she is."

"So what's your point?"

"Nothing. I was just messing with you. It's all good, bro."

"Can we get back to work now?" Lucas asked, wondering how Griffith managed to land such a gorgeous trophy wife. She was ten years younger than Griffith and had a stellar homegrown body that supermodels would envy. To keep her satisfied, he assumed Griffith was packing a 10-pound wonder dog or a plentiful balance sheet. Either way, Lucas was jealous.

Lucas stood in front of Griffith's lab door and planned his actions carefully. Griffith had several close friends on the Advisory Committee, any one of whom could shut down his experiment with a single phone call. He knocked twice and took a deep breath to steady his nerves.

Be nice, but not too nice, he told himself.

Griffith answered the door, wearing a wrinkled white lab coat and cheater glasses. His cheap black toupee was sloped forward, threatening to cover his brown, rheumy eyes. His right hand was on the door handle while his left was filled with a cordless soldering gun and a coil of resin. But what caught Lucas' eye was the heavy smear of ink on the smiling man's cheek. It stretched from just under his eye clear down to his chin. Lucas had to manufacture a cough to cover up his involuntary laugh. It seemed to work.

"Hey, Lucas!" Griffith said, his face beaming with a smile. "It's wonderful to see you. Do you need my help with something? Wow, you look especially handsome today. How is your project coming along? I hear you're getting a new lab tech tonight. How's your mother feeling? What were those Marines delivering? They sure looked impressive in their uniforms, didn't—"

Lucas was in a rush, but couldn't afford to be rude. *Keep it simple and to the point,* he decided. "I'm fine, the project's fine, Drew's fine, we're all fine. If you're not using it, can I borrow your hand truck?"

"Sure, go right ahead. It's right by my desk."

He kept a safe distance away from Griffith to avoid his constant hand touches. The man smelled of cleaning chemicals; some of them were probably toxic, even fatal. Lucas was barely inside the door, and already his nasal passages were flooded with noxious fumes. He minimized his breathing.

"Do you need me to help? Did you know I work out regularly and can lift heavy objects? You should be careful with your back. Be sure to lift with your legs. Hernias can happen easily."

Lucas stopped listening as Griffith continued to ramble, talking aimlessly about anything and everything. Lucas nodded and smiled, adding the occasional "Mmhmmm, yes, yes, fascinating" at the appropriate times. He just needed to find the hand truck and get back to Drew. Nothing else mattered.

He found it right where Griffith said it would be, spun it around with one hand to face the door, and pushed it ahead of him. *Focus on the door, nothing else,* he told himself. *Just get back to Drew.* He kept his head down to avoid eye contact.

The hallway wasn't far, but Griffith was still right on his heels, yammering on about absolutely nothing. Truth is, on any other day, the endless jabbering without a breath between sentences might have been impressive—today, it was just annoying. Lucas knew the man was going to follow him into the corridor and possibly into their lab. He needed an excuse. He turned around and held out his hands while standing near the exit.

"Sorry, but this delivery belongs to Dr. Kleezebee and contains classified material. Nobody else is allowed within twenty feet of it."

"Okay, I understand. Take your time. Just return the dolly when you're done. I won't need it for at least a week. When you stop by again, we should go to lunch—"

Lucas rolled his eyes in relief when he heard Griffith's lab door close behind him.

Drew was waiting for him in the hallway, laughing quietly with the back of his hand covering his mouth.

Lucas scowled. "Glad you're enjoying yourself. Now let's get this stuff inside already."

Drew slid his access card through the security scanner. After a loud buzz and a hollow click, the double doors swung open automatically. He used his wheelchair as a stop block to keep them from closing.

It took all of Lucas' strength to load and center the three containers onto the hand truck. He hauled them into the center of the lab, being careful not to lose the heavy load along the way. Drew followed him inside with the doors closing behind his wheelchair. Lucas slid the stack off and left the boxes sitting on the floor next to a rectangular worktable. Before he could put the first container on the table and open it, the security scanner guarding the lab doors buzzed.

Lucas turned around in a flash. "Crap, what now?" he muttered, wondering if Griffith might be popping in for an unscheduled visit.

When the doors opened, he knew instantly it wasn't the annoying Griffith—it was worse. It was Randol Larson of the Advisory Committee. The pencil-thin attorney was carrying a clipboard and gold-colored pen as he walked into the lab, his head tilted slightly back.

"I guess it's up to me to deal with this guy," Lucas mumbled when he didn't see Kleezebee tagging along. He waved a quick hello to Bruno, who was standing just outside their door with his Master Security Card in hand. Apparently, Bruno had used it to let Larson into their lab.

Larson, who appeared to be about ten years younger than old man Kleezebee, was dressed in a form-fitting blue pinstripe suit. His medium-length blond hair was neatly feathered front-to-back on the left side. It adhered to the side of his head, defying both gravity and air pressure as he moved. He had blue eyes, a sharp, pointed nose, and high cheekbones covered with acne scars. He looked like a nervous bird, scanning the area for insects to gather up in his narrow beak.

Lucas assumed Larson's spotless presentation was intentionally calculated to distract people from noticing the scars on his face, which made his cheeks look like the surface of an asteroid after a yearlong meteor shower. He agreed with Kleezebee's earlier assessment of the attorney: it was hard to believe this frail-looking man was a former gunnery sergeant in the Marines.

Larson brought his eyes around and looked at Lucas. "Dr. Ramsay, I presume? I am Randol Harrison Larson the Third, lead council for the University's Advisory Committee for Theoretical Research."

"Yes, sir, I'm Dr. Ramsay, and this is my brother Drew. What can we—?"

"Where's Kleezebee? He was to meet me here thirty seconds ago."

Lucas looked at his brother and then back at the attorney. "I don't know, sir. I know he intended to be here to show you around in person. I'm sure he'll be here any second."

Larson clicked his pen frequently as he walked slowly around the room, stopping periodically to transcribe something onto his clipboard.

Lucas figured Larson needed to document the contents of their lab, possibly for insurance purposes, but he wasn't sure. He considered asking the man, but decided to let Kleezebee handle it when he arrived.

Larson stopped in his tracks and stared through the ten-foot-wide window that led into the adjoining chamber. He scribbled a long series of notes before clicking his pen one final time and sticking it back in his shirt pocket. He whirled around and went to Drew's location, leaning in close to Drew's face. "All right, then, let's get on with it."

Drew rolled his chair back a few feet and didn't respond.

"Come on now, I don't have all day," Larson said, louder this time, pulling the pen from his pocket again.

Lucas moved in front of Drew, chest expanded, fighting the urge to strike the pushy bureaucrat. It was an instinctive reaction brought on by years of torment in the orphanage. "Can I help you with something?"

Larson took an uncoordinated step back, lowered his head, and began fiddling with his gold pen while shuffling through several layers of his paperwork.

This guy's a former Marine?

Larson cleared his throat before looking at Lucas. "I've just received this lengthy, attorney-prepared disclaimer agreement from the Defense Department. Obviously, I need a comprehensive briefing concerning the nature of your project and its need for the material in these three containers. Liability must be assessed. Damage must be mitigated."

Goddamn attorneys, Lucas thought, remembering the family's hefty legal bills to defend his dad's failed pest control invention. He'd thought about hiring a lawyer to fight the insurance company over his mother's denied medical claims, but hated the idea of lining some future politician's pocket with what little money he had.

Then a new thought popped into his head. Maybe he should team up with one of the chemical geeks down the hall and invent a bio-toxin that targeted only insurance executives and lawyers. He liked that idea— would probably make him rich in the process, since everyone would want a lifetime supply.

Larson continued, "Which one of you wants to explain this to me? I need to know who authorized this."

Before Lucas could respond, Kleezebee buzzed in and bolted through the lab entrance. He pushed at the doors, not waiting for them to open fully on their own.

"Damn it, Larson, I'm here. I told you earlier I'd handle this. Let's step outside and let these guys work. I'll explain it all to you— probably very slowly, so you'll understand."

Kleezebee took Larson by the arm and led him out of the lab.

Lucas looked at Drew, who was sitting in his wheelchair, smiling. Lucas took a deep breath and then let the air seep out through his lips. He rolled his eyes after realizing Kleezebee had come to their rescue as he'd done countless times before. It seemed like any time they needed help, Kleezebee would somehow know and magically arrive just in time to assist.

"That was a close one," Drew said with a concerned look on his face.

"Yeah, tell me about it. Thank God Kleezebee showed up in time. I never know how to talk to people like that. All I wanted to do was deck his ass."

Just then, the lab doors opened again and Kleezebee walked through. He looked pissed. "Next time, run the paper by me first," he said to Lucas. "You're lucky nothing in it violated this project's confidentiality agreement."

"Sorry, boss," Lucas said, assuming Larson had just told Kleezebee about the paper he'd posted online. The professor returned to the hallway as quickly as he came in.

"What was that all about?" Drew asked.

"Nothing. I'll tell you later. Let's get to work."

Lucas and Drew began their shift by dressing in their customary white lab coats and logging into the computer network.

4

A short while later, Drew was seated next to Lucas at the lab's center worktable when the lab doors buzzed behind him again. He prayed it wasn't that jerk of an attorney, Larson. He didn't think Lucas would be able to keep his temper in check this time, assuming the man came at him like before.

When he turned his wheelchair around, he saw Trevor and a lovely young Asian woman standing next to each other. His heart nearly stopped beating. She was a petite, black-haired beauty with an adorable figure and dark, soulful eyes. She flashed a bright, alluring smile, revealing a gorgeous set of sparkling white teeth.

"Hi," she said to Drew.

Drew's tongue shriveled up and swallowed the words in his mouth, leaving him to muster an uneven grunt. His lungs suddenly forgot how to breathe properly, taking shorter and shorter breaths. He desperately wanted to say something, but he just sat there, staring at her like a creepy dumbass.

As she moved into the lab, her hair shimmered under the fluorescent lights like heat waves rising up from the desert sand. Her curly, flowing locks wrapped around her neck and cascaded gracefully down the front of her shoulder, drawing his eyes lower and lower until they found her curvy chest. Drew couldn't believe his eyes: She was a vision, a goddess who wore a yellow flower just above her right ear.

Lucas extended his right hand when she arrived at the worktable. "Hi, I'm Dr. Lucas Ramsay. Welcome to Project AG-356-12."

She bowed her head slightly and then gripped and shook Lucas' hand. "Hello, I'm Abby Park."

She looked at Drew. He dropped his paperwork.

Lucas let out a short laugh, then put a hand on Drew's shoulder. He shot a casual smile at the new girl. "And this slobbering member of the male species is my little brother, Drew."

"Hi Drew. It's nice to meet you," she said, looking as though she was waiting for a return greeting.

Drew tried to speak again, but his tongue still wouldn't cooperate. He felt his face turn an even darker shade of red, if that was even possible. He looked at Lucas, sending him a subtle 'help me' look.

Lucas didn't hesitate, turning to Trevor to draw attention away from Drew's embarrassing stumble. "I assume you've already introduced yourself to Abby?"

"*Ja*, I did."

"Have you signed your non-disclosure agreement?" Lucas asked the girl.

Abby nodded.

"Well, then, let's get started," he said, motioning for her to follow him toward the reactor chamber, only a seven-step walk. It was on the side of the room opposite from the lab's entrance doors.

Drew remained behind with Trevor to organize the items scattered across the top of the rectangular worktable in the center of the room. He still couldn't take his eyes off her.

* * *

Lucas began Abby's introduction with the control station located just to the right of the reactor chamber's door. It featured a seven-foot-wide stainless steel counter with a flat panel computer screen at each end and was attached to the wall below the viewing window. In front of each console was a black wireless keyboard and matching mouse, and between the two stations was an angled instrument panel covered with switches, knobs, instrument gauges, and the like. Two rolling desk chairs were offset to the left, leaving room for a third to be added on the right end of the counter.

"This is the Primary Control Station, where all the action happens. Drew sits to the right, and the other console is mine. The chair in the middle is yours."

Abby opened her spiral notebook and started taking notes. "What about Trevor?"

"He usually stands over there and monitors his system," Lucas said, pointing at three heavy-gauge steel shelving units installed on the wall to the left of the reactor chamber. They were loaded with rack-mounted computer equipment actively processing data, with their LED lights flashing and their hard drives whirling. A retractable network console was located waist-high in the center rack, with its hideaway keyboard pulled out on sliding rails.

"Trevor designed the system from the ground up and it controls our reactor. Everything else is networked to the university's mainframe and we share CPU time across all active experiments."

Lucas guided her to a pair of tall red-and-blue storage cabinets on the other side of the room. He opened the first storage unit, which contained an assortment of hand tools, cleaning supplies, paper, pens, and other miscellaneous materials.

"If you ever need any supplies, you'll find them in here."

He removed a clipboard hanging on a magnetic hook inside the cabinet's door. "Just be sure to write down what you took in this inventory log. Dr. Kleezebee wants every penny accounted for."

He opened the second cabinet, which held an array of equipment, wire, and other electronic parts. He pulled out a handheld device the size of a DVD case and held it up in front of her. "Radiological detector. Hopefully, we'll never have to use this puppy."

"How likely is that?"

"Not very. We've spent the past eighteen months making sure this experiment is perfectly safe."

"But there're always risks, right?"

"Sure, but I wouldn't be too concerned. Kleezebee made sure we took every precaution."

Abby scribbled some more words into her notebook. "Can I see the reactor?"

"Sure. I was planning on showing you that next."

He walked to the door to the reactor chamber. Drew followed along behind them. Lucas led Abby into a smaller room just inside the chamber's entrance; Drew stayed outside. He and the girl were standing in a closet-sized room that resembled a two-door airlock system, like those found aboard a submarine.

"The reactor's a clean room, so we use this decontamination chamber each time personnel or material enters the chamber." Lucas reached around her and closed the thick outer door. He turned around and powered on a twelve-inch LCD monitor to the right of the inner door. Drew's face appeared on the screen once the image stabilized.

"He's sitting in front of his console at the Primary Control Station," Lucas told her, pointing.

Lucas opened a cabinet to his left and gathered one of the six yellow protective suits hanging inside. Below them were several pairs of steel-toed boots and chemical-resistant gloves. A handful of voice-operated microphones and earpieces were sitting on the top shelf.

"A Hazmat suit?" she asked.

"Yes, Level A. Provides airtight protection from all forms of chemicals, including gasses and vapors. Safety protocols require we use them inside the reactor."

He pulled out a second suit and gave it to her. "We even have one in your size. Here, put this on. Let me know if you need assistance," he said, spinning around to give her privacy.

* * *

Five minutes later, both of them were wearing their protective gear, including boots, gloves, and the voice-activated communication devices.

"Abby, can you hear me? Is your comm unit working?"

"Yes, it is. Can we go inside the reactor?"

"Wait until Drew sets everything up. He'll give us the all-clear signal when it's time." Lucas looked at the pea-sized camera mounted above the video monitor. "Okay, bro. We're ready in here."

An upward stream of air blew past them as the process began. Thirty seconds later, Drew gave his brother a thumbs-up signal. Lucas entered a five-digit numerical code into a keypad next to the video monitor and waited for the inner door to unlock and slide open. They both stepped inside.

The reactor was a gray metal sphere the size of a commercial walk-in freezer, with a series of cables and heavy industrial piping above it that fed into the backside of the unit. There were dozens of valves, conduits, and other industrial components leading to and from the reactor's base.

"What kind of material is this?" she asked, tapping on the reactor's housing with her pen. She pinched her eyes with a look of curiosity on her face. "It's not like any metal I've seen before."

"It's one of Dr. Kleezebee's inventions. He calls it VX-312. We call it tri-tanium."

"Like in *Star Trek*," she quipped.

"Exactly. It's a chemically altered blend of hardened titanium and tungsten composites, which have been infused with a series of interwoven membranes of nanocrystalline diamond fiber. It can withstand fusion-level temperatures and intense gravimetric shear."

"That's impressive. Dr. Kleezebee is full of surprises."

"There's more where that came from, believe me. The man's a walking enigma."

She adjusted her headgear, then pointed to one of the eight black rectangular devices installed evenly around the perimeter of the reactor in forty-five degree increments. "What are these? I'm assuming they're some kind of magnet, right?"

"You got it. Superconducting electromagnets, to be exact. They've been specifically calibrated to allow us to control our gravity wave experiment."

Lucas saw her looking up at the elongated silver tube attached to the dome of the reactor, which extended to the ceiling at a forty-five degree angle. He continued his introduction. "That fires a focused, cold neutron beam at the core. It's what jump-starts the experiment."

He unlatched and slid open a protective shroud covering the midsection of the reactor. Inside was a white, egg-shaped receptacle the size of a thermos bottle. It was being held in place at the exact center of the reactor by a surrounding lattice of non-metal struts.

"What goes inside?" she asked after examining the interior of the reactor. "The reactive element?"

"Right again. You catch on quick—I'm starting to see why Kleezebee assigned you to our team."

She smiled.

So did he. "What goes inside is the really cool part of this whole setup. Follow me and I'll show you."

They completed decontamination procedures and removed their Hazmat suits before stepping out of the chamber. They returned to the center worktable where Trevor was standing. Drew joined them, maneuvering his wheelchair up under the worktable.

Lucas pointed to the three metal boxes near his feet, then looked at Abby. "These were just delivered today. You couldn't have picked a better day to join the project. We've been waiting months, and now they're finally here."

"Just dumb luck, I'm afraid. I never thought Dr. Kleezebee would pick me. I'm sure he had lots of applicants."

"Probably not as many as you think," Lucas said, thinking about the professor's reputation as a demanding perfectionist. "Trevor, would you do the honors?"

Trevor picked up one of the boxes with ease and put it on the worktable before cutting the bands of yellow security tape with a pair of shears. He unsnapped three metal clasps along the front of the box, opened its hinged cover, and then pushed the box closer to Lucas with one hand.

Lucas slid on a pair of safety gloves before removing the surface layer of the packaging material. Inside was a perfectly round black sphere the size of a baseball. He removed it with both hands, straining to lift the object up high enough for all to see.

"This material is called 'Unbiunium,' which is a new super-heavy element recently discovered by the U.S. Navy. Its atomic weight is 121, which is why we call it 'Element 121' or E-121 for short."

Abby narrowed her eyes and furrowed her brow in what Lucas was beginning to recognize as her go-to look of concentrated scientific curiosity. "I thought elements larger than ninety-two on the Periodic Table were theoretical and didn't occur naturally. Even if they could be synthesized by fusing two heavy elements together, wouldn't it be unstable and instantly decay into lighter elements?"

Lucas' arm muscles couldn't support the weight of the material any longer. He lowered the sphere down to chest level, locking his elbows in tight to hold it still for her inspection. "Yet here it is, stable, and in solid form. Kleezebee said he pulled a lot of strings to get us access to these samples."

"Where'd the Navy get it?"

"In an unexplored deep sea trench off the coast of Mexico, near Chicxulub, just off the Yucatan peninsula. From what Kleezebee told us, the Navy found a substantial amount of it."

"Chicxulub? Isn't that where they found the impact crater that killed off the dinosaurs?"

Lucas nodded. "Yep. Sure was."

Abby stared at the ground before responding in a softer tone, "I do remember reading something about a gravitational anomaly found at that impact site. I suppose it's possible that E-121 may have had something to do with that." She leaned over and peeked inside the shipping container.

Lucas was excited to be sharing his talisman with the appreciative new assistant. "This special material has some very unique properties, which are essential to the last phase of our project. Without it, we can't run the experiment. Super-heavy elements like E-121 have an ultra-strong gravity field that extends well beyond the perimeter of its atom, making it accessible. Just like any other field in the electromagnetic spectrum, E-121's gravitational wave has a specific frequency and amplitude. Since we can access it, we plan on using the reactor to control it."

"Are you trying to manipulate the element's strong nuclear force to bond its particles together?"

"No. We plan to morph the actual gravity field itself," Drew replied, picking up an egg-shaped capsule sitting next to him on the work surface. He unscrewed the capsule's domed-shaped lid before holding out the bottom half with both hands.

"Don't you think Trevor should take it from here?" Lucas asked.

"Nope, I got it," Drew replied, resting his elbows on the table.

Lucas wanted to say something else, but didn't. He put the E-121 sample into the container and screwed on its lid. Drew tugged the capsule across the tabletop and put it in his lap, partially wedged between his legs.

Lucas told Abby, "We'll use E-121 as the catalyst for our experiment. We hope to compact one side of the element's immense gravitational field under the control of the powerful electromagnetic system, which will in turn push out or bulge an equal and opposite reaction on the other side. While the quantum morphing occurs, we expect the surrounding subspace to counteract the change in force and effectively push against our material to maintain spatial equilibrium."

Abby nodded several times while writing in her journal. She folded her arms with the notebook pressed flat up against her chest. "Assuming I understand you correctly, in theory that could result in transmutation of the laws of gravity, or 'anti-gravity,' as it were. Like what would happen if you pushed against the side of a floating soap bubble."

Lucas nodded. "We hope this will lead to a revolutionary new type of interstellar propulsion system, which is why NASA agreed to fund this project in the first place."

"The power requirements must be enormous," she said.

"That's where the cold neutron beam comes into play. While an atom's strong nuclear force is trillions of times stronger than gravity, we believe there's an underlying quantum energy stream that's even more powerful."

Drew was smiling when he added, "So powerful in fact, we should be able to use it to manipulate E-121's gravity field."

"Did you say quantum energy stream?" she asked Lucas.

"If we can precisely match the frequency of E-121's gravity wave, the beam should be able to wedge open a crack between the exposed section of the gravitational field and the element's perimeter. This should allow us to tap into the energy matrix connecting our universe to the next. With it, we should have an endless supply of energy to power our experiment."

Abby's mouth dropped open and she did not respond.

Lucas smiled internally. He'd finally impressed her, which he was learning wasn't easy to do. Kleezebee had chosen her well. Not only was she much better looking than Gracie, but she was smarter, too.

5

Drew shot a covert glance at Abby across the worktable, just as the lab's security system buzzed. He turned his head in time to see the double doors spring open. Dr. Kleezebee breezed in, carrying a black three-ring binder with the phrase PROJECT AG-356-12 written on a white label affixed to the cover.

"How are things progressing?" Kleezebee asked with an unlit, stubby cigar hanging from the corner of his lips. The professor made his way to the worktable and stood next to Lucas.

"Perfectly," Lucas replied. "We're just about ready to load the core."

"Excellent. Let's get to it," the professor said, placing the binder on the table. "I've finished reviewing your work, and everything appears ready to go. Nice work, you two. I only changed a few things with respect to power utilization. Let's begin with the flow regulator set at fifty percent. We can always increase it from there if needed."

Lucas and Drew nodded.

Kleezebee winked and smiled at Drew. "Time to man your station. Abby, you go with him to observe."

"Yes, Dr. Kleezebee," she answered crisply.

Drew gave the E-121 container to Trevor and wheeled himself to the Primary Control Station. He sat in front of the right console; Abby sat down to his left. When she scooted her chair closer to his, he could smell her strawberry-scented perfume. It reminded him of his mother's backyard vegetable garden.

Abby was looking over her right shoulder when she whispered to him, "What's the deal with Trevor? He sort of gives me the creeps."

"Trevor? Oh, he's harmless. He's a big teddy bear and would never hurt a fly."

"But he just stands there with his arms folded and never says anything."

"That's just the way he is. Sometimes he goes an entire day without saying a word."

"I'm glad you're not that way," she said, touching her hand lightly on his shoulder.

Drew felt his face flush when she smiled at him. He had difficulty stabilizing his hand when he reached for a series of red switches located on the riser panel in front of her. When he pulled his arm back after turning on power to the chamber's video system, his forearm grazed her shoulder. The tiny black hairs on his arm tingled, sending a wave of shivers throughout his body.

He waited for his LCD screen to fill with four equal-sized windows. Three of them contained camera feeds showing the exterior of the reactor; the fourth was a shot of the reactor's core.

"So what happens next?" Abby asked, opening her documentation journal.

Drew hadn't looked closely at her journal before. This time, though, he noticed it was a blend of normal and unique: the notebook inside was filled with typical college-ruled paper, something anyone could buy at a store that sold school supplies. But the cover was made of tanned leather, with faded Asian characters stenciled into the front. It was dark and worn, like an old saddle. He wondered where it came from. It was clearly old—a family heirloom, perhaps? He'd have to ask about it later.

He changed the upper-left video feed to show Trevor and Lucas standing inside the decontamination chamber. Lucas was holding the E-121 container while Trevor put on his triple-XL Hazmat suit.

"It's time to load the core," Drew told her.

He brought up a command window on his computer screen, obscuring all the video feeds except the one monitoring his brother. He waited until he received the thumbs-up signal from Lucas before entering a series of programming commands into his wireless keyboard. Thirty seconds later, the decontamination sequence was complete.

* * *

Lucas stepped through the inner door first and led the way back to the reactor. He unscrewed four wing nuts securing the reactor's protective shroud and slid it open. He stood aside and waited for Trevor to place the E-121 container inside the core's main housing. The container fit perfectly inside the precision-made receptacle.

"The material's in place. Closing the core now," he announced over the communication system.

Lucas closed the heavy shield, secured it, and the two scientists headed for the exit. They followed established air-lock decontamination procedures before removing their safety gear and leaving the chamber.

"All set, boss. We're good to go," Lucas said, sitting down in front of the left console. He was only a few feet to the right of the chamber's door. Abby was seated to his right, with Drew on the other side of her.

Lucas spent the next several minutes preparing his workstation for the experiment, but was distracted by Abby and Drew babbling away. Occasionally, the chatter was interrupted by one of Abby's giggles. He looked back to see Kleezebee talking with Trevor near the center worktable. Lucas couldn't hear their conversation, but based on Kleezebee's body language and the professor's frequent glances at Drew, he suspected a problem.

Lucas leaned around the front of Abby and quietly told his brother, "You need to concentrate on the work. Kleezebee's watching, and he looks pissed."

"Sorry," Drew said, straightening himself up in his chair.

A short while later, Kleezebee and Trevor had finished their conversation and joined the crew at the Primary Control Station. "All right, then, let's fire this baby up," Kleezebee said.

Drew opened the procedure manual, licked his forefinger, and used it to turn to the first page. It contained almost forty pages of instrument checks, startup protocols, calculations, and notes to run the experiment. The first order of business was to boot the various systems and reset the instruments. Kleezebee's procedure manual included extensive notes regarding startup protocols and baseline readings.

"Control systems initiated. Stage one complete," Lucas reported after calibrating the final set of instruments.

Abby documented every facet of the experiment in precise detail. As was true with most scientists, Lucas despised the tedious documentation requirements mandated by the advisors and often chose to shortcut the process by avoiding it altogether. He was pleased to see direct evidence of Abby's detail-oriented nature, knowing she would save him a tremendous amount of grunt work.

Kleezebee was standing watch over Lucas' shoulder, his arms folded high across his chest. He was grinning and seemed proud of their accomplishments. Lucas felt the same way. They both had good reason to be proud. They'd worked their asses off to get to this point, and if everything went the way they thought it should, their team was about to rewrite the laws of gravity.

"Go ahead and remove the atmosphere from the core," Kleezebee said.

Drew started typing into his keyboard and seconds later, the custom-built reactor engaged, filling the lab with a momentary swooshing sound.

Lucas' pulse began to race as excitement took control. He checked his instruments to verify the reactor's core had transformed into a space-like vacuum. "Core's ready, Professor."

"Now let's flood it with the gas," Kleezebee said.

Drew turned to another page in the procedure manual and pressed a series of bright yellow switches in order from left to right. Then he twisted two quarter-sized control knobs and pressed a black button labeled **FLOW**. "Flow regulators are set. Releasing the Radon gas now," he said, typing commands into his console.

"Radon gas?" Abby asked Drew.

"We use pressurized inert gas to stop unwanted chain reactions from occurring."

"Status?" Kleezebee asked.

"Seals holding. All systems report green," Drew replied after checking his instruments.

"Lucas, fire up the EM system, and make sure it's calibrated properly," Kleezebee said.

Lucas activated the electromagnets surrounding the core by lifting eight toggle switches simultaneously. Within milliseconds, he could hear the reverberating hum of the superconducting magnets starting their power-up sequence. As expected, a series of low-pitched tremors started in the floor and tickled his feet. Within seconds, the vibrations intensified, shaking the console desk and sending a jar of pencils and a pad of sticky notes off the edge. Abby bent down in her chair to pick them up off the floor.

"This is the point of no return. Let's have a full systems check before we proceed," Kleezebee announced to the team, his voice unsteady from the mounting rumble in the room.

Drew reviewed each subsystem. "Calibrations are . . . good. Power levels . . . check. Monitoring and safety systems are active and ready. E-121 is stable and pressures are holding. It looks like everything is working perfectly and within specs. I think we're good to go."

Lucas checked his watch: 10:24 p.m. He enshrined the time in his mind. This was it. The moment of truth. If this worked, all would be right with the world—his world—a world in which Drew and his mom were the two most important things. The fact that he'd royally screwed up by impulsively submitting the paper to Dr. Green's journal wouldn't matter anymore. His mistake would quickly disappear into the background and be buried under the enormous success of this project. It would make their entire team famous and bring instant respect among their peers. He'd be able to take care of his brother and his mother for as long as was necessary—no more living in a rent-free apartment and eating cafeteria food on a meal plan.

Lucas put a halt to his runaway excitement, returning his attention to the chamber. First things first. Prove the theory, verify the results, then report the success. That's the order a true scientist follows.

After a long exhale, Kleezebee said, "Set the beam's power to Level One. When the capacitor is charged, let 'er rip."

Lucas reached forward and unlocked a palm-sized black control knob attached to the vertical portion of the control station. He twisted it counterclockwise and set its indicator to **LEVEL ONE** before locking its protective cover back into place. He pushed a neighboring red **CHARGE** button and waited for the capacitor's power meter to increase. When it reached capacity, a green **READY** light lit up on his panel. He looked back at his boss. "We're all set, boss."

Kleezebee nodded.

Trevor scrunched up his face and took a giant step backward, as if he expected the chamber to explode. Trevor's movement surprised Lucas, because he'd never seen Trevor scared of anything. He couldn't think about that, though. He needed to focus on the task at hand.

The project comes first. Everything else comes second.

Lucas steadied his finger and pressed the green **READY** button. A short, pulsating whirr resonated from deep inside the chamber, signaling that the capacitor just released its stored energy. "Almost there," he mumbled with excitement. He could feel his chest tightening, making it difficult to breathe.

Soon the monitors in front of him began to stream multiple columns of numerical data up from the bottom. The numbers crawled up the screens like a swarm of digital army ants on the march toward imortality.

When the final set of results appeared, Lucas took a double-take to make sure he was reading the results correctly. He was—there were no results. He couldn't believe it. Not a goddamn thing. He stood up and yelled, "Shit!" and threw his safety glasses across the room with a side-armed throwing motion.

Abby flinched. "What's wrong?"

Lucas raised his hands against the sides of his head. While looking to the heavens, he said, "Nothing. That's what happened. Two years of work, and then—" He struggled to bring his emotions under control, but they were too powerful to hold back. "Nothing! We got nothing!"

Kleezebee put a firm hand on his shoulder. "It's okay, Lucas. Have patience. It's only our first attempt with E-121."

The professor turned to Drew. "What's the status of the core?"

Drew checked the reactor instruments. "Looks good. E-121 remains viable and the core's adequately pressurized. Should we try again, possibly at full power?"

"No, not yet. We don't want to get ahead of ourselves. At this point, there's no guarantee that doubling the power will accomplish anything."

Kleezebee began to pace the room while everyone else remained silent. He shuffled to the far wall and back, looking immersed in thought, his hands folded behind his back. Then he stopped pacing and addressed the group. "Before we do anything, I need you to perform a complete systems analysis of the available data. Let's see if we can tell what, if anything, happened. We might have missed something. Remember—details are everything. For now, let's power down the EM system but leave the core pressurized."

Kleezebee's cell phone rang. He opened the phone's flip cover. "Go for DL." Partway through the conversation, he held his hand over the phone's microphone and told the crew, "I need to go take this call. I'll be back in a few."

* * *

Half an hour later, the team was huddled around the center worktable after concluding their detailed systems analysis. Kleezebee still hadn't returned from his private phone call.

"Let's run through it one step at a time," Lucas told his team after a long exhale.

Drew's shoulders slumped as he read from a list of notes. "I checked the core's internal data feeds and didn't detect anything anomalous. The core's material remained viable throughout the test and the internal housing was structurally sound. The core's internal pressure held steady and was right on mark, but our instruments failed to show any notable change in E-121's EM field."

Lucas sensed his brother had more to report. "Anything else?"

Drew nodded. "The really odd thing is that with all the energy released, you'd think our instruments would've recorded something. If nothing else, it should've at least registered a power spike when the core was bombarded. But zilch. All that energy had to go somewhere. It's as though the beam never fired."

"Drew had me review the operational logs," Abby said. "According to the project specs, the capacitor's power level was precisely where it was supposed to be, and the beam frequency was tuned perfectly. All readings indicate the energy was discharged and the beam fired."

"I check magnets and calibration matched. Power okay. No failure," Trevor added with his thick accent skewing some of the words.

"Okay, then, let's recap what we know," Lucas said. "Everything was calibrated perfectly. The core and E-121 were stable. We had the proper amount of power. All our readings were normal before, during, and after the test. The capacitor's energy discharged and engaged the core, but no power was registered."

Lucas rubbed his temples. "Damn, that makes no sense. What are we missing?"

"Nothing. Everything went perfectly according to plan. It should've worked."

"I know, this whole thing is fucking nuts."

"What do we do next?" Drew asked, looking as perplexed as Lucas felt.

"What about full power?"

Drew hesitated, his eyes tightening into a long stare. "Worth a shot."

"Yeah, it's possible the beam's energy level wasn't sufficient enough to morph E-121's EM field. But we'll need to crunch a whole new set of numbers."

"We could also try reversing the EM polarity?" Abby asked with a look of confidence.

"Maybe use inverse wave frequency?" Trevor added.

Lucas took a minute to consider the merit of each suggestion. After a short pause, he decided a politically correct answer was in order. It would keep everyone happy and help cover up his indecisiveness. He wasn't ready to make a decision. Not one of this magnitude.

"Hmmm, all three ideas have potential. But we need to run them by DL to see what he wants to do, if anything. I will—"

Before he could finish the sentence, the room started to shake violently. The procedure manual slid off the console desk and the storage cabinets' metal doors rattled and flung open. Several items fell off the shelves and landed on the floor. Abby grabbed Drew's arm.

The tremor lasted less than ten seconds.

"Was that an earthquake?" Abby asked, letting go of Drew.

"It felt like one, but that's not what it was. We started feeling those tremors about a month ago. We checked with the USGS, but they said there hadn't been any seismic activity in the area," Lucas replied.

"We think the NASA group down the hall must be firing up one of their experiments. Some type of underground test, mostly likely," Drew said.

"I wonder what they're working on?" she asked.

"Nobody knows," Lucas said. "If you go past our lab and around a few more corners, you'll see their security checkpoints. There must be something big going on there, because they have a full complement of guards on duty around the clock. I'm pretty sure it's the most secure place on campus."

"So I take it you've never been down there?" she asked.

"No. Never. Those guards and their assault rifles are a great big sign that says *stay the hell away*."

Drew added, "We call it 'the Zone.' If they think you're a threat, they'll charge at you with their guns drawn. Several people have been arrested for just taking a wrong turn and not following their commands quickly enough."

Before anyone could respond to Drew's comment, the lab's telephone rang. It was mounted on the wall, next to the entrance. Lucas sprinted over to it and snatched its receiver from the cradle.

"Dr. Ramsay speaking," he said, turning sideways and leaning his right shoulder against the wall. To balance himself, he crossed his right leg over his left. He remained silent until the very end of the conversation. "Okay, I'll let the team know," he told the caller before slamming down the receiver. "That was Kleezebee. He said our project is on hold indefinitely, at least until he can convince the damn Advisory Committee to let us continue our work."

"What? How can that be? They've already approved this project," Drew snorted.

"Apparently that shit stain of an attorney, Larson, just got in touch with the committee chairman and somehow convinced him to suspend our experiment, pending a formal review. Kleezebee said it has something to do with government liability and the E-121 samples," Lucas said, figuring there was more going on behind the scenes than just that. Probably had something to do with his paper to Dr. Green. "All I know for sure is Kleezebee told us to shut down for now. He thinks it might take a while to talk some sense into the group. He said we all might as well head home for the holidays."

"But we're so close. How can they do this to us now?" his brother asked.

Lucas was sure it was his fault. He'd give anything to go back in time and stop himself from hitting the 'send' button on his laptop, but it was too late now. His heart had been in the right place. He was trying to take care of his family, but it completely backfired. He felt like such an idiot. Now his actions were going to affect everyone involved in the project, not just him. How could he have been so stupid? He wanted to tell Drew the truth but didn't want to disappoint him, not in front of the rest of the team—especially not in front of the new girl, Abby.

"There's no way to tell with these bureaucrats," Lucas said, choosing to keep his secret quiet for a bit longer. "Could be any number of reasons, and probably nothing to do with science either. Let's hope DL finds a way to work it out."

"I can't believe this is happening. We deserve better than this."

"I hear you, bro. But we'll have to wait a few days until Kleezebee gets back. He said he was heading to Washington right away to meet with the entire Advisory Committee. I guess they're at some technology conference in the Pentagon."

He turned his attention to the techs. "You two can leave, if you want. There's nothing more for you to do right now. We'll call you when the project's back on." He looked at Trevor. "Kleezebee said he wants you to call him right away."

Trevor nodded.

Abby slipped Drew a folded piece of paper before gathering up her belongings and walking to the door. Trevor held the door open and waited for her to walk through, then they both disappeared to the right as the doors closed behind them.

6

After Abby left the lab, Drew opened her handwritten note and saw a phone number with a tiny heart symbol drawn just below it. His face flushed, then his breath turned shallow as his palms began to sweat. A thousand fantasies leapt unbidden into his mind.

"So, what do you think we should do?" Lucas asked.

Drew thought about Abby's smile, the swell of her breasts in her tight t-shirt, the sway of her hips as she walked, and the alluring way she'd wiggled into the Hazmat suit as he'd watched over the monitor. He had no idea how she'd managed to make the ugly suit into something sexy, but she had.

"Hello? Earth to Drew," Lucas asked.

Drew snapped out of his reverie. "What?" He glanced down at the slip of paper in his hand, memorizing the number before folding and stuffing the note into his shirt pocket.

"I asked . . . what do you think we should do? About the experiment?"

"Not sure. After all those months of planning and testing, I really expected this to wo—" he said, pausing as an idea took shape in his mind. He knew it would be risky, but he didn't see another way. There was no guarantee Kleezebee would ever get approval from the Advisory Committee to resume the project, so that left only one choice. They had to try again, right then, before they were locked out of their own lab. For all he knew, their security codes might've already been cancelled, meaning they'd never get back into the lab once they left for the evening. He wouldn't put it past a weasel like Larson.

Plus, Drew's Quantum Energy thesis was due in less than a month, and he needed the neutron beam technology to show positive results. Otherwise, he'd never be awarded his PhD at the end of the year. Everything he'd worked for his entire collegiate career depended on it.

He looked at his brother, but didn't say anything.

Lucas flared his eyes. "Hey, I know that look. You got something, don't you? Come on, brother, out with it."

Drew cleared his throat, doubling checking with himself that he actually wanted to utter the words that were about to erupt from his lips. After careful reflection, he let 'em fly, adding in a mix of conviction and anger to his tone. "Well, we can't quit now. We're so close I can taste it. We've worked too darn hard for too darn long. If they shut us down now, our project will be a total failure. I've never failed at anything in my life, and I'm not about to start now! If it were up to me, I'd re-engage the EM system, charge the capacitor, this time to full strength, and hit it again. Unless someone checks the power logs, which is highly unlikely, nobody will ever know about it unless we succeed."

"Holy crap! Where did all that come from?" Lucas said with a look of shock on his face.

"I don't know, it just did. Stress I guess."

Lucas smiled, like he understood the motivation. Or maybe the desperation. "Try again? Full power? I don't know about that. Kleezebee's orders were very specific."

Drew had never used an obscenity in his life, but was ready to cuss like a sailor if it would persuade his brother to try again. He'd do anything to convince Lucas he was right. "I know he was, but what are our options? Just give up and give in? Let someone like Larson ruin our lives? You know as well as I do that we may never have this chance again. There's no guarantee Kleezebee will ever be able to get the committee to give us the go-ahead. Who knows how they're gonna react."

"I hear what you're saying, but—"

"You know what Dad always said? Don't be afraid to go after what you want, because nobody else will do it for you."

Lucas sighed but didn't answer. He shook his head slowly.

"Please, we're running out of time, Lucas. We have to try before they lock us out of our own lab. I've got a bad feeling about this. Larson wants us shut down. Permanently."

Lucas still didn't respond.

"Look, if it works, we can sell the patent and pay off Mom's medical bills. If it doesn't work, no one will ever know we even tried. I think this is what's called a win-win proposition."

Lucas appeared to be considering the idea. After a minute, he said in a matter-of-fact way, "It would be nice to get rid of those vultures, once and for all. I don't know how else we're gonna clear all that debt. Certainly not with my measly paycheck."

"Then you agree?"

Lucas shrugged. "I don't know. Maybe . . . So, you think full power is the way to go?"

"Absolutely. There's no sense in replicating what we just did. We have to make some sort of change if we expect a different result, and running the experiment at full power seems like the simplest thing we can do in the limited time we have. They could lock us out at any minute. This might be our one and only chance."

"All right. Let's go for it. I'm with you a hundred percent," he said, giving Drew a knuckle bump. "All for one and—"

"One for all," Drew finished, wearing a full smile.

The brothers spent the next forty-five minutes preparing for their next attempt. They crosschecked and completed each step in the procedure manual, except this time around, they charged the beam's capacitor to full power.

Drew completed the last step and was ready to begin. He recorded the new time into the logbook: 11:52 p.m., December 21.

Just then, Drew wondered if Abby's suggestion to reverse the polarity might actually work. He knew her proposal was a long shot, but it was worth considering. He flipped through the procedure manual, stopping on page sixteen to review the equations. Then something caught his eye.

"Hey, wait a minute. That can't be right," he mumbled. He reached into his backpack and pulled out a copy of their original work. After comparing the two versions of the manual, he said, "Holy cow, DL changed our calculations."

"What?"

"How the heck did I miss this?" Drew asked, using a yellow marker to highlight the changes. He handed both copies of the manual to Lucas. "Here, see for yourself. He changed our wave displacement factors."

Lucas spent a minute reviewing the calculations. "You're right. Why would he do that and not tell us?"

"I have no idea. But it might have caused the failure."

"It certainly would explain the conflicting data."

"We should use our original equations and run it again."

"Do you still want to use full power?" Lucas asked.

"Yes, definitely," Drew said, plowing forward on his keyboard to enter the correct calculations.

They spent the next fifteen minutes reconfiguring their experiment.

"Okay, we're ready," Drew said.

"Let 'er rip," Lucas replied in an old man's voice, sounding like he was trying to do an imitation of Kleezebee from earlier.

Drew pressed the green **READY** switch to fire the charged neutron beam, listening for the sound of the pulse. Once he heard it, he sat back to watch the steady stream of data fill the center monitor.

So far, so good. Everything was going according to plan. Maybe his idea to run the experiment at full power was going to pay off. Then a few of the readings changed. His excitement started to change into nervousness. Then more of the readings scrolled into view, but were off a bit. Then he realized something wasn't right. He wasn't sure what it was until some anomalies in the data values jumped out at him from the right column. His heart skipped a beat. The reactor's internal mass readings were low—much too low.

No, he thought. *That can't be right.* Maybe the monitor was malfunctioning. It would explain the change in numbers. He scrambled to enter commands into his keyboard, trying to validate the readings. But the checksums validated—the numbers shown on the monitor were correct.

He sat forward to lean in close to the screen, looking over the data values one final time, making sure he wasn't misinterpreting the results. There was no denying it—the mass of the material inside the reactor had dropped by almost a hundred percent.

He changed the screen to show the video feed from inside the core. He was afraid to look, but did anyway. "Are you kidding me?"

"What's wrong?" Lucas asked.

Drew pointed his finger at the screen. "Look, it's gone!"

"What's gone?" Lucas asked, scooting his chair closer to Drew's station. "You need to be more specific."

Drew couldn't stop the barrage of cuss words he'd been storing up his entire life. They came flying out of his mouth with force. "The goddamned, bitch-ass E-121 is not fucking there anymore!"

Lucas' jaw dropped, his face frozen in time like he'd just seen a UFO.

Drew looked at his brother and shrugged, pretending he didn't know what had just stunned Lucas. "What?"

"I don't believe what I just heard. You spewed like a drunken sailor."

A sickening feeling began to churn in Drew's stomach. "Yeah, I know. Sorry about that. I feel awful, but I couldn't help it. It just came out before I could stop it."

Lucas chuckled with a smirk on his face. "It's okay, bro. You made your point. It's gone. I get it. Now I need you to show me what the hell happened."

Drew turned his attention to the video replay, using frame-by-frame mode to show the recording from inside the chamber. The evidence showed that just before E-121 and its container disappeared, an instantaneous white flash of light filled the core. It originated as a microscopic point near the center of the container before expanding vertically and then horizontally, like a four-pointed star. A few frames later, the brightness vanished, and so did E-121 and its receptacle.

"Where did it go?" Lucas asked.

Drew zoomed in the camera. "Beats the shi—I mean crap—out of me."

"What's that stuff covering the base?"

"Looks like some type of black film."

"I need to get in there," Lucas said, pointing. "Prep the chamber."

Drew flipped several switches on the riser panel to power down the reactor's subsystems.

* * *

Lucas rushed to get into the safety gear, before snatching two electronic devices from the equipment cabinet and a plastic sample container from the supply cabinet.

He went to the chamber, stepped inside and completed decontamination procedures before hurrying back to the reactor. When he arrived, he paused to take a few deep breaths before opening the core's protective shield. He didn't want to face reality, but it was about to look him dead in the face. Drew was never wrong, but Lucas still couldn't keep himself from wishing that wasn't the case, just this once. His entire future was inside the core—at least it used to be.

When he looked inside, he confirmed the reactor was empty. Shit. No sign of E-121 or its container. Only the black residue remained. He couldn't help but stare at the emptiness, hoping the material would somehow return to set things right. But it didn't. He gulped, wondering how he was going to explain this to Kleezebee.

A series of painful flashes from his past roared through his thoughts, making him relive some of the more difficult moments from his days in the orphanage: the beatings, the lonely nights, the crappy food and the overcrowded bedrooms. Everything he'd survived thus far had led up to this moment, and now . . . complete failure. He took another few seconds to let it all sink in. Then he decided to press on and try to determine what happened.

Lucas used the portable multi-spectrum analyzer from storage to scan for all known forms of radiation, but found none. Next, he used the Radon detector to check for signs of the toxic gas. He held up its sensor probe while walking the length of the chamber, but the results were negative.

He turned to Drew and gave the thumbs down signal, waiting to see his brother's reaction. Maybe Drew wasn't as disappointed as he was, but his brother's face told a different story. Drew looked downright depressed, which was saying something since he was usually the happiest man in the room. Even at a funeral, Drew could somehow push through the heartache and project an upbeat attitude. Drew's happy demeanor was usually infectious, but it was nowhere to be seen today. Not now—not after this.

Lucas opened the plastic container and used his glove-covered finger as a scoop to retrieve a sample of the black powder. He left the reactor with the specimen in hand, completed decontamination procedures, and changed back into his clothes.

He put the sample container on the desk in front of his brother, trying to think of something witty or clever to say to alleviate the suffocating tension in the room. However, the words failed him, so he went with an old standby line. "Here, don't say I never gave you anything."

Drew picked up the plastic container, held it close to his eyes, and shook it gently. "What do you think happened to E-121?"

Lucas sat down and leaned back in his chair while rubbing the back of his neck and shoulders. "I have no clue. Do you think we used too much power and vaporized it?"

"I wish I knew."

"Kleezebee's going to be royally pissed."

"Yeah, at me. This was my idea," Drew said, looking petrified.

"That's not how it's gonna be, bro. DL put me in charge and ultimately, I'm responsible."

"Are you sure? Because that doesn't seem right. I talked you into this."

"Look, I know you want to be a stand up guy and all, but bottom line, this was my call. I need to take the heat, not you. Besides, I don't want anything to jeopardize your PhD candidacy," Lucas said, thinking about the thesis he submitted to Dr. Green. Blowback from the article was coming and this latest failure was the least of his worries. If he was going down for it, might as well be for everything. No reason to let Drew's future be affected. "Trust me, this isn't the first time I've screwed the pooch, or the last. I'm sure it'll all blow over eventually. It's not like they're going to fire me. They need us. Both of us. It's all good, bro."

Drew hesitated, then let out a concerned smile. "Thanks, Lucas. I owe you one."

"But it probably wouldn't hurt to figure out what happened and see if we can't reverse it. Or stop it from happening again in the future. Mistakes happen in labs all the time. That's how breakthroughs and discoveries happen—on the heels of failure. We're no different, right?"

Drew nodded.

They spent the next hour checking the available data logs, instrument readings, and video feeds.

"The answer has to be in here somewhere." Lucas flipped through the final pages of data on the computer screen. He sat back in his chair, yawned, stretched, and then rubbed his watery eyes. When he looked back at the computer screen, he noted a single nonconforming data value just below the top edge of the screen. He almost missed it. He scrolled back a page and found another strange value just above it.

"Holy shit!"

"What?"

"There was a massive power spike inside the reactor."

"Are you serious?"

"Yes, deadly."

"How massive?" Drew asked.

"According to the readings, about a trillion times the level we were using at the time."

"That's not possible. You must be misreading the results."

"Hey, all I can tell you is what the log says. Somehow, the reactor was hit with a huge power spike."

Drew tilted the computer screen toward him and stared at it for good minute, before flipping through several of the data pages. "You're absolutely right. The spike's timing does seem to coincide with E-121's disappearance. Now what?"

"Well, a few minutes ago, I was thinking we should run it again, and try to recreate the conditions that led to the sudden loss of mass. However, the energy spike changes things," he said, handing the black powder container to Drew. "I think the first thing we need to do is figure out what this stuff is. You should go see if Griffith can identify it."

"Why me?"

"Because it's your turn. I've had my fill of Griffith for the day," Lucas said, smiling. "Have fun, little brother."

* * *

A short while later, Lucas was leaning back in his chair with his eyes closed when he heard Drew come through the lab door. He sat up and turned to face the entrance. "What's the verdict?"

"It doesn't exist."

"What the hell does that mean?"

Drew gave the container to Lucas. "It means it doesn't register at all. Griffith ran it through his mass spectrometer, but it didn't detect any chemical or biological compounds. It's as though the stuff wasn't even there."

"Okay, let me ask you this. If we don't know what this stuff is, how do we know if it's safe to be handling it right now?"

"We don't. There's no way to tell."

"Well then, I guess if it doesn't exist, it can't hurt to inspect it a little closer," he said, opening the lid. He retrieved some of the black substance and rubbed it around between the tips of his fingers. It felt smooth, almost like baby powder, but heavier. He held his fingers up to his nose and took a whiff. "Kind of smells like . . . oranges."

Drew leaned in and sniffed the sample. He shook his head. "I don't smell anything."

"Well, I do. Your sniffer must not be working."

"So what's next?" Drew asked.

Lucas reattached the container's lid and cleaned off his fingers with a paper towel. "I don't know about you, but I'm totally spent right now and can't think straight. It's been a brutal night. Let's close up shop and come back tomorrow to see if we can figure this out before DL gets back from Washington."

"Sounds like a good plan. But we'll have to wait until Sunday to come back, though."

"Why?"

"Mainframe? Servicing? Tonight? Did you forget?"

"Oh crap, that's right. Okay, we'll come back Sunday, then."

Lucas backed up their instrument readings and data logs onto a USB flash drive in case he wanted to review the data later. He unzipped Drew's backpack and put the thumb drive and the black powder container into it.

The brothers followed established shutdown procedures for their equipment before leaving the lab and heading back to their apartment.

Lucas was looking forward to crawling into bed. He hoped when he woke up in the morning, the events of the day would turn out to be nothing but a bad dream. A long, painful, never-ending nightmare. One he planned to forget ever happened.

7

Saturday, December 22

The next morning Lucas stepped out of the handicapped-accessible shower stall in their apartment, wiping himself off with a beige terry-cloth towel. The bathroom was filled with rising steam trails after his long, hot cleansing, flooding his nostrils with moisture.

He closed his eyes and slid in front of the mirror, never wanting the relaxing moment to end. The tranquility raced into his soul, filling him with peace. He took a few moments to let the comforting feeling soak in and register, because he knew when he opened his eyes again, reality would return with a vengeance.

There was a good possibility his life might never be the same again after this blissful moment passed. If he was right, he needed to remember what it all felt like before the balance of his own history began to write itself into the annals of time. A future history filled with ramifications from a series of poor decisions.

Lucas sucked in a deep breath and held it for a three count before letting the air out in a slow release. He repeated the same methodical breathing process two more times, thinking of nothing but the tepid humidity caressing his skin. When he was done, he felt invigorated and ready to face the day. It was time to open his eyes.

He wiped off a spot on the mirror with the towel, clearing a path to witness the pain. There it was—the look of disaster—staring back at him. A face littered with the aftereffects from the previous day's debacles.

There was nothing he could do about all that had happened except move forward and take destiny on with all he could muster. And that's what he decided to do—right there, right then—it was time to man up.

He slipped on his boxer briefs and a pair of ankle-high white socks he had sitting on the bathroom counter. Then he wiped off the rest of the mirror so he could keep watch on his hands as they lathered up his face with shaving cream.

"What do you wanna do for breakfast?" he yelled to Drew, almost smearing some of the cream into his right eye.

"Hang on a minute, I'm on the phone," Drew yelled back from the other room.

Lucas scraped the five-bladed razor across the middle of his chin, trying not to cut open any of his childhood scars. The blade pulled and ripped at his stubble, reminding him to buy replacements at the campus drugstore. When he finished, he rinsed off his face, toweled it dry, and then waited for signs of blood to appear. There were none. He ran a blast of hot water through the blades and tapped the razor twice against the edge of the sink.

Drew rolled into the bathroom and squeezed past the back of Lucas' legs, positioning his wheelchair between the sink and the toilet. Their apartment had an oversized handicapped accessible bathroom, its only redeeming quality. Drew put his maroon-colored shaving kit on the edge of the sink, along with a can of air freshener. The can was still shrink-wrapped, with a price sticker on its side.

"Round two?" Lucas asked, sending a wide smile at his brother.

Drew laughed. "I should've known better than to have those onion rings yesterday."

"Can you wait a minute? I just need to brush my teeth."

"Sorry, can't. I've been holding on too long already. I think that's the longest shower you've ever taken in your life."

"Yeah, got lost in my head for bit. Sorry. Needed to chill."

"You should probably get out of here. What I have to do ain't gonna be pretty."

Lucas laughed, appreciating the delicate touch in his brother's words. He was usually much more graphic about his bowel movements, like any other college student would be. He gave Drew an extra roll of toilet paper from under the sink. "Here, sounds like you might need this."

* * *

Lucas was on the couch when he heard the toilet flush and the air freshener canister go off in three long bursts. He went into the bathroom and stood next to Drew, who was washing his hands in the sink.

"I think you need to use more of the spray. It's hard to breathe in here," Lucas said, holding the shirt collar over his nose.

"I don't smell anything."

"You never do. Like I said yesterday in the lab, your sniffer ain't working."

Lucas dodged his brother's left arm as Drew removed his pajama top. It was all part of his brother's shaving ritual. After that, Drew would spend a good ten minutes brushing each of his teeth twenty-one times.

"Damn, how many push-ups did you do today?" Lucas asked, seeing Drew's pumped up biceps.

"Three hundred seventy-five, a new personal best."

Lucas looked at his physique in the mirror. "I'd be lucky to do fifty. Plus it would take me all day."

"I had a lot of extra energy today."

"Maybe you should think about wearing a short-sleeved shirt, to show off those guns to the ladies."

"Nah, I don't think so."

Lucas flexed his right bicep in the mirror, but it was barely noticeable. "I know I would if I had your biceps. It seems like no matter how hard I try, I can't put on any weight. I still look like I did in eighth grade. Even my koala bear birthmark looks the same. Nothing ever changes."

"Except you're a foot taller."

"Seriously, dude, you should think about it. I see major hotties checking you out all the time."

"I doubt that. Besides, I don't care about them. I figure I've found the only girl for me."

"Who?"

"Abby."

"Our new lab assistant?"

Drew smiled.

"Granted, she's smokin' hot, but you just met her. She could be a bunny-boiler for all you know. Besides, how do you know she's even interested?"

"Because she gave me her phone number yesterday and I just called her. We're meeting this morning for coffee at the Wildcat House."

Lucas was impressed by his brother's initiative, especially since Drew didn't drink coffee. His brother was more of a milk and cookies kind of guy.

"Am I invited?"

"Are you serious? It's sort of a date. I'd look totally lame if I brought my brother along to help me out. Besides, I'm pretty sure she's only expecting me."

"Yeah, you're right. Maybe I'll just grab something here."

"I guess it would be okay, though. It's up to you. She probably won't mind if you join us."

"No, you go ahead. I'm gonna make some cinnamon oatmeal. Maybe even fry up a slab of bacon," Lucas said, trying to flex his non-existent chest muscles in the mirror. "You might want to bring her a gift."

"What kind of gift?"

Lucas smiled. "Like a dozen red roses wrapped in a big yellow bow. She obviously likes flowers since she wears them in her hair."

"I don't know. That sounds expensive. Can't I just get her something small?"

"Maybe a box of chocolates?"

"I'll think about it," Drew said, thumbing through the dust inside his wallet. "Hey, when Mom calls later, be sure to find out what the cardiologist said. I was planning to ask her, but since I won't be here—"

"Do you really think you'll be gone that long?"

Drew grinned. "I hope so."

* * *

Drew waited for the shuttle driver to retrieve his wheelchair from the rack on the front bumper of the bus. After getting in his chair, he thanked the driver and tipped him a dollar, not knowing if gratuity was appropriate or if the amount were sufficient. Lucas normally took care of fetching his wheelchair from the rack and gratuities, so tipping the driver was uncharted territory for him. Either way, the buck was all he could spare.

He made his way along the sidewalk next to the science lab. To his right was a flower garden flush with the glowing reds and enchanting purples of mums, pansies, petunias, and some other flowers he did not recognize. Perhaps the botany department was experimenting with some new type of flora, genetically modified to burst open with vivid colors and fragrances. He strolled next to the flowerbed, reached down, and snapped off one of the more radiant red flowers. He placed it across his lap, then un-tucked his shirt and used it to hide the gift.

Drew resumed his trip, entering the west end of the Student Union, where he rode the elevator up two levels and found Abby sitting at a table near the front of the Wildcat House restaurant. In front of her were two jumbo-sized Styrofoam cups of coffee and a plate of muffins.

He hesitated for a moment, wondering if he could really go through with it. She was more gorgeous than he remembered, and was wearing a low-cut pink sweater and pair of what looked like tight blue denim stretch jeans. Her long black hair fell over her clear skin in a soft cascade, and her red full lips stirred feelings inside his body that he wasn't used to dealing with in the wild, so to speak.

She smiled when they made eye contact. Drew blushed. She stood up and walked over to greet him, catching him off guard when she wrapped her arms around his shoulders for a tight hug. Drew went to hug her back, but missed the opportunity when she let go before he could react. She looked into his eyes, as if he needed to say something.

He swallowed hard, scrambling for something cool to say. Something that would cover up the fact that he failed to hug her back and may have embarrassed her. "Wow, it's nice in here," he said, loud enough for everyone to hear—not what he expected his lips to say.

Arggg, could the words have been any less cool? I'm such a geek.

"Haven't you been in here before?" she asked, looking away as if she just became disinterested in him. Then her eyes returned, and so did her smile.

He relaxed a bit, slipping into the comfort of her gaze. "No. We always eat in the cafeteria on the first floor. I try to avoid stairs whenever I can. Tough on the knees, if you know what I mean."

She laughed, glancing at his wheelchair for a second.

But he wasn't trying to be funny. Oh well, her eyes were totally focused on him so he decided to just go with it.

"Well, in that case, I guess it's up to me to show you the ropes. I know all the coolest hot spots and how to avoid being on your knees," she said, winking, then handing him one of the cups of coffee when he reached the cozy two-person table. "I love this place. It's my favorite place to sit and chill on campus."

He smiled, then put the cup on the table before sliding his wheelchair under the edge. He was sitting directly across from her, only an arm's length away. He wasn't sure if the time was right, but couldn't wait any longer. He reached under his shirt to retrieve the flower he'd picked from the garden outside, then gave it to her. "This is for you."

"Oh Drew, it's so beautiful. Thank you sooooo much. Nobody has ever given me flowers before."

Drew smiled. "To be honest, this is the first time I've ever given someone flowers." The instant those words left his lips, he felt like such a tool. Smooth, he thought. Let her know exactly how inexperienced you are. *Could you be any more of a total goof?*

"What kind of flower is it?"

"I really don't know. But when I saw it, it made me think of you. It's breathtaking." He wasn't sure where those words came from, but he was impressed with himself. Just when he thought he couldn't be more lame, he actually sounded smooth and charming, as if he'd done this before. Lucas would be proud of him. So would his adoptive father, if he were still alive.

Abby gently hugged the flower across her chest. She stood up, came to his side of the table, and then hugged him again, though this time she lingered much longer.

He took a deep, slow breath and let the aroma of her hair filter into his nose. Apple was the scent he detected, and the touch of her smooth skin made him blush again—but this time he felt the blush hit his entire body.

A second chance, he thought. *Don't mess up.*

He wrapped his arms around her, finding her tiny body soft and inviting. The warmth of her gentle breath caressed his neck and her sweet perfume was intoxicating. The combination of everything made him tremble, and he was glad she couldn't see his hands or read his thoughts. He was in heaven, praying she'd never let go. But she did.

Drew wasn't sure what to say next, so he just smelled his cup of steaming java, hoping she might continue the conversation. The coffee blend had an enjoyable aroma. If it tasted half as good as it smelled, he might actually like it.

He took a sip, and then understood why he avoided coffee, as a rule. It was nasty. It tasted like feet. Old feet that had been wrapped in the same pair of socks for a week. He wanted to spit it back into the cup, but figured that wouldn't look too cool on a first date. Abby had just said she loved the place, so he needed to play along. He smiled at her, then sucked in another mouthful. The java was scorching hot, burning the roof of his mouth. He hated it. Every last drop.

"Do you like it? It's my favorite," she said.

"Yes. It's really delicious." He tore open and dumped four packs of sugar into it. He took another drink, wondering if he'd ever get used to the disgusting taste. It was bitter and pungent. The four packets of sugar didn't help take the edge off. "Yum," he said. "They sure know how to do it right in this place."

"Yeah, I come here all the time. It's always packed. Did you have any trouble getting here?"

"No, I took the shuttle. It dropped me off a block away."

"Lucas didn't drive you?"

"No, we don't have a car. But the shuttle's pretty handy. Not expensive, either."

"Do you live close by?"

"We're just north of Speedway, in an old apartment building Dr. Kleezebee owns."

"He owns an apartment building? I never would've guessed that by the way he dresses. Looks like he shops at Goodwill."

"Don't let his appearance fool you; Kleezebee's loaded."

"Really? Dr. Kleezebee?"

"It's true. Have you ever heard of BTX Enterprises?"

"Hmmm," she said, then hesitated. "Actually, I have seen their signs all over town. At construction sites and stuff, I think. Are they a developer or something like that?

"They have their hands in a bunch of things. It's Kleezebee's company."

"It's his?"

"Yep. He owns it."

"Wow, impressive. If I remember right, aren't they building the new Atlantis World Mall halfway between here and Phoenix?"

Drew nodded. "They are. I can't wait to see it. It's going to be the world's largest indoor mall by the time they're finished. Kleezebee told me they're building a really cool science exhibit for the kids, too. I hope it includes a telescope for some decent nighttime viewing. The kids will love that. I just wish it was going to be closer."

"Is your apartment nice?"

"Not really. It's old and small. But it does have a bathroom big enough for my chair. I need handrails and stuff. Kleezebee lets us live there for free, so we can't complain."

"That's very generous of him," she replied with a surprised look on her face.

"He does that for a lot of his staff. Bruno and Trevor live in our complex, too. He even keeps a place there, though I'm not sure why. He's never there. I think he sleeps in his office most nights."

"I see he wears a wedding ring. Is he married?" she asked.

"Yeah, supposedly. That's the story, at least. I don't think anyone's ever seen his wife, though. I've been in his office and his apartment, but there aren't any pictures of her or any kids. To tell you the truth, I'm not sure what the deal is."

Drew's eyes wandered away from Abby on their own, looking beyond her at the checkout counter along the back wall of the Wildcat House. A broad-shouldered man with a Mohawk haircut was standing in line, talking to two female students in front of him. Drew recognized him. It was the jerk rugby player from the altercation in the cafeteria— the one who had shoved his wheelchair across the room. His heart raced and he started to sweat.

Not now, he thought. *Not in front of Abby.*

If the rugby player decided to pick on him again, he'd be humiliated. He should have invited Lucas along for the date.

"Is it a two-bedroom?" Abby asked.

Drew slumped down in his chair and leaned to his right, using Abby as a shield. If the jock turned his way, he'd be hidden from view. He looked down at his muffin and coffee. He'd read somewhere that if you don't stare at someone, they're less likely to turn around and look at you. Some kind of psychic connection, the article said.

"Did you hear me?" she asked.

"I'm sorry, what did you say?"

"Is your apartment a two-bedroom?"

"No, it's only a one. Lucas and I share a room, just like we did as kids. What about you?" Drew kept his eyes on Abby and prayed Mohawk man was preoccupied with the girls he was talking to. Abby's smoldering eyes drew him in and he focused on the soothing sound of her voice.

"I live in Cochise Hall. It's just on the other side of the Science Lab."

Drew took a full bite of the chocolate chip muffin and washed it down with another sip of the revolting coffee. His throat wasn't working properly, making it difficult to swallow. He was worried that if he choked or coughed—if he made any move or noise at all—the rugby player might notice him.

Then he realized he was sweating like a pig and his face was red. He was sure Abby could sense his nervousness. He went to take another sip of coffee to wash down the muffin, but accidentally swallowed more than he could handle. He choked, coughed, and had to grab his napkin from the table to wipe the coffee dripping down his chin, sending his fork clinking onto the floor.

Great, he thought. *There's no way Mr. Mohawk didn't hear that. My date: ruined. My ass: toast.* He cringed, closed his eyes, and waited for the jock to come over to their table. The moment stretched into two moments. Nothing happened. He opened his eyes, and all he could see was Abby.

"Drew, are you okay?" she asked, using her foot to retrieve the fork. She bent down, grabbed it, and put it on the table.

It took a few moments to get his voice working again. "I'm fine. Just went down the wrong pipe. And I got something in my eye. Sorry about that."

"It's okay. Was kinda cute, actually."

"It was?"

"Yeah. It's nice to know I'm not the only one who's a little nervous. I don't usually go out on coffee dates, like ever. Or any real dates, either. You know, with studying and all there just isn't much time. Plus most guys I meet are complete selfish jerks. But this is nice."

Drew smiled. He was relieved. Maybe his date wasn't ruined after all. He reviewed their conversation in his head—she'd just told him she lived in Cochise Hall. He decided to pick up right there, not knowing if he should address all her nice comments. "What's it like living in Cochise? I've never been in that dorm. Are there single rooms or doubles?

"Doubles, mostly. I have a roommate, just like you. Her name's Jasmine. She's a pre-med student from Colorado. I'm lucky. I've heard so many roommate horror stories, but she's really fun and we get along great. Her dad's in the military. Some general, she said. I've never met him face to face, but he called once and I answered."

"Are they close?" Drew said, thinking of his deceased father.

"Not really. He's too busy, I think."

"Are you from Colorado, too?" he asked, checking the checkout line. Rugby player was still busy working his way through.

"No, I'm from Milwaukee, Wisconsin."

Drew wasn't much of a sports fan, but felt confident he could fake it. He guessed at some facts, hoping he remembered them correctly. "Oh yes, the home of the Packers and the Wisconsin Badgers. Do you get home much?"

"Only during the summer when I can drive back home. It's too expensive to fly over the Christmas break."

Cool, Drew thought. *She'll be on campus over the break.* Just like him and Lucas. He wouldn't have to wait long for another date, assuming he didn't mess this up and she wanted another date. *Just keep the conversation moving,* he thought—*no awkward pauses.* "My mom lives up in Phoenix. Usually she drives down and picks us up for the holiday, but she had heart surgery recently and can't drive. So we plan to stay here and work on our project over the break."

"Is she okay?"

"Yeah, she's doing great. One of our neighbors watches out for her. The doctors say she should be able to get back to work soon."

Drew glanced at the counter again. The rugby player was still chatting with the girls in line. So far, so good, except now his stomach was turning flips. He might need to make a run for the bathroom soon. Not a bad idea, he thought. It would make a good place to hide—for a while a least. But what would happen if that guy followed him into the restroom? He'd be cornered, alone, and helpless. He decided to remain where he was—plenty of other people around.

"What's your mom do?" Abby asked.

"She's a mathematics professor at Paradise Community College in Phoenix."

"And your dad?"

"He died two years ago."

She reached over and squeezed his hand. "I'm so sorry, Drew. I didn't know."

"It's okay. There was no way you could have."

"Still, I shouldn't have asked. I'm sorry," she said, rubbing her soft forefinger across the top of his hand. He looked at her and she smiled back with a glaze of tears in her eyes.

"It's okay, really. We've put it all behind us as a family. It was tough, though. Kinda came out of nowhere. Dad went into the hospital one day for a routine test, and never came out. They were doing an angiogram on his neck and something went wrong. We never really got the whole story."

"You must really miss him."

Drew stared into his coffee while swirling it around with a thin red straw. He looked up, but couldn't see the bully through Abby's head. "Yeah, very much. Besides my brother, he was my best friend. We used to spend all day working on inventions in his workshop. Those were great times."

"Your dad was an inventor?"

"Well, he tried to be, but he never really had much success. He did come up with this cool self-cleaning toilet, but nobody was interested. I guess electricity and bowel movements weren't meant to go together."

She laughed.

He continued with confidence. "Dad's best invention was a sonic pest control system. He even found some investors for it, but the EPA chased them away when their field testing showed it liquefied dog brains."

"Gross," she said, slurping from her cup.

"I know, right. It was epic."

"Do you ever think about continuing his work?"

"Sometimes Lucas and I talk about it, but we've never had the time. We've both been so busy with school. I guess we should, though. The idea is solid, and I'm sure we could work out the kinks. All his equipment is still in the garage back home. After he died, Mom couldn't bear to part with any of it."

He thought he was talking too much about himself. "How about you? Are your parents back in Wisconsin?"

Her smile vanished and her shoulders slumped. "They both passed away my senior year in high school. I miss them so much."

Drew tried to respond, but couldn't find the words. His throat went dry and he felt a stab of compassion for her. She looked so sad. He wanted to comfort her, but he didn't know if he should hold her hand or roll over to her and give her a hug. He did neither. He felt useless.

"I'm sorry for your loss, Abby. I can tell you really loved them."

Abby wiped a tear from her cheek. "Mom died from colon cancer. Dad passed away in his sleep six months later. I think he died of a broken heart. They were together almost forty years."

"I've heard that's pretty common for couples who've been married for a long time," he said with a soft tone in his voice. "Sounds like they loved each other very much."

A smile washed over Abby's lips. She nodded quickly. The joy returned to her eyes. "Yes, they did. And we were close. I was lucky growing up. We were a happy family."

Drew took another swig of coffee. It didn't taste quite as bad this time. It still wasn't pleasant, but at least he no longer wanted to spit it out. "Anyone else? Sisters or brothers?"

"I'm an only child, just like my dad. My mom had a sister, though, but she died when I was really young. Some horrible dump truck accident. I don't remember her at all. What about you? Any aunts or uncles?"

"Nah. Just me, Lucas, and Mom. Oh, and Grandpa Roy. But we never see him anymore."

"Why not?"

"I don't want to bore you with family drama."

"I'm curious. I want to know more about you."

"You sure?"

"Yeah, unless I'm prying." She paused. "I'm sorry, am I being too nosy?"

"No, not at all." Drew tried to wrap his mind around the idea that an attractive girl was interested in his family life. He didn't understand why, but decided to tell her anyway. "Well," he began, "we haven't spoken much since the time we almost had to call the police on him."

"Oh my God." Abby raised her eyebrows. "What happened?"

"It was Thanksgiving, four years ago. Everything was going along just fine until Roy decided to open a second jug of wine. It wasn't long before he and Dad were totally sloshed, and then all hell broke loose. They started cussing and shoving each other, then Roy took a swing at my dad. Next thing I know, they're beating the crap out of each other and Mom is screaming at them to stop. Lucas jumped in to break it up, but he took one in the jaw—knocked him out cold. The fight stopped on its own at that point."

"What started it?"

"Seemed like every time Roy stayed with us, he'd harp endlessly about Dad getting a real job. He's a real traditional guy. He didn't approve of Dad being an inventor and working from home. He thought the husband's job was to work, and the wife's job was to stay home, raise kids, and cook and clean. He didn't approve of my mom's teaching career, either. Most of the time my dad just brushed it off, but when he drank, he had less tolerance for Roy's constant criticism. That night, he'd just had enough. He got tired of it and said something he shouldn't have."

"I can see why Roy's not welcome anymore."

Drew continued. "He's a high-ranking Army intelligence officer and moves around a lot, so we wouldn't see him much anyway. I think he's back East somewhere right now. The last time we saw him was at Dad's funeral. He arrived late and sat in the back of the church. He left before the service was over."

"That's too bad. Family's important, and you'd think he'd want to stay in touch, especially after your dad died."

"Actually, he and Lucas started talking again recently."

"They did?"

"Yep, but Lucas doesn't know I know. Last week, I stumbled across a few emails hidden in his spam folder by accident."

"He puts them in the spam folder?"

"I guess he figures I wouldn't look there. But I probably shouldn't have told you. I'm sorry. Don't say anything, okay?"

"I won't," Abby said. "Have you ever thought about calling Roy?"

"To be honest, never. He and I have nothing in common. I'm into science and he's career military. Lucas is into all that stuff, but I could care less."

"You and Lucas seem to get along well."

"Yeah, we do. I don't know what I'd do without him," Drew said, missing his brother more than ever at that moment. He checked the counter line again—Mohawk man was still there. He wished he'd just go away.

"I take it you're older than your brother?" Abby asked.

"A lot of people think that. Actually, he's six months older than me."

"You guys look so different."

"That's because he's Irish and I'm Italian. I'm sure Dr. Kleezebee didn't tell you . . . but we're both adopted."

She paused, giving off a look of surprise. "Oh, that makes sense. I thought you were stepbrothers or something."

"I'm sure a lot of people think we're brothers from a different mother, which of course we are, just not in the way they think. But we don't go around advertising."

"I don't blame you. It's really nobody's business, including mine."

"It's okay, Abby. I want you to know everything about me." He suddenly felt like he'd said something wrong. "Was that too much?"

"Not at all." She smiled. "Is it too much that I want to know everything about you?"

"No," he said. "I like it."

"Good," she said. "So go ahead. Tell me."

He decided to start at the beginning. "It's simple, really. The state put us together as roommates when we were really little. Lucas barely said anything to me the first month. But he finally came around. I guess I grew on him. We've been best friends ever since."

"Your parents adopted both of you, together?"

"Yeah, we were a package deal. It doesn't happen that way very often. We lucked out." Drew checked the counter again—the miscreant was next in line at the cash register. He thought about faking an excuse to go home, but didn't want to leave Abby there all alone. What if the rugby player tried to hit on her? Or worse, what if he spotted him leaving and followed him outside?

The rugby player opened his wallet and handed a few bills to the checkout girl, who was chewing gum and blowing six-inch pink bubbles with it.

Drew's heart sank. It wouldn't be long before Mr. Asshole spotted him. Sweat dripped from his temples and his hands shook. He decided to roll up his sleeves to expose his biceps. They were still pumped up from that morning's pushups and might be enough to dissuade the troublemaker from stopping at their table. It was a long shot, but it was the only idea he could muster.

"Wow, you have really strong arms," Abby said with a curious look on her face.

Drew felt blood swelling in his cheeks and forehead, certainly turning his face a beet-red color. He was worried she might think he was showing off. "Uh . . . yeah, it's a little hot in here with all the coffee and stuff. I'm still a little sweaty from my workout this morning. I hope I don't smell."

She touched his hand again. "Sweetie, you smell really nice."

"Thanks, I was a little worried there for a moment." Drew wiped the sweat off his face with the folded red napkin sitting in front of him on the table.

She smiled back at him. "Can I ask you something? You don't have to answer this if you don't want to."

"No, go ahead. Ask me anything."

"How did Lucas get that horrible scar on his face?"

Drew laughed. "Which one?"

Abby pointed to her right cheek, just under her eye. "The big one."

"It came from this boy, crazy Dave, who never stopped picking on us in the orphanage. He was a lot older than we were, but it didn't seem to matter. One day, when Lucas was protecting me, the kid picked up a piece of broken glass and stabbed Lucas in the face. Cut him all the way to the bone. It took sixty-three stitches to sew him up. Thank God the house monitor guy jumped in to stop it. He held on to Dave until the police showed up and took him to juvy."

"It must've been awful growing up in that place."

"It wasn't easy, that's for sure. Luckily for us, Mom and Dad came along and adopted us. I'm not sure either of us would've survived much longer."

Just then, someone bumped into the table, lifting it up about two inches. Drew grabbed his and Abby's coffee cups, catching them both before they tipped over. When he looked up to see who smashed into the table, the breath ran out of his lungs. It was the rugby player. Drew ducked his head, figuring a punch to his jaw was next.

"Sorry, my bad," the man said, trying not to spill the three coffee cups on his tray. He squeezed behind Drew's wheelchair and scooted by. The two girls with him followed suit.

"Nice catch," Abby said.

"Got lucky," Drew said, trying to catch his breath. He kept an eye on the player as he walked through the side entrance and sat outside at a table on the terrace. The girls took seats on either side of him.

"Do you remember your biological parents?" Abby asked.

"Not really. My bio-mom died in a car accident when I was like eighteen months old or something. At least that's the story I was told. I was in the car with her, but I don't remember anything. Supposedly, she fell asleep at the wheel while we were on our way home from daycare after she'd worked a double shift at the hospital. The car flipped over several times and landed in a ditch. My legs were pinned underneath. Would you like to see a picture of her?"

"I'd love to."

He reached inside the collar of his shirt and pulled out the leather pouch hanging from his neck. Inside was a pristine picture of a beautiful, dark-haired woman. He handed the photo to her.

"One of the orphanage's volunteer workers found her picture and had it laminated. Lucas made the pouch for me."

Abby studied the photo. "She's beautiful. I see where you get your good looks."

Drew wasn't prepared for her compliment and didn't respond right away. "Her name was Lauren Falconio. She was an ER nurse and was studying at night to become a doctor."

Abby turned the photo over. "What's this date? February 12, 1985."

"The day she died. I wanted to remember it," he said, then pointed down at his legs. "The same day this happened."

Abby didn't say anything as she gave the photo back to Drew.

He slid it into the leather pouch and tucked it inside his shirt.

"Hang on a sec," she said with a furrowed brow, reaching into her purse. "There's something I want to check." Her fingers were now holding a smart phone, which she promptly turned on and started typing into.

"Something wrong?" he asked.

"Nope. That date . . . sounds really familiar to me."

Drew waited while she swiped at her phone.

"I thought so," she said, flipping the device around to show him something. "Remember the dump truck accident I was talking about? The one that killed my aunt?"

Drew nodded, staring at the device. A newspaper article and photo was on the screen showing a mangled pileup of vehicles at an intersection.

"Same day," she said. "February 12, 1985."

"Jesus, what happened?"

"Some dumbass in the dump truck ran a red light and smashed into a city bus that my aunt was riding in. My mom said she was in Tucson that week for a job interview."

"I'm sorry, Abby. That's terrible."

"Thanks," she said, turning the phone around and looking at it for a good fifteen seconds. Then her eyes moved up and met Drew's. "So what do you think the odds are that both of us lost somebody in two different traffic accidents on the same day and in the same town?"

"I don't know. Beyond astronomical, I guess."

"It's like we're linked together somehow. Across time and space."

He didn't believe in all the cosmic connection stuff but wanted to be supportive. "I think you're right. Some kind of linkage."

"We must've been destined to meet. Right here. Right now, in Tucson."

Drew smiled, not sure what else to say.

She put the phone away, then looked up at him with a face that no longer looked sad. It was almost as if she flipped off the emotional channel inside of her. "But enough about me and my family drama. So, your biological mom was studying to be a doctor? Tell me everything."

"That's what I was told. Working a lot of hours, I guess."

"Was she married? Boyfriend?" she said in a friendly, excited voice.

"I doubt it. Supposedly Mom was artificially inseminated at some fertility clinic. Apparently, she wasn't into men and decided the turkey-baster method was the way to go."

Abby laughed, nearly choking on her coffee. The tension at the table was suddenly gone.

He smiled. For some unknown reason, Drew felt very comfortable talking with her about everything, painful or not. Even about subjects that were taboo with his brother. That's why he couldn't stop the next string of words that shot out of his mouth. "Lucas' mom was a drug addict who died of an overdose, and his dad died in prison. I think he was a grifter. Lucas doesn't like to talk about them much."

Abby didn't respond right away, obviously deep in thought. "Sounds like you both had really tough childhoods. I don't know how either of you made it through in one piece."

"We had each other, thank God."

"I thought I had a difficult past, but mine was nowhere near as traumatic as yours."

"It sounds worse than it is, really. We've all had our share of drama, right?"

She nodded. "Hey, I was going to ask you . . . tonight my roommate Jasmine and I are going to the midnight movie at the Gallagher Theatre. Would you and Lucas like to join us?"

"Sure," Drew said before thinking it through. He'd never been inside the student-run theater, even though he passed by it every time he ate in the cafeteria. The box office was just to the right of the Student Union's main entrance. "Well, I should probably check with Lucas first. I'm not sure if he'll want to go."

"You should tell him Jasmine's *really* pretty. And she doesn't have a boyfriend right now."

"Still, I'll have to ask him first. Can I call you later and let you know?"

"Sure, that's fine."

While Abby went on to tell him about her parents and blistering cold winters in Wisconsin, Drew's mind wandered. He envisioned their future together. He imagined they were on their honeymoon in Hawaii, sitting on the beach and holding hands. She was drinking a margarita and he, a virgin Daiquiri. Both of their glasses were garnished with tiny paper umbrellas that would dance around the rim whenever a sip was taken.

His insides ran soft as he listened to her, sending a warm tingle across his spine. He wanted to sit there forever, staring at her big, beautiful eyes, while each syllable from her glistening lips washed over his body like a gentle summer breeze. Even the tone of her voice was enchanting. In fact, she didn't have a single flaw that he could see.

The next two hours flew by quickly. They chatted about everything, never taking their eyes off each other. Each time she smiled at him, more shivers radiated throughout his body. He'd seen dates like this in movies and on television—dates where two people instantly connected and couldn't stop talking or smiling at each other. He always thought that kind of stuff was pure Hollywood make-believe, but now he wasn't so sure. Everything she said seemed to make sense, and every word she spoke made him feel all gooey inside. He'd never felt so comfortable with another person his entire life, except maybe Lucas.

* * *

Sometime later, Drew went home and found Lucas sitting at the study desk in the apartment after he unlocked the door and went inside.

"Nice timing. You just missed Mom's call," Lucas said.

"How's she doing? What did the cardiologist say?"

"She's doing excellent. Just needs to keep taking her meds."

"Awesome news."

"So how'd it go today? You were gone awhile, bro."

Drew considered telling Lucas about the encounter with the rugby player, but decided against it. It would only upset him. "It was actually really nice."

"Did you get any?"

"No," Drew said wholeheartedly. "We just sat and talked. She's not that kind of girl."

"What? Does she have a penis?"

"Shut up."

"Did you at least kiss her or get a hug? Something?"

"She held my hand."

"Well, that's a start. You gonna see her again, Romeo?"

"Yes, tonight, for the midnight movie on campus. Her roommate's coming, too."

Lucas laughed and smirked. "Sounds like loads of fun. Better you than me, brother."

"Actually, I was hoping you might go with me."

"Sorry, I don't do blind dates. Not my thing."

"Please, Lucas. I really need you to go."

Lucas closed his eyes and shook his head, biting his lower lip.

"I'm way too nervous to go by myself," Drew said. "Come on, I'd do it for you."

Lucas took a deep breath and let out a long exhale. "What's the movie?"

"*Eraserhead*. Some low budget surreal horror flick made in nineteen seventy-seven."

"Never heard of it. Must be a real pile of crap."

"I don't know, it just started playing at the theater."

"So who's this roommate?"

"Her name's Jasmine. She's a pre-med student. Abby says she's really nice."

"Dude, you do realize that anytime a girl uses the word 'nice' to describe someone they want you to meet, it means she's totally hideous. So which body part is she missing?"

Drew laughed, though he didn't want to. "Abby says she's super pretty, too. I think she works at the Pussycat Palace on Speedway."

"Isn't that a strip joint in the red light district?"

"I think so. Supposedly, she makes really good money, which pays for all her schooling."

"Pussycat Palace, huh?"

"That's what I was told. And she doesn't have a boyfriend."

Lucas smiled and raised one of his eyebrows. "Okay, I guess I'll go. Since she's pre-med and all. What time are we meeting them?"

"Eleven forty-five. They'll be waiting for us in front of the theater."

* * *

Drew and Lucas were late as they made their way across campus to the student-run theater. They would have left a few minutes sooner, but Lucas had to wait for his brother to finish combing his hair, and then spray it down. Once Drew was into his personal hygiene ritual, nothing could stop him from finishing.

"Why so gloomy, brother? This is supposed to be fun," Lucas said, sidestepping a pile of dog crap sitting on the sidewalk. It was covered in flies and looked fresh. Lucas figured there might be more landmines along the way as they got closer to the grassy mall area.

"I'm not sure about this, at all," Drew said, his face red and stiff.

"Just relax and go with the flow."

"That's easy for you to say. I have no clue what I'm supposed to do."

"Didn't you just spend the whole morning with her?"

"Yeah, but we just talked."

"I thought you held hands?"

"She held mine. I never moved."

"Then I'm sure Abby will take care of everything," Lucas joked, trying to relieve his own nervousness.

"That's what I'm afraid of. She's going to expect me to react in a certain way, but I'll probably misread her signals and ruin everything."

"It's simple, really. When she tries to stick her tongue down your throat, let her. How hard is that?"

"You're not helping very much," Drew said, rolling his chair forward. "When am I supposed to put my arm around her?"

"As soon as the movie starts. Did you bring a condom?" Lucas wisecracked, knowing Drew's penis was one of the few things still working properly below his waist. Luckily for Drew, his bio-mom's car only crushed his legs and not his spine or pelvic area.

"No, I didn't. Was I supposed to? See, I already screwed up."

"I was just kidding," Lucas said, patting his brother on the back. "Look, there's no reason to panic. It's obvious she's really into you."

"How can you be sure?"

"Look, she gave you her phone number in the first place, right?"

"Yeah."

"And the coffee date went well—"

"I guess."

"Then she asked you to this movie?"

"Yep."

"Okay, then. Trust me. She wouldn't have asked you out tonight if she didn't like you. And she definitely wouldn't want you to meet her friends if she wasn't into you. Just be yourself and you'll be fine."

"I guess you're right."

Lucas had to hide his own reservations about a blind date with a strip club worker. He'd only been with one woman before, the university's librarian. It was in December of his freshman year, while she was working the graveyard shift. He stopped to comfort the forty-year-old woman, who was going through a tumultuous divorce and crying behind her desk.

It began as a simple hug and ended with him losing his virginity on the floor in the last row of book stacks. He had no clue what he was doing and just went along for the ride, literally. During the brief encounter, Lucas learned the basics but still wasn't confident in his ability. He recalled very little from the few minutes he'd spent with her, except how slippery and soft she felt on the inside. However, one thing always puzzled him. Why did she run off afterward, sobbing the entire way?

Her first name was Robyn, but Lucas never knew her last name. In fact, it was the one and only time he ever saw her. He went back to the library the following night, but she wasn't there. Her replacement said she'd quit her job that morning and was moving out of town.

* * *

Lucas waited for Drew to catch up as they approached the Student Union. Even from a distance, the building's towering all-glass foyer was impressive, overlooking a hundred-foot wide set of cement stairs leading up to its main entrance. To the right was Gallagher Theatre, where a sea of film enthusiasts waited to enter through its turnstiles.

"There's Abby," Drew said, pointing at the left side of the movie crowd. Then he moved his finger slightly to the left. "And that must be Jasmine."

Lucas brought his eyes down and followed the line from Drew's arm to the middle of the stairs. The girls were right where Drew was indicating, on the third step from the top. Abby was bouncing up and down, wearing a pink-colored pullover jacket and waving her arms over her head. She was holding a spread of movie tickets in her hand.

Lucas checked the Student Union's clock tower. The time was 11:50 p.m., barely enough time to purchase popcorn and Cokes and find seats together. "Damn it. Late again," he mumbled, hoping they weren't relegated to the front row of the theater.

Jasmine was several inches taller than Abby and wore a navy blue Denver Broncos football jersey with a white 10 emblazoned on the front. If Jasmine were truly a fanatic, it might pose a problem since Lucas knew zip about football. Lucas much preferred the speed and grace of professional ice hockey, specifically the Los Angeles Kings, who had just started their season, hoping to defend their back-to-back Stanley Cup titles. He'd just have to fake it if she brought up football.

Her jet-black shoulder-length hair was pulled back into a single, understated ponytail. Lucas was still too far away to decide if she was as attractive as Abby had promised. Nevertheless, he did detect some prominent curves hidden beneath her casual apparel, leading him to believe the blind date had real potential.

If she was really pre-med, then she'd be able to carry on a decent conversation, too. He could easily talk about high-energy processes in warped space-times around black holes, but most girls weren't into that stuff. Maybe she would be, though. He tried to keep his mind open, but he was starting to have doubts about himself, his date, and the evening in general. He imagined her staring at his forehead as if he had a third arm growing out of the middle of it while he rambled on about physics.

He wished he knew more about football.

He looked to his left, but Drew wasn't there. He turned around and found Drew sitting still, about six feet behind him. He looked scared to death. "Bro, relax. It's only a movie. Don't worry. I've got your back."

"That's not it. Look!" Drew said, pointing again, this time at a group of three men standing two steps below Abby and Jasmine. "It's those guys from the cafeteria. The ones you almost got in a fight with."

"Are you kidding me? Not again," Lucas said. He looked around and didn't see any campus police. He'd have to face these assholes alone. He hoped nothing would happen. Not now. Not tonight. There was no chance Jasmine and Abby would be impressed if he got into a fight on their first double date. Especially if he got his ass kicked.

The theater line advanced forward as the patrons ahead of the girls navigated their way through the rope-style stanchions leading into the theater. Abby and Jasmine turned to face forward, then stepped back into line to keep pace with the procession. They were almost to the top step, and the rugby players were still two steps behind them in line.

"What do we do?" Drew asked.

"We ignore them, that's what we do. Walk right past them. Don't give them the satisfaction. Come on, we need to hurry. The girls are almost inside. Let's double-time it," Lucas said, moving behind his brother to grab the wheelchair handles.

Drew nodded. "I wish those guys would just go away, forever."

Lucas glanced up at the girls, and at that exact moment, a blinding, white-hot light shot out from the steps, right behind where the girls were standing.

Before he could react, a deafening, high-decibel squeal nearly ripped his eardrums apart. He let go of the wheelchair handles, raising his hands to cover his ears. It felt as though his head were in a giant microwave oven and someone had turned it on full blast, cooking his brain from the inside out.

His equilibrium gave way, buckling his legs and sending his kneecaps crashing into the cement sidewalk.

A few seconds later, both the intense light and the deafening sound subsided. Immediately after, a sudden breeze pulled him toward the theater, but dissipated quickly.

He lowered his hands, opened his eyes, and looked to his left and right. Dozens of people on either side of him were lying on the ground; all but two appeared to be unconscious. One of those still awake pointed at the Student Union.

Lucas swung his eyes forward to check what the person was looking at.

His jaw dropped open. "Holy shit."

The entire front section of the Student Union and most of the theater's façade had vanished, like someone had used an ice cream scoop to carve out a huge section of the building. With the exception of an untouched section on the right, most of the concrete steps had vanished, too. Even though the visual proof right was right there in front of him, he found it hard to accept what he was seeing. So much destruction.

He brought his gaze down in search of Drew. He found him directly in front about six feet away, slumped over in his chair and not moving. Lucas ran in front of the wheelchair and spun around with his back to the Student Union. He found Drew's head tilted down, with blood dripping from his left nostril. The sight of his helpless little brother sent a stabbing pain into his chest.

Lucas' head started spinning with gut-wrenching flashes from his past: his dad lying dead in a hospital bed, his mother hooked up to an endless series of tubes and wires after open heart surgery, and now his foster brother was unconscious and bleeding. He didn't think he could take much more.

Drew had to be okay. He had to be. Drew was his only true friend. His only confidante. The only person who accepted him for him and expected little in return.

Lucas shook Drew's shoulders gently, trying to wake him up. "Drew? Drew? Can you hear me?" There was no response. Lucas wiped the blood off his brother's lip and shook him again. "Come on, little brother, wake up. Talk to me."

Drew finally opened his eyes. "What happened?" he asked in a throaty, half-awake voice.

Lucas felt the crushing mound of worry leave his chest. He put on his best poker face, wanting to appear strong and composed for Drew. That was his job—he promised his father he'd always be there for Drew and keep him safe. "You passed out. Are you all right?"

Drew rubbed his forehead. "My head's spinning and I have a wicked headache . . . Where's Abby?"

He centered himself in front of Drew to block his view, not wanting him to see the destruction across the front of the Student Union. "We should head back to the apartment."

"Why? What's wrong?" Drew asked, trying to peer around Lucas.

Lucas stayed in front of him. "We need to turn around and go home. Like right now."

"What happened?"

"Trust me. You don't want to see what's behind me. Nobody does."

"Move, Lucas. I need to see. Move, please!"

Lucas didn't want to step aside, but Drew shoved him out of the way with his powerful arms.

Drew's face froze, his eyes locked in a state of fright for a good three count. "Oh my God, Abby!" he screamed, putting his callused hands on the wheelchair's push rings. He began gripping and releasing in powerful thrusts, racing past Lucas as he quickly propelled himself forward. "Abby! . . . Abby! . . . Abby!"

Traumatized and a bit unsteady, Lucas followed behind his brother, though at a much slower pace. His heart was breaking for Drew, knowing the emotional pain must've been unbearable.

8

Lucas initially thought the blinding white light flash might have been some type of terrorist attack, possibly a suicide bomber hell-bent on payback. But that prospect seemed unlikely since he hadn't seen or heard an explosion, nor had there been any type of shockwave following the event.

He stopped walking just before what remained of the steps to take a look at the damage. There should've been building rubble and debris everywhere, but there was none. Not a speck. It was almost as if a giant vacuum had come down from the heavens and cleaned the area the instant the flash was over.

The front of the Student Union stood exposed in cross-section, like an architect's drawing, but this architect had a twisted imagination. The glowing edges of the building's framework were holding together, at least for now, but he wondered when they might surrender to gravity or burst into flames.

Inside, some of the theater's second-floor patrons were huddled together, close to the exposed edge. They seemed oblivious to the trails of smoke invading their space and the precariousness of their position.

"Hey!" he yelled up to them. "Get back! The edges are hot." They gawked at him but didn't respond, obviously still too stunned by the flash of devastation to think clearly.

A scruffy young man on the third level was standing between a rolling office chair and a metal desk that had been sliced in half. Based on the equipment and metal spools nearby, Lucas assumed the longhaired man was inside the projectionist's booth.

Lucas was amazed his scrawny neck could hold up the weight of his head, given the bushel of hair hanging from his scalp and the medley of jewelry decorating his face. His right hand was holding the waistband of his saggy blue jeans, while the piercings covering his earlobes, eyebrows, nose, and lips twinkled in the moonlight.

The projectionist walked to about a foot away from the ledge and looked around with a glazed look on his face. He stood there, motionless, for at least thirty seconds, then stepped back to the desk and pulled his shirtsleeve up to peel off a white patch on his left bicep. He tossed the covering away before opening one of the few remaining drawers to take out a cigarette. He lit the joint with the smoldering edge of the desk, then sat in the rolling desk chair and inhaled a long drag, making the tip of the cigarette glow red-hot. He puckered his lips to puff out floating smoke rings, one after another.

* * *

When Drew arrived at the steps, he flung himself out of his chair, landing chest-first on the cold cement, which nearly knocked the wind out of him. He grimaced when his right elbow landed directly on the edge of a step, sending numbing pain up his arm and into his shoulder.

Even though he only had partial feeling in his legs, the cement stairs still hurt his kneecaps. But the pain was nothing compared to the howling emptiness swelling in his heart and the boiling knot in his stomach. He'd finally found a girl who was interested in him. A pretty girl who was smart and funny. And now she was missing. His eyes were telling him one thing, but his brain refused to accept it.

Scattered along the stairway was a trail of body parts, as if a tree shredder had shot them out from its chute. He saw an arm, a leg, a severed ear, and part of a skull. The scene was right out of a macabre horror movie, but one thing struck him: there was no blood anywhere. He tried to convince himself the fragments were only mannequin parts, but his self-trickery failed when the unmistakable odors of seared meat and burnt hair assaulted his nasal passages. He almost gagged and felt like he needed to throw up, worrying the smell might become permanently etched into his brain.

He searched the steps on his hands and knees, inspecting each body fragment to see if it belonged to Abby. As far as he could tell, none did. But of course, for some of the pieces, he couldn't be sure. He scoured the open pit in front of the theater, but again, he found no sign of her. She was gone.

* * *

Lucas moved to the lower edge of the crater and looked inside.

"How the hell?" he asked, seeing a familiar black film covering the bottom of the depression. He bent down to sample it, rubbing the powdery substance between his fingers. Then he smelled it.

"Oranges again," he said, wondering if it was the same substance he'd found inside the reactor core. Before he could answer his own question, a dark, sickening notion washed over him. He tried to ignore it, but it was too powerful, pushing its way to the forefront of his thoughts.

Was the second run of the E-121 experiment connected to this? Whatever this was?

He pondered the question for a moment, then pushed it aside, not ready to dwell on it or accept the possibility of a 'yes' answer. More data and study was needed.

Can't jump to conclusions, he convinced himself, needing to turn his focus to Drew. His brother was priority one right now. *Pull it together dickhead. Drew needs you.*

He walked to Drew and knelt down beside him. He wanted to console his brother, but he couldn't find the proper words. They were all jumbled up and backward, flailing out of control just beyond the tip of his tongue.

The same thing had happened when he'd tried to comfort Drew after their adoptive father had passed away years before. He knew he sucked at consoling people, but he needed to push past his anxiety and step up, now more than ever. Whether it be with words or actions, he needed to try. For Drew and for himself. Anything was better than nothing when a loved one was suffering from unimaginable pain.

He rubbed his brother's neck, hoping Drew would know he was there for him. That he loved him. That he'd never leave his side. However, when his normally effervescent brother looked up with tearful eyes, Lucas almost broke down as a flood of emotions pushed up from his heart. He gave Drew a one-armed hug, fighting to remain strong and steadfast; it wasn't easy. He needed to look away, trying to find something else to focus on so he wouldn't totally lose it.

A few yards to his left, a lifeless body wrapped in a bloodless Denver Broncos football jersey—number 10—sat slumped over in a twisted heap. The mound of unresponsive flesh was leaning to one side, resting against the upper step, with only its right leg and arm still intact. The left side of the skull and neck were missing, making it an even more gruesome sight than it already was.

The corpse belonged to Abby's roommate, Jasmine. She'd been wearing the same jersey only moments before *it* happened. He could see the girl had been sliced in half, as if by a molten hot guillotine, and there wasn't a drop of blood anywhere. Her head was tilted back and pushed to one side, exposing the brain matter clinging to the inner membrane lining her skull. Her right eye was open and dilated, looking directly at Lucas.

He covered his mouth with his free hand, trying to ignore the nausea swelling in his gut. But his body had its own idea. A small amount of stomach bile erupted, slinking its way up his esophagus and into his mouth, leaving a rancid taste that sickened his tongue. For a moment, he thought that was going to be the end of it, but the pressure in his belly continued to grow exponentially. More was coming. Lots of it.

Lucas let go of Drew and stood up in a hurry before moving away. He bent over just as the flood arrived, sending a stream of foul-smelling puke across the steps. Part of his stomach contents had stuck to his lips and was now dripping slowly from his mouth. He wiped it off with the back of his hand and stood upright to compose himself, taking a series of deep breaths and letting them out.

It took some time, but he managed to shake off the nausea and let the scientist within him assume command. He wiped his hand on his pants, then turned and went back to her body.

Even though only half of her face remained, he could see she'd been a gorgeous young Hispanic woman—a promising medical student who'd been cut down in the prime of her life. Her death had been brutal, but he figured she wasn't aware or plugged into her consciousness when death came to collect her. No more than if she'd been standing on the train tracks and was flattened by a speeding locomotive from behind. Instant death meant no pain—one good thing amongst all the tragedy filling the steps of the Student Union.

Lucas scanned the area for the rugby player and his cohorts, but found no sign of them. He went down to the base of the stairs, stepping over a string of cell phones and designer purses. There was a red-and-blue backpack still attached to a slender arm and shoulder, which had a heart-shaped pink tattoo that read "Billy."

On the second-to-last step, he found a pair of half-full water bottles, each with a severed hand wrapped tightly around it. To his right was a pair of unattached legs sitting at an odd angle, as if they were propped up by something.

Lucas moved closer and found they were resting on top of a severed head. It was mostly bald except for a streak of yellow hair down the middle, telling him what he needed to know. It belonged to the Mohawk rugby player. The skull must've rolled down the steps after it was decapitated, though he couldn't fathom how the legs ended up on top of it. Perhaps they tumbled down the stairs, too.

But in the end, what did it matter? All he knew for sure was Drew got his wish—the man was gone forever, almost as if the universe had been listening and took action to erase him from existence.

Lucas took a few steps back to view the entire scene in one frame. The visual evidence across the front of the building spoke to him:

when the flash obliterated the theater's entrance, it had encompassed nearly the entire movie line, taking with it anyone unlucky enough to be standing inside its perimeter. Those persons straddling its outer edge were cut in two pieces, vertically, like a lamb shank being chopped by a cleaver on a butcher's block. The leader of the rugby players must have been bent over—probably laughing or tying his shoe—when the flash happened, separating his head from its body.

Then, out of nowhere, his logic was replaced with a stampede of thoughts supercharged with emotion.

The flash of light—shit—it was the same type of burst they'd seen when they reviewed the video recording of the experiment. The one that coincided with the phantom power spike inside the core. Plus, there was the black powder residue appearing in both places after the flash. It must have been some type of byproduct of the energy release. And last but not least, the strange scent of oranges. Drew couldn't smell it back in the lab, and probably couldn't smell it now. But Lucas could, helping to firmly connect the two events in his memory.

A sense of dread slammed into Lucas' spine. He tried to stop it but couldn't as his chest tightened and his face went numb. His lungs began to take in a series of rapid, shallow breaths. One after another, the air rushed in, making his head swim and every muscle in his body ache. He dropped to his knees when his eyes blurred out of focus, his heart no longer able to deny the facts lying right there in front of him.

The E-121 experiment must have caused this.

This was all his fault.

He killed these people.

He didn't want to believe it, but it was true. He was the person responsible for the bloodless massacre. He knelt there, gasping for breath, while his mind tried to process the magnitude of what he'd done.

Just when he thought he might remain frozen on the steps for the rest of his days, he heard the sound of a boy sobbing and moaning. It was Drew—behind him.

Lucas snapped out of his emotional fog, suddenly able to think clearly again. He struggled to his feet, fighting against a pair of wobbly knees and sweeping muscle fatigue. He shook the pain from his heart and turned to his brother, who was sitting in a ball, staring at the open crater with a face full of tears.

The look of despair on Drew's face said it all—he was beaten and besieged by what had just happened. It was a completely normal reaction to a horrific set of events. Any normal person would've been sitting right next to Drew, bawling their eyes out, too.

But not Lucas. He couldn't allow it, no matter what he was feeling inside. He needed to press on and find strength. Somehow, some way, he knew he needed to figure this out and make it right. For him and his brother, and for the families of all the victims. He had no idea how he was going to do it, but he had to do something because if he did cause this, he'd never be able to live with himself.

He looked around at the carnage, forcing himself to concentrate on what to do next. Then new thoughts popped into his head.

What if this wasn't a onetime event?

What if this was just the start—of something?

How many more people might die?

How many more deaths would he be responsible for?

Just when he thought he was in control, the pain in his chest returned, this time doubling in intensity after those additional thoughts soaked in. His brain seemed to start moving in slow motion as an intense sense of doom took control of his body.

He closed his eyes and fought back with all his remaining strength. He needed to find a way to stop the guilty swell; dwelling on it wouldn't do anyone any good.

Not now. You gotta get a grip, he told himself, getting pissed at his emotional weakness. Then he made himself a promise. *Never again will you let the guilt take control. Turn it off. Shut it out. It's the only way. You have to be strong and figure this out. For the victims and for Drew.*

He ran his hands over his face and eyes, trying to wrestle control from his emotions. It took a few fist slams against his chest, but he managed to push past the random flashes of insidious thoughts and find his logic again.

Come on, asshole. You're a scientist, he told himself. *Observe, document, and verify. Science is based on facts. Observations and conclusions. There has to be an explanation. Think it through.*

But how would he gather the facts?

He glanced down and found the answer right in front of him: an expensive-looking, high-resolution video camera on the bottom step. Its black safety strap was cut four inches from the digital camera's padded handgrip. Two fingers and a thumb were lying on the ground next to the unit, probably the owner's.

Lucas flipped the unit over to examine it. Everything appeared to be in one piece. Its red REC light was on, with display numbers steadily increasing. The thing was still recording despite being dropped several feet onto the cement stairs.

Step One, he thought, *documentation.* It wasn't much, but it was a start. Logic and control were returning. Guilt was being pushed aside. *Find a way to fix this.*

He slid his right hand into the narrow safety grip and aimed the camera at the demolition zone. He started by slowly panning from left to right across the exposed sections of the theater, making sure he stood back far enough on the mall's grass to record all the damage.

Then he walked up to the crater, knelt down, and filmed a close-up of the black powder. He got a shot of his fingers scooping up a handful of the substance and letting it pour through the palm of his hand. He finished by documenting the precise location of each body fragment lying on the steps.

Lucas removed the camera's flash drive and slid it into his pocket. He intended to review the evidence captured on the drive once he and his brother returned home. With any luck, the camera's owner was facing the right way when the flash appeared.

The faint echoes of emergency sirens began in the distance as they wailed and whooped through the heavy night air. Someone had obviously called 9-1-1. He bent over to put the camera on the step and caught a glimpse of a crowd of onlookers taking refuge in the middle of the grass. Most of them were clustered together, arm in arm, trying to comfort each other. He wanted to feel compassion for them but wouldn't let the emotion take root. He couldn't. Not after the promise he made himself. He ignored the feelings, sending them into the blackest corner of his heart.

The emergency sirens howled suddenly in his ears, no longer a faint echo. Reflections of swirling red and blue lights danced off the building façades surrounding the grassy mall when police cars, fire trucks, and ambulances flew over concrete curbs, cut across sidewalks, and ripped up grass with their tires to reach the scene. It wouldn't be long before the place was crawling with news media, too, and hundreds of Good Samaritans and gawkers. He needed to grab Drew and get him back to the apartment.

Lucas turned back toward the theater and out of the corner of his eye, spotted Trevor galloping toward him from the east end of the Student Union. The former wrestler was wearing a red muscle shirt and weightlifting belt, his sweat-soaked physique bulging and glistening with each stride.

"You damaged?" Trevor asked when he arrived, breathing heavily from his sprint.

"No, I'm okay and so is Drew, but I'm pretty sure Abby Park is dead."

Lucas quickly explained what had just happened. He told his friend about the blinding flash of light, where Abby and Jasmine had been standing, and the bloodless body parts. Even though Lucas suspected this incident was related to their lab incident, he wasn't going to tell Trevor about it, at least not yet. He wanted to review the video evidence in private, first. He needed to have verifiable facts and a solid theory before he shared his conclusions with anyone else. If he was going to take the blame for this tragedy and invite a mountain of scorn upon his soul, he had to be sure—one hundred percent sure. Until he was, there was a slim chance this wasn't his fault. Maybe that was just wishful thinking, but his heart and his mind needed to hang on to something positive. And that's all there was at the moment.

Lucas continued with Trevor. "I'm going to wait here for the police to tell them what I saw. But Drew is in no shape to deal with the cops right now. Can you do me a huge favor?" he asked, pointing at his brother. "Get him home *right now,* before all hell breaks loose."

Trevor agreed and headed up the steps. Lucas kept an eye on him as he carefully tiptoeing through the sea of body parts until he reached the top. He knelt down next to Drew, picked him up with the strength of ten men, and carried him down the stairs to his wheelchair. Moments later, he and Drew slipped into the building shadows along the west end of the Student Union.

Lucas ran to the first police car that was now arriving in a skid, waving his hands above his head. He approached the driver's side door just as the officer shoved the gearshift into park and turned off his siren. The emergency lights were still flashing, making it difficult for him to see inside the driver's window.

When the male officer got out of the cruiser, Lucas looked up a steep angle to make eye contact with him. The bald cop with a thick mustache was a few inches shorter than Trevor, and not nearly as muscular. The officer put on his police cap and repositioned his duty belt.

"I'm Sergeant Cherekos. Can you tell me what happened here?"

"Yes, I can," Lucas answered in his most serious tone as dozens of other vehicles closed in on his position. Several of them slid sideways, nearly hitting each other, as the dew-laden grass lessened the tire traction when they tried to stop. One by one, police cruisers and emergency transports took position, surrounding Lucas on three sides, with the Student Union behind him.

The officer took out a pad and pen and began to write. "Let's start with your name."

"Lucas Ramsay."

"Okay, son, what did you see?"

"I was walking across the mall when suddenly a bright light exploded out of nowhere in front of the Student Union and nearly blinded me."

The officer glanced at theater. "How long did the light last?"

"Maybe two seconds."

"Where were you at the time?"

"I'd guess about a hundred feet from the Union's steps. Close to where those girls are standing over there," Lucas said, pointing to three people, probably in their twenties, standing on the grass.

"Where would you say the light originated from?"

"Well, it was really intense and only lasted a second, but I think it was near the center of the crater."

The sergeant looked at the hollow crater for a few seconds before turning his eyes back to Lucas. "Was there an explosion?"

"No, the only sound I heard was this high-pitched squeal. It started right after the flash happened."

The officer hesitated, scratching his temple with the pen. "A squeal you say?"

"Yeah, it was like being trapped inside a room with a thousand kids screaming at the top of their lungs. The pain was so intense I fell to my knees. When I looked around, there was a bunch of other people lying on the ground, too. Luckily, I didn't pass out, but almost everyone else did."

Cherekos nodded his head while wearing a slight smirk on his face, scribbling more notes into his incident report.

Fire and rescue personnel ran past the two of them carrying hoses, stretchers, ladders, and medical equipment. News reporters were now on the scene, too, jogging across the mall with their cameras and microphones in tow.

Some were out of breath, which Lucas assumed was due to them having to park several blocks away. The mall was a pedestrian-only zone; civilian vehicles didn't have access.

"How large would you estimate the light to be?" the officer asked after watching a trio of EMTs race by.

"That I'm not sure. It was so bright, I couldn't look at it directly," Lucas replied, turning his neck to stare back at the theater while thinking about it for a few moments. He brought his eyes back to the officer's. "But I'd say about the same size as the area that's missing. Maybe a bit smaller?"

"Did you see anything unusual before the flash? Like someone who didn't belong? Someone acting suspicious, perhaps?"

Lucas shook his head. "All I remember seeing was all the students lining up for the movie."

Helicopters buzzed in overhead, flooding the scene with swirling spotlights. Lucas knew he'd have a difficult time hearing the cop over the deafening rotors now chopping through the cool desert air.

"How many students were in line?" Cherekos yelled.

Lucas shouted back, "Best guess? Maybe two hundred. The line was fairly long."

Cherekos seemed to be making a visual count of the human remains along the steps. Then he said, "What happened to the rest of the students?"

"They vanished into thin air, just like the building."

Cherekos shook his head slightly and mouthed the words "vanished into thin air" as he wrote a few more notes. Two additional officers joined Cherekos and stood to his left. Based on their body language, Lucas thought they were waiting for instructions.

"What happened next?" Cherekos asked.

"I felt a breeze pull me toward the Student Union."

"Pull you? Do you mean push, like in wind?"

"No, it was more like I was being sucked into the crater. It pulled at me, from the front. I'm guessing when the building and steps vanished, the resulting spatial vacuum created a negative air pressure event. If I'm right, then not only did the physical matter disappear, but the surrounding air mass did as well."

The officer stopped writing and looked at Lucas with his left eyebrow raised. "Sir, I need to know, have you been drinking tonight?"

"No, Sergeant, I don't drink. *Ever.*"

Cherekos clicked his pen, put it into his shirt pocket, and closed his incident report with more force than necessary.

"I know it sounds crazy, but I'm telling you the truth."

"Okay, sir, I think we have all we need."

"Do you want me to stay here?" Lucas asked, wondering why the cop didn't ask him for more information in case he needed to get in touch with him later. He assumed the man was a little traumatized by what he was seeing and wasn't thinking clearly. Or he thought Lucas was totally and completely nuts.

"Hold on," Cherekos said, stepping away and beginning a private discussion with his officers. Lucas saw him reach for the radio transmitter clinging to his upper chest.

Lucas scanned the area and noticed that the police had erected a series of sawhorse-style barricades around the scene, and they were in the process of linking them together with bright yellow police tape with **DO NOT CROSS** written on it in black block letters. He felt like he was being hemmed in, making his feet want to take off running. But he held his position, not letting his guilt take over.

Stay cool, he thought. *Now was no time to panic.*

After a minute, Cherekos and his fellow officers broke their huddle to escort Lucas and the ever-growing number of paparazzi to the other side of barricades. Lucas waited there for fifteen minutes as thousands of civilians filtered into the mall area and congregated on his side of the barricades. Many of them snapped photos and shot video of the scene with their smart phones.

Lucas yawned, barely able to keep his eyes open. It had been a long and stressful day. His legs were tired and his feet were hurting. He decided it was time to walk the mile and a half home before he fell asleep standing up by the police barrier. There wasn't any more he could he here. Plus, he needed to check on Drew. He turned and headed for their apartment.

* * *

When Lucas arrived at his apartment complex, he didn't feel like waiting for the elevator, so he climbed the three flights of switchback stairs and went down the hall to his place. He unlocked the door, removed his shoes, and walked through the central room with an adjoining kitchenette. The door to the lone bedroom was sitting ajar a few inches. He pushed it open and went inside, slipping past his brother's bed. Drew was snoring as he lay on his left side, his back to the center of the room.

Lucas sat at the study desk and turned on his computer. While he waited for the sign-on screen to appear, he pulled the flash drive out of his pocket and put it on the desk, being careful not to damage it. Once he logged onto his laptop computer, he connected the flash drive with one of the two dozen electronic cables he kept stuffed inside the bottom drawer. He turned down the computer's speaker system and began to play back the video footage on the screen. The audio was just loud enough for him to hear if he leaned forward with his ear near the tiny built-in speaker.

The video camera's operator had been waiting in the movie line with his three friends—two young women and one older guy who wore a baseball cap with a two-inch, block, blue-and-red-letter "A" on the front. The camera captured them laughing and joking around about the movie they were about to see.

It was hard to watch the events unfold without feelings of guilt and responsibility trying to find a home inside his heart. He needed to push them aside like he'd done before. It took a few seconds of intense concentration, but his mind was able to overcome the distress and flush them back into the waiting darkness.

He began to put the pieces together, hoping—no, scratch that—praying they wouldn't fit. But deep down, he knew better.

What had started with a single email—an impulse to make things right for himself and his family—had somehow ended in *this*. It began with his online paper submission, which led to Dr. Green's scathing criticism, which led to the attorney named Larson getting involved and having their lab project suspended. That was bad enough, but then it got worse with Drew's subsequent pleas of desperation to run the E-121 experiment again. That, of course, led to his total cave and a second run at full power after changing the specs back to their original equations, which made the E-121 module vanish into thin air. And with his luck, it probably landed somewhere it shouldn't have, somehow kick-starting . . . *this*. A bloodless massacre on the steps of the Student Union. All from a single email. It was too insane to believe, but he decided to run it through his mind anyway.

A sphere of E-121 missing—his fault.

The Student Union in shambles—his fault.

Dozens of innocent college kids dead—his fault.

Jasmine cut in half—his fault.

Abby dead or missing—his fault.

Drew in emotional panic—his fault.

All because he'd pressed the send button.

How did he let *this* happen? Whatever *this* was.

Then his mind shifted gears, possibly out of self-preservation—or maybe it was denial. He couldn't be sure. Not that it mattered. There was work to be done and since sleep wasn't going to be an option right now, he decided to let the facts take center stage. After all, maybe he was jumping to conclusions. Maybe he wasn't responsible. Maybe he was drawing lines and connecting facts incorrectly. Scientists don't assume, and they never guess. They quantify the data and correlate the facts, then suggest a theory. That's what he needed to do. Run it by the numbers to be sure.

To do that, he needed to study every last detail in the video data. Perhaps there was something hiding between the frames. Something he couldn't see with his naked eye when the flash happened. Something that might prove this event wasn't related to the E-121 experiment. That it was something completely new and different and all just a sick, twisted coincidence.

Lucas fast-forwarded the recording to a frame just before the flash appeared. The camera's time stamp read 11:52 p.m. He reviewed the incident in super slow motion, playing the recording frame by frame, until he came to the first appearance of blinding light. It started as a microscopic point of light, just to the left of the Student Union's entrance door, before stretching vertically and then horizontally until the camera's lens was inundated with light.

His suspicions were confirmed: the theater flash, though more powerful and larger, was a near-perfect copy of the one they'd seen inside their reactor's core. He'd realized it back at the Student Union, but the video evidence confirmed it. Combine that with the black powder he'd found both inside the crater and in the reactor's core, and there was no way around it. The evidence was as clear as the scent of oranges.

They were related.

It was all his fault.

Fuck!

He went to his brother's bed and shook Drew's arm several times. "Drew, you need to wake up. This can't wait. We have to talk."

9

Sunday, December 23

Lucas woke up Sunday morning after a lousy night spent drifting in and out of light sleep, mentally replaying the previous night's horror show repeatedly until he finally drifted off somewhere around 4:30 a.m. He wasn't ready to get out of bed yet, so he slid deeper under the covers and curled up in a ball, squeezing a second pillow between his arms. A few seconds later, he realized the room was dead quiet—too quiet. He wasn't hearing his brother's snoring or any other sounds in the room.

He sat up in a flash and looked at Drew's bed. The covers were pulled back and it was empty. He scanned the room quickly, but didn't see any sign of Drew or his wheelchair.

Shit. Where'd he go?

Lucas hopped up, got dressed, and checked the top drawer in Drew's nightstand, but his brother's wallet, keys, and shuttle pass were all missing. It wasn't like Drew to venture off without informing him first. Something was wrong. He could feel it deep in his bones.

In the main room, he found the TV on but the sound had been muted. He swung his eyes around and saw the remote control on the kitchen table, next to a small plate with two slices of toast. One of the pieces had a bite missing. Plus, there was a nearly full glass of milk sitting next to a open tub of margarine and a used butter knife.

Lucas thought about the facts for a moment and realized Drew had gotten up to eat something. He must have sat the table with his plate of toast and turned on the TV with the sound off. Just after adding the butter and taking the first bite, something must have caught Drew's eye on the tube. That's when he took off. But to where?

The front blinds were closed and so was the front door, though Lucas found its two-sided deadbolt unlocked. He opened the door, went outside, and wandered barefoot along the catwalk to the elevator. He could see dozens of people out front, loading their vehicles with belongings.

From his view, it looked like everyone was leaving town. He couldn't blame them. He would've joined them if he could after what had happened to the front of the Student Union. He was sure the news was claiming it was a terrorist attack or some other localized threat by now, sending the Tucson residents into a fleeing frenzy.

He checked the laundry room on the first floor—no sign of Drew. He knocked on the manager's door, but no one answered. He asked several of his departing neighbors if they had seen Drew, but none had.

Lucas went out front where he ran into little Cindy Mack. He waved at her while she stood beside her father as he packed the trunk of their car. In a flash, she came running up to Lucas, wrapping her arms around his waist. He bent down to give her a hug.

She started crying. "Lucas, I don't want to leave. But my dad says we have to go."

"It'll be okay, Cindy. Your dad's right, it's not safe for you to stay here."

"But I'll never see you again."

"Sure you will," he said, looking her in the eyes. "When this is all over, I'll be right here waiting for you by the swing set. Okay?"

She smiled at him, sniffed, wiped off her tears, and then ran back to her dad.

Cindy was one of four kids in Kleezebee's apartment complex, and the only one Lucas liked. Maybe it was because she was the only one who liked him, despite his nasty cheek scars. Her parents both worked during the day, leaving her to play by herself on the swing set in the back of the apartment after school. He'd gotten to know her a few months earlier when she'd fallen off the swing and scraped one of her knees. He was on his way out to the dumpster with a bag of trash when he found her sitting on the ground, crying. He used the complex's garden hose to clean out the dirt and gravel from her wound, and then found a bandage to cover the scrape.

She took a shine to him and they'd talked at least once a week ever since, usually by the swing set on trash day. She was a quiet but cheerful girl in the fourth grade, who carried an empty white purse with her everywhere she went. He worried for her safety since she was left alone for two hours each day after school, until her parents came home from work. He often looked out the bedroom window to check on her while she played on the swings.

He went back upstairs to the apartment to change clothes, still thinking of Cindy's arms wrapped tightly around him. He already felt bad enough about all the death and destruction, but if something happened to her because of his actions, he'd never forgive himself.

No more deaths, he told himself, grabbing a pair of socks and his shoes from the bedroom. Once he had his shoes and socks on, he changed clothes, then went to the main room and stood in front of the TV. He turned on the sound and hit the remote control to scan through several channels. Every station was broadcasting live from a different location around the Student Union. He stopped on the fourth channel, which featured a cameraman in a helicopter circling above the devastation. The feed from overhead allowed him to take in a wide angle view of the damage.

"Shit, it looks much worse from the air," he said, feeling a stinging pain in his belly again. His heart tightened in his chest, making breathing a chore. He realized there were no body fragments littering the theater's steps like before. CSI must have collected the evidence and taken it back to their lab, he decided.

Lucas settled in to watch, taking a seat on the edge of their saggy old couch. News correspondents were interviewing campus officials and law enforcement. He sat back and put his arms up on the sofa's back cushion, catching a whiff of his left forearm. Even after last night's hot shower, he could still smell the stench of burnt hair and severed flesh on his skin. He wondered how many scrubbings it would take to get rid of the stink.

Most of the network's reporters and a few of their interviewees offered opinions on what had happened. Some believed last night's event was merely an accident, like a gas explosion, but most thought it was a terrorist attack, with some form of incendiary device as the weapon.

He was flabbergasted when no one mentioned the lack of building rubble or the bloodless body parts. He wondered if anyone was actually paying attention, or just running their mouths without thinking. The missing evidence was just as important as the tangible facts, and he couldn't believe none of them were discussing it.

When law enforcement officials were asked for a cause, they declined to comment, giving the police department's typical response: "I can't comment right now. The investigation is still ongoing."

Lucas could see the Tucson Bomb Squad in the background, milling about, working their detection equipment, scanning inch-by-inch for chemical and radiological evidence.

The local police were straining to hold back the crowd of thousands surrounding the scene. Many observers were snapping photos and recording their own video footage. Firefighters were keeping watch on the theater's exterior, equipment at the ready, while smoke still billowed out from the sides of the damaged structure.

When the camera swung around to the front of the theater's steps, it showed two FBI agents chatting with the police chief. One of the FBI agents looked a lot like the redheaded security guard who'd broken up the skirmish with the rugby players in the cafeteria.

"Damn, that guy could be his twin," Lucas mumbled.

Then the camera panned down to show Drew sitting in his wheelchair. He was talking with the FBI agents.

"Drew, what the hell are you doing?" he yelled at the screen.

Randol Larson, the pretentious attorney from the Advisory Committee, was standing only a few feet behind Drew.

"Damn it," Lucas said, clicking off the TV and throwing down the remote control. He raced out the door, down the hall, down the stairs, and ran the 1.5 miles to the Student Union. He was out of breath when he arrived.

He checked the pandemonium to figure out the shortest route he had to Drew, but he couldn't see over the crowd. He climbed up on a short retaining wall to his right. He held on to the branch of a nearby tree to balance himself while he stared over the mass of people. He could see the front of the Student Union, but not Drew. There were too many students blocking his view. He figured he needed to swing around to the right to bypass as much of the horde as possible, cutting through the crowd's outside edge to get to Drew.

He jumped down from the cement wall, which caused a slight pain in his right shin. After narrowly avoiding a broken beer bottle and a well-concealed sprinkler head, he navigated his way to the front right sector of the mob. He said, "Excuse me," "Pardon me," and "Coming through," as he worked his way through the multitude with an outstretched arm.

A police barricade stopped his progress when he reached the front row. He could see the back of Drew's head only fifty feet away. He called out Drew's name several times, but his brother didn't react. The crowd noise and the helicopters whirling overhead were almost deafening.

One of several police officers standing guard was a few feet to his left and just inside the perimeter. He hoped to convince the cop to let him inside the barricade but needed to think of the proper excuse. Then it came to him.

"Hi, Officer, I'm Dr. Ramsay of the Astrophysics Department. I may be able to help you figure out what caused this."

The man looked at Lucas and laughed. "Yeah, right. Astrophysics Department. What are you, eighteen?"

Lucas pushed closer to the man. "I know I look young, but trust me, I'm a physicist with the university. I can help you, but you need to let me inside."

"That's not going to happen. Now step back."

Lucas reached for his back left pocket, realizing instantly he'd left his wallet in the apartment. While he was considering his options, the crowd noise faded and became silent. The only sounds came from the helicopters. Then, like a tidal wave traveling atop the ocean, each bystander around him turned in succession to face the east end of the grassy mall.

Lucas spun to see what they were all looking at, but stopped when an earsplitting scream caught his attention. Instantly, his eyes locked onto the girl who'd just screamed. She was pointing east and looked frantic. He followed her finger until he spotted something about a half mile away, at the east end of campus. His jaw dropped when he realized what it was—a towering dome of intense, white-hot light. His feet froze in place, unable to move. The mountain of energy looked like the top half of a giant, glowing white cue ball stuck into the ground. He couldn't see all the way through the dome but could make out an intense mass of energy swirling around inside it, shimmering like the surface of the sun.

The swarm of students around him panicked and began screaming when they, like him, realized the dome was headed their way. Lucas bolted to the Student Union and pressed his back up against its south wall as the frenzied mob ran wild in all directions.

Above the screams, he could hear buildings and other structures tearing loose from the earth as the energy field barreled west through campus. Along with the buildings, he could see and here the energy field tearing up trees, cement, and pavement as it moved. Everything it encountered was swallowed up inside.

His knees shook as he watched the gigantic energy mass advance on his position. He needed to run to Drew, but couldn't convince his body to move. Nor could he take his eyes off the monster destroying the campus. It was still several blocks away, but the anomaly's size dwarfed the top of the majestic mountain chain standing beyond it. The dome had to be at least fifty stories tall, yet it seemed to move with grace and purpose, even as it swallowed up everything around it. If it kept on its current course, he estimated it would just miss the south side of Student Union where he was standing, but it was headed straight for the science lab at the other end of the mall.

As the area began to clear, he saw a handful of injured students lying on the ground. One was a pregnant woman who was bleeding from her forehead. Four others had stopped to help her, bringing the expectant mother to her feet.

Lucas decided it was time to move. He ran to Drew, who was sitting alone by the theater steps. There was no sign of Larson or the FBI agents.

"Are you okay, Drew?" he asked loudly.

His brother's hands were shaking. "I'm fine. What is that thing?"

"I don't know, but we need to get the fuck out of here, and fast." Lucas grabbed the wheelchair handles and pushed his brother west along the front of the Student Union.

Drew pointed to the injured students. "What about them?"

"I'm sure the police will help them. We need to go!"

A few steps later, Lucas heard a loud, familiar squeal. It was coming from behind him, dwarfing the sounds of buildings being ripped from their foundations. It was the same debilitating shrill he'd heard the night before, when the brilliant flash took Abby from the steps of the Student Union.

He was starting to get dizzy but couldn't cover his ears while pushing the wheelchair. He kept his hands on the wheelchair grips, hoping his equilibrium would hold out long enough to get Drew away to safety.

With the sound of death breathing down his neck, he looked back to check the progress of the energy field. All he could see was a rolling wall of shimmering energy closing the gap behind him. He couldn't see the field's top or sides; it was too close and too massive.

A pair of bicyclists whizzed past him on the left and then cut across in front as they pedaled furiously along the sidewalk. Fifty feet ahead of them was a pair of young women who were stumbling forward arm-in-arm, helping each other remain upright. When the bicyclists nearly ran the women over, Lucas wondered if the earsplitting squeal was affecting their vision.

Seconds later, both the bicyclists and the girls made it around the corner, making a sharp right in front of the science lab to head north and away from the carnage. Lucas intended to use the same escape route, if he had enough time. His thigh muscles were burning and he could hardly maintain his balance, but he kept his legs pumping to push the wheelchair even faster than before.

Twenty seconds later, he and Drew were still alive when they made it to the end of the grassy mall. He aimed the chair to the right, almost tossing Drew out of the seat when they made the ninety-degree turn and hurried north between the science lab and the far end of the Student Union.

"Hang on, little brother. We're almost there!" he yelled, hoping Drew could hear him above the noise. But his brother didn't answer.

One look down and Lucas knew why. Drew's head was hanging and bobbing as they moved—he must have been unconscious again. Lucas figured the dome's high-decibel shrieking knocked him out. The same thing had happened the previous night when they approached the steps of the Student Union. He pushed Drew's chair as hard as he could, but it wasn't easy, not while gasping for air and pushing through the pain boiling in his thigh muscles.

Just when a cramp started to form in his right leg, the squeal behind him stopped. Lucas slowed his hobble and looked over his right shoulder to see what was going on. He saw the enormous crown of the dome just beyond the top floor of the Student Union. It had stopped moving and was now a blistering orange color, like it was mad and changing its mood.

There was a pair of news helicopters on the far side of campus, circling high above the giant intruder. Lucas wondered why their pilots weren't affected by the squeal. The sound seemed to disable nearly everyone else in the vicinity, at least on the ground. Perhaps it had limited range. It was also possible the dome's shrill was unidirectional and only people directly in front of it could hear it.

A heartbeat later, Lucas heard a swooshing, hum-like sound as the dome vanished. The hum was followed by a rush of wind that sucked him back toward the dome's position—again, much like what happened the night before when the flash vanished from the steps. His chest constricted as he realized this was another bloody connection to the E-121 lab experiment. The facts were piling up, and all of them meant more death on his hands. It was becoming crystal clear he couldn't outrun his legacy of failures. No matter how hard he tried, or how many lies he told himself, destiny was coming for him and it was painted in a sea of red. All he could do right now was try to protect his brother from whatever was coming next.

Drew woke up a few seconds later and rubbed his forehead. "Whoa, my head's killing me. Where are we?"

"We're just north of the lab. We're safe. For now. I think."

Drew looked back in the direction of the Student Union. "What happened to that thing?"

"I don't know. It just stopped moving and then vanished. Just about the time you woke up."

"We should go back and see if anyone needs help."

Lucas didn't answer right away. He needed to think it through. Even though his logic was screaming at him to keep running and get as far away as possible, he knew he couldn't. Not after his guilty conscience had just teamed up with his breaking heart, keeping him right where he was—both in mind and spirit.

When facing a mountain of debt, a good man chips away as best he can in an attempt to repay what he owes. Even if it's a foolish, fleeting endeavor. A good man faces adversity head on and never gives up, no matter the odds, and that's what he planned to do.

"Okay, we head back. But if another one of those energy domes appears, we don't stick around for a second. Agreed?"

Drew nodded.

Lucas stretched out his leg muscles, ridding them of the cramping sensation so he could stay effectively mobile. The brothers reversed course and went back to the south side of the Student Union.

When they turned the corner to face the mall, Lucas' eyes locked onto a horrific sight. He couldn't help but stare at the long, shallow, devastated channel in front of them. It was about three hundred feet wide and perfectly straight, and appeared to stretch clear to the east end of the mall near Campbell Avenue, and probably far beyond.

All the buildings along the north side of the grassy mall were intact, but most of the campus buildings along the mall's south side had been obliterated, including the four-story library and the old Bear Down basketball gym. He wondered how many students had been inside when the buildings were destroyed.

Too many to count, he decided, facing a rising, seemingly endless death toll. Yet he wouldn't allow his mind to focus on it—it was too painful and too debilitating to his thought processes. He needed to be cold, calculating, and deliberate, if there was any hope of making it through the events unfolding across campus. Deep down he knew there was more to come, and he needed to stay sharp. He turned to his analytical side, hoping it would squash the emotions bubbling within.

As Lucas had predicted, the energy field just missed consuming the Student Union. There was an eight-foot-wide strip of undisturbed grass between the event crater from the previous night's theater event and the wreckage from this latest incident. Everything else caught in the dome's path had vanished. Again, there was no visible rubble.

"Looks like more of that black residue," Drew said, pointing to a film of black powder covering the bottom of the entire channel.

Lucas saw something else: a tall, pyramid-shaped mass near the dome's endpoint. "Let's go check it out," he said, pointing at the discovery. His feet took him closer, though his logic wanted him to turn tail and run.

"Oh my God. Is that what I think it is?" Drew asked, as a throng of onlookers closed in around them.

"Yeah, it is. A pile of bodies, at least bits and pieces of them," he answered, turning his head away for a few moments to process the ghastly sight without hurling. The move seemed to work, allowing him to bring his eyes forward again.

The stench coming from the pile was overpowering, and based on the reactions of those around him, everyone was getting a nose full. Drew was the first to lean over and vomit, barely missing the side of his chair. Four of the other witnesses sent out their own puke, covering the grass in bile and food chunks.

Drew sat upright and wiped off his chin, "What the heck's going on here, Lucas?"

"I'm not sure exactly," he answered, scooping up a handful of the black residue. He looked around to make sure no one was within earshot before he spoke again. "But like we talked about last night, I think it's all related to our E-121 experiment."

Drew said quietly in his chair, looking stunned.

"There are just too many similarities. All of it is tied to this black residue somehow. This kind of shit just doesn't happen by coincidence."

Lucas studied the pile in front of him. The facts seemed to indicate the dome had expelled an eight-foot-high mound of semi-liquid human remains. The heap oozed down its sides as gravity pulled at its gooey consistency, made up of organs, muscle, tissue, fingers, skulls, bones, brain matter, and intestines, intermingled like a bloody tossed salad. The coroner's office was going to be busy for months sorting out the remains.

He couldn't see any signs of clothing in the bloody pile, but he wasn't sure if that was a good thing or not. On one hand, it eliminated any hope of visually identifying Abby, or the other half of Jasmine. On the other, the lack of evidence protected Drew in his fragile emotional state. Lucas decided it was probably a good thing Abby's pink windbreaker wasn't visible in the dome's waste pile. Drew would still have hope and that's all he could ask at this point.

"Do you think it'll happen again?" Drew asked.

The answer was yes, but he didn't want to come clean with his brother. He chose to spin his answer a bit, lessening the blow. "I don't know, maybe. It all seems a little too fantastic to even comprehend. I sincerely hope this is the end of it, but we shouldn't wait around to find out. Let's get out of here."

10

On the way back to their apartment, Lucas noticed a white broadcast van parked a few hundred feet past the science lab, on a side street to the left. The vehicle sat behind two other news vans from competing stations, all of them facing the opposite way.

"Hey, check it out," Lucas said, pointing at the back of the vehicles.

"You think they caught anything on camera?"

"There's only way one to find out. Let's go."

When they arrived, they found the first van's cargo door open, partially covering up the faded black stenciling on the side which Lucas determined to be 'Channel 9 News.'

Inside were two clean-cut young technicians wearing jeans and T-shirts. They seemed to be taking order from an older man with a bad comb-over and a belly hanging down to the front pockets of his slacks. All three were sitting close together in front of the mobile studio, watching the center monitor.

Lucas poked his head inside, clearing his throat before he spoke. "Hey, guys. Is that footage of the energy field that just tore up the mall?"

The older man flinched, then turned around. He had the red cheeks and weary, bloodshot eyes of a long-time alcoholic. "Yeah, it is. Who the hell are you?"

"Dr. Lucas Ramsay. I'm with the Astrophysics Department," Lucas said, climbing up and in while leaving Drew sitting outside in his wheelchair.

"Seriously?" the man asked. "I'm supposed to believe that?"

"Yeah, because it's true. I really am a physicist. Part of Dr. Kleezebee's crew. I'm sure you've heard of him. He owns BTX Enterprises, and you've had him on your news broadcast at least a dozen times. He's my boss and the Dean of the Astrophysics Department."

The man looked him over from head to toe, but didn't say anything.

Drew stuck his head inside the opening, leaning forward and still seated in his chair. "My brother's telling you the truth. You can pull his name up on the Internet if you want. He's listed as part of the staff. Go ahead, check it out: Dr. Lucas Ramsay. It'll be listed under the University of Arizona Physics Research Team."

The old man's concerned look faded. He gripped Lucas' hand and gave it a shake. "I'm Don Wenzel, Field Producer. Channel 9 News."

Lucas nodded and gave him a half-smile. "Can I take a closer look at the video? I may be able to explain what happened."

"Sure, Doc, why not? Provided we get the exclusive."

"It's a deal."

Wenzel used his left hand to nudge one of the techs out of his chair before motioning to Lucas to sit down, which he did.

"Can you restart it at the beginning? It would help if I can see everything you have," Lucas asked, turning his head to check on Drew.

His brother was sitting outside the door, trying to peer around Lucas to see the screen in front. Lucas brought his eyes back to the equipment and decided to shift the chair a few inches to the left. If the news crew managed to capture the tragedy in digital form, he needed to block Drew's view.

The last thing he wanted was for the horrific images to burn a hole in Drew's memories for all of eternity. There would be no way to un-see what was sure to appear on the screen in the next few seconds. Lucas felt it was best if he was the only member of the Ramsay family to carry that burden. His job was to protect Drew, and this was one of the ways he could do just that.

Wenzel restarted the playback, showing an overhead feed from one of the helicopters circling the mall. The first few minutes showed the energy dome working its way west from Campbell Avenue, gobbling up street signs, cars, campus buildings, fencing, and most of the university's newly renovated aquatic center. It was hard for him to watch as a handful of students scrambled to get away from it. Some made it, others didn't—snuffing their lives out in an instant.

The helicopter caught up to the dome and then flew directly over it. When its camera tilted down, Lucas could see deep inside the phenomenon through a opening in the crown. The aperture was like the eye of a hurricane, showing debris being carved out along the dome's inside edge and, while suspended in midair, twisted and compacted into a long, winding rope of matter, before being flushed through a swirling black vortex in the center.

He watched partially consumed buildings collapse along the south side of the mall, but only after the energy field moved past them. While the dome was in contact with them, the damaged structures seemed to defy gravity and remain erect, leading Lucas to believe the energy field's perimeter was acting like a stabilizing force, keeping the buildings upright until after it passed.

Lucas leaned in closer when the recording showed the energy field rumbling across the mall, consuming every inch of grass, trees, cement, and pavement, all of it stripped from the earth and wedged through the sphere's powerful vortex.

Just then, on the screen, he saw himself in miniature on the ground. He was running up the right side of the monitor as he pushed Drew in his chair along the front of the Student Union, heading west. The perspective was a little disconcerting. He'd never seen himself on video before, and seeing his size relative to the massive dome and its destructive force made him feel small and insignificant. Sort of how he imagined the rest of the scientific community viewed him now after Dr. Green's scathing comments about his thesis.

On the left side of the screen, two injured females—one of them pregnant—were struggling in the grass, trying to get up before the energy field reached them. Lucas had to look away from the horror when they didn't make it. He was obviously wrong earlier when he'd told Drew the police would help those injured in the mass exodus.

The dome continued up the video screen, slaughtering people unable to escape its maw. Lucas held his breath as their bodies were ripped apart like string cheese, then mangled and distorted as they were sucked through the dome's violent eddy.

After the miniature versions of him and his brother disappeared off the screen, the energy dome stopped moving, turned an orange color, and then dissipated a few seconds later. The news camera zoomed in for a dramatic close-up of the mound of bloody human remains left behind—the same pile they'd seen earlier when most everyone started puking.

Lucas felt like he was watching a science fiction movie, one that featured a fictional report from a war zone half way around the world, somewhere in a developing nation—somewhere remote and disconnected from real life. He had to remind himself that he'd just seen the events happen with his own eyes—and it was real, all of it within what was supposed to be the safe and peaceful confines of a university campus. A campus within the borders of the most highly developed country in the world.

Lucas looked at the producer. "Could you burn a copy of the footage onto a DVD for me? I'd like to analyze it."

"Sorry. Can't do it. Not without my station manager's okay. I'm sure he's gonna wanna see it first."

"We don't have time for that. Look, I'm not going to steal it. If you want, watermark the footage with your station's logo and copyright. Just don't obscure the important stuff."

Wenzel hesitated before he finally agreed. Three minutes later, the producer handed a DVD to Lucas. "Can you tell me what this thing is?"

Death from above; a stupid mistake; the end of his career were the phrases that first popped into Lucas head, but he chose to hold them all back. "I'm not sure yet, but once I've had a chance to analyze your video, I should be able to. Give me your number and I'll call you later with the results."

Wenzel gave Lucas his business card. Lucas shook his hand, then climbed out of the van.

"What did you guys see?" Drew asked.

"I'll show you later. Let's head back to the apartment so I can check this out better."

Neither of them said anything until after they crossed Speedway Boulevard on the north side of campus. That's when Lucas decided to break the eerie silence. "Earlier, when I saw you with the FBI . . . What did you tell them?"

"I didn't tell them anything except that my girlfriend was on the steps when the accident happened."

Lucas thought the use of the term "girlfriend" was a little premature. One breakfast did not constitute much of a relationship, certainly not one that would qualify her as Drew's girlfriend. But seriously, what the hell did he know about relationships, let alone members of the opposite sex. So he let it go. Besides, there were more important things on his mind right now. "Did you tell them you saw it? That you were there at the theater?"

"Yeah, I sorta had to. It was the only way they'd talk to me. I'm sorry, but I just couldn't stay away. I had to see if there was any news about Abby."

"What else did you say?"

"That was it. I didn't mention E-121 or our accident in the lab," Drew said as his eyes welled with tears. "Do you think we're really responsible for all this? That we killed Abby and all those other people?"

"There's no *we* in this, brother. If the E-121 experiment is somehow responsible, then this is all on me. I'll be the one to take the heat. Not you."

"But—" Drew said.

"No, we talked about this before. It was my call. End of story. I don't want to have this conversation again."

"Okay, but I still think you're wrong. Brothers should stick together, no matter what."

"I appreciate it, but no. I've got this. When they come, they come for me . . . alone. Understood?"

Drew nodded, though his face clearly indicated he wasn't happy about it.

"Let's focus on what to do next, okay?" Lucas asked, wanting to shift gears and get back on track.

Drew winkled his nose. "Maybe we should leave town?"

"What are you saying? Hide out? Like lowlife criminals?"

"Seems like the right move to me."

"No, we're not running."

"Okay, then, call it leaving town for safety reasons."

"And go where? We don't know if this thing will happen again, or where. If it starts jumping around, then no place is safe. Besides, if we did cause this, then the honorable thing to do is stay and find a way to stop it."

"You're right," Drew said, letting his face run soft.

"And the only place we can do that is right here, in our lab."

Just then, Drew seemed to find emotional strength. His body language, face and tone of his voice changed, almost as if the reality of the situation had taken root and charged his resolve. "That's true. We have to stay. It's our duty to stop it. For Abby and everyone else. That's what Dad would've wanted us to do."

Lucas nodded. "It's time to man up. And the only way we can do that is to focus on what we do best—figuring this out. Let the police and the emergency crews deal with the rest. We can't afford to get caught up in the middle of all this insanity. We've got work to do."

* * *

Fifteen minutes later, Lucas heard their phone ringing when they made it to the front door of their apartment. He struggled to find his keys, but eventually opened the deadbolt lock and ran inside. But by the time he made it to the phone, the caller had hung up.

He turned to Drew, who was just arriving in his chair. "I'm guessing that was probably Mom."

"Knowing her, she saw the news and has been calling every five minutes. She must be worried sick."

Lucas gave him the phone receiver. "Why don't you give her a quick call while I make backups of the news footage?"

"What do I tell her?"

"Just tell her we're okay, but don't mention anything about E-121 or our lab accident. If she asks about us coming home, tell her we need to stay here and help. If she gives you any grief about it, remind her that Dad would've wanted us to pitch in and help the victims in any way we can. She won't like it, but she'll understand. It's the honorable thing to do."

"Okay, I can do that."

Lucas went to his desk and logged onto the laptop computer. He then proceeded to copy the DVD evidence to his hard drive. Once it was on the hard disk, he uploaded the video files over the Internet to his private cloud storage space, which Kleezebee had given him for their computer's weekly offsite backups. Lucas kept backup copies of all their research material stored there as well.

Drew rolled over to the desk after hanging up the phone. "Mom's good, but you were right. At first, she didn't like the idea of us staying here, but once I mentioned Dad, she understood. I told her we'll watch out for each other so she didn't need to worry. You done yet?"

"Just about," Lucas said, opening the desk drawer. He searched through the pile of junk in the drawer, tossing items aside with his fingers.

"What are you looking for?"

"Have you seen the sixty-four gigabyte thumb drive we just got from Trevor? I want to make a copy of everything so we have it all in one place."

"It's still in my backpack. I'll get it."

Lucas craned his neck up when he heard the pound of footsteps walking across the floor of the apartment above them. A few seconds later, his upstairs neighbor flushed the toilet, sending a loud stream of water gurgling down the sewer pipes in the wall. But the noise didn't stop there. The squeal of a chair rang out from above as it was being pulled across the floor.

Drew tapped Lucas on the arm, bringing his eyes down from the ceiling. He gave the flash drive to Lucas. "If you need the space, delete my study folders from last semester. I don't need them anymore."

"Why don't you see what the news is saying?" Lucas suggested, pointing at the TV. He inserted the flash drive into his computer's USB port. "The remote's on the couch. Hit the MUTE button so I can work in peace."

Drew rolled to the couch and did as he was told. A few minutes later, he called out to Lucas in a concerned tone. "Hey, you'd better come see this."

"What's wrong?" Lucas answered with only partial interest. He was still in the middle of his USB drive's download.

"They're setting up roadblocks around campus."

Lucas grabbed his laptop, flew out of his chair, and raced over to the couch, where he set his computer down in front of him on the coffee table. The broadcast showed four soldiers patrolling the street in front of the north entrance to the university, while two other soldiers erected sawhorse-style barricades from one side of the street to the other. Three Humvees were parked perpendicular to the street, just behind the barricade.

"Hey, isn't that our entrance on Speedway?" Lucas asked. "The one we just went through?"

Drew nodded. "Good thing we got out of there when we did."

Along the bottom of the screen, the news ticker displayed the words: *"BREAKING NEWS: Suspected Terrorist Attack in Tucson . . . National Guard Activated . . . Arizona Governor Declares State of Emergency . . ."*

Lucas rolled his eyes and tossed his hands up. "Now we'll never get back into the lab."

"Maybe we should call Dr. Kleezebee. I'll bet he can get us in."

Lucas liked the idea and dashed to their wall phone, snatching the receiver from its cradle. He didn't have Kleezebee's hotel information in Washington, so he dialed the professor's cell phone, only to have his call redirected to the professor's voice mailbox. He left a message. "Dr. Kleezebee, this is Lucas. Please call me at the apartment when you get a chance. It's urgent."

Next, he tried calling Bruno on both his cell phone and his home phone. There was no answer on either number. "Damn it, where is everybody?"

"You could try Trevor. We both know he's home," Drew said, looking up at the ceiling.

"Worth a shot," Lucas said before grabbing a broom leaning against the wall next to the fridge. He walked to the center of the room and stood between the couch and coffee table. Above him, the ceiling was covered with dozens of shallow, nickel-sized indentations. He picked a new spot, then raised the broom handle and rammed it into the ceiling three times, careful not to punch a hole in the drywall. "You know this would be a lot easier if he'd just get a damn phone. I mean seriously, how hard is that?"

Drew shrugged, turning his eyes back to the TV broadcast.

Lucas sat down on the couch and checked his laptop to see if the video download had finished. The progress bar showed 100% complete. He removed the USB thumb drive and put it into his front pocket.

Less than thirty seconds later, there was a knock at the door.

"Trevor?" Drew asked. "That was fast."

"The dude must've sprinted down here."

When Lucas opened the door, he was surprised to find Dr. Kleezebee standing there, holding one of the E-121 transport cases.

Lucas cleared his throat, knowing he was in trouble. Kleezebee never came by their apartment unannounced. "You back from Washington already, Professor?"

Kleezebee unlatched the container's lid and opened it. "Where the hell is it?"

Lucas needed a few seconds to think, but his mind wasn't cooperating. "Why don't you come in, boss?"

Kleezebee scowled and breezed past him. The professor took the middle seat on the sofa while Lucas sat down across from him in a wooden rocking chair his father had made for them in the workshop back home in Phoenix.

Kleezebee put the material case on the coffee table. "With President Lathrop closing campus, I went to your lab to retrieve the E-121 samples. Imagine my surprise when I found this container empty."

Time to come clean, Lucas thought. There was no way around it. He needed to address it head-on but choose his words carefully. He didn't want to implicate anyone else. Namely his brother. Oh, and Trevor.

He cleared his throat, again, then swallowed to buy himself a few extra seconds of think time. The words finally came to him and he was ready. "Professor, there's something I need to explain. But before I do, I need to tell you that Drew, Trevor, and Abby had nothing to do with it. It was my decision, and I take full responsibility for everything that happened."

"Wait, Professor—" Drew said, trying to join the conversation, but Lucas held out his hand, making sure to stop him.

"No, Drew," Lucas said. He spoke in a soft tone. "I'm not letting you take the fall for this."

"But we did it tog—"

"Not how I see it, bro. I was the man in charge and it's my responsibility. Not yours."

"What the hell did you do?" Kleezebee snapped, his cheeks turning red.

"Friday night, after you left for DC," Lucas said, taking a moment to formulate the rest of the words, "I—and I alone—decided to run the experiment again. Drew had nothing to do with this."

"You did what?" Kleezebee said with a stunned look on his face. "No. No. No. Tell me I didn't just hear those words come out of your mouth."

"Maybe it's best if I show you," Lucas said, queuing up the reactor's video feed on his laptop. The recording showed the core's flash of light in slow motion, and the disappearance of E-121 and its canister.

Kleezebee's nostrils flared and his face turned an even deeper shade of red. He just sat there, shaking his head with his jaw clenched, staring at the wall across from him.

Lucas thought his boss was about to blow a gasket, so he quickly explained, hoping to diffuse the situation. "I felt like I had to try again while I still had access to the lab. With the committee shutting us down and you heading to Washington, I thought I might never get another chance. So I convinced Drew to help me. We cranked up the juice and used full power."

"And we corrected your wave displacement calculations," Drew said.

"Again, sir, it was all my decision," Lucas added.

Kleezebee lowered his head and began to rub his forehead with his hand. Almost a full minute later, he said, "You know, there was a damn good reason why I changed your specs. I specifically told you to only use half power. You never should've made any modifications without checking with me first."

"Yes, sir, I know. I'm sorry. But there's more I need to show you," Lucas said, starting the video of the theater's flash event using frame-by-frame mode. He stopped the playback at the point right before he used the student's video camera to capture close-up footage of the body parts. He wanted to prepare the professor for what came next.

"How'd you get this?" Kleezebee asked.

"Drew and I were on scene when it happened."

"Why were you there at that time of night?"

"We were meeting Abby and her roommate at the theater for the midnight movie. It was a double date of sorts."

Kleezebee sighed. "Were the girls already there?"

"Yes. She was on the steps with her roommate when the flash appeared. I'm afraid they're both gone, sir," Lucas said, lowering his head in shame. He waited for a reprimand, but it never came.

Lucas brought his head up and looked at his boss. Kleezebee's mouth was hanging open with his eyes transfixed on the floor.

"Somebody should call Abby's parents," Lucas said thirty second later.

"She doesn't have any. They're both dead," Drew replied.

"So I take it one of you brought the video camera to the scene?" Kleezebee asked, breaking his silence.

"No, Professor. I found it there, on a step. It belonged to one of the people waiting in line. They were using it when the . . . the event happened."

"Then what?"

"I recorded the scene. Here's what I shot," Lucas said, clicking the **PLAY** button on his laptop's screen. "Notice how there's a complete lack of rubble and blood. Only body parts. Clearly, this wasn't an explosion. Despite what the police think, I doubt a terrorist cell could've caused this type of destruction."

Kleezebee gasped and then turned away when the close-up shot of Jasmine's severed torso appeared on the screen. "Okay, enough. I get the picture."

Lucas canceled the rest of the playback, then queued up the Channel 9 news video before asking Kleezebee, "Did you hear about the energy field that leveled the mall this morning?"

Kleezebee nodded, his eyes squinting.

Lucas played the video footage. "This was shot from one of Channel 9's news helicopters. Notice the dome's transparent crown and how it lets us see what's happening inside. It may be a possible weakness or an entry point that could be exploited somehow. Inside, you can see matter as it's stripped from the Earth, then it gets twisted and compacted before being sucked through the vortex." He stopped the playback just before the grand finale.

"Did you notice any change in air pressure following the event?" Kleezebee asked.

Lucas didn't expect that question, taking a second to frame a response. "Yeah, as a matter of fact, I did—both times. It felt like I was being pulled toward ground zero, not pushed."

Kleezebee smirked, as if he'd expected the answer.

"There's something else you might find interesting," Lucas said, replaying the last few seconds of the video. He froze the recording just after the camera zoomed in and revealed the pyramid-shaped heap of tissue and bones. "The energy field leaves behind some form of bio-excretion when it dissipates."

Lucas double-clicked his laptop mouse pad to replay the video file containing the theater's flash event. He fast-forwarded to the very end, and then paused the recording on a scene showing the black powder sitting inside the crater. He looked at his brother. "Grab the sample."

Drew opened his backpack and took out a plastic container. He gave Kleezebee the sample of black powder.

"We found the same black residue inside the reactor core after E-121 vanished," Lucas said.

"Did you analyze it?" Kleezebee asked.

"Yeah, with Griffith's mass spectrometer across the hall," Drew replied. "But the results were inconclusive. It didn't detect any chemical or organic compounds. It's as if it doesn't even exist."

Kleezebee held up the container and shook it before his eyes, much like Drew had done earlier in the lab.

"We also found the same substance inside the theater's crater, and it was all over the mall today after the energy field tore across campus," Lucas said.

Kleezebee opened the container and smelled the residue before rubbing some of it between his fingers. "It certainly appears E-121's disappearance is somehow linked to the two incidents on campus. Wouldn't you agree?" he asked Lucas.

"Yeah, it does. Have you ever seen a substance like this before, Professor?"

"Once, a long time ago, when I was about ten years older than you are now. We never were able to identify it," Kleezebee replied, closing the lid to the container. "I'd like to run this by an old friend to see what he can make of it. Substance identification has come a long way in the past fifty years and maybe he might be able to tell us what it is."

"There's one more thing you should know," Drew said. "Right before E-121 vanished in the reactor's core, there was a massive power surge."

"How massive?"

"Hard to say. It was off the chart."

"Give me an estimate."

"Based on the power acceleration curve, and factoring in the composition and density of E-121 and its receptacle, I'd say at least six times 10^{31} terajoules."

"That's over a trillion times more energy than our sun releases in an hour. How is that possible?"

"I don't know. But that's what the values indicate."

"What was the source of the spike?"

Drew shrugged. "We have no idea."

"Was it from some type of cascading reaction?"

"We don't think so," Lucas answered. "We reviewed all the data, but found nothing to suggest that. I just don't see how our experiment could've generated that level of energy. It wasn't designed for anything close to that."

"I hope you realize I can't just cover this up. We'll have to report everything to the Advisory Committee, and to the authorities. Larson is going to want your heads on a silver platter, and I don't think I can protect you from that festering pustule of a man."

"We understand, Professor," Lucas replied in a solemn voice.

"I need you to put together a copy of all the evidence and get it to me ASAP. I want to review it with my colleagues on the committee and get everyone's input."

Lucas retrieved the thumb drive from his pocket and gave it to Kleezebee. "It's all on here, boss, including the data logs." He was hopeful the committee's senior professors would be able to assist. Two of them were Nobel Laureates who had won for the prize for physics.

Just before he walked out the door, Kleezebee turned and said, "Let's meet tomorrow morning in your lab. 9 a.m. We can sit down and go through the data together."

"How are we supposed to get past the roadblocks? The military's never going to let us through," Lucas said.

"I'll figure something out and let you know in the morning."

11

Monday, December 24

The next morning Lucas untangled his feet from the sheets and flew out of bed when the wall phone rang, waking him from a deep sleep.

"Who the hell is calling so damn early?" Lucas groaned in a rusty, thready voice, hearing his brother stirring in the bed across from his. "It better not be another one of those damn political polls."

He stumbled in the dark to the main room and lifted the receiver. He intended to be rude to the caller but changed his mind at the last second, just in case it was someone he knew. "Lucas Ramsay speaking."

"Lucas, I'm glad you're up. It's DL. I don't have time to explain, but the meeting's been changed to seven a.m. I've already sent a car to get you. It'll be there shortly. Make sure you bring Trevor along. Understood?"

"You got it, Professor; see you then," Lucas replied, his head still running in slow motion after the call woke him up. His lips had answered on their own before his brain had a chance to store the information relayed by his boss. He called the mental condition *Autopilot Amnesia*—a curse of intellectuals who disappear into their own thoughts on a moment's notice, while carrying on in the physical world like normal people.

He took a second to replay Kleezebee's words, finding them rattling around inside his head as fading echoes of reality. He was able to latch onto them and memorize the details before they vanished from his thoughts completely.

The fact that he'd been able to doze off the night before was something of a miracle after everything that happened. The events kept replaying over and over in his mind like some miraculous breakaway goal in the Stanley Cup Playoffs. Somewhere along the way his eyes finally closed and his brain shut off, letting him drift off into the blissful state of unconsciousness. His decision to finally tell Kleezebee everything probably had something to do with it.

Confession is good for the soul.

He was thankful for the bounty of shuteye, because facing another day with the load of blood on his hands wasn't going to be easy. The last thing he needed was to be dragging his body around like the walking dead.

Lucas went across the main room and stuck his head into the doorway of their bedroom. "Hey, Drew! Get your ass up. Kleezebee's changed the meeting to seven."

Drew stirred momentarily under the covers, but didn't respond.

"Dude! Get up! We need to get moving, now!"

"Okay. Okay. I heard you the first time," his brother said, turning over and sitting up.

Lucas turned to face the refrigerator, which was just outside the door to their bedroom. He snatched the broom next to the fridge, then walked to the center of the room and rammed it into the ceiling three times to call Trevor. A few seconds later, the broom was stored away and the fridge was open. He found a can of grape soda sitting on the top shelf. He grabbed it, tapping the top of the can with his finger five times before popping the tab. Three powerful gulps later, the can was empty.

"Nectar of the gods," he said after letting out a thunderous belch that rattled his throat.

"Nice one," Drew said, cruising into the room in his chair. His hair was sticking out in all sorts of directions. "Do you know why DL changed the meeting?"

"Nope, not a clue," Lucas said, tossing the aluminum can in the recycle bin. "Where's our notebook?"

"It's on the desk."

Lucas found the red and blue spiral notebook right where his brother said it was. He slipped it into Drew's backpack and began to wonder what might explain the sudden change in Kleezebee's plan. Not that it mattered. Nothing was going to change what Lucas had to do next.

First, protect Drew.

Second, man up and face the wrath of the Advisory Committee.

Third, try to convince everyone it was all just an accident, and he never intended to hurt anyone with the experiment. They'd have to understand, right?

After all, they were all scientists and every scientist knows that mistakes can happen in the lab. Sometimes people even get hurt or killed, especially in the field of advanced theoretical physics. And besides, the experiment had been sanctioned by the committee and by the feds in the first place. How could anyone have expected him to anticipate the results?

He liked his argument. It all sounded logical and reasonable. For a moment, he thought everything might just be okay.

Then his intellect took control, reminding him of other, more troubling facts. Facts that weren't going to help his case: his paper submittal to Dr. Green. Larson shutting down the experiment. Ignoring direct orders from Kleezebee. The vanishing E-121 material from the reactor. Then the endless blood, death, and destruction on campus.

Lucas gulped, knowing he was totally and completely screwed. The kind of screwed that often leads to courtrooms, endless hate mail, and jail time.

He turned and looked at the door, half-expecting the police to come crashing through and arrest him for mass murder. He waited, but nothing happened. Then he shook his head and told himself he was overreacting about the earlier than expected meeting. DL probably had other things to do today and simply moved the meeting up a few hours to accommodate his schedule.

Positive thoughts, he told himself. Everything would work out. Just stand up and tell the truth. Kleezebee would protect him—he always did. It was all just a horrible, freak lab accident.

Lucas quickly dressed and sat down on the couch to wait for his brother. He powered on the TV and changed the channel to one of the network news stations.

There was an African-American female correspondent standing in a crowded parking lot filled with emergency vehicles. Superimposed across the bottom of the screen was the phrase *NORTH HANOVER, NJ LEVELED. MCGUIRE AFB SPARED.*

The broadcast switched to an overhead feed from a helicopter, which showed a familiar-looking trail of black destruction several blocks long that cut through the center of the city. Lucas' heart sank as he watched the all-too-familiar scene play out on the screen.

"Another war zone in the heart of the U.S.A., brought to you by Dr. Lucas Ramsay. A totally fucked Dr. Ramsay—soon to be breaking rocks in some harsh outdoor labor camp sponsored by the State of Arizona," he mumbled to himself.

A minute later, he watched a group of firefighters wandering around the scene, then turned his head to call to his brother who was digging around inside the fridge for something to eat. "Looks like another energy dome has appeared."

"Where? Tucson?"

"No. This one is in New Jersey."

"Jersey? That's like two thousand miles away."

"I know. Not good. It's spreading."

Drew came cruising over to the couch. His right wheel slammed into the side next to Lucas. "Was anyone hurt?"

"Looks like it. The dome took out a small town," Lucas answered, wondering how much more guilt he'd have to endure. He wasn't sure his conscience could take much more.

"Any more black residue?"

"Oh yeah, it's there."

"I wonder why it moved to New Jersey?"

"No clue. But it looks like I was right. No place is safe."

"What about Mom up in Phoenix?"

"We'll have to deal with her later. The chance of something happening to her versus the rest of the planet is virtually nil."

"But still?"

"Look, the best way we can help her is to help everyone. And that means we focus on figuring out how to stop this before it happens again. Trust me, nobody on this planet wants to solve this more than me."

"We'll need to convince the professor that we can. Otherwise, I don't think he'll let us anywhere near the lab. I'm sure he's lost faith in us."

"I know. But he has to. For everyone's sake. All we need is a second chance."

"Like Dad needed."

"Exactly. I figure the universe owes our family one. You ready to go?"

Drew nodded, right before Trevor knocked on the door. The three of them went down to the first floor to wait for Kleezebee's driver. They were just outside the main entrance, next to the manager's office, when a four-door sedan picked them up for their short commute to the science lab.

They traveled south toward the cordoned-off university and used the driver's credentials to pass through the north checkpoint. Military troops had set up roadblocks and checkpoints to limit access to campus while forensic investigations continued. The driver pulled up to the front of the science lab to drop them off.

Inside, the three of them met up with Bruno, who was guarding the security entrance as usual, standing next to two of his beefier staff members.

"Dr. Lucas, I'm to escort you to NASA's security station. There are several people waiting for you. DL said he'll meet you there."

"NASA?" Drew asked.

"Ah, that ain't good," Lucas said, feeling the knot in his stomach tighten. He'd never been within fifty yards of NASA's section of the building. He'd often wondered what stealthy projects were underway, but never imagined he'd actually have the opportunity to walk the halls of the top-secret wing.

Trevor put one of his enormous hands on Lucas' shoulder, gripping it gently as a friend would do.

Despite his uneasiness, Lucas forced himself to remain calm. He cleared his mind and took a few deep breaths. He needed to be one hundred percent on point, or no one would listen to him. The meeting's new location meant the situation had escalated. NASA would never have granted them access unless the circumstances left them with no other choice.

Bruno led Trevor and the Ramsay brothers past their own lab and continued on to NASA's checkpoint, where he stopped to shake each of their hands. "Good luck today, boys. I need to return to my station before my guys run amok. Hopefully, DL will allow me to send them home soon."

After Bruno left, a two-man crew of armed MPs frisked Lucas, and then they searched Trevor and Drew, before instructing the trio of scientists to go through another gauntlet of scanning equipment.

Lucas walked through first, holding his breath. He hated these things, always feeling like his organs were being irradiated. No alarms sounded and he was cleared for entry. A guard handed him a dark blue NASA visitor's badge, which he clipped to his shirt pocket.

Trevor picked up Drew and carried him through the two screening devices. Once again, the security devices remained silent. Trevor put Drew back in his chair and the guards handed them visitor's badges to wear as well.

They were escorted down two connecting hallways before arriving in front of a metal-grated freight elevator. Lucas knew there was only one reason for the single-story building to have an elevator. They were about to travel underground. He boarded the lift and stood with the small of his back pressing against the rear handrail. Lucas could smell a lingering cigar odor. Actually, it was a nasty cigar stench. That meant only one thing: Kleezebee must have ridden the elevator recently.

One of the guards pressed the control panel's bottom-most button, illuminating the number 20. As the lift descended, Lucas thought about NASA's lengthy ten-year construction period. There was plenty of gossip floating around campus, but nobody seemed to know the reason it took so long.

Now he knew: building a secret twenty-story subterranean bunker directly under campus was an impressive feat. It also corroborated the rumor that secret underground tests were being run, which had shaken their lab like a bartender finishing a James Bond martini. He wondered if Kleezebee had known what was happening right under their feet, possibly damaging the science lab's foundation and putting all their lives in jeopardy.

Lucas felt a body-wide flush when they stepped off the elevator on the 20th floor and were greeted by Mary Stinger, Kleezebee's executive assistant. The same young woman who held the starring role in many of Lucas' late night sexual fantasies.

She smiled. "Hello, Dr. Ramsay. I'm to escort all three of you to the conference room, which is at the far end of this floor. Please follow me." She held out her hands in the MPs' direction. "I've got it from here, boys. You may return to the surface."

Lucas couldn't keep his eyes off Mary's body. He'd been preconditioned to appreciate a beautiful woman's appearance, just like every other male of the species. Even in a tense, dire situation like this, it was difficult to stop his eyes from wandering. Then again, maybe a temporary diversion was just what he needed right about now, so he decided to set them free.

Mary's silky orange blouse was unbuttoned deep below her neckline to expose a sizable portion of her upper breasts. He snuck several peeks, trying not to appear obvious, but it was difficult not to stare. Her cleavage wasn't only magnificent, it acted like a magnet for his eyes.

He kept a close eye on her as she started to walk down the hallway. She swayed her hips with purpose, walking with a distinct bounce in her step, as if she were strutting down the runway at some New York fashion show. He listened to the rhythmic clatter of her six-inch heels smacking the cement floor, which, when combined with the metronome-like stride of her tan legs, was almost hypnotizing. He'd gladly follow her anywhere.

* * *

Drew waited to let Lucas file in behind Dr. Kleezebee's assistant, Mary, knowing his brother would appreciate the priority view of her figure. His assumption proved correct when Lucas flared his eyebrows and gave him a quick thank you nod.

Before Drew followed his brother and Mary down the corridor, he took a look back at the MPs waiting inside the elevator for the doors to close. The sharply dressed men were standing in the rear of the car with their keen, hawk-like eyes trained on him. But there were fewer men in the lift than he remembered. Somehow his earlier head count had been off by one.

He wasn't sure how he'd made such a simple mistake, but figured it must've had something to do with his mind being too preoccupied with other matters. It was obvious his focus was slipping and he needed to better his concentration since this might be his one and only visit inside NASA's underground complex.

As they moved deeper into the facility, Drew micro-focused on the details around him, wanting to remember everything until the end of time. He tried to peek inside the various labs along the way, but couldn't because most of their doors were closed. Fortunately, on two occasions, he was able to catch a glimpse inside an open door when a person in a white lab coat just so happened to be entering or exiting as he cruised by.

Inside the first room was an elderly woman sitting behind a desk. She was stirring the contents of a black coffee mug while leaning forward with her face unusually close to the computer screen. A row of five-drawer filing cabinets stood watch behind her, and there were hundreds of shoebox-sized boxes stacked up all around the room. Each brown box had a red, white, and blue priority mail sticker on the side. Before the door swung closed, she turned to gaze at Drew, slipping on a pair of glasses that had been hanging on a chain in front of her chest.

The second room featured two heavyset men—maybe Native Americans, judging by their long black hair and dark skin. They were standing in front of a transparent grease board, scribbling equations in red and blue marker ink. The board was at least a foot taller than they were, and framed in wood, with a set of casters for mobility.

Drew could only see a portion of their work, but recognized it. They were attempting to control virtual protons in a quantized field—not an easy feat given the infinite number of excitation waves that could be produced or annihilated. If he wasn't expected elsewhere, he would've stopped to inform them their energy absorption rates were off.

He brought his eyes forward and noticed an abundance of Marine personnel roaming the halls. He hadn't expected such a strong military presence inside a scientific facility. Granted, both the military and NASA were funded by the Congress, and NASA was nominally considered a defense agency, but it didn't explain why there appeared to be more Marines than scientists.

The journey continued, with his hands gripping and releasing to push his wheelchair forward one thrust at a time. Out of habit and to maintain his bearings, Drew kept track of their location as they moved deeper into the facility. He thought it prudent to calculate where they were in relation to their own lab on the ground floor, and to memorize the path back to the elevator. Just in case it was needed later.

* * *

Lucas led his brother into the waiting area outside the conference room. The seating area was just to the left of the conference room's double doors. The space had been adorned with eight fabric-covered chairs and a glass coffee table sitting between them. Two stacks of magazines were lying on the table, the top of which was lying open with a photograph of a man standing in an aluminum boat on a lake, fishing.

"Go ahead and take a seat," Mary said, pointing. "They'll call for you when they're ready."

The three scientists followed Mary's instructions and found seats in the waiting area along the wall. Lucas and Drew were next to each other, with Trevor on Lucas' left. Mary was now seated in the chair directly across from Lucas with her legs crossed lady-like.

Lucas locked his eyes on Mary's chest, studying the official NASA ID badge she was wearing. Since the ID had her name on it and included her photo, it meant she wasn't simply a visitor. She'd been granted specific security clearance, and by extension, Kleezebee must possess it as well.

Obviously, there was a lot Lucas didn't know, and it was starting to make him question everything. The nagging feeling in his gut was telling him that what he didn't know about his mentor and his job at the university was more important than what he did know. The whole experience of being Kleezebee's hired assistant was starting to feel like an exercise in humility, or futility, depending on how he wanted to look at it. Working in the dark, especially for a cryptic, emotionally detached man like the professor, is never easy.

Lucas' planned recap of what had happened in the lab with the E-121 experiment was starting to rattle apart in his memory. It all sounded good when he rehearsed it earlier in his head, but now the words seemed meaningless and insignificant, sending his confidence running for the shadows. He needed to know a lot more about the nature of this meeting and who was attending. It was the only way to know for sure if he should change any of the details in his planned explanation or not.

"Excuse me, Mary," he said, waiting for her eyes to meet his before continuing. "I was wondering who we are meeting with besides Dr. Kleezebee?"

"I'm sorry, but I'm not at liberty to say," she answered in a sharp, deliberate tone, almost as if she'd been expecting the question.

"Okay, but can you at least tell me how many people are inside? Are they from NASA, the university, or from someplace else?"

"Sorry, can't say. It would mean my job. I hope you understand."

"I do. Just trying to get a feel for what to expect. Please don't take offense."

A weak grin grew on her lips. "I don't. In fact, if I were in your shoes, I'd want to know as well."

"Yeah, this waiting around and not knowing ain't gonna be easy, that's for sure."

Mary nodded, her face indicating she was deep in thought. "Well, there is one thing I *can* tell you. The group inside has been in conference for well over an hour. It probably won't be long now."

Lucas nodded, feeling his worry level skyrocket. "So we need to be ready, for whatever this is."

"That would be my suggestion."

Drew tapped Lucas on the arm, then leaned over and spoke in a whisper, "Did you see all the soldiers on the way here?"

"You mean the Marines?"

"Yeah, that's what I said."

"No, you said *soldiers*. Marines aren't soldiers. Calling them that is fightin' words."

"How do you know?"

"I read. Remember? They prefer to call each other jarhead or grunt or something along those lines. Just not soldier," Lucas answered.

"Sorry."

"Easy mistake. I catch myself doing it all the time. Yeah, but you're right. It does seem a bit odd. Why so many?" Lucas angled his head in Mary's direction. "Did you notice her ID badge?"

"Sure did. This whole thing makes me nervous."

"Maybe the Marines have some joint venture project with NASA? After all, they're all part of our government. It's probably not the first time they've pooled their resources."

Drew looked down at his lap and began to rock back and forth, clutching the leather pouch hanging from his neck.

Lucas recognized his brother's familiar response. Drew was slipping away into his secret, dark place, trying to conceal himself from reality. He gave his brother a small hug. "It's going to be all right, little brother. I'll take care of it. I always do."

"Drew okay? Need help?" Trevor asked Lucas, finally breaking his customary silence.

"He'll be fine. Just give him a few minutes," Lucas said. "But thanks for asking, and for being here. You're a good friend."

Lucas turned to face his brother. He hoped that by interrupting his brother's ritual, Drew would snap out of his funk. He nudged him on the shoulder. "Can you hand me the notebook?"

Drew stopped rocking, unzipped his backpack, and pulled out the multi-colored notebook they'd brought from the apartment. He gave it to Lucas. There was a faded purple stain on the lower half of its cover, next to the torn right edge.

Lucas and Drew had exhausted the previous evening formulating a number of unorthodox theories regarding the nature of the energy fields the day before. They knew conventional thinking wasn't going to provide them with answers, let alone a solution. They'd considered every conceivable possibility, no matter how irrational or preposterous.

They'd discussed cascading reactions, antimatter annihilation, subspace fractures, micro singularities, quantum rifts, subatomic space-time turbulence, and even the possibility of third-party sabotage. They developed multiple theory paths and mapped them to an elaborate decision tree, which they could implement depending on how future events unfolded.

At the time, Lucas thought it was an ingenious, well-conceived plan that would impress Kleezebee. Now he wasn't so sure. Especially since neither of them could explain the massive energy spike that triggered the E-121 incident. The energy levels were off the charts and he knew mentioning it would make them sound like incompetent amateurs.

"Would you mind if I ran through some of these theories with you, Trevor?" Lucas said, turning to the third page. "We need a fresh pair of eyes to help us check their accuracy and make sure our assumptions are valid. You can be our sounding board."

"Go ahead. I help."

* * *

Twenty minutes later, Mary's digital pager began to beep. She reached for the unit and disabled its alarm.

Lucas wondered why she was using such an antiquated device. Perhaps a dampening field was in place to block cell phone reception for security reasons. On the other hand, it may have been due to heavy terrestrial interference. A digital signal would degrade significantly having to penetrate twenty floors of thick cement and rebar. A second later, Lucas heard at least two other pagers going off, though they sounded distant, possibly down the hall.

"Are they ready for us?" Lucas asked her.

She shook her head with a concerned look on her face. "That wasn't them."

"Is something wrong?"

"NASA just ordered everyone to evacuate the building."

Lucas put his hands on the chair's armrests. "Do we need to leave?"

"Not sure. Let me check," she replied before standing up, adjusting her blouse, and walking to the conference room door. She knocked twice, then leaned through the doorframe, as if she were waiting for permission to enter. She stepped inside and was gone less than a minute before returning with a folded piece of white paper. She handed it to Trevor. "This is from Dr. Kleezebee. He says it's for your eyes only."

Trevor stood up and moved away before unfolding the paper and reading the note.

Mary told Lucas, "They're almost ready for you. Should only be a few more minutes."

"Then I take it we're not evacuating with everyone else?"

"No, you're to remain here until they call for you."

"What is taking so long?" Drew asked. "They're wasting time. We really need to be in the lab, finding answers."

"It takes time to set up an execution," Lucas mumbled before he could stop his lips from muttering the words. He looked at Drew, but it didn't appear his brother heard his accidental comment.

Trevor walked back and whispered something into Mary's ear, after which the two of them hurried down the hall and disappeared around the corner.

"What was that all about?" Drew asked.

"Who knows? This just keeps getting stranger by the minute. All we need now is for your friend Griffith to show up with one of his toxic chemical experiments," Lucas said, sitting back in his chair, thinking about the energy dome chasing them on campus. He was happy to be deep inside a hardened military-style shelter with thick, reinforced walls, far below ground where it couldn't reach them. But he worried for everyone else across the planet who was stuck on the surface with nowhere to hide.

Drew clutched his leather pouch again and resumed rocking.

Lucas expected the next hour of his life to be one he'd always remember. It was either going to be a career-making meeting—if one of their notebook theories proved to be the solution to the energy fields—or career-ending. Prison could be the result, too. He didn't know how this was all going to unfold, but it was clear the gut-wrenching stress was going to be his companion for a while.

Just then the conference room doors swung open and Dr. Kleezebee poked his head out. His face looked numb and pale, like he'd just seen a ghost. "Guys, it's time. Come on in."

Lucas took a deep breath and steeled himself.

12

The windowless conference room was encased with gray padded fabric along the interior of its walls. Lucas presumed it was some form of soundproof material, which was understandable given NASA's secret activities. More than likely, NASA was employing several layers of security countermeasures to safeguard today's meeting.

In the center of the room was an oval mahogany table, featuring a four-sided television platform built into its center. A 3D NASA logo was spinning on the screen facing him, acting like a bouncing screen saver.

Lucas waited for Drew to select a spot at the table and roll into position, then he took the open seat next to him. He took a deep breath, then let his eyes wander around the table to greet the faces staring back at him. He recognized everyone.

Directly across from him was Dr. Kai Suki, an undersized Korean fellow. Suki was the chairman of the university's Advisory Committee and Kleezebee's immediate boss. Two years earlier, Lucas had dropped Dr. Suki's advanced calculus class when he discovered that Suki barely spoke English. The man was brilliant, but good luck understanding what he was saying with his back turned to the class while his hand was cranking out complex equations across a mammoth grease board.

Lucas knew better than to continue with a teacher he couldn't understand. He'd made that mistake his first year in college, when he struggled to pass a physics class taught by a chubby Italian professor whose lectures were littered with broken syllables and misused pronouns—not a good start to his college career. It was the only grade lower than an A on his entire transcript. Lesson learned.

Kleezebee was seated to Suki's right, dressed in a shiny blue suit with a matching tie that was partially obscured by the man's thick gray beard. Lucas had never seen his boss dressed in formal attire before. In fact, he couldn't remember a time when he hadn't seen Kleezebee in his customary flannel shirt and redneck coveralls. He figured Kleezebee's closet only contained a dozen or so copies of the same outfit, at least until now.

DL cleans up well, he mused silently, trying to cover up his anxiety with some humor. It wasn't working.

On the opposite side of Dr. Suki, was Randol Larson, the abhorrent Legal Counsel for the Advisory Committee. The man's right eye was watering and blinking rapidly, as if something were stuck in it. Larson pulled at his eyelid with his fingers. Lucas held back a chuckle by covering his mouth with his hand and coughing.

Next to Larson was Dr. Judith Rosenbaum, chief scientific advisor to the President of the United States. Lucas recognized her from a recent magazine article on the effects of greenhouse gases on the planet's atmosphere. The article mentioned her winter home was located in Green Valley, Arizona, a retirement community thirty miles south of Tucson. He'd never been there but had heard all the jokes about the golf-cart driving old folks clogging up the city's streets.

Rosenbaum's wrinkled cheeks sagged down to her jaw line like a deflated balloon. Her face was riddled with liver spots, as were her tiny forearms. Her most prominent feature was her two-foot beehive hairdo, much like the animated character Marge Simpson wore, except Rosenbaum's was gray instead of royal blue.

To the woman's left was Hudson Rapp, a famous African-American astronaut who'd just been named by the U.S. President as the Director of NASA. The man was big. Trevor-sized big. If he hadn't gone NASA, he probably would've ended up playing professional football somewhere. He was an Arizona native, a local hero of sorts. He'd been dominating the local news lately with claims of having discovered extraterrestrial life. His team had found traces of silicon-based microbial life hidden inside a porous meteorite that crashed recently in northern Oregon. Rapp was scheduled to be the university's keynote speaker at next semester's graduation ceremonies.

Lucas knew the stakes had been raised when he craned his neck to the left and saw a bank of jumbo-sized teleconference screens along the wall. Each one contained a different high-ranking Washington official who appeared to be transmitting from a separate location.

Dennis M. Hubbs, President of the United States, looked out from the center screen. The trim forty-five-year-old was seated behind his desk in the Oval Office. He was flanked on the left screen by William Myers, Director of Homeland Security, who appeared to be in a heated conversation with a slender blond woman in a wilderness location. The elderly General Phillip Seymour Wright, Chairman of the Joint Chiefs of Staff, stood tall in his uniform on the right screen, though his eyes were dragged down with heavy, dark bags under them, making him look half-asleep.

Given the attendees, Lucas assumed Kleezebee chose the meeting's new location to take advantage of NASA's superior communication network and security systems. Microphones and video cameras circled the meeting area, allowing for real-time transmission to all interested parties. A lengthy electronic whiteboard hung on the opposite wall from the teleconference screens. The university used the same technology, which was capable of digitally transcribing anything written on it, and then transmitting the contents to remote locations.

With everyone focused on him, Lucas felt a little self-conscious. He dropped his eyes and let his hand brush across the tabletop. Its surface was silky smooth and polished, the polar opposite of how his insides felt at the moment. Someone had taken great care to buff and polish its shine until every blemish had been removed, something he wished he could do with his nasty cheek scars. The mahogany wood was a deep reddish color, and its individual planks were edge-glued, using a book-match technique, much like a butterfly's wings. It was a stunning piece of workmanship.

There were stacks of reports spread out in front of him, along with yellow markers, pencils, legal pads, and several unlabeled bottles of water. He could also smell a hint of ammonia in the air.

He finally found the courage to look up, locking eyes with his longtime mentor and boss, Dr. Kleezebee. He'd hoped to find a generous supply of support looking back at him, but the professor's face instantly went cold after he whispered a single word: "Sorry."

At that moment, Lucas felt like a defenseless rabbit who'd just hopped into a clearing, only to find the meadow was surrounded by a pack of hungry wolves. The room's temperature suddenly seemed a bit high, and the walls were much too close for comfort. Yep, it was an execution all right, and his ass was firmly planted in the electric chair.

President Hubbs spoke first. "Dr. Ramsay, I wish to thank you and your brother for joining us here today."

Lucas' throat ran dry as he tried to utter a response, but the words stuck in his throat. It felt like someone had just dumped a mattress full of cotton into his mouth. He stuttered like an idiot. "Happy..." he coughed, "...to be . . . here . . . Mr. President."

He decided he needed a drink to calm his nerves and unstick his lips. When he went to open one of the water bottles in front of him, the plastic cap squirted out of his fingers and shot across the table. He tried to lunge for it as it bounced away from him, but missed. It rolled across the floor and into the far corner.

"Fuck," he snapped before he could stop the vulgarity from leaving from his lips. He was mortified, realizing all he could do now was sit back in his chair and act like nothing had happened.

Play it cool, he told himself. Maybe they didn't all notice his fumble, and the F-bomb.

He drank a healthy swig of water, praying his throat would remember how to swallow properly. Otherwise, he'd look like a drooling idiot. It did, thank God, sliding down properly to quench his raging thirst.

The President cleared his throat. "I had planned to remain for the duration of this meeting, but unfortunately, I have a press conference to give. Dr. Rosenbaum will handle it from here," the President said before standing up and removing his lavalier microphone. All three teleconference screens went dark a second later.

What a stroke of luck—the President wasn't sticking around. The last thing Lucas wanted was to face the President of the United States and admit his mistakes. It was bad enough having to come clean and face the wrath of Kleezebee and the rest of the people seated at the table, but President Hubbs was a former prosecuting attorney with a near-perfect record of convictions. Lucas would've wilted under direct cross-examination by the Commander-in-Chief, only making matters worse.

Lucas kept his head down to avoid eye contact until he pulled himself together. He opened his red-and-blue notebook and scanned through the first few pages, pretending to be interested in the equations. He felt like an unprepared student, hiding in the back of the classroom, praying the teacher wouldn't notice him. Maybe if he kept quiet, everyone would forget he was in the room, too.

Without thinking, he picked up a #2 pencil from the stack on the table and began to chew on the middle of it. The soft wood surface gave way as his teeth clenched around its perimeter. Without warning, his eyes wandered up on their own, looking directly into the eyes of Dr. Rosenbaum.

She didn't miss a beat. "Dr. Ramsay, we're here to investigate the recent tragedies on campus. Dr. Kleezebee has assured me we can expect your full cooperation as we address the cause of these horrific events. Rest assured, we *will* get to the bottom of this," she said in a gravelly voice that sounded older than she looked.

The woman reached for a remote control sitting in front of her, then spoke. "There have been some new developments overnight, of which you may not be aware. Please direct your attention to the screen in front of you."

She clicked a button on the remote while pointing it at the table's video carousel. The screens flickered for a moment, just before the video playback started with the word **MUTE** in the upper left corner of the screen. "This first report is from France and was filmed by one of their local news agencies."

The broadcast showed aerial footage of a devastating gouge that cut through a crowded neighborhood in Paris. Portions of a school and a playground were missing, exposing a bank of lockers and the floor of a gymnasium.

"As you can see, another energy field has appeared and killed thousands of French citizens as they slept. Pay close attention to the last segment of the report."

Lucas had seen the carnage from New Jersey, but the dome terrorizing France was news to him. Things were spiraling out of control, piling more and more guilt onto his already overloaded shoulders.

The camera zoomed in on a mound of shredded bodies left behind by the dome. The organic material was seeping out and percolating in the afternoon sun. The pile appeared to be at least twice the size of the one Lucas had seen on the grassy mall.

"This next report is from Sydney, Australia. It was captured by an American tourist with a video camera."

The recording showed an energy field unleashing its might along the city's waterfront. The dome wasted little time consuming the city's marina before leveling two restaurants and a parking lot crowded with vehicles. Not much remained after it passed, leaving the shoreline a disaster area.

The final report was from South Africa, where a city security camera captured an energy dome flattening downtown Cape Town. It obliterated at least a dozen high-rise buildings and consumed a city park, trees and all.

Rosenbaum clicked a button on the remote control. The video playback paused as she continued. "In addition to last night's reports, we've just received word that subsequent energy fields have reappeared in each of these areas, killing thousands more. Beijing, Moscow, and Baghdad have also reported their first incidents, and the list of cities continues to grow. Each time a dome appears, its size increases. So does the duration of the event, as if they are building toward something even more catastrophic."

"Or searching for something," Kleezebee added. "I question whether we've gathered sufficient evidence to make any formal conclusions about anything as yet."

"Possibly," Rosenbaum said in an annoyed tone, slipping on her reading glasses and opening a thick manila folder sitting in front of her. She took a few moments to scan through the paperwork before addressing Lucas. "Dr. Kleezebee has given us a detailed briefing as to the nature of your E-121 project. He also informed us that you believe these energy fields are linked to the second test of your experiment. Is this still your assessment, Dr. Ramsay?"

"Yes, ma'am. While there's no direct proof, we believe E-121's disappearance and the recurring energy fields are connected in some fashion. The timing of the events, the similar energy levels, the black powder residue—it can't all just be coincidence. It's a good bet they're related . . . somehow."

"When you say *related*, do you mean E-121's disappearance caused the energy fields?"

Lucas chose his words carefully, wanting to sound like a seasoned investigator and not the newly hired physicist he actually was. "Yes, given the facts, one could draw that conclusion. But it may not be the only ex—"

"Was your second test sanctioned by the university, Dr. Ramsay?" she asked in a louder tone, not letting him finish his answer.

"No, it wasn't. But—"

"Then would it be correct to assume that if you hadn't violated protocols and run the experiment a second time, we wouldn't be sitting here today?"

"Yes. However—"

"Then by extension, would it be accurate to conclude that your unauthorized actions led to the deaths of thousands of innocent civilians and hundreds of billions of dollars' worth of damage?"

Lucas didn't answer right away. He needed time to think. It was clear she wasn't there for answers and certainly had no intention of letting him speak and explain the facts. Her agenda was obvious—she needed to pin the deaths on somebody and his name was the only one on the suspect board. He was screwed no matter what he said.

Even so, she *was* right. This *was* his fault. He was the one who disobeyed Kleezebee's orders. There was no denying it. He decided not to fight it. It wouldn't make any difference, anyway. He needed to take it like a man, and deflect responsibility away from his little brother. He looked at Drew, who was staring down at the edge of the table in silence.

Lucas took a deep breath and let it out slowly before answering in a nervous voice. "Yes, ma'am. It's my fault. I'm the reason all those people died. My brother had nothing to do with any of this. I take full responsibility for ignoring Dr. Kleezebee's orders and running the experiment without authorization, and everything else that's happened as a result."

Rosenbaum nodded as if pleased with herself. She leaned forward in her chair like a courtroom judge who was about to render sentencing. "Do you have anything else to add, Dr. Ramsay?"

He was surprised she opened the floor for a response. "As a matter of fact, yes, I do. There was an unexplained energy spike in the reactor just before the material vanished. It may have overloaded the core, which might explain why E-121 disappeared."

"What was the origin of the spike?"

"Unknown, ma'am."

"Then how can you be certain there actually was an energy spike?"

"Because our instruments recorded it."

"Isn't it possible your equipment may have malfunctioned and reported a spike when in fact there was none?"

"No, Dr. Rosenbaum, they were functioning properly."

"Who, may I ask, built these instruments?"

"We did. They're our own design and we spent months perfecting them."

Rosenbaum pulled out a sheet of paper from her folder. "Your logbook reported the spike to be at least six times 10^{31} terajoules. Is that correct?"

"Yes, I believe so."

"Were your instruments designed to handle that amount of energy?"

Lucas shook his head, wondering how the old woman knew everything. "No, they weren't. But trust me, my brother ran the calculations and he's never wrong."

"Even if there was a massive energy spike, as you claim, does that in any way mitigate your responsibility for running the experiment without permission?"

He wished he could answer yes to her question, but couldn't. "No, ma'am, it doesn't."

The woman was relentless. Lucas suddenly felt like the chair he was sitting in was six sizes too large for him. His blood pressure skyrocketed as his chest began to squeeze down on his heart. He suddenly felt the need to make a run for it. He checked to see if the door behind him was open. It wasn't.

Shit. Trapped.

Rosenbaum closed the folder with added force, then made eye contact with each of her colleagues seated at the table. "Dr. Ramsay, this council has spent the early morning hours reviewing the available video and scientific evidence with President Hubbs and his advisors. It is our conclusion, as well as the President's, that your experiment indeed triggered the energy vortexes, which are, at this very moment, spreading across our planet. You were correct earlier when you stated that the facts in evidence are not merely coincidence. We agree. They're much too specific to be random, unrelated events. Your unauthorized E-121 test caused these tragedies."

Lucas had intended to present the council with their notebook of theories, but he changed his mind when it became clear Rosenbaum's sole intent was to crucify him. He decided it would be best if he waited until after the meeting, when he could discuss the notebook privately with Kleezebee. Maybe DL could reason with her.

Rosenbaum continued in a stern voice, "Based on our projections, if this phenomenon continues at its current pace, the entire surface of our planet will be leveled in a little over two weeks. Thanks to you two, the human race is on the verge of extinction."

She took a sip from a half-empty water bottle. "The press is all over this with their doomsday predictions. We're hearing reports of riots, looting, religious hysteria, and mass suicide in every major city around the world. As this phenomenon spreads, power grids are beginning to fail, along with key transportation and communication systems. We have foreign heads of state promising retaliation for what they believe is a planned attack. Our society is on the brink of social and spiritual anarchy. . . ."

She was right, Lucas thought, but damn. She didn't need to rub his nose in it and do so in front of everyone. He'd already admitted he was dead wrong and had taken full responsibility. What more did she want? He couldn't possibly feel any worse than he already did about all the death and destruction. As it was, he had no idea how he was going to live with the consequences of his actions.

Deep down, he knew he wasn't a murderous criminal, even though she was painting him out to be one. He was a good person who always tried to do the right thing, even when his temper got in the way. People make mistakes, right? Everyone does. This was all just a horrible accident that started with one really bad decision. Now his entire life had been turned upside down and gone completely haywire. How the hell did all this happen?

He looked at her, wanting to say something, but he couldn't find the words to defend himself. All he could do was sit there like a wounded duck, wondering if he should even try. It was pointless. She wasn't going to listen. Neither would anyone else at the table, except Drew. And possibly Kleezebee. But they weren't in charge. She was.

Hell, if he thought if it would make a difference, he'd gladly stand up right then and there and offer to give up his life in exchange for all the others who'd died.

Then another idea popped into his head—a foolish one. Maybe he could invent some type of time travel machine and voyage back into history to undo the mistakes he'd made. Oh, how he wished that were possible, but the laws of physics weren't going to allow it. No, he was totally screwed. There was no way out of this mess.

Just then, there was a knock at the door.

Lucas swung his head around to see who it was.

The door behind him opened partway and Mary Stinger stuck her head inside. "Excuse me, Dr. Rosenbaum. I have an urgent report to deliver to Dr. Kleezebee."

"Come in," Rosenbaum said, "but make it quick."

Mary walked around the far side of the table and handed the report to Dr. Kleezebee. Her hair swayed from side to side as she walked quickly back to the door. She smiled and winked at Lucas.

Now she notices me? Seriously? Now?

Kleezebee spent half a minute reading the contents of the folder before addressing Rosenbaum. "Dr. Rosenbaum, this is a preliminary DNA report for the human remains left behind on campus. Thus far, we have positively identified a hundred and five victims. There appear to be twenty-two additional DNA samples, which we have yet to identify."

Kleezebee handed the folder to her. "I caution you, there are some rather graphic photos attached to the back of the report."

Rosenbaum opened the folder and spent a few minutes reviewing it. She seemed to be unaffected by its contents. She turned the folder sideways to look at the photos attached in the back.

"Dr. Rosenbaum," the attorney Larson said, leaning forward in his chair. "If you don't mind, I'd like to see that report next."

She closed the folder and slid it across the table to Larson. It landed in his outstretched hand with a sliding swoosh.

She turned her focus to Kleezebee. "May I have a word with you in private?"

Kleezebee stood up and the two of them moved to the far corner of the room. Lucas couldn't hear what they were saying to each other.

Meanwhile, Larson was slowly scanning the report with his right index finger. When Larson's hand stopped moving, he pulled out his cell phone and tried to use it.

Lucas knew there was no way Larson was going to get cell signal all the way down in the sub-basements, but he didn't say anything. Let him try. Dumbass.

Larson closed his cell and reached for the house phone sitting in front of Dr. Suki. He dragged it closer to him by the phone cord before picking up the receiver. "Do I need to dial nine first to get an outside line?" he asked Suki.

Suki nodded.

Larson dialed the phone, and a few moments later, he began a conversation. "I need to speak to Rafael; is he available? . . . This is his brother-in-law, Randy . . . I need to get a message to him . . . Tell him I'm sorry to report that he was correct all along. He'll know what it means."

Larson hung up the phone and walked past Lucas on his way out of the conference room.

Drew leaned over and whispered into Lucas' ear, "See if you can get a copy of the DNA report. I need to know if Abby's name is on the list."

Before Lucas could respond, he heard a faint rumble above him, and it was getting progressively louder. Moments later, his fingertips felt an uneven vibration in the conference room table. At first, Lucas thought NASA was firing up one of their underground tests, but he soon realized he was wrong when the intensity of the quake increased dramatically. The tremor was far beyond anything he'd ever experienced before.

Kleezebee and Rosenbaum, who were still engaged in a private conversation along the wall, both fell over and landed on the floor.

Lucas was shaken out of his seat and landed next to Drew's wheelchair. He reached up for his brother's arm and pulled Drew down beside him, allowing them to crawl under the mahogany conference table together for safety.

As soon as they were underneath, a series of events happened almost at the same time: one of the padded ceiling tiles came crashing down and landed on Drew's empty wheelchair, with the pointed corner of the tile hitting first. It tore a penny-sized hole in the fabric seat. Then a teleconference screen broke free from the wall and smashed into the floor with a bang, and a moment later, glass lenses from two of the cameras shattered into pieces after the video units shook loose from their ceiling mounts and hit the floor next to the table.

The destruction continued to escalate, with lawn mower-sized chunks of cement raining down from above, splintering into dozens of pieces when they hit.

It was getting hard to breathe with streams of cement dust spewing into the air. Lucas coughed right before the room suddenly went dark. He heard a few more items come crashing down around him.

Drew immediately latched onto Lucas' right arm. "Another energy field?"

Lucas nodded, even though Drew couldn't see his face. "Oh yeah, and it's close."

Before the last syllable left his mouth, the dim emergency lighting kicked in. Lucas looked behind him to see if everyone was okay.

He saw Kleezebee and Rosenbaum kneeling together under the table. They were next to Hudson Rapp, who appeared to be unharmed, though his face was covered in a film of white dust, making him look like a mime.

LINKAGE   173

Lucas didn't see Dr. Suki, not at first. Then he spotted a bloody hand sticking out from under a pile of cement chunks. Since everyone else was accounted for, the arm must have belonged to Suki. But Suki's hand and fingers weren't moving—probably dead.

One more death on my hands, Lucas thought.

He could feel the cement floor moving beneath him as the tremor's violence increased. As far as he knew, they were on the bottom-most floor, with nothing but bedrock underneath them. However, if something manmade were down there, they could fall through.

Drew tapped him on the shoulder and tried to tell him something. But Lucas couldn't hear the words clearly due to an intense, brain-splitting squeal that suddenly filled the room. Now he knew what gophers felt like when someone used ground-penetrating sonar on the surface.

It wasn't long before Drew blacked out and fell against his thigh. Soon after, Kleezebee and Rosenbaum also lay unconscious. Director Rapp was awake and vertical, but his left ear was bleeding heavily from its center, almost like someone had stuck a screwdriver inside his ear canal.

Another volley of debris fell onto the table above Lucas. It sounded like some of it may have smashed into one of the TVs built into the tabletop, shattering a screen.

A few seconds later, the tremor stopped and so did the squeal, just as the conference room doors swung open on their own. The room was now quiet, except for the moans of those around him. Outside the entrance, he could see Larson lying on the ground, face up—apparently unconscious, or maybe dead.

Lucas poked his head out from under the table, hoping another piece of concrete wouldn't shake loose and put a dent in his melon. His eyes ventured up, noticing a heavy bundle of cables hanging through one of the gaps in the ceiling. The place was a mess, with cement, ceiling tiles, glass, insulation and other building debris spread across the conference table and the floor. Despite the sweeping devastation, the ceiling and walls were holding together somehow. But he knew that fact could change at any moment. Especially if another energy field spawned and tore across campus.

13

Lucas helped Drew back into his wheelchair after he woke up. The chair's leather seat held Drew's weight despite the puncture in its material. They were lucky the falling debris hadn't caused more damage to Drew's only mode of transportation.

"You in one piece, brother?" he asked Drew.

"Sort of."

"Must have been another energy field attack," Kleezebee said.

"Yeah, and right above us," Lucas said, eyeing what was left of the ceiling.

"Do you think it damaged the science lab?" Drew asked.

"Yep. You can kiss our experiment goodbye," Lucas said, coughing twice from the dust swirling in the room. "I can't believe it affected us twenty floors underground. I thought we would've been safe down here. Boy, was I wrong."

"Gives you an indication of its destructive power," Kleezebee replied, grimacing.

"Professor, your leg!" Lucas said, seeing his boss walking with a severe limp. Blood had soaked through the cuff on the same pant leg.

"One of the video screens landed on my ankle and I heard something snap. I'm pretty sure it's broken. It hurts like hell, but I'll live. Everyone else okay?"

"I'm not injured," Rosenbaum said, dusting herself off with her wrinkled hands. Sprinkles of debris had been trapped in her beehive hairdo, much like in a spider's web.

"Dr. Suki's in pretty rough shape," Rapp said, grunting to remove hunks of heavy cement covering the frail man. A two-foot section of rebar was sticking out of the upper right quadrant of Suki's chest. He checked Suki's pulse. "His vitals are weak. We need to get him to medical, and soon."

"Thank God," Lucas said, feeling relieved. Suki's death wasn't on his head, after all.

"I'm sorry, what?" Rapp asked. He was clearly taken aback by the callous-sounding comment.

Lucas froze for a moment to consider the timing of his words, then decided to elaborate. "I mean, thank God he's alive, right?"

Rapp's annoyed look evaporated. "Yes. He's alive. Barely."

Kleezebee picked up the receiver to the house phone and listened. "No dial tone. Switchboard must be down. Someone's going to have to go up top and get help."

"I'll go," Lucas said, watching dust trails trickling down from the ceiling in a swirling pattern. "But I'm taking my brother with me."

Larson walked gingerly into the conference room, his face looking weary. "How? The power's out and I doubt the elevator is working."

NASA Director Rapp pulled out an ultra-thin computer from a leather bag he had sitting underneath the table. He powered up the unit and wrinkled his nose. "We shouldn't be on emergency lighting right now. This facility is self-contained and has its own nuclear power plant and air-filtration system. Something's wrong."

"Did you say nuclear?" Larson asked.

"Yes. Something must've caused the reactor to go offline."

"There wasn't a meltdown, was there?" Larson asked.

"If there was, we wouldn't be having this conversation right now," Rapp snapped.

"Do you know the location of the reactor?" Kleezebee asked, hopping on his good leg to move closer to the NASA director.

"I should have the building's schematics on my iPad. Let me see if I can locate it," Rapp said, using the device's touch screen. "What was that horrible sound earlier? It made my ears bleed."

"I've heard it a few times now," Lucas said. "At first, I thought it was being generated by the dome's energy matrix and only extended out in front of the dome. Now I'm starting to think it's more like ground-penetrating sonar. Almost as if the anomaly is searching for something."

"Searching for what?" Larson asked.

"Probably you," Kleezebee said with an annoyed look on his face.

Lucas laughed. Drew didn't.

"Looks like the reactor's two floors up," Rapp said, breaking through the tension.

"Do you have the plans for it?" Kleezebee replied, pointing at the man's iPad.

"Roger that. It's all right here."

"Then I might be able to get it working again."

"Excuse me, Professor," Lucas said, thinking about his mission to go get help. "If the science lab was destroyed, then I doubt the elevator's going to work, even if it has power. There's nothing left at the top of the elevator shaft."

"What about stairs?" Drew asked.

"Yes, they're next to the elevator," Rapp said.

"Are you nuts? It's twenty floors up," Larson whined.

"The rest of you should go. I'll never make it to the top with this ankle," Kleezebee said. "I'll stay behind and see if I can get the reactor working again. We're going to need it for the ventilation system. We could be here a while."

"I agree. We don't want to suffocate before we're rescued," Larson said.

"I'll assist you, Professor. I can't climb all those steps, either," the elderly Rosenbaum said, shaking the dust and debris from her high-profile hairdo.

"I'm staying, too. Someone has to look after Dr. Suki," Rapp said, staring at Kleezebee's injured leg. "We should see about getting your ankle into a splint. You should probably sit down. Keep it elevated.

It's gonna swell like hell once the body sends fluids to incapacitate the area around the injury."

"Then I guess it's just the three of us," Lucas said to Drew and Larson, picking up the theory notebook from the table. He blew off several layers of dust from its cover, in the direction of Larson, unintentionally—well, sort of.

Larson coughed and waved his hands in front of his face. "If there's this much damage down here, do you really think the stairwell is clear all the way to the top? I think not. It's nothing but a goddamn waste of time and energy." He folded his arms and pinched his nose and lips together. "No, I'm gonna wait right here until help arrives."

Lucas was more than happy to leave Larson behind. He held up the notebook in Kleezebee's direction. "Professor, this contains a few theories that Drew and I put together regarding the energy fields. You might want to review them while we're gone?"

"Why don't you keep them for now? I can't do anything with 'em down here."

"Sure," Lucas answered his boss before slipping the notebook into the zippered section of his brother's backpack. It was still hanging on the back of the wheelchair.

Lucas turned to Drew. "Do you remember the way back to the elevator?"

Drew shook his head. "Yeah, I memorized it on the way here. I'll draw you a map."

"No, you're coming with me."

Drew shook his head. "You should go alone. I'll just slow you down."

"No chance, bro. I'm not leaving you behind," Lucas said, looking at the others in the room. He knew with Rosenbaum and Rapp staying behind to help Kleezebee and Dr. Suki, that would leave only Larson to look out for Drew's safety. And that asshole was the last person he'd choose to watch his little brother.

Drew looked down at his wheelchair. "If the elevator's disabled, how am I supposed to get up the stairs?"

"I'll carry you on my back if I have to. Wouldn't be the first time, now would it? Besides, there's no way in hell I'm leaving you down here. We're going to stick together, no matter what. It's what Ramsays do."

"You two need to get moving. Once you let the emergency crews know where we are, find Trevor. He'll get you someplace safe," Kleezebee said.

"Sure, but what if we can't find him?" Lucas replied.

"Then get as far away from Tucson as you can," Kleezebee said, tossing a set of keys to Lucas. "My car's in the rear parking lot of the apartment complex."

Lucas shook his head. "We can't just run from this. Drew and I need to find a way to help stop what's happening. We have to do something."

"Let me worry about that. For now, I need you to get help and then find Trevor. Understood?"

"But, sir—"

"This isn't open for discussion. I've made my decision. Now, go get help and then get as far away from here as you can. That's an order."

"Yes, sir," Lucas said, not wanting to agree.

"The professor owns a car?" Drew asked quietly.

Lucas shrugged. "Yeah, who knew? I always see him traveling around campus on foot."

"How will we know which one it is?"

"Good question," Lucas replied, turning to Kleezebee to find out.

The professor beat him to it. "It's a yellow eighty-two Volvo. You can't miss it. There's a three-foot crack across the windshield. You can drive a stick, right?"

Lucas nodded. "Sure, Professor, no problem." He remembered seeing a faded, piss-yellow four-door sedan parked next to the dumpster whenever he took out the trash. It had numerous spider webs stretching from its undercarriage to the pavement, and a year's worth of bird crap all over its hood. He doubted whether the Volvo would start—its battery was probably dead.

He slid a chunk of cement out of the way and pushed his brother out through the conference room door and into the waiting area.

"So we're really just gonna leave town?" Drew asked.

"You heard DL. He wants us to get help and then get as far away as possible."

"What about finding a way to stop this?"

"I don't like it any more than you do. But we have our orders."

"So let me get this straight. You pick right now—this very instant—to start blindly following the professor's orders? Without question?"

"Yep. Seems to me that if I'd listened to him before, none of this would be happening right now. All those people would still be alive, including Abby."

"Good point."

"For once, let's just do what we're told. I can't handle anything else at this point. One man can only take so much."

"I know you think you're alone in this, but you're not. I'm with you every step of the way, Lucas. It's time for me to have your back, like you always do for me. We're the Ramsay brothers, remember. No matter what, we stick together and figure this out one step at a time."

"Thanks, buddy. That means a lot. You have no idea."

There was much less debris in the hallway as they made their way back to the elevator through the maze of connecting corridors. When they arrived, the elevator doors were compacted to half their normal height and bent outward into the hallway.

"Looks like we were right. There's nothing connecting to it up top," Lucas said.

"I wonder if anyone was in it?"

"Let me check," Lucas said, peeking into the partially separated elevator doors. He cupped his hands around his face to block out the hallway light. "It's too dark in there to see." He pressed his right ear against the crack in the doors and listened. "I don't hear anything, either. We should keep moving. Got a long way to go."

"Do you think Bruno was at his station when the energy field hit?"

"I don't know. I can't think about that right now," Lucas said, not wanting to dwell on the possibility of yet another friend getting hurt. He shifted his focus to Kleezebee's note—the one the professor gave to Trevor right before the meeting started. "I wonder where Kleezebee sent Trevor and Mary earlier?"

"You don't think they were in the science lab, do you?"

Lucas shrugged, wishing his brother would stop with all the death questions. He opened the doorway to the stairs and walked inside. Above him was a seemingly endless series of switchback metal stairways that stretched as far as he could see.

"Holy shit," Lucas said, hearing his voice echo. Light in the stairwell came from emergency lights installed above each level's entry door.

"Are you sure you wanna do this?" Drew asked.

Lucas bent down with his back to Drew. "Hop on, like when we were kids. Just don't squeeze my neck too tight."

"Don't forget my backpack," Drew said, climbing up onto Lucas' back, piggyback-style.

Lucas removed the knapsack from the wheelchair and handed it to Drew. "Can you put this on, or do I need to put you down first?"

Drew slung the pack over his right shoulder. "Nope, got it."

Lucas began the long climb, making it up six flights of stairs before his leg muscles screamed at him to stop.

"Where's Trevor when you need him?" he asked, gasping for air while leaning against the handrail for a few seconds. Stenciled on the entry door in front of him was the sublevel floor number—14. "For a little guy, you weigh a ton. It's probably all those push-ups every morning. Or maybe it was all those burritos."

"You can put me down for a minute if you need to."

"No, I wanna keep moving. Just give me a second. Gotta catch my breath."

Lucas took a few more deep breaths before resuming the ascent with his brother's arms wrapped around his neck. He pressed on, floor by floor, ignoring the occasional twinge of pain in his lower back, stopping every two minutes to rest and recharge his lungs. Each flight of stairs was a bit harder than the last, taxing the remaining strength in body.

He wasn't sure he'd make it to the top, but continued anyway, hoping to find the energy. He didn't have a choice.

* * *

Kleezebee and Rosenbaum huddled in the control room on Sublevel 18, sitting in front of the twenty-foot-wide operator's control panel for NASA's underground power reactor. The front half of the room was crammed full of screens, gauges, switches, knobs, and instruments, surrounding Kleezebee on three sides. It reminded him of NASA's launch control room in Houston, which he'd seen in person several years before.

Kleezebee's injured ankle was resting on top of an upside-down trash can, while a homemade crutch—fashioned from an old janitor's mop and duct tape—leaned against the control desk. There was power to the room, keeping the bank of instruments running, while red, green and yellow lights flashed on and off like someone sending Morse Code. He scanned the systems, one by one, taking the time he needed to assess the situation as Rosenbaum watched.

"Can you tell what happened?" Judith asked.

"Looks like the reactor scrammed on its own. The Boron control rods dropped into the core to stop the reaction."

"Can you get it restarted?"

"I think so. The coolant pumps are running on backup power, so the water is still circulating through the core. All we should need to do is reset the trip condition, and then pull out the control rods sequentially to restart the reactor."

"Do you know what order to pull them out?"

"Luckily, it's all computerized." He showed her the schematics on Rapp's touch-screen computer. "All I have to do is tell the computer to initialize the power-up sequence, and it'll pull the rods out in the correct order. Then the reaction should resume automatically and start superheating the water."

"How hot does the water need to be?"

Kleezebee looked at the schematics for a few seconds, then changed screens to pull up a saturated steam table on the iPad. "The reactor's coolant system is pressurized to 1600 PSI, which means the water temperature will need to reach 480 degrees Fahrenheit. Otherwise, it won't be sufficient for the steam pressure to power the turbine."

"How long?"

"It's a controlled buildup in temperature, so I'd say about an hour or so."

Dr. Rosenbaum looked around the room and asked, "So . . . where exactly *is* this reactor?"

Kleezebee checked the computer tablet again, then pointed. "It's a hundred feet down the hall, in a separate room."

"Is it safe to be in here while the reactor's powering up?"

"We'll be fine. The reactor is surrounded by a thick, reinforced wall of concrete and there's a three-quarter-inch metal plate lining the inside of the room. There's virtually no risk of being irradiated."

"Finally, some good news," she said.

Kleezebee used the touch screen interface embedded in the reactor's control station to change the computer display until it read REACTOR FAST RESTART in bright red letters. "Trip condition reset. I'm ready to power up. We'll know shortly if this is going to work," he said before pressing three different button icons on the touch screen. The phrase REACTOR INITIALIZING started blinking green the center of the screen.

Kleezebee waited a minute. "Looks good. The control rods are retracting."

"Should we head back to the others now?" Rosenbaum asked. She seemed to be in a hurry.

"Not quite yet. Let's wait here for a bit to make sure there are no surprises."

* * *

Lucas carried Drew past the access door as they made it to the third sublevel. He looked up and realized the path above them was much too dark. "That's not a good sign," he said, pointing up. "There should be more light." He hated to admit it, but it looked like Larson was right. This was a giant waste of time.

They made it up two more flights of stairs before they were forced to stop. The stairwell was almost completely blocked by a twenty-foot-high mound of cement, dirt, gravel, and other debris from above. He could see random office supplies and equipment hanging out from the pile: parts of a two-decker coffeemaker, a flattened stapler, the opening to an electric pencil sharpener, and a mangled toner cartridge box for a laser printer. Just above those items was a baggie with what looked like a squished ham and cheese sandwich. It was out of reach but looked edible, making his stomach growl.

Despite the cave-in, the path wasn't blocked completely. A steady stream of light was shining through a gap at the very top of the heap. He pointed at the opening. "That may be our only way out."

Lucas bent down to allow Drew to slide off and sit on the landing. He welcomed the chance to straighten up his sore lower back and then rub the area just above the top of his belt, kneading it with both hands to see if he could loosen up the knot forming inside. If he had to carry Drew much farther, he feared he might never walk upright again.

There was a twisted section of metal stairway sticking out of the wreckage at a downward angle. The lowest part of it was about ten feet off the ground. He thought they might be able to use it as a ladder, if they could figure out a way to reach it. "The stairs must have broken loose from above," he said, scooping up a handful of loose dirt and gravel. "All this must have come from up top."

"You'd think it would've been sucked up by the dome."

"It might've been just beyond the reach of the energy field. The dome probably shook it loose and it fell down the stairwell. There's no telling what's piled up, up there."

"Maybe we should go back?"

"Hell no. I just hauled your butt up seventeen floors. Let's just take a minute and think."

Lucas looked up and studied the hole where the light was shining through. It appeared to be about two feet in diameter and might be big enough for someone to crawl through it.

"Drew, if I can get you up there, do you think you can squeeze your ass through that opening?"

"Me?"

The brothers both had thirty-two inch waists, but Lucas' shoulders were wider, despite Drew's powerful biceps. He wore a large shirt and Drew a medium. "Yes, you. I'll never fit."

Drew wrinkled his forehead and shook his head. "I don't know. Looks awfully small to me."

"Well, you need to try. I don't see any other option, do you?"

"Let's assume for a moment I can get through—what about you?"

"I'm hoping you can crawl up a couple more flights and yell for help. We're not far from the surface. The dirt and stairs had to fall in from somewhere. I betting it's open up top."

"And if it's not?"

"We'll cross that bridge when we come to it," Lucas said, bending down to let Drew shimmy back up on his back.

Lucas worked his way up the wreckage by using the fallen cement blocks as footholds. It was difficult to maintain his balance with

Drew hanging off him, but he managed to climb up to within a foot of the metal framework he wanted Drew to use as a ladder.

"It's time to put all those pushups to good use. See if you can reach it."

14

Drew put his left hand up and grabbed the lowest part of the fallen metal. He let go of his brother's shoulder with the other hand and hung with both hands from the framework, like a monkey. He pulled himself up three rungs before wedging his right elbow between two V-shaped sections of the metal scaffolding to catch his breath and plan his next move. A flat section of metal was to his left, which he could use as a resting platform.

He swung his lower body like a pendulum and plopped both of his feet over the front edge of the horizontal surface. He had only minimal control over his legs, but was able to slide his knees and his thighs onto the ledge. *So far, so good,* he thought. He just needed to maneuver his head and shoulders under a metal support rail to get his entire body onto the metal landing, then he'd be safe.

He loosened his elbow grip and tried to slide his head and back under the railing, but the knapsack caught the underside of the metal above his head. He twisted and contorted his upper body to compress the backpack, forcing it under the rail and through.

"You okay?" Lucas asked.

"I'm good. Come on up," Drew replied, removing the bulky knapsack.

Lucas leaned away from the face of the debris pile and wrapped his fingers around the bottommost metal bar. Drew watched as he tried to pull himself up, making it partway, but then his body slid back into its hanging position. "I'm not strong enough," he said, craning his neck up at Drew.

"See if you can lift your leg and grab hold of the bar above you. It'll take some of the dead weight off your hands."

Lucas grunted, lifting his right leg and wrapping the hollow of his knee around the metal bar next to his hands. "Okay, now what?" he asked, in a strained voice.

"Now reach up and lock your arm over the next strut. Your center of gravity will change and you should be able to pull yourself up."

Lucas tried twice to reach for the bar. "Can't reach it. Maybe I should have had a power bar this morning."

Drew feared Lucas would soon lose his grip; his arms had to be getting tired. One slip and they would be having wheelchair races in the hospital. "Try swinging your body to shift your weight. Then lunge for the bar. You should be able to reach it."

Lucas rocked his body back and forth, each time swinging a little higher. He reached up and wrapped his right arm around the metal bar, locking himself into place with the crook of his elbow. He climbed the rest of the way up.

"I knew you could do it," Drew said, relieved.

"Glad that's over with. I thought I was going to lose my grip," Lucas said, looking down.

Drew could feel the temporary platform swaying beneath them. "We should get moving before this thing decides to give way."

Together, they climbed up the rest of the makeshift ladder until they reached the top of the debris pile.

"Can you get in there?" Lucas asked, pointing to the bright opening just above him.

"It's going to be tight, but I'll try."

Drew used a piece of rebar protruding from a slab of broken cement to pull himself up. He inserted his head into the passage, but he had to jerk his head back and slam his eyes shut when a beam of sunlight burned into his pupils from the other side.

"What do you see?" Lucas yelled from behind.

"Give me a minute. Right now, all I can see is sunlight from the other side." Eventually, Drew's eyes adjusted and he could see properly. "Looks like a dirt cave, but I think I can crawl through."

The aperture was barely wide enough for his chest and shoulders to fit. It was about six feet in depth, and there were several jagged objects sticking out along the top of the opening. He went into the cavity head first, on his back. He slithered deeper and deeper into the hole, barely missing the edges of the sharp objects threatening to slice open his chest. He made it to within a foot from the far side of the hole.

"Can you get through?" Lucas yelled from behind.

Drew turned over on his stomach. "There's something in my way."

Part of a fluorescent light assembly had fallen into the passage and was blocking the exit. He gave it a shove with his right hand. It moved, but only slightly. He tried working the light back and forth to see if he could move it. Each time he shoved at it, the housing would slide a little farther away from him. It took several more tries, but eventually he worked the light free, sending it crashing through the far side of the opening.

"I'm clear," he shouted.

"Go get help," Lucas replied.

"What about you?"

"I'll be fine. Now go."

Drew slid headfirst, out of control, down the far side of the debris pile, scraping his elbows and forearms on cement chunks, rocks, rebar, and other objects in the wreckage. He was almost upside down when he reached the bottom. After he flipped his body around to sit up, he felt something wet around his waistline. He put his hand inside the back of his trousers and when he pulled it out, it was slick with blood. He'd been injured somewhere, yet he wasn't feeling any pain.

He checked the rest of his body, looking for the wound. He found a six-inch rip in his pants just above his left thigh. He pulled the material apart, revealing a deep gash in his thigh muscle. It was bleeding in spurts and he could see the bone underneath. He clamped his hand around the wound to keep pressure on it, hoping to stop the deep red ooze from dripping down his leg.

When he looked up, he could see clear up to ground level. The surface opening was triple the size he was expecting, perhaps due to the massive surface collapse. It would explain the overabundance of dirt and rocks in the stairwell.

"Hello? Anyone up there? We need help down here!" he yelled.

A man wearing bulky firefighter gear peeked over the ledge and looked down at him. He then turned away for a moment and said, "We have a survivor over here!" The man looked back at Drew. "Are you injured?"

"I'm bleeding from my leg and can't walk."

"Are you alone?"

"There're seven of us down here. One's in pretty bad shape."

"Hang on, we'll send someone down," the man said, before disappearing from view.

It wasn't long before the surface opening was crawling with emergency personnel. A rescue worker wearing a full-body harness was lowered down by rope to Drew's position.

"My name's Alan," the rescuer said, swaying in midair before his feet touched the ground.

"I'm Drew."

"Where are the others?"

"My brother's just on the other side of this cave-in. There are four more people down on the twentieth floor. One critical."

Alan was carrying another harness, which he took off his shoulder. "I need you to put this safety rig on."

"No, I'm not leaving without my brother."

"Trust me. We'll get to him, and the others. But first, we need to get you to the surface. Looks like you're losing a lot of blood."

Drew struggled to prop himself up on his feeble legs. "You're going to have to help me."

Alan grabbed Drew by the belt loops and tugged him up the rest of the way to his feet. Then he helped Drew slip his lower body into and through the two leg holes, and then put the V-shaped shoulder straps over Drew's head. He latched the waist belt around Drew's midsection and clipped Drew's harness to his own.

"Hang on tight," he said, whistling to his colleagues on the surface, who were now standing around the opening, looking down with intense gazes. Once Alan gave them a thumbs-up signal, they were winched slowly up to the surface.

Drew studied the dark-haired man's face as they made their way up to the surface. He seemed familiar in some way. "You wouldn't happen to have a brother who's a security guard on campus, would you?"

"No, why?"

"I know it sounds weird, but you look like you're related to this man who stopped a fight between my brother and some rugby players— except that guy had red hair."

"Sorry, no relation. I don't have a redheaded brother."

"I guess it's true what they say. Everyone has a twin."

* * *

Kleezebee and Dr. Rosenbaum joined Rapp, Larson, and the injured Dr. Suki in the lobby on Sublevel 20, just outside the NASA conference room. Kleezebee's left armpit was getting sore from the makeshift crutch rubbing against it. He switched it to the other side.

"Were you able to get the reactor started?" Rapp asked.

Kleezebee nodded. "The power should be online soon."

"Excellent news. Any problems?" Rapp replied, taking the iPad computer from Rosenbaum.

"None," Kleezebee said as the lights sprang to life. He felt a rush of fresh air blow past from the vent above him. "Whew, that's better. It was getting pretty stuffy in here."

Larson asked, "Now that the power's back, can we take the elevator up to the surface?"

"The elevator was destroyed," Rosenbaum replied. "Dr. Kleezebee and I had to take the stairs up to eighteen."

"Any news from Dr. Ramsay or his brother?" Rapp asked Kleezebee.

"No, but at least they haven't come back empty-handed. Hopefully, they made it to the surface and will send help."

"So we just sit here and wait?" Larson asked.

"Hey, you had your chance to leave earlier," Rapp said sharply. "So unless you have a site-to-site transporter and can beam us out of here, we're not going anywhere."

Larson stormed off, throwing his arms up in the air and mumbling to himself as he walked down the hallway.

Kleezebee smiled at Rapp and proceeded to mock the attorney by waving his arms like a gorilla, then arranged his hands as if he were holding a loaded rifle that was aimed at Larson. He pretended to pull the trigger, simulating the gun's recoil.

"How's Dr. Suki doing?" Rosenbaum asked Rapp, wearing a smile on her lips.

"He's hanging in there, but his pulse is weak and he's lost a lot of blood."

"Should we take him to the stairs?"

"No, we probably shouldn't move him again. I'm afraid the rebar might shift and cause more damage."

"Is there anything I can do to help?" she asked.

Rapp shook his head.

Kleezebee checked the house phone attached to the wall next to him—there was no dial tone. "Phone's still out."

"Then it's up to Lucas," Rapp said, tending to Suki. "But he better hurry."

Kleezebee limped to the closest chair in the waiting room and took a seat. He slid one of the magazine stacks to the right on the coffee table, making room for his injured leg as he brought it up and put it on the surface. He leaned back in the chair, closed his heavy eyelids, and let his head fall gently rest against the wall.

* * *

Two sweat-covered firefighters tugged at the rope as Drew and Alan were winched over the ledge and onto the ground just beyond the stairwell's entrance.

"Thanks for the lift, guys," Drew said, waiting for someone to help him out of the safety gear.

Lucas' earlier prediction of the science lab being leveled was correct. From the looks of it, the energy field had torn through the west side of campus, leaving only a fifty-foot section of the NASA building intact. The stairwell's shaft appeared to be just beyond the energy field's reach, though a sizable portion of the surrounding structure had collapsed into the hole.

A female EMT, wearing an orange reflective vest, pushed a gurney toward Drew, while her partner ran alongside her, carrying a pair of red medical boxes. After Alan unclipped Drew's harness, she helped Drew remove the harness and sit back on the gurney.

Alan told his colleagues, "There's another survivor on the other side of a blockage, plus a few more down on the twentieth floor. You're going to need excavation equipment and a medical team."

Drew watched rescue crews rally quickly with shovels, picks, and other equipment. Seconds later, two men were lowered into the hole. He hoped it wouldn't be too long before Lucas came up and out.

"Thanks for getting me out of there," Drew said, shaking Alan's hand.

"No problem. Just doing my job," Alan said. "EMT Dana will take good care of you now."

Dana used a pair of scissors to cut away his pants from around the wound. "That's a pretty deep cut. We need to get you to a hospital."

Drew pushed her hands away. "I'm not leaving without my brother."

"We need to stop the bleeding," Dana said. "Can I at least clean it out and wrap it?"

"Okay, but I'm not leaving until Lucas is out of there," he said, as his head began to spin and his chest ran cold.

The second EMT opened one of the medical boxes, pulling out gauze and other supplies. He gave them to Dana.

"Let me know if you need something for the pain," she said, dabbing the gauze on the wound. The pad turned a dark red color almost immediately.

Drew leaned back to rest his head on the pillow. His eyes closed unexpectedly and everything went black.

* * *

Lucas had been sitting alone for almost an hour, dwelling on all the problems he'd caused, when he finally heard muffled sounds of tools clanking against rock and cement above him. He used a rebar stump to pull himself up to the opening at the top of the debris pile. He yelled through the cavity, "I'm here! I'm here! Can someone hear me?"

A male voice from the other side shouted back, "We can hear you. Hold on, we're digging our way to you."

"How's my brother doing? Is he okay?"

"He tore up his leg pretty bad, but the paramedics took him to the hospital. You might want to stand back in case some of this stuff shakes loose."

Lucas nearly jumped off the wreckage in excitement, quickly descending to the ground. While he was waiting for rescue, someone tapped him on the shoulder from behind. He gasped a quick breath and turned around. It was Larson. "Shit, you scared the hell out of me."

"Sounds like rescue crews on the other side," Larson said in a gleeful tone. "Hopefully, they'll have us out of here soon."

"What are you doing up here?"

"I got tired of waiting. Do you have a problem with that?"

Lucas shook his head.

"No, I didn't think so," Larson said with a smug look on his face.

Lucas fought back the urge to punch Larson in the face.

Larson used his forearm to nudge past Lucas, moving closer to the base of the cave-in. He just stood there with his hands on his hips, looking up at the opening at the top of the wreckage.

Lucas moved to within a step of the man's backside. He raised his hands together and considered wrapping his fingers around Larson's neck. He wondered what it would feel like to squeeze Larson's throat until the asshole stopped wiggling.

Larson shuffled back a step.

Lucas did the same, lowering his hands so he didn't bump into him.

Larson looked over his shoulder at Lucas. "What the hell's wrong with you? Stop crowding me, you little twerp."

When Larson spun forward again, Lucas flipped him the bird and mouthed the words, "Up yours!"

* * *

Sometime later, Drew woke up in a hospital room to the sounds of medical equipment beeping all around him. He found a clear plastic tube running from a catheter stuck in his left arm to a metal stand next to his bed. At the top of the stand was a clear bag of liquid and it was about half full, emptying slowly through the drip chamber below it. He felt groggy and guessed the IV bag contained more than just fluids— probably a hefty dose of painkillers, too.

His other arm was being squeezed by a blood pressure cuff as its automated system pumped air into it. A set of thin black wires snaked its way from the cuff to a high-tech looking machine flashing his vital statistics. He watched the pattern of his heart rate moving across the display screen, keeping time with the beeping noise he heard when he first woke up.

A throbbing pressure was pounding at his thigh with every heartbeat, which was odd since he only had minimal feeling in that part of his body. When he reached down, he found a pressure bandage wrapped around his leg.

He sat up and found a smiling friend sitting in a red-colored easy chair near the foot of his bed. "Trevor, you're alive!"

Trevor winked at him, but said nothing.

"What happened?" Drew asked.

"You lose much blood. Ambulance bring you here to medical center."

Drew read his patient ID wristband. He was in the University Medical Center, less than a mile north of campus. "No, I meant what happened to you when you left the NASA meeting?"

"Kleezebee send me on errand."

"I thought you might've been in the lab when it was destroyed."

"No. I vas south of town."

"Where's Lucas? Did they get him out of the elevator shaft? Is he here with you?" Drew asked, his eyes darting around the room, looking for clues that his brother had been there.

"They rescue him. He be here soon."

"Then he's safe, right?"

"*Ja.*"

"Thank God. What about the others?"

"They will get them out, *ja.*"

A doctor and nurse walked into the room before Drew had the chance to ask him any more questions.

*   *   *

A hour later, Lucas strolled into Drew's hospital room, pushing a wheelchair with a can of grape soda, a jumbo Snickers bar, and a bag of barbeque chips sitting on the seat. He'd just bought the food from the vending machines near the entrance to the hospital. Drew's backpack was hanging off the back of the chair.

"Hungry, little brother?" Lucas asked with a huge grin on his face.

"Lucas!" Drew cried out.

Lucas leaned down to give Drew a hug. "I'm glad you're okay, buddy."

"You got my chair?"

"Sure did."

"How?"

"Kleezebee made sure the rescue crews brought it up."

"Thanks. I'm kinda partial to that thing."

Lucas pointed to the gash in the seat made by the falling ceiling tile. "And now it has a battle scar, like you." He laughed, then turned to Trevor and shook his hand. "Glad to see you're still in one piece, too, big fella. Thought you might've been in the lab when it was sucked into oblivion."

Trevor stood aside and offered his chair to Lucas.

"No, thanks. I think I'll stand for a while."

"How's Dr. Kleezebee?" Drew asked Lucas.

"Last I heard, they were putting a cast on his ankle."

"And Dr. Suki?"

Lucas groaned. "He's not doing so well. They took him into surgery," he said, fluffing his brother's pillow. "How are you doing?"

"The doctor said I can leave in the morning. They want to monitor me overnight."

"How come?"

"They're worried about infection," he answering, nervously pulling at the wide bandage around his upper leg. "Mostly because of where I got this. With all the dirt and metal, they don't want to take any chances. They're pumping me full of antibiotics and just gave me a tetanus shot. You know, just in case."

"Then I guess I'm bunking here tonight," Lucas said, opening the can of grape soda and giving it to Drew.

Drew took a drink, and then let out a low-pitched belch.

"Sounds like you're feeling better already," Lucas said, smiling. He held up the candy bar and the bag of chips. "Which one do you want?"

"I don't think I'm allowed to eat those in here. Don't I need the doctor's permission first?"

"Come on, pick one. I know you want some," Lucas replied, dangling them in front of Drew. He continued to tease his brother until Drew snatched the Snickers bar from his hand. "I'm surprised you didn't pick the chips. They're your favorite."

Drew tore open the wrapper with trembling hands, took a huge bite, and began to chew it. He smiled. "Normally, I would've, but I totally needed a sugar fix. I can tell my blood sugar is low, which is why my hands are shaking."

Lucas pried open the bag and ate a handful of BBQ chips. He licked his fingers afterward. "They're a little stale, but edible."

There was an orange suitcase sitting along the wall next to the door. It was a wheel bag the size of a footlocker, with a black pullout handle and a pair of casters on the bottom. They didn't own a piece of luggage that size, so Lucas presumed it belonged to Trevor. "You wouldn't happen to have a change of clothes in there for me, would you?" he asked, pointing at the bag.

Trevor shook his head. "Sorry, no clothes."

15

Tuesday, December 25

Lucas woke early the following morning in his brother's hospital room with sunlight streaming through the window. It gave the room a livelier feel than the previous afternoon, when the fluorescent lighting had made everything seem muted and antiseptic.

He found himself slumped in the red armchair next to Drew, who was snoring peacefully in his hospital bed. Lucas felt foggy and didn't remember sitting down in the chair, let alone falling asleep in it the night before. He sat up and looked around for Trevor, but his friend was missing, as was the man's big orange suitcase. He assumed Trevor had slipped out during the night, not wanting to wake him.

There were twinges of soreness in his lower back and on the side of his neck, probably from sleeping in the chair. The pain in his neck was the strongest, feeling like someone had slashed it repeatedly with a hockey stick. He rolled his head around in a circle, trying to stretch out his neck muscles. When that failed, he started rubbing the sore spot with his right hand, hoping to loosen it up, which finally worked after several minutes of kneading it like bread dough. In the process, he discovered some type of tacky residue on his hand. It felt sticky, like leftover glue had partially dried between his fingers. He figured it must've come from the grape soda or the BBQ chips he'd eaten before he fell asleep in the chair.

He walked into Drew's private bathroom, closed the door to muffle any noise, and then washed his hands under the faucet. It took several rounds of lather up, scrub, and rinse, but he finally got rid of the gooey crap between his fingers.

When he moved to the towel rack to dry his hands, his right shoe stuck to the floor. He pried his shoe loose and lifted his leg up to find a string of residue hanging between the rubber sole and the tile floor. It looked like chewing gum, but was a semi-clear orange color. He took a few sheets of toilet paper from the dispenser and pulled the gunk from the tread, then tossed it into the waste basket next to the commode. He washed his hands again for good measure.

When he opened the bathroom door and returned to the room, he found Drew wide awake and talking to a short, chubby nurse with plump cheeks and a Santa Claus hat sitting at an angle on her head. She reminded Lucas of an elementary school teacher, or maybe Santa's wife down for a visit from the North Pole, especially with the reindeer pin blinking rapidly on her shirt. Her nametag ID'd her as Rose.

"Mrs. Claus, how nice of you to visit us down here in the desert," Lucas joked.

She glanced over her shoulder, busy taking Drew's temperature. "Ho, ho, ho," she said. "You must be Lucas. The brother."

"Yes, ma'am. I am. The one and only. How's he doing?"

"Looks like he gets to go home today," the nurse said after reading the thermometer and scribbling something into Drew's chart. She checked the time on her watch. "Blood test results look good. No sign of infection."

"That's a relief," Lucas said.

"Today? As in this morning?" Drew asked with eyes beaming.

"Yes, as soon as Dr. Marino discharges you."

Lucas asked her, "We'd like to be home in time for Christmas dinner. Do you think it's possible?"

"Shouldn't be a problem. There're only a handful of patients left with the evacuation underway. It's been a complete madhouse out there."

"Yeah, I can imagine," Lucas said, thinking about the energy domes and the widespread destruction they'd caused in town. "I'm surprised this place is still open for business."

"It takes time to stabilize and transfer a thousand patients," she said, writing something else into Drew's chart. Before she left the room, she told Drew, "You can go ahead and get dressed, if you like. But be careful. That's a nasty cut and it's going to take time to heal. You don't want to undo Dr. Marino's fine needlework."

Lucas held up Kleezebee's car keys in front of Drew's eyes. "As soon as we get out of here, we're going back to the apartment and pack for Phoenix. I've had enough of Tucson for a while."

"It'll be nice to spend some time with Mom," Drew said.

While Lucas was helping Drew out of his hospital gown, he noticed Drew was missing something. "Hey, where's your leather pouch?"

Drew felt around his neck and chest. "I didn't even realize it was gone. Is it in the clothes bag on the counter?"

Lucas searched the clear plastic bag, but only found his brother's pants, shirt, comb, watch, socks, and shoes. "It's not here. When was the last time you remember seeing it?"

Drew didn't respond right away. "Back when I first got rescued. I was sitting on a gurney by the stairwell."

"Then what happened?"

"I remember feeling really dizzy when a nurse put gauze on my leg. The next thing I know, I'm waking up here in this bed with all these machines doing their thing. I didn't even think of it 'til just now."

"Maybe the EMTs took it off you for some reason. Do you remember the name of the ambulance company? We should call their lost and found."

"I don't remember. I was pretty out of it," Drew said with a deep look of concern on his face. He shook his head and pinched his nose. "Geeze, I can't believe I lost it. After all these years."

Lucas knew it was unlikely they'd ever see the pouch again. It'd probably been misplaced during the chaos of the rescue from the elevator shaft. He didn't want to worry Drew, though, so he patted him on the back and said, "I'm sure it'll turn up."

"No, it won't. It's probably buried down the hole somewhere. Or someone just threw it in the garbage."

"Let's keep positive thoughts, bro."

"But you made it for me. And I lost it. Like a moron."

"Hey, there was a lot of crap going on. Don't beat yourself up. Besides, I can make you another one. No sweat."

"Yeah, I know, but it had my bio-mom's picture in it. I can't replace that. What am I gonna do, Lucas?"

Lucas rubbed Drew's back, knowing this conversation was going nowhere. "We'll figure something out."

While they waited, Lucas turned on the TV. He scanned the channels to see if there was any new information about the energy fields. There was. The local news channel was reporting that dozens of domes were destroying cities all over the globe and each time they appeared, they were getting larger and lasting longer.

"You see that?" Drew asked him.

Lucas nodded. "They keep spreading and getting worse," he said, not wanting to think about all the deaths on his hands. "But at least there's no sign of any more of them around here."

"Maybe they're done with Arizona."

"Let's hope. The sooner we can get away from here, the better. In fact, we should probably take Mom away from Phoenix and go hide in the mountains somewhere. The domes seem mainly interested in large cities. Give us a chance to figure out the next step."

"One of us should call her and let her know I'm getting released."

"I'll take care of it. Hand me the phone."

* * *

Two hours later, Lucas and Drew were still sitting in the hospital room, waiting for Dr. Marino to sign off on Drew's discharge. Lucas got tired of waiting, so he tracked the doctor down, finding him near the nurse's station, looking over a chart. He gently reminded the doc that they wanted to get home in time for Christmas dinner. Marino apologized and thirty minutes later, Drew was released.

"How's your leg doing?" Lucas asked without thinking, pushing the wheelchair across the parking lot in front of the emergency room entrance.

"It's still sore."

Lucas was shocked by his brother's response since Drew only had marginal feeling in his lower extremities. "Wow, if you can feel it at all, then it must be a deep gash."

"Oh yeah. It definitely hurts," Drew said, right before his stomach growled loud enough for Lucas to hear. "Can we stop and eat on the way home? I'm starving. The hospital food was terrible, and all I had yesterday was that junk food you brought."

"Sure, assuming we can find something that's open. Most people who have any sense at all are long gone by now. Like we should be."

Half an hour later, after passing a string of businesses and restaurants that were closed, the only place that seemed to be open was a Dairy Queen. Its interior lights were on.

Lucas learned forward from behind the wheelchair and pointed an outstretched arm at the building. "Looks like you might have to settle for more junk food, little brother. I doubt anything else is still serving," he said, steering Drew's chair across the empty parking lot.

"Figures. More empty calories."

"Huh, that's strange," Lucas said, walking up to the door. "I don't see anyone inside." He grabbed the door handle and pulled at it, swinging it open. "Someone must have been in a major hurry; they forgot to lock up, too." He looked around for signs of looting, but there was none. "I'm surprised this place is still in one piece."

"I'm thinking a couple of extra large Oreo Blizzards are just what the doctor ordered," Drew said in a matter-of-fact way, wheeling his chair forward. "But you'll have to help me reach the toppings."

Lucas closed the door and stood in front of it before Drew could get inside. "No, we're not going to steal."

"Come on, I'm starving."

"I'm sorry, but we're not doing this."

"Are you serious? Where else are we going to get food? You said it yourself; everything's probably closed by now with the city in evacuation mode."

Lucas shook his head and folded his arms across his chest, but he didn't answer.

Drew threw up his hands. "Look around. This place is a ghost town. Who's gonna know?"

"We will."

"Look, I get the whole honesty thing, especially after what happened in the lab. But after all, the owners *did* leave the place open and the lights on. It's not like we'd be trespassing."

"Okay, I'll give you that one."

"I'm sure there's a legal precedent somewhere about an unlocked, abandoned restaurant. It's practically an invitation to just help yourself, right? A great big welcome sign."

Lucas nodded. His brother had a point.

"Besides, we'd be doing them a favor," Drew said, sounding like an attorney driving home a point.

"How do you figure?"

"Well, first of all, it's our civic duty not to let all this ice cream go to waste. Someone's got eat it. Why not us?"

Lucas laughed, but said nothing.

"And second, we should make sure nobody's hurt inside and needs help. Then figure out a way to lock up the place. Maybe there's some keys inside."

"Okay, I like that idea. It's the responsible thing to do."

"Besides, who's to say that helping ourselves wasn't their intention when they left the place wide open like this? I'm pretty sure if they thought the energy fields would return and level the area, they wouldn't care what happened to their store, right? Might as well feed a few people before it's gone anyway."

Lucas took a minute to consider his brother's argument. Drew's points made sense, though there were certainly plenty of other explanations that would fit the current situation.

However, he was tired and didn't have the energy or the patience to debate anymore. Plus his belly was running on empty, too. He needed food. So did Drew. They'd both be able to think better with a full stomach, even if it was only ice cream and chocolate. "Okay, but make it quick," he said, stepping aside and holding the door open as Drew rolled inside.

After making and eating their sugary treats, they walked the rest of the way to their apartment complex and pressed the call button for the elevator. It didn't light up.

"The electricity must be out. Looks like I'm carrying you up more stairs," Lucas told Drew.

He carried Drew up the third floor, then returned to the ground level to fetch the wheelchair. Once Drew was back in his chair, Lucas followed him to their apartment door, unlocked it, and they both went inside. Lucas opened all the blinds to let sunlight in so they could see what they were doing.

"You get started packing. I'll grab the laptop and few of our books," Lucas said, taking Drew's knapsack off the back of the wheelchair. He unzipped the center pouch and put it on the study desk next to the computer. He slid the molded plastic chair out and sat down.

He ran his hands through his short-cropped hair, drawing in a long, slow breath, and then exhaled—it soothed him. He let his mind drift to thoughts of recent events as he brought his fingertips down to brush them across the smooth, wood-grain surface.

So much had happened—it was hard to process; his emotions were a tangled mess. He tried to remember life before the campus tragedies but couldn't seem to recall it clearly in his mind. He felt like he was on the outside looking in, viewing the memories as if they belonged to someone else. Nothing felt as it should, not even his own skin.

Deep down he knew the visions were his, but now they seemed foreign, tainted in some way. Even his own heartbeat felt off—a strange sensation, to say the least. Certainly, his life wasn't what he expected when he enrolled at the university as a wide-eyed teenager. No, this was something different. Something twisted and surreal.

He wondered what constituted a normal college life. Was it the endless beer bongs and hookups, or was it something more? If he had to do it over, would he join his classmates in the occasional alcohol-induced, three-day bender, or would he stick to the original plan? One path was about hangovers and unchecked venereal disease, and the other was about duty and responsibility.

It was easy to fantasize about a different life when currently treading in quicksand. A life filled with playful days of innocence and guilt-free Sunday mornings. Yet, he knew it was a hopeless illusion.

You are who you are, and there's no going back in time and starting over.

Life is a series of endless decisions and mistakes—some critical and others, not so much. He'd certainly made his share along the way but hoped if someone dissected his life, they'd find he always tried to do right by Drew and his adoptive parents, even if things spun sideways.

He knew exactly who and what he was—a man with a bit of a temper who sometimes overreacted to situations. But in reality, everyone did that from time to time, especially when family was involved.

Was he really so different from everyone else? He'd certainly met people who were far more volatile than he was, some needing to just go away forever—and some had, like the Mohawk-wearing rugby player from the cafeteria.

Let's face it, everyone struggles with their own personal demons, some are just better at hiding them than others. His inner demons rarely gave him any warning before they were about to erupt, and until recently, hadn't gotten too far out of hand. Yet, given what he was dealing with right now, it was understandable why he was having issues with them, right?

He was a certainly a work in progress, trying to gain control over his life, his emotions, and his own actions, but everything *normal* seemed just out of reach, as if his grip on reality was slipping. He wondered if he sat perfectly still and listened hard enough, would he hear the malignant shadows closing in around him? He wasn't sure why things always seemed to go haywire, but they did.

Maybe the universe was studying him closely and then picking the perfect time to torment him with sudden twists of fate. Almost like it was focusing on him for some reason. Of course, for that to be true, he'd have to be important enough for the universe to give a shit, which seemed unlikely.

When he boiled it all down, he didn't know where his future was headed. Would it end in death? Triumph? Something in between?

He pushed all those thoughts aside. They weren't helping and he was getting off track. He knew whatever was going to happen wasn't going to be easy. What he was facing right now was the certainly the hardest test he'd ever faced in his life, and he'd had his share growing up in the orphanage.

What was it that his old man used to say? Oh, yeah . . . "It's how you handle the difficult moments in life that defines you."

Lucas wasn't afraid to face the facts, or their consequences. That's what a scientist does. A scientist puts it all out there on the line, then waits to see the outcome after his theories are scrutinized and dissected by some of the greatest minds on the planet.

The same humiliating process of exposure and evaluation happens in life, too. Like when he stood in front of NASA and some of the most prominent scientists in the country and took responsibility for his actions. He was ready for whatever the powers that be—and the universe, for that matter—were going to throw at him.

He just hoped Kleezebee would let him join the fight to help to unravel the mess he'd made across the planet. He was ready to do whatever it took to make things right.

* * *

A few minutes later, Lucas stood up from his study desk and leaned forward with his thighs pressing hard against the center drawer. He thumbed through the physics material on the top shelf of the bookcase, looking for his quantum field theory book. He found the thick red six-hundred page book next to his reference notes on spatial anomalies and slid it out. He remembered the day he'd bought it from the bookstore, feeling like he'd finally made it. He was finally someone important. Someone his adoptive parents could be proud of.

He opened the book and slips of yellow notepaper fell from between the pages, scattering like forgotten dreams across the river of unpaid medical bills on his desk. He gathered the notes, trying to put them back where they belonged, when he realized they no longer mattered. Neither did his anti-gravity research. Years of accelerated graduate study, plus eighteen months of tireless research, gone in a flash—literally.

He started thumbing through the pages, hoping for some facts or a theory to jump out at him. Something that might help stop the energy domes or lead him down a solution path. He'd just started going over the introduction on wave functions, where the author discussed the probability amplitude of position, momentum, and other physical properties of a particle.

He wasn't three sentences into the text when someone started pounding furiously on the apartment's front door. The abrupt noise made him jump, and the book slipped from his hands. It landed perfectly flat, making a loud bang ricochet through the room like a gunshot. His heart pounded at the walls of his chest, trying to break free from its cage.

"Dr. Ramsay, we need to speak with you. It's urgent," a man shouted from the other side of the door in a commanding voice.

Lucas walked to the door and looked through the peephole, but could only see a close-up of a man's face—maybe Hispanic. Lucas didn't recognize him.

"Dr. Ramsay, please open up," the man insisted. "It's urgent."

Lucas hesitated, then decided to open the door, expecting it to be someone from the university. Immediately, a second man, a white guy with a dimpled chin, scrambled into view with a rifle pointed at Lucas' face. Both men were wearing combat fatigues, tactical vests, and helmets with the letters MP stenciled on the front in white letters.

"Wait, don't shoot!" Lucas said, raising his hands above his head.

"Are you Dr. Lucas Ramsay of the Astrophysics Department?" the Hispanic soldier asked.

"Yes, I am."

"Is your brother with you?"

Lucas moved a step closer to them with his hands touching both sides of the upper doorframe. He looked past the soldiers, down through the open railing bordering the catwalk outside his apartment, and saw two green Humvee trucks parked outside the manager's office on the ground floor. To the west and south, massive fires burned as looters took to the streets. Thick plumes of black smoke rose to the sky from more locations than he could count.

Lucas took a deep breath to calm his nerves before he spoke to the MP, hoping to show strength. "He's in the bedroom. What's going on here?"

"We're here to take you into custody by order of Major General Rafael Alvarez."

"Who's that? Why the guns? Custody? What the hell for?" Lucas asked.

"For the murder of one hundred and twenty-seven people on campus. Both of you need to come with us, immediately."

"Look, you need to understand. It was an accident. I was running an experiment, and something went wrong. My brother had nothing to do with it."

The lead MP opened a pair of handcuffs. "My orders are to detain both of you. Turn around and place your hands behind your back."

Lucas tightened his grip on the doorframe and braced his feet.

The other MP pressed the open end of the barrel against Lucas' forehead.

Lucas stood firm. He didn't believe the soldier would shoot.

The MP cocked the rifle and flared his eyes. His face burned a deep red color. "Just give me a reason, asshole." He pressed the barrel hard against Lucas' scalp.

"You really need to let me cuff you before my trigger-happy partner decides to redecorate your face," the lead MP said. "Trust me. He wanted to just kick down the door and open fire. You're lucky to be alive right now."

Lucas didn't respond. He needed a moment to think.

"You don't have a choice here, Dr. Ramsay. You're both coming with us—one way or the other. Doesn't matter how."

"Okay, okay. Just don't hurt my brother," Lucas said, taking a step back from the doorway with his hands high in the air.

The MP pulled the rifle back. Lucas turned and overlapped his wrists behind his back. He heard the ratchets click as the shackles were tightened around his wrists, tearing into his skin. He grunted, feeling a trickle of blood run down his hand.

The white MP pushed past Lucas and went into the apartment. Drew was confronted by the soldier the moment he rolled into the room in his wheelchair.

"Hold it right there!" the MP shouted, aiming his gun at Drew. "Hands up where I can see them."

"Drew, just do as they say. These guys mean business," Lucas said.

Drew nodded and put his wrists together above his lap and allowed the MP to handcuff them to the arm of the wheelchair. The soldier stood behind Drew as if he were getting ready to push the chair, but instead, he opened a Velcro pocket along the front of his equipment vest and pulled out a syringe. He jammed the needle into Drew's neck.

"What are you doing?" Lucas screamed, struggling to wriggle free from his captor. The Hispanic MP grabbed Lucas' head and pushed it to one side.

A second later, Lucas felt a sharp pain on the exposed side of his neck, followed by a warm sensation spreading out under the skin. He was about to pass out when a black hood was pulled down over his eyes.

* * *

Sometime later, Lucas felt a blast of cold liquid splash into his face. He thought it was water—not a lot, maybe a cup full. It hit him right between his eyes, then trickled down his cheek. If it wasn't water, he didn't want it causing any damage so he kept his eyes closed.

"Time to wake up, Ramsay," a male voice said. Someone kicked him in the ribs twice, hard. "Eyes open, punk. You're gonna watch this."

Lucas did as he was told and opened his eyes while gasping for air. Two sets of car headlights were trained on him, piercing the darkness about twenty feet away. The light burned at his retinas, making him look away for a few seconds until his pupils adjusted.

Once his brain caught up to his vision, he realized he was lying on his side with his right cheek buried in loose dirt. His hands were restrained behind his back and he could see frosty breath billowing out into the cool night air each time he exhaled.

For some reason, his whole body ached and his thoughts were agonizingly slow. Then he remembered why: the sharp pain in his neck from the MP's needle, and the warm sensation that followed.

Shit, he'd been drugged, then hauled here in the dead of night. Wherever here was.

Someone grabbed the back of his shirt, forcing him to sit upright. He couldn't see anything beyond the vehicle headlamps except the silhouette of a three-fingered saguaro cactus rising up to block a portion of the star-clustered sky. Two desert bushes were in view, one between the two vehicles in front of him, and another just to his left. His wrists hurt where the handcuffs dug into his skin, and his ribs were aching from the kicks to the gut he'd just received.

Then his eyes found Drew. His brother was sitting on the ground to the right, about ten feet away, with a gag in his mouth. Streaks of dirt were smeared across his face and the collar of his shirt had been torn. Someone had roughed him up, sending Lucas' blood pressure skyrocketing.

When they made eye contact, Drew's face went wild with fright. His brother tried to yell something at him, but only muffled groans escaped through the cloth clamping down against his tongue.

A heartbeat later, Lucas knew what his brother was trying to tell him when he noticed a rectangular hole about six feet in length sitting behind Drew. A pile of brown dirt was next to it, with a long-handled shovel sticking out of the top.

A series of flashes hit the video player in the back of his mind—all of them bloody and none of them good. He knew what a hole like that was dug for, but he couldn't bring himself to acknowledge it. Not with his little brother sitting helplessly in front of it.

A heavy shadow of a person approached Lucas, possibly a man judging by the size, interrupting the high-beam glare as he moved from right to left.

"Who are you? What do you want with us?" Lucas asked, squinting to catch a glimpse of the man's face. He hoped he could reason with these men and talk his way out of whatever this was.

"I'm Major General Rafael Alvarez, commander of the Arizona National Guard," the man said with a haughty, self-important air, as if Lucas should recognize his name.

Lucas thought about Larson's cryptic phone call in NASA's conference room just before that area of campus was leveled. He flashed back to Larson talking to someone named Rafael and wondered if this Rafael was the same person. "Larson's Rafael?"

"My sister's husband," Alvarez said with a slight Spanish accent, sounding like he wasn't proud of the fact.

"What do you want?" Lucas asked the burly man, wondering why he didn't just call Larson his brother-in-law.

"Payback."

"Payback for what?"

"Jasmine Lynn Alvarez."

"Who?"

"My daughter."

"Sorry, but I don't know who you're talking about."

Alvarez grabbed the underside of Lucas' chin and pulled it up with force. "You killed my sweet innocent girl, you son of a bitch. The least you could do is acknowledge that you knew her."

"But I don't, I swear. You've got the wrong person."

"Bullshit. You two were on a date the night she was killed. Don't lie to me."

Lucas finally realized who the general was referring to and replied, "Jasmine? You mean Abby's roommate, the stripper?"

Alvarez punched him on the left side of the mouth, sending him crashing into the dirt. Lucas spat out blood before someone pulled him back up into a sitting position. His head was ringing, and his jaw was stiff with pain, but he didn't think it was broken since he was able to loosen it up with several open-mouth jaw extensions.

"She was a bartender, you asshole," Alvarez said, shaking his right fist in Lucas' face.

"Okay. Okay," Lucas said, turning his chin away to avoid another strike. "You're right. We were on a date, but it was a blind date. I never actually met her."

"I doubt that. Her personal journal mentioned you by name and included explicit details of your relationship."

Jasmine must have been as nuts as her old man. Either that or she'd been stalking him. Maybe Abby and Jasmine were both stalking them, setting up him and his brother for whatever was going on. But that didn't make any sense. "I don't know what she wrote or why, but I swear on my brother's life, we've never met. I only knew Abby, and I'd never even heard Jasmine's name until that day."

"Stand him up," the general said to one of the two soldiers with him.

Lucas looked over his shoulder and realized the man holding his arm was the same soldier who'd drugged Drew earlier, in the apartment.

"Wait a minute," Lucas told the general, trying in vain to pull away from the guard who'd just pulled him to his feet. "You've got this all wrong. I didn't kill your daughter. It was an accident, we—"

"I know all about your supposed *lab accident*. Randol filled me in on all your lies," Alvarez said, pulling his sidearm from its holster. He checked its ammo clip, then cocked it. "Gag him, Thompson."

"Wait, you don't have to do this—" Lucas snapped, before Thompson stuffed a thick cloth into his mouth.

The general walked to where Drew was sitting and pressed the barrel of his weapon against Drew's left temple, then looked back at Lucas. "You took my precious little girl away from me, and now I'm going to return the favor."

Before Lucas could scream at him to stop, the general pulled the trigger, and the weapon recoiled as the gunshot echoed across the barren landscape.

Lucas gasped and the muscles across his chest tightened all at once when he saw the far side of Drew's skull blow apart in a spray of red. His brother's limp body tumbled sideways, disappearing head-first into the unmarked grave.

All the energy ran out of Lucas' body, sending him to the ground on his knees. He felt a stabbing pain pierce the ventricles of his heart, causing his logic to shut down in an instant. His jaw seized up and he suddenly couldn't breathe, or think—his mind was a jumbled blur. He couldn't take his eyes from the edge of grave, hoping Drew would somehow climb out of it, unharmed.

His heart needed to weep for his brother, but his brain and mouth had other plans. They fought back the flood of emotions wanting to escape his body, holding them in and letting them fester and mix together. All he could see was red in his mind as something inside snapped, taking him to a deep, dark place where he'd never been before. Revenge was the only thought on his mind as his heart turned from sorrow to pure hatred.

"Mother*fucker*, I'll kill you!" he screamed at the general, but the gag muted his words to an indecipherable level. His adrenaline spiked as he tried to shake free from Thompson's powerful grip, thrashing from side to side, but he couldn't break the man's hold. If Lucas had still been standing and not on his knees, he figured he might've been able to use his legs for added leverage.

A second later, Alvarez swung his head and sent Lucas an evil, sadistic smile, then turned his focus back to the hole where Drew's body had landed. He fired two more shots.

BOOM! BOOM!

The reverberating sound of the gunshots echoed across the desert terrain and tore an even bigger hole in Lucas' heart. His lungs were now pumping at full tilt, and so was his heart, thumping well past its red line. Insanity was next, if his heart could hold out that long.

Alvarez turned to Lucas and aimed the sights of his weapon at him. "Now you know what it feels like to have a loved one ripped from your life. Before I kill you, too, you're gonna watch us piss on your brother's body. Then I'm gonna bury you both and leave you to rot in the dirt."

Before Lucas could suck in another angry breath, the general's cell phone started ringing. Alvarez pulled the device from his pocket and looked at the phone's display and promptly answered it.

"Alvarez here," he said, his eyes and body language indicating it was someone important. He turned and walked to the front of his Humvee, then climbed up the hood and across windshield, coming to a stop on the roof. He was now facing away from Lucas, looking off in the distance with the phone stuck to his ear.

"Yes, I see it," Alvarez said into the phone.

The call continued for bit, then ended with, "Yes, ma'am, right away." The nimble general jumped down from the vehicle and told the second soldier, "Rodriquez, you're with me."

"Is something wrong, sir?"

"That was the governor. Another energy field is heading toward the capitol building. She wants us there ASAP."

"Sir, what do you want me to do with this one?" Thompson asked, still holding on to Lucas.

"Finish him, then bury him with his brother," Alvarez said before sliding into the front passenger seat of the Humvee.

"Gladly, sir," he answered with exuberance.

The general's driver, Rodriquez, sat behind the wheel and started the truck. He shifted it into reverse and spun the tires hard, sending a hail of rocks and dust at Thompson and Lucas. The Humvee made a one-eighty before darting off in the same direction as the general had been looking when he was perched on top of his vehicle.

Lucas knew he was running out of chances and decided to use the distraction of the speeding vehicle to gain the upper hand. He stood up and tried to turn around to attack Thompson, but the soldier punched him in the left kidney before he could complete his spin. Lucas gasped and fell back to his knees once again.

Thompson moved in front of him, pressing the razor-thin edge of a long-handled knife to Lucas' throat. "Britney and Carl Junior," he said with fury in his words.

"What?" Lucas mumbled through the gag, trying not to scrape his throat muscles across the man's blade.

"My wife and unborn son. Two of the people you killed on campus."

Lucas' mind filled with a vision of the pregnant woman and her friend being swallowed up by the energy field eating its way across the grassy mall.

Thompson leaned in close, forehead to forehead. "I'm going to enjoy bleeding you, slow."

It was time to act, Lucas decided, whipping his head back and bringing it forward in an instant. He rammed the center of his forehead into the soldier's nose, making Thompson stumble backward with a stunned look on his face. He landed flat on the ground, face up.

Lucas sprang to his feet and hustled to Thompson's position. He jumped high into the air, aiming both of his knees at the man's face. He heard a crackling snap when they made impact.

He rolled off the soldier, dodging a steady stream of blood jetting out of the man's nose. Thompson's eyes were closed and his limbs weren't moving, but Lucas could see the soldier's breath puffing into the night air. Thompson's knife was a few feet beyond his head, thrown clear by the man's tumble.

Lucas' heart howled for revenge, demanding he finish Thompson off for his part in Drew's death.

An eye for an eye, his temper screamed. *Go ahead and do it; do it now. No one will blame you. This man, along with Alvarez and Rodriquez, deserves to die.*

His logic agreed, temporarily blinded by the rage coursing through his veins. Lucas was eager to play the role of the Reaper and take this man's last breath away. He raised his right foot until his thigh was level with his waist, ready to crush Thompson's face with every ounce of strength remaining in his body.

The instant before he unleashed his wrath, sanity broke through the cyclone of fury consuming his thoughts and stopped him. He lowered his leg to the ground and stared at the unconscious man's bloody face, seeing him not as a guilty soldier, but as a young husband, not much older than Lucas was. He thought about Thompson's pregnant wife and unborn son, killed by the rampaging energy dome.

If they'd been his family, wouldn't he have responded the same way? In fact, wasn't he about to do the very same thing—wield the sword of vengeance for a loved one?

If he took Thompson's life, then he'd be no better than those who'd just murdered his brother. He wasn't a killer; he was a scientist, his logic yelled at him. How could he ever live with himself?

The answer was . . . he wouldn't be able to. Not after promising to do everything he could to man up and make the situation right for the deaths he caused on campus and everywhere else. And killing a man out of revenge was wrong—no matter what Thompson had just done.

Then his brain connected more of the dots, reminding him none of this would be happening if he'd just followed orders and not run the experiment a second time. Everything up to this point was his fault, not Thompson's. That included Drew's death.

Lucas backed away, his heart no longer consumed with exacting revenge. Even though he was insane with grief over the death of his brother, he'd rather kill himself than become a cold-blooded murderer like Alvarez.

He was suddenly filled with an overwhelming desire to hold his little brother in his arms. He needed to say goodbye, then take Drew's body back home for a proper burial. He wasn't sure how he was going to face his mother and explain what had happened, but he'd have to find a way.

He knelt down next to Thompson to search the man's pockets. Lucas' hands were still cuffed behind his back, making it difficult to see what he was doing. He found an aluminum key in a third pocket; he hoped it was the right one. He fumbled with the key, trying to insert it blindly into the handcuff's keyhole. It took several attempts, but he managed to unlock the restraints and free himself.

He removed the gag from his mouth and ran to Drew's grave. When he looked into the hole, his brother's body wasn't there; only a muddy pool of red liquid remained along the bottom.

"What the hell?" he said, staring at the emptiness, trying to wrap his head around what he was seeing. Or more accurately, what he wasn't seeing—a corpse.

Before Lucas could decide what to do next, he heard rustling behind him. He turned to see Thompson's limbs squirming in the dirt. He ran to the soldier and punched him in the jaw, making sure Thompson stayed unconscious. Then he used the empty pair of handcuffs to secure the man's hands, before standing over the man to admire his conquest.

He was proud of his self-restraint for not killing Thompson when he had the chance. But after additional consideration, he decided a smashed nose and sore jaw wasn't sufficient punishment. He pulled his leg back and kicked Thompson in the ribs hard—just like Thompson had done to him earlier. He desperately wanted to hurt this man more but kept his hunger for all-out revenge in check.

He considered, for the briefest of moments, picking up the soldier's KA-BAR knife and carving his brother's initials—DR—into his forehead. It would serve as a constant reminder of Thompson's role in Drew's death. But cutting into a man's face was too disgusting and he couldn't bring himself to do it. Drew wouldn't have wanted him to do it, either. Not on his behalf and certainly not at the hands of a fellow Ramsay. Lucas hoped he'd never become the kind of sick, twisted animal who was capable of disfiguring another human being.

Lucas went back to the grave and searched in and around the clearing for his brother's body, scouring every inch of dirt within a two hundred foot radius. But he found no evidence of Drew's body anywhere—no footprints, no drag marks, and no blood trail. Nothing.

He didn't understand it. Somehow, Drew's body had simply vanished.

16

Lucas opened the driver's door to Thompson's Humvee and found the keys in the ignition. When he started its engine, the dashboard displayed the time as 11:11 p.m.

The GPS system installed into the center console beeped twice, then booted its operating system. Moments later, he knew his exact location—thirty-five miles northwest of the Phoenix metropolitan area. He used the GPS interface to plot two courses: One was to the capital building in downtown Phoenix, where he knew General Alvarez was headed. The other was to his mother's home in north central Phoenix.

Both destinations required him to take the same route southeast to Phoenix until he ran into Interstate 17, giving him about thirty minutes to decide on his final destination. If he chose to go home, he still had time to make it there before midnight to wish her a Merry Christmas, and it would give him time to rehearse what he was going to tell his mother about Drew's death. On the other hand, if he decided to hunt down Alvarez, he'd have time to devise a stealthy approach.

He stepped on the gas and drove off across the desert in the same direction as General Alvarez. The road, if you could call it that, was filled with gullies, sand, and rock, sending his head crashing into the Humvee's padded ceiling numerous times. Tumbleweeds, bushes, and a few cacti careened off the truck's grill guard as he plowed through everything in his path.

Just when he thought the uneven terrain would never end, he came across a paved, two-lane highway. He turned left and headed southeast toward the freeway.

He drove about a mile down the road, then over the crest of a steep hill near one of the state's manmade lakes. A skyline view of the Phoenix metro area opened up before him, catching him off guard for a moment. It was a stunning nighttime panorama of the sprawling desert metropolis. The spectacular view would have been jaw-dropping beautiful and soothing, if not for the pair of killer energy domes glimmering in the distance and the fresh wound from Drew's death squeezing his heart. Death and destruction seemed to be all around him and following his every move.

Shit, they're back. More blood on my hands.

One of the domes appeared to be devouring the downtown Phoenix area, while the other was near Scottsdale, a suburb thirty miles east of Phoenix. Pockets of the city's power grid were now failing, flickering off and leaving dark, featureless voids across the brilliant nightscape.

* * *

Twenty minutes later, he arrived at the north side of Phoenix, where he turned right and took the south access ramp onto I-17. Downtown Phoenix was straight ahead and still a bit of a drive. He jammed the gas pedal to the floorboard, plastering his back against the driver's seat.

The opposite side of the freeway was crammed with a long line of cars and trucks, each filled with people trying to evacuate the city. He appeared to be the only one dumb enough to be heading south, directly toward the chaos.

Ten minutes later, he was nearing the point in his trip where he needed to make a choice—track down General Alvarez or go rescue his mother? A mile ahead was the Thunderbird Road exit, the point of no return if he wanted to drive to his mother's house.

The terrain blurred by his window, seemingly speeding up the passage of time. The tires churned and the engine roared, taking him forward at high speed. Second by second ticked by, until he could see the exit ramp approaching on the right. Reason and rage battled within him. He didn't know what he was going to do. Which path should he take?

Suddenly, his mind detached from his body, filling his consciousness with the sensation of being outside of himself. He was now floating high above the truck, looking down through the top of the windshield like an observer. He could see his dirt-covered fingers gripping the steering wheel as the momentum of the Humvee took his body forward into the future.

Without warning, his flight path changed, swinging him around the driver's side of the truck and lowering his viewing angle. He could now see himself working the steering wheel, his face smothered in emotions.

At that instant, he knew what his body was thinking about: his mom, his dad, and his brother—everyone who was important to him.

What would they want him to do?

Alvarez or rescue Mom?

The answer came to him the instant the Humvee swerved to the right, down the Thunderbird Road exit ramp. Family first, he decided.

His out-of-body sensation passed, and he was now back behind the steering wheel and in full control—full control of the vehicle, his emotions, and his future.

Intersection after intersection flew by, and so did the traffic heading the opposite way. He was now only a minute from his mother's house.

The rest of his plan was simple—get Dorothy out of town and away from the energy fields. He needed to save what little family he had left, and do it now. Then find the words to explain to her what had happened to Drew.

* * *

Lucas arrived on the street to their family home just short of midnight. Dorothy was normally in bed around 9:00 p.m., but he figured she was still awake. He imagined her sitting on the plastic-covered living room sofa, staring out the front window, sipping eggnog from her favorite coffee mug, which had a nonsensical mathematical calculation on its side with the humorous caption, "Friends Don't let Friends Derive Drunk."

Dorothy was probably worried and still awake after he and Drew failed to show up in time for Christmas dinner. There was sure to be a pile of homemade oatmeal cookies sitting on the coffee table, next to a cold glass of milk with his name on it. Oatmeal Crispies were his favorite and she made them for him every year. It was a Ramsay family tradition, one started by his Grandfather Roy, back before the gruff old man was banned from the household.

The thought of cookies and milk stirred in his brain, making his stomach growl with hunger. If he was going to face his mom without Drew at his side and explain his death, he needed a sugar fix first, to bolster his energy. Then he got an idea, wondering if the general's men had any food in the Humvee. A second later, the vehicle's center console was open and he found two power bars tucked under a pair of sunglasses. He ripped off the wrappers and wolfed them both down in seconds as he crept closer to Dorothy's house on the right.

His foot eased off the gas pedal a bit when he saw a white van parked along the curb in front of his mother's house. The streetlights were still blazing, providing ample light to identify the vehicle—a campus security van. If its driver was someone he knew, it would make explaining the night's events all that much easier.

He intended to pull behind the van and park, but changed his mind when he noticed two armed guards standing next to it, on the side facing the house. His mother was being escorted out of the house by another pair of men, one alongside her and supporting her right arm as she moved, and the other was two steps behind, carrying a pair of suitcases, and a knapsack over his left shoulder.

As the Humvee cruised a little closer, Lucas realized the person escorting his mother by the arm was Bruno, his favorite campus security guard and king of the sugar junkies. Lucas studied the face on the other man to see who it was. He recognized him, too, but did a double-take to confirm . . . yes, the man carrying the baggage was him!

"What the hell?" he snapped, frowning in confusion. Maybe he'd been hit on the head while he was drugged? His mind must've been playing tricks on him, that's all he could figure.

He decided to check a third time in order to convince himself he wasn't going crazy. He closed his eyes tight, took two deep breaths to calm himself, then looked again. Shit, he wasn't seeing things. The man carrying the suitcases was *him*.

This isn't possible, he told himself. *Is it?*

It was clear from Dorothy's smile and demeanor that she believed her escort was Lucas. But how could she not know the man walking with her was an imposter? A mother knows these things, right? She knew Lucas better than anyone else in the world, except for maybe Drew. That meant only one thing: the charlatan wasn't simply an actor, and his resemblance must've been more than just superficial. His mother was being fooled and probably in trouble, he decided.

Lucas lowered his head and drove past the house, hoping to avoid detection. There was plenty of ambient light from the moon, but nobody seemed to notice him or the Humvee as he drove slowly by the house.

At the end of the street, he turned off the truck's headlights and made a U-turn, parking behind a dented and scratched four-door GMC Dually truck on the opposite side of the street. A stack of inner tubes was tied down inside the bed of the gas-guzzler using bungee cords, and its front wheels were parked up on the sidewalk at a sharp angle, probably due to the driver having one too many six packs at the indoor water park Lucas knew was only a mile away.

He got out of the stolen Humvee and snuck along the street until he made his way to the house next to his mother's. He crouched down behind the three-foot-tall hedge separating the two lawns, giving him a clear view of the front yard and the waiting van. The sliding side door was open, but shadows cast by the halogen streetlamps partially obscured the interior from view.

Bruno opened the passenger door and helped Dorothy into the front seat, then walked around the front of the van and got in the driver's seat. A black laptop computer case with an LA Kings' hockey sticker on its front pocket was slung over his shoulder. Lucas recognized the computer—it was his. He'd put the sticker on the case just a few months before.

The red-haired man impersonating him approached the vehicle's open side cargo door. The phony handed both suitcases to one of the armed guards already inside, then stepped up and entered the vehicle himself. Seconds later, the other guard joined them and the sliding door slammed shut.

Part of Lucas was impressed. The man pretending to be him moved exactly like he did—his walk, his mannerisms, his facial expressions, everything. But only part of him was impressed—the rest was furious about his mother being kidnapped under the guise of friendship and family. He wasn't about to let this charade continue and needed to expose it, but first he needed a plan. Those armed guards wouldn't like someone sneaking up and causing hell, so caution was in order.

Lucas went back to the Humvee and waited to turn on his headlights until after Bruno flipped a U-turn and drove down the street in the opposite direction. Lucas put the transmission into drive and followed the university van for the next hour as Bruno worked his way through traffic, traveling west across the north side of town. Lucas kept the Humvee back at a safe distance, trying not to be spotted as a tail. His plan seemed to work. It wasn't difficult to blend in with the numerous Army trucks interspersed within the civilian traffic.

Bruno made a sudden turn and drove south along the access road bordering the Loop 101 Freeway until he reached the Glendale Hockey Arena's front-side parking lot. The van drove down a sharp incline and

JAY J. FALCONER226

disappeared into an underground garage. To the right of the ramp's entrance was a twenty-foot-wide sign that read:

ARENA RENOVATION
General Contractor: BTX ENTERPRISES

Lucas knew Dr. Kleezebee's development company had purchased the vacant hockey building and was in the process of renovating it, but he'd never set foot inside the arena. He'd seen it on TV many times, the last being two years earlier, right before the Arizona Coyotes filed for bankruptcy—a second time—and then relocated to Mexico. Nobody expected the financially strapped team to thrive in Mexico, but it did. To this day, he never got used to saying "Los Coyotes."

Lucas waited five minutes before driving the Humvee down the entrance ramp. Inside, he only found one other vehicle—Bruno's security van. It was parked backward in the very last row, only about twenty feet from his current position. He could see the empty front seat of the van and its cargo door. The van looked abandoned.

He looked around to see where Bruno and crew had taken his mother. There were only four exits on the sublevel, including the entrance ramp behind him. At the far end of the garage was the main elevator and its adjoining stairs, but the white university van wasn't parked anywhere near them. The only other choice was a closed orange door, which was about ten feet on the other side of the van.

Lucas pulled forward slowly and parked the Humvee nose-to-nose with the van. He set the parking brake and got out. The soldier's gun was in his right hand as he looked through the van's driver-side window. No one was inside. He tried peering inside the van's rear windows, but they were heavily tinted and the garage lighting was poor. He couldn't see much of anything. He went to open the double doors on the back of the van, yanking hard, but they were locked.

He walked to the orange door he saw on the way in and put his left hand on the doorknob. The plan was to carefully open it and sneak inside, but he stopped his hand from turning the knob when he heard voices coming from the other side. He leaned in close to the door and pressed his left ear against it to listen.

One of the voices he heard was a perfect rendition of his own. There was a friendly argument happening between the imposter and Bruno—something about who "should go first." He didn't know what they were talking about, but they were kidding around like old chums at happy hour. The imposter certainly had everyone fooled—except him. He listened for his mother's voice but didn't hear the familiar melody of her words.

A handful of seconds later, an electrical hum rattled the doorframe, startling him for a second. Inside, a female's voice said, "Please step onto the pad. Activation sequence will begin in thirty seconds. Remember not to hold your breath." It wasn't his mom's voice. It was someone else.

Lucas slowly twisted the doorknob, trying to open it, but it wouldn't budge. It was locked.

Again, he heard the same female speak on the other side of the entrance. "Please step onto the pad. Activation sequence will begin in thirty seconds. Remember not to hold your breath." Both times the woman spoke, she used the exact same inflections and timing, making her voice sound artificial, like a recording.

He waited and listened for another few minutes, but heard nothing else from the other side. It was time to break in, he decided, kicking at the metal door. But it wouldn't open. He tried again and again, each time getting nowhere. A new plan was needed, so he hustled back to the Humvee and searched it for tools. There wasn't much useful inside other than a heavy-duty scissors jack stuffed in a recessed sidewall compartment behind the rear seat, and a three-foot-long tire iron with a tapered end like a screwdriver. It was wedged inside a form-fitting cutout just below the scissors jack. A second later, the steel bar was in his hands and he was sprinting back to the orange door with the intention of using it as a crowbar.

He took aim, then jammed the bar's tapered end into the doorjamb with a single thrust, splitting the metal seam next to the lock. He wiggled and pushed the tire iron farther into the crack before leveraging his weight against the bar. It worked; the door popped open with a creak of metal and a crack as the lock assembly finally broke in half. He flattened himself against the outside wall and waited to see if anyone came running after all the noise he'd just made.

No one came.

He let out the breath he'd been holding in his lungs and put the bar on the cement floor before walking inside with the loaded gun out in front of him. He snuck along the brick wall lining the hallway until he came to a chamber about the size of a 7-Eleven convenience store.

Inside, he discovered two stacks of blinking electronic equipment with a metal desk and computer console sitting in front. It was all black and chrome and looked incredibly high-tech—definitely out of place in an abandoned sports arena. He checked the room, but there was no sign of his mother or anyone else—the place was empty. He didn't understand how, but it was.

A clear cylinder about the size of a phone booth stood in the center of the room. It was a few feet taller than Lucas and resembled an oversized pneumatic tube, like those used by a bank in its drive-through lane.

On the left side of the tube, a bundle of gray-and-black cables snaked their way along the floor, connecting the tube to the electronic equipment. The cylinder's base was a round pad about three inches thick and four feet in diameter. Its surface was shiny and appeared to be made of glass, or possibly an acrylic. The pad was sectioned off into four pie-shaped triangles of different colors: red, blue, orange, and green.

When Lucas approached the cylinder, its enclosure rotated automatically, revealing two clear, overlapping glass tubes, one inside the other. The glass rings continued moving in opposite directions until a man-sized opening appeared. The device wanted him to step inside. He was tempted, but decided to wait. More information was needed.

He went to the computer desk, where a rotating 3D font was spinning on the computer's twenty-inch monitor. The phrase **BTX ENTERPRISES** danced across the screen in block letters, taking turns bouncing off the four edges of the display. He didn't see a mouse or keyboard, so he touched the screen to deactivate the screen saver. The computer display changed to show:

NETWORK CONSOLE: JUMP PAD 13

Destination: Silo 3	Status: Online / Ready
Comm: Sync	Stream: Outbound
Core: Charged	Buffer: Waiting

ENGAGE   CANCEL

"Jump Pad Thirteen . . . Comm Sync . . . Buffer waiting," he mumbled aloud, working through the details in his brain. The device must be some type of streaming communication system, he decided, and it was connected to a silo. Apparently not the only one Kleezebee owned, either, since it showed silo number three.

He used his finger to press the ENGAGE button. A female voice instantly said, "Please step onto the pad. Activation sequence will begin in thirty seconds. Remember not to hold your breath." Her voice came at him from every direction and was obviously being artificially generated by the technology in the room. His eyes darted from left to right, scanning the walls and ceiling, but he didn't see any speakers.

The computer's voice spoke again. "Please step onto the pad. Activation sequence will begin in thirty seconds. Remember not to hold your breath."

"Ah, I don't think so," he said to her, taking a step back while thinking about the contents of the screen and the fact he was alone in the room. Then the answer hit him square in the forehead. The machine must have been some type of telepod or transporter. It would explain how they left.

"Must have taken it to Silo Three, wherever that is," he mumbled.

The computer spoke again, issuing the same commands as before. He ignored it like before, returning to the vertical cylinder to consider his options. There were two choices: step onto the pad and take a ride, or abandon his intention to rescue his mother. If he gave up now, where would he go? What would happen to her if he didn't chase after them? After a few more moments of deliberation, he decided the only choice was to risk the transporter, if that's what this thing actually was.

He stepped into the device, making sure the handgun he was holding did not damage the glass. Lights flashed and a high-decibel alarm blared through the room. Then the same female's voice said, "This is a weapons-free zone! Please discard your weapon immediately. You have twenty seconds to comply or a nerve agent will be released."

A steel door slammed shut from the ceiling above, blocking his access to the entrance hallway. He was trapped inside the room. Then a four-foot-wide metal drawer slid open along the wall next to the electronic equipment.

Lucas didn't need to be told twice. He flew off the pad, ran to the deposit drawer, and tossed in the handgun. The drawer closed as soon as the weapon clanked along its bottom. He listened for the computer to respond, but she didn't.

"I just gave you the gun," he shouted to the room, hoping she'd cancel the nerve agent threat. But he heard nothing. He waited for it, but didn't hear the sound of gas being released. Maybe he was in the clear. He went back to the pad and stepped inside. This time its enclosure rotated closed without any alarms or warnings, allowing his heart rate and supercharged lungs to slow a bit.

He closed his eyes and waited for the machine to do its thing while concentrating on his breathing, making sure to inhale and exhale normally as the computer told him to do. Everything was going fine until he started thinking about the 1986 movie *The Fly*. He suddenly worried he might come out the other end of the system as a hybrid organism, like the movie's Brundle-Fly creature—half-human, half-fly. He opened his eyes and listened for insects buzzing around the telepod. There were none.

Then the equipment powered up while he was checking for insects, making him hold his breath. He began to feel lightheaded, as if he were in a dream, floating above the clouds. It was almost a spiritual experience, which was more than strange since, unlike his brother, he didn't believe in a supreme being. He preferred the hard reality of science and couldn't fathom how his mother and brother could blindly follow church doctrine without a shred of proof or assurance.

A long second later, he heard the same computerized female voice say, "Welcome to Silo Three."

Lucas pried his eyes open, expecting the worst. He looked down and checked all his body parts—each was intact and still human. *So far, so good,* he thought, as a wave of dizziness came over him. He stumbled a bit before throwing out his hands against the clear glass enclosure to catch his balance. A second later, the enclosure began to rotate open and he stepped out in a flash.

He was in a room much like the one he'd just left: electronic equipment installed in wall-mounted enclosures along one side of the room and a stubby computer desk with a flashing monitor sitting on top of it.

Lucas walked to the only door, opened it, and stepped into a featureless gray concrete hallway. Two people—a thirty-something male with thick, horn-rimmed glasses and a mousy looking younger female with her auburn hair pulled back in a tight bun—were approaching from his right. They were lab techs of some sort, judging by their identical white tunics and turquoise-colored surgical pants.

They were shuffling their feet forward at half-speed, obviously in no hurry to get where they were going. The woman was eating a bagel while her colleague carried the conversation.

It was too late to go back inside the room, so Lucas decided to stand there and act natural—maybe they wouldn't notice him. However, a moment later, the man turned his eyes toward Lucas. It sent a wave of panic down Lucas' spine.

"Hello, Dr. Ramsay. Enjoying your visit so far?" the man asked, giving him a friendly, welcoming smile.

Lucas was stunned for a second, then realized the man thought he was the imposter. He pushed through his surprise and glanced at the man's nametag to play along. "Yes, I am, Doctor . . . Khoury."

The girl flashed him a grin, too, but didn't say anything as they cruised past him, heading down the hallway to the left.

Lucas waited till they made the corner, then decided to head in the opposite direction, following three different colored floor stripes— red, orange, blue. They were painted down the middle of the cement floor and about four inches apart from each other.

When the stripes branched off from each other, he went with his instinct and followed the red stripe, only because red was his favorite color. He needed to pick one, knowing that without additional data, the odds of selecting the correct stripe were thirty-three percent in his favor. Of course, the pessimist lurking inside his gray matter would say it was sixty-six against, but he chose to think positive. The red line led him down two more connecting hallways where he eventually found a half-dozen closed doors lining the wall on the right.

The first door was labeled with a sign that read LAUNDRY. He kept on walking until he came upon another door that read SUPPLIES. He opened it and went inside.

The room's interior was just as he expected, two floor-to-ceiling metal shelves with cleaning supplies on one and office supplies on the other. There was a janitor's mop and bucket, several worn yellow sponges, a pair of dirty yellow Converse sneakers that appeared to be older than he was, and a handful of fly-fishing magazines sitting under a box of Handi Wipes. A blue baseball cap with a crusted ring of sweat was draped over the end of the mop's handle.

Several waist-high rectangular signs were leaning up against the wall next to the door. Some of the printing was faded beyond recognition, but Lucas was able to make out TITAN II MISSILE SITE AZ-18 stenciled across the top of each sign. Just below the title was a single number, varying from 1 to 8, depending on which sign he looked at. Below each number was a differing floor plan with footprint icons leading to exterior doors.

"Floor schematics," he mumbled, wondering if the signs belonged to the building he was in. He'd visited the Titan Missile Museum just south of Tucson during his freshman year of college and recalled what the tour guide had explained that day. When the Department of Defense decommissioned various missile silos around the country, they often sold the property to citizens at pennies on the dollar.

He wondered if Kleezebee's company had bought one of them and refurbished it. If his boss had, it would explain the *Silo* name on the telepod's control screen. And since the professor had given its name the number three as well, it meant he'd likely purchased several of them—at least three would be a safe guess.

"Okay, I'm underground in an old missile silo, but where?" He inspected the office supplies and found they were all from the same supply store in Tucson. He recognized the address as just south of campus on Broadway Boulevard, telling him he was probably still in southern Arizona. Good news. He wasn't far from the university.

He went back outside and continued down the hall, turning right around the next corner. He could see an elevator at the far end of the corridor with a woman standing in front of it. To his immediate left, there was a door marked ARMORY.

"That's more like it!" he quipped before ducking inside the door. The room was only slightly larger than the shared bedroom in his apartment but much better stocked. An overcrowded weapons rack with machine guns and semi-automatic handguns was hanging on the far wall. In addition to the rack, there was a generous supply of other combat gear, including handheld radios, ammunition, night-vision goggles, smoke and flash grenades, helmets, and Kevlar protective vests.

He'd hit the mother lode.

On his way to the rifle rack, he bumped into a case of odd-looking handheld weapons sitting on top of two black corrugated storage containers. The guns were dark gray, almost black, with a blocky, right-angle appearance, much like a police-issued Taser. He picked up one of the weapons and balanced it in his hand. It was much heavier than expected.

A pea-sized lever stuck out on the side of the gun and just above the handgrip. He pressed it with his thumb, releasing a two-inch rectangular cartridge from the bottom of the stock. The cartridge was glowing green, warm to the touch, and fit into the palm of his hand. He snapped the cartridge back into its chamber, then pointed the weapon at the empty wall next to the closed door.

He wasn't paying attention to his fingers and accidentally pressed the trigger, sending a crackling blast of white energy out of the gun's barrel. When the energy ball hit the wall, it scattered across the surface like static lightning frolicking across the night sky. It raced around the room, spreading out and fading in intensity as it went, until it became only a memory.

"Holy shit!" he muttered, staring at the energy weapon. He smiled, then tucked the gun inside the back of his waistband and pulled his shirt down over it to conceal the bulge. He also grabbed a black 9MM handgun from the weapons rack and checked its ammo. All fifteen rounds were loaded into the magazine, which he rammed into the gun's stock.

Lucas took a moment to admire the precision engineering that had gone into building the semi-automatic firearm, letting the importance of the moment settle in and register. The two weapons he was now carrying suddenly made everything seem more real.

What came next wasn't going to be easy and he wondered if he was ready. Not that it mattered; he didn't have a choice. He needed to venture forth into hostile territory, and do so without backup or support if he hoped to save his mom and figure out what the hell was going on. He'd already lost Drew and wasn't about to let someone take the last member of his family away.

"This is it. Time to get serious," he told himself, his hands shaking and knees feeling weak. He took a deep breath and exhaled slowly, calming his nerves a bit. "Playtime is over."

Overall, he felt good about his progress thus far. He'd made it past the sentry door in the underground parking garage, figured out how to use a high-tech transportation device, then fooled two lab techs in the hall. Now came what he assumed would be the lethal stage.

He stuffed the 9MM inside the front of his belt and returned to the hallway, where he continued down the corridor toward the elevator, keeping track of the armory's location in case he needed to return.

When he reached the end of the hall, the elevator door opened and a security guard walked out, whistling a happy tune. "Can I help you find something, Dr. Ramsay?"

Lucas cleared his throat, trying to act cool and play the part of the imposter. "Have you seen Bruno?"

"Last time I saw him, he was down on Sub-Eight, in surveillance."

"Thanks."

"Of course, anytime," the guard said, walking away. Then the man stopped and turned around. "Hey, didn't I just see you down there? How did you get up here so fast?"

Lucas pretended he didn't hear the guard's question and quickly stepped into the lift. He just needed the doors to close before the man asked him a second time. He pressed the Number 8 button on the panel, then smiled at the guard as if everything was normal. The guard brought a hand up with his index finger pointed as he went to say something, but the elevator doors closed before he could get the words out.

Shit, that was close. I'd better hurry.

The lights on the elevator showed he'd been on Sublevel 5, and it was only a matter of seconds before he reached Sublevel 8. A bell chimed and the door slid open.

Lucas expected to see another hallway, but instead the lift opened directly into a warehouse-sized room filled with a 5x4 grid of twenty massive video screens covering the far wall. He stood there speechless, with his jaw hanging open, watching the sweeping array of technology.

He'd seen control rooms like this in the movies plenty of times, but the reality of where he was now and how he got there was a lot to take in. The screens featured a wide variety of images: some were only displaying numbers, charts, and graphs, while others showed energy domes wreaking havoc and destruction across the planet.

Between Lucas and the video feeds was a group of six technicians—all men. They were seated side-by-side in front of a control station that stretched from one side of the room to the other. Like the three men standing behind them, they were facing forward, with their backs to Lucas. Everyone in the room looked to be focused on either the huge wall of video feeds or the control panels in front of them. No one seemed to notice his arrival in the back of the room.

Lucas recognized the three men standing with their heads tilted up toward the active screens. One of them was Kleezebee, who was leaning on crutches, wearing his patented flannel shirt and coveralls. One of his pant legs was cut off just below the knee to make room for the white cast wrapped around his ankle. Bruno was standing between Kleezebee and the imposter who had carried his mother's suitcases from the house up in Phoenix.

Before the elevator doors closed, Lucas quickly moved forward, aiming his 9MM handgun at the back of Kleezebee's head.

"Someone mind telling me what the hell is going on here?" he shouted, making Kleezebee turn around in a lurch.

17

Kleezebee's eyes flew wide, as did Bruno's and the imposter's, all three of them now facing the business end of Lucas' gun.

"L? What are you doing here?" Kleezebee asked.

"You're supposed to be dead," Bruno added, looking like someone had just walked over his grave.

"You mean like my brother?" Lucas asked, sending an angry scowl with his words.

"Exactly," the redheaded imposter said with attitude.

"Sorry to disappoint, but I'm alive and kicking. It's obvious to me now, you're all in cahoots with General Alvarez. I should shoot all of you for what you've done to my family."

Kleezebee put out his hands, like he was trying to stop a runaway truck. "Wait, it's not what it looks like, L."

"Yeah, what does it look like?" Lucas replied. It startled him that Kleezebee called him L. He'd never done that before. "And what do you mean, L? You know perfectly well what my name is."

"Please, put the gun down and let me explain," Kleezebee said.

"Where's my mother?"

"She's safe and resting upstairs."

Lucas pointed the gun at the imposter. "Who the hell are you?"

"I'm you. The real you," the freckled man answered, looking like he was about to start laughing.

"What? What do you mean, the real me?"

"You heard me. You're not you. I'm you," he answered with a full smile on his lips.

"You think this is funny, asshole?" Lucas asked.

"Yeah. It's hysterical. I know for a fact you're not going to shoot."

Lucas waved the gun, wanting to drive his point home. "I wouldn't be so sure about that."

Just then, the elevator's arrival bell chimed behind him. Lucas didn't turn to look at it right away. Instead, he slid four steps to the left to maintain a defensible position. If a security team was arriving next, he needed to be ready.

A second later, he swung his eyes to the elevator doors when he heard them swoosh open. Then he saw it—a wheelchair with a handsome young Italian man in it. It was his little brother, looking at him with his big, handsome eyes.

Lucas' mind froze, trying to make sense of what he was seeing. He lowered the weapon a few degrees and loosened his grip, almost dropping the gun on the floor. "Drew? You're alive? How can that be?"

A smile erupted across Lucas' face, but vanished just as quickly when he realized the person sitting in the wheelchair could be another imposter. He regained his wits and tightened his hold on the pistol.

"What the hell's going on here?" he asked, pointing the firearm first at the kid in the wheelchair, then at Kleezebee, and then at his double. He was usually an excellent problem solver, but this situation had him stumped. He wasn't prepared for any of it and didn't know what he should do next, so he kept shifting targets to buy time while he figured out what was happening.

Bruno took a step toward Lucas, but Kleezebee stopped him with an arm bar maneuver.

Lucas pointed the gun at Bruno and held it there. "That's close enough, big fella. Everyone just stay right where they are until I get some answers. Trust me when I say that my emotional state right now isn't something any of you should bank on."

"Easy now, let's all take a breath and not do anything rash," Kleezebee said, stepping between Bruno and Lucas. "We're all friends here."

Lucas turned to the boy in the wheelchair, who had a heavy bandage wrapped around his leg. "Who the fuck are you and what are you doing in my brother's chair?" It was all he could do not to pull the trigger and blow a hole in whoever was sitting in front of him.

The Drew imposter smiled. "It's me, Lucas, your brother. Please put the gun down before someone gets hurt."

"Not a chance," Lucas said, shifting targets again. This time, the professor's forehead was the focus. "Someone better tell me what the hell is going on here before I let my trigger finger do all the talking."

"That wasn't me out there with Alvarez," fake Drew said. "I never got shot."

"You're going to have to do better than that," Lucas said, shaking his head. "I saw my brother's brains get splattered all over the desert after Alvarez's men drugged us and took us out there against our will. You can't be him. I was there. I saw him die. It's something I'll never forget. The general took everything away from me, and now this?"

"Please, L. Let me explain," Kleezebee said, his face frantic.

"Yeah, why should I listen to you? Everything you've been telling me all along has been nothing but a lie. I should shoot all of you right now. Fuck this."

"Wait! Wait! Wait! Just give me a chance to explain. I'll tell you whatever you want to know."

"Bullshit. It'll just be more lies on top of lies, Professor. It never ends with you."

"He's telling you the truth," Bruno said in a calm, steady voice.

"So you're in on this too?" Lucas asked his friend, not wanting to believe it.

"Just hear him out. Please," Bruno said.

Lucas could see the sincerity in the guard's eyes. His heart wanted to believe his friend, but his logic had other plans. "And why should I do that? Why should I believe any of you?"

"Because the fate of the human race depends on it," Kleezebee said, this time with more confidence in his words. "All I need is five minutes and I can prove it."

Lucas stood motionless and silent, considering the request.

"I'll answer all your questions. Full disclosure. I give you my word," Kleezebee said.

Lucas thought about it for a short minute, then decided to take a chance on the man and listen to what he had to say. "Fine, by all means. Enlighten me, Professor. But no sudden moves. From any you."

"Why don't we start with how you got away from the situation in the desert?" the professor asked.

Lucas decided to play along, hoping his mentor would give him some answers before he started spraying and praying. His nerves were completely frazzled and his patience was wearing thin—almost microscopic. He finally understood what the phrase *itchy trigger finger* meant. He could feel the power of the gun building in his hand, coming alive and ready to strike.

He locked eyes with Kleezebee. "After Alvarez shot Drew and left, I overpowered his guard and took his Humvee. Then I went to Mom's to get her and saw you guys escorting her out, so I followed you to the hockey arena." He gestured to Bruno. "Nice transporter, by the way."

"Did you kill him?" Bruno asked.

"Who? Alvarez?"

"No, the guard."

Lucas shook his head. "I sure as hell wanted to, but I decided to just cuff him and leave him in the desert with a canteen of water. I didn't want to sink to their level."

"Then this ain't over, boss," Bruno told Kleezebee with a worried look on his face.

"We'll deal with that later. The boys are safe as long as they remain here with us."

"I'm still waiting for an explanation," Lucas said, wiggling the gun to get their attention.

"Bruno, it's time to show him," Kleezebee said.

"Sure, Chief," Bruno said, stepping forward in front of Kleezebee.

Lucas took a step back as the overweight man extended both of his arms straight out from his shoulders, then tilted his head back and closed his eyes like an evangelist preparing for deliverance. His arms and legs started to quiver slowly at first, then gradually built in intensity until Bruno was in a full-blown, full-body seizure.

The contours of his face and body twisted and contorted, morphing its symmetry into something unexpected. His body mass shrank, decreasing to two-thirds of its original size. The convulsions calmed before he brought his head forward from the tilted position. Bruno, or what was left of him, looked at Lucas with a devious smile, his cheeks now soft and smooth.

It took Lucas' mind a full second to catch up to what his eyes were reporting. The old Bruno was gone, replaced by version 2.0. Only this version was a hard-bodied female with curves in all the right places.

Somehow Bruno had just transformed himself from a fat, lovable security guard into a gorgeous female in mere seconds. But not just any female—he was now Mary Stinger, Kleezebee's assistant. He, or rather she, was dressed in a short plaid skirt and sheer pink blouse. But that wasn't all. She wasn't wearing a bra and the pair of six-inch stiletto heels almost leveled her height with Lucas.

The video equipment illuminated her body from behind, allowing Lucas to see much more of her figure than he'd ever dreamed of, or wanted to, given the circumstances. A gut-wrenching pain wrapped his abdomen when reality sank in about the metamorphosis from manly plump to stunningly sexy. It was the most bizarre thing he'd ever witnessed in his life. And considering what he'd seen the past few days, that was saying something.

"How do you like my figure now?" Mary asked, using Bruno's grizzled voice. She stepped out of Bruno's duty belt, which had fallen past her slender waist and landed on the floor.

"What the hell is this?" Lucas gasped, regretting every lustful fantasy he'd had about Mary for the past couple of years. How could he ever trust his eyes, or his raging hormones, again?

"Bruno is one of our infiltrator units," Kleezebee said in an even tone.

Lucas pointed the gun at Mary. "An infiltrator unit? So he's . . . she's . . . what? A cyborg?"

"Not exactly," Kleezebee said. "Bruno's a genetically engineered bio-morph. A synthetic replica of the original biological entity."

The red-headed imposter with cheek scars who claimed to be him laughed out loud. "I had this exact same conversation just a little while ago. Talk about *déjà vu.*"

Lucas poked Mary in the arm to see if she felt real. "A bio-morph?"

Kleezebee replied, "He has the ability to mimic different organisms and assume their identity. He looks and acts just like the original but can be programmed to carry out a specific mission."

"So which is he, a clone or a robot?"

"He's neither. And both. He's something in between. Bruno's what we call a 'synthetic.' An artificial being who can transform at will to assume any identity or shape—whatever the mission demands. All he needs is a good supply of sugar to generate the energy needed to sustain each transformation."

Lucas smirked, letting out a sarcastic laugh. "What a complete load of horse shit. You can't possibly expect me to believe any of this. I've heard some whoppers in my day, but this one is biblical."

"Okay, smart guy. You tell me: how do you explain what you just saw?" the professor asked.

Lucas thought about it for a bit, but came up with nothing. "Nice try, boss. But it's not up to me to explain. I'm the one holding the gun, remember?"

"Look, my old friend, everything I told you is true. Just take a minute and run it through that analytical mind of yours. Weigh the facts and let them align themselves until the answer runs clear."

"And if I don't agree?"

"Then by all means, shoot us all."

"What?" Mary asked Kleezebee in Bruno's voice. "Don't plant ideas—"

"Just give him a minute. Trust me on this. L will come around."

Lucas ran it through in his head, sifting through all the bizarre and curious facts he'd accumulated while being part of the project, not only recently but over the entire time he'd been working for the professor. He wanted to prove Kleezebee wrong, but he couldn't. Everything seemed to line up perfectly to support the professor's claims. He stared at Mary, or Bruno, or whatever name he should call the person in the dress.

She smiled and winked. "It's all true, Dr. Lucas. All I need is a supply of sugar for the energy to complete the transformation."

Lucas nodded. Slowly at first, but with more vigor as time passed. It was all starting to come together. Lucas understood why Bruno was addicted to all things chocolate. The security officer consumed mounds of donuts and candy for the sugar rush, then used the energy to transform and assume different identities. Lucas was astonished when he thought about how human Bruno had acted for the past eighteen months. He never would've guessed the fat man wasn't human.

"How many infiltrator units are there?" Lucas asked, watching Bruno change back into his regular self. He knew he'd never look at Bruno the same way, at least not without thinking about Bruno's alter ego, who was no longer standing there in a short skirt and heels.

"Bruno's not the only one. However, the exact number is classified, and on a strict need-to-know basis."

When Lucas thought about Bruno and Mary being the same person, he discovered a discrepancy in Kleezebee's story. "Wait a minute. Something's not right here."

"What's that?" Kleezebee asked.

"A few days ago, when we were escorted to NASA's facility, Bruno was up on the surface and Mary was waiting for us down on sublevel twenty. How could he, or she, be in two places at once?"

"Let me show you," Kleezebee said, calling forward one of his video technicians to stand next to Bruno. Lucas hadn't realized it earlier, but all the video techs looked like brothers and were wearing the same oversized, pentagon-shaped watch as Bruno.

Bruno extended his left arm and the tech his right. Their index fingers touched in the middle as if they were plugging into each other's bodies. Their fingertips fused together into one scarlet-colored mass, which resembled the semi-liquid substance found inside a lava lamp. The blob shimmered as it slithered across the connection, slowly encasing the tech's arm, then spread to his torso. Eventually, the goop smothered his entire body.

For the next fifteen seconds, the tech's body fluctuated under the gelatinous layer like a waterbed mattress swaying in an earthquake. When the spasms subsided, random sections of the gooey substance disappeared, revealing more and more of Bruno's appearance from underneath. When all of the scarlet material had dissipated, the tech was gone, having been replaced by an exact replica of Bruno, clothes and all. The only things missing were the duty belt and sidearm.

Both copies spoke to Lucas in perfect unison, using Bruno's deep, raspy voice. *"We are one. We are many. We are whoever we need to be. Hopefully, now you understand."*

It took Lucas a few seconds to process what he'd just seen and heard. "So you can make copies of copies, like a Xerox."

"Yes, exactly," Kleezebee answered.

"Okay, I get that. I don't believe it, but I get it. Regardless, it still doesn't explain what happened in the desert with Drew."

The red-haired imposter wearing his freckled face stepped forward. He pointed at both Bruno copies and said, "Jesus Christ. Don't you get it yet? You're one of them. You're a copy. So was the Drew that Alvarez shot."

Lucas didn't say anything. He needed a moment to think.

"Trust me, you two are replicas and were sent there to die," the imposter added. "So the real me and him could live," he said, pointing at Drew in his chair.

Lucas rolled his eyes, then turned to the professor. "Okay, let's assume for a moment I believe you, which I don't. How did you know Alvarez was going to kidnap us?"

"We have a spy inside the general's unit. He tipped us off when Alvarez was coming after you. Remember my note to Trevor outside the conference room? I had him go make contact with our operative," Kleezebee said. "That night in the hospital, Trevor replicated both of you while you two were asleep. We knew Alvarez was gunning for you, but we didn't know when or where he'd strike. It was the only way to protect your Authentics. Alvarez had to think Lucas and Drew were dead; otherwise, he'd never stop looking for them. That meant we had to let him kill you. Since we needed you and D to act like your Authentics, we couldn't let you know you were copies."

Lucas remembered the sticky stuff on his hand when he woke up in the chair in Drew's hospital room. His mind flashed to a vision of the gooey material he stepped in when he was washing his hands in the bathroom sink. And his sore neck and back when he woke up in the red chair. Then he remembered seeing Trevor's big orange suitcase and wondering what was inside it. If his lab assistant hadn't brought a change of clothes for him and Drew, why take a suitcase to a hospital?

Even though the facts were compelling, he still didn't believe he was the copy. Or maybe he didn't want to believe it. His body felt real. His thoughts felt real. His emotions felt real. He'd watched his brother get shot in the head, for fuck's sake, and had his guts ripped out over it.

He'd felt anger, sadness, rage—the whole gamut. Plus he'd almost killed a man, and almost carved his brother's initials in the asshole's forehead, but compassion rose up inside him and he stopped himself, like a righteous human being would do. How could a copy go through all that? How could a bio-morph, as Kleezebee called them, feel and experience everything that he had recently?

A copy couldn't, he decided. Kleezebee must've had the two of them confused. "No, I don't buy it. I'm not the copy. I'm the real Lucas." He pointed at the imposter grinning back at him. "He's the fake, not me."

"Maybe you need to show him the Med-Lab, boss," Bruno said to Kleezebee.

Kleezebee did not respond. Instead, he walked to the front left corner of the room and stood near an eight-foot wide section of empty wall space. In front of him was a red, wall-mounted fire extinguisher. Kleezebee opened a sliding compartment hidden underneath the extinguisher's nameplate. Inside was a digital security keypad and biometric scanner. He entered a numerical security code and pressed his left thumbprint against the scanner.

The empty wall segment slid up and disappeared into the ceiling. Lucas realized the hidden segment was actually a thick, reinforced metallic door covered in fabric that matched the wall, creating a perfect camouflage. Beyond the door was a room roughly the size of Lucas's E-121 project lab.

"Welcome to our Med-Lab," Kleezebee said.

Two seven-foot long stainless-steel surgical tables stood in the center of the med-lab. Their smooth, polished surfaces reflected light shining from directional units beaming down from the ceiling above. Their edges were raised like coroner's tables, with depressed sections spaced evenly across their surface.

Runoffs for blood, Lucas decided.

Above each table, robot-like medical equipment hung down from the ceiling. A well-stocked mobile surgical cart sat between the two tables, adorned with instruments and supplies. Scalpels, scissors, forceps and hemostats shared space with gauze bandages, plastic tubes, and syringes still in their wrappers.

What Kleezebee called a Med-Lab was looking more and more like a torture chamber.

Metal shelves lined three walls of the room, packed with clear glass containers. Each container was about the size of a janitor's mop bucket and was two-thirds full of a scarlet-colored liquid. The ceiling carried a supply of two-inch diameter tubes, which connected the containers to a furnace-sized machine along the back wall. An enormous, blond-haired technician was standing in a lab coat in front of the machine with his back to the entrance.

Lucas walked into the lab and pointed the gun at the male technician. "Turn around and let me see your hands."

The tech turned around and smiled. It was Trevor, their Swedish lab assistant.

"Seriously? So what, everyone knows about this except me?" Lucas asked.

"We know this might not be easy to accept," Kleezebee said. "Let us show you. Then you'll come to understand."

Trevor fetched a glass container from the shelf closest to him and poured the red substance into one of the surgical table's depressed areas. It oozed out of the container like semi-frozen red pudding.

Kleezebee called in one of his operation techs from the video room and had the man roll up his sleeve. Kleezebee submerged the tech's hand into the scarlet material and held it there for a good twenty seconds.

"We call this substance BioTex. It's synthetically engineered living latex," Kleezebee explained. "Once his hand is submerged, the BioTex processes his DNA and begins the replication process. It requires at least fifteen seconds of contact in order to create a genetic map of the donor's body. Plus, it downloads the donor's memory engrams at the same time."

"Living latex?" Lucas asked.

Kleezebee withdrew the tech's hand from the BioTex. "We prefer to call it BioTex, which is short for Bio-mimetic Latex."

Lucas stood there, watching the BioTex coagulate and thicken as it spread itself across the length of the table. It rose up from the table like bread dough and progressively assumed the shape of a featureless human body.

Soon after, a facial structure began to materialize and show through the scarlet substance, like a person's face pushing up through a silk sheet. Mouth, eyes, and nose formed first, then hair sprouted and grew to full length. Eventually, the entire body, including genitalia, took shape.

The final step was the appearance of a lab coat and clothing. When the transmutation was complete, an exact copy of the male technician lay before Kleezebee on the table.

Lucas shook his head. "If the replica is a perfect copy, right down to its DNA, how do you tell the copy from the original?" he asked, thinking about himself. He wondered if he could somehow switch places with the imposter without anyone knowing, or vice versa.

Kleezebee picked up a handheld electronic device the size of a paperback book. "This is a BioTex scanner. We use it to check the validity of any subject. When it senses the bimolecular resonance of BioTex, it lights up red. When it senses an authentic human, it lights up green." Kleezebee aimed the device at Bruno's chest. After three seconds, the unit lit up red. "Red means he's a replica." He pointed the unit at the imposter. "Green means he's an Authentic. If I pointed it at you right now, it would light up red."

Lucas took a sharp step back to avoid the scan. He already knew the answer and didn't need a piece of unfamiliar equipment telling him who or what he was. *He* was the authentic, not the imposter. He was sure of it, and he wasn't going to let a piece of machinery he'd never seen before try to convince him of anything different.

Kleezebee held up the scanner. "May I scan you to demonstrate? It'll only take a few seconds, L."

Lucas pointed the gun at Kleezebee. "I told you to stop calling me that. It's not my name. How many times are you going to make me say it?"

"Okay, okay. I'll call you Lucas if you prefer," Kleezebee said. "Just relax. We're all on the same side here. Everything we've done is for your benefit and your brother's. If you'll let us prove it, you'll see we've been trying to protect you."

"By calling me 'L'?"

"That's simply the naming convention we use for replicas. We call them by the first letter of their donor's name. Is it okay if I approach? It's the only way to resolve this situation and bring you into the fold."

Lucas paused, then finally agreed. He lowered the gun but kept his finger on the trigger, pointing the weapon at the professor's kneecap.

Kleezebee aimed the scanner at Lucas' chest and activated the device. It lit up red, just as the professor said it would.

Shit. Maybe they're right. Maybe I'm not me.

Lucas took his finger off the trigger and lowered his hand, aiming the gun's barrel at the floor.

A second later, Bruno tackled Lucas from the side, pinning him spread-eagled to the floor. Then Trevor jumped on a half a second later and inserted a four-pronged electronic device into Lucas' neck.

Lucas screamed in pain, feeling an electric discharge coursing through his body right before his hands, legs, and arms went limp.

"Get off me," Lucas gasped with his face and chest pressed hard against the floor. The combined weight of the two men on his back was making it tough to breathe. He watched his fingers slowly melt away, turning into the runny scarlet substance.

It was true—*he was the replica.*

He craned his neck to look down along the side of his torso and then he saw it happen. His body began to lose cohesion as it dissolved into a runny blob of BioTex. Moments later, his mind went blank and his vision went dark.

18

The authentic Lucas looked at the puddle of BioTex lying underneath Bruno and Trevor on the floor. "I sure am glad that's over with. I never realized what a stubborn son of a bitch I can be." He turned to Drew. "I'm sorry for being a life-long pain in the ass."

"You're forgiven," Drew said, laughing. "Besides, if you weren't a total pain in my butt, I'd think you'd been abducted by aliens and replaced with a normal guy."

"You mean a boring guy, right?"

"Sure, that's one way to look at it. One thing's for certain, life just wouldn't be the same around here without my high-speed, low-drag brother watching my back, even if he gets a little edgy at times."

"Edgy?" Kleezebee asked. "That's the term you chose?"

Drew shrugged. "I was trying to be nice."

"You guys don't have to tip-toe around me and sugarcoat everything. I know perfectly well who and what I am. So don't sweat it. It's all good. No worries," Lucas added, hoping to sound like the jab Drew just took at him didn't hurt. It did sting a little, but he pushed past it. He knew Drew didn't mean anything by it. His little brother didn't have a mean bone in his body. That was Lucas' job, as well as a few others in his diminishing circle of trust.

Bruno rolled out of the BioTex sludge. "Well, that was interesting. For a moment there, I thought your copy was going to shoot us all."

"He sure was one mixed-up dude," Lucas said with a half-smile.

"Wouldn't you have been, given the circumstances?" Drew asked.

"Not a chance. If I was starting at two of you, I'd know the real Drew."

"I doubt that, considering replicas are perfect copies, right down to their synthetic DNA."

"Trust me, I could tell. No problem."

"Guys, now that L's been handled, we need to get back to business," Kleezebee said.

"Sure, Professor, sorry," Lucas said.

"So then. Before we were so rudely interrupted by L, you said you still had some questions?"

Lucas had to think for a minute. With everything that just happened, his memory needed a wake-up call. "Oh yeah, now I remember. Does it always take ten minutes to replicate someone? Or can you speed up the process, if needed?"

"Yes, ten minutes, but only the first time a synthetic duplicates someone new. After that, as long as the replica maintains its sugar supply, its bio-mimetic programming remains intact. It only takes a few seconds to resume any of its previously copied identities, switching from one to another, almost at will."

"Even clothes? How?"

"From the Authentic's memory. The BioTex scans the subject's mind and determines what the donor was wearing at the time of replication. It then synthesizes the clothes just like the rest of the body."

"What about memories and emotions? Are they replicated, too?"

Kleezebee nodded, changing to his methodical professorial voice like he was about to start an hour-long lecture. "Since memories and emotions stem from physical structures in the brain that register levels of certain chemicals being manufactured by the body in response to stimuli, they are copied as well. These structures are all part of the whole. A bio-morph is a perfect replica of the original, right down to the cellular level, including every cell and neuron in the brain, which include memories and emotions. Blood, bodily fluids, voice, brain patterns, and memory are mimicked perfectly. Even a human DNA analysis wouldn't be able to detect the difference. Only a bimolecular resonance scanner like ours can distinguish the replica from the original."

Lucas thought about his brother's disability and wondered about a cure. "What about genetic defects, and things like injuries and diseases?"

"We can program the BioTex to repair any physical defects during the replication process. However, we usually leave the imperfections in place to help make the impersonation more believable. Diseases are irrelevant and don't affect the replica, since it's not a real human being."

"Can your bio-morphs impersonate anyone? Like the President?"

"Well, yes, they can. But there are issues when replicating a high-profile individual. First, we need prolonged contact with the donor to process its genetic makeup and download its mind. With someone as well-protected as the President, that wouldn't be possible. Then you have the issue of what to do with the original. We wouldn't want to have two of them running around the White House. Obviously, that would cause problems."

"Yeah, no doubt."

"If you remember, I told you Bruno needs an ongoing supply of sugar in order to transform and maintain his identity. The same would be true with a copy of the President. The replica would need to consume significant amounts of sugar to maintain its form and not revert to pure BioTex. Someone would certainly notice the sudden change in the President's eating habits if he became a sugar junkie overnight."

"Okay, makes sense," Lucas said, nodding.

Drew asked, "Once the replica reverts back to its native form, what would happen if someone inserted their hand into it? Wouldn't it start to duplicate them?"

Kleezebee shook his head. "The BioTex can't be used again without the introduction of a reactivating enzyme that only we possess. It's one of our fail-safe mechanisms. The enzyme, and the knowledge to make it, is kept locked away under tight security. It's as important as the

BioTex itself. We certainly don't want our own technology used against us, so we take every precaution."

"Did you invent this stuff?" Drew asked.

"Yes and no. But I'm afraid that's all I'm at liberty to say at this point. I'm sure you'll agree, our BioTex and its unique properties are beyond top secret. The rest of the details are on a strict need-to-know basis."

"I understand, Professor," Drew said, "No need to explain. You're the boss."

Lucas remembered reading somewhere that latex could either be a natural or synthetic substance. It was made up of several ingredients, including sugar, which explained Bruno's chocolate requirements for genetic transformation and cohesion. Nevertheless, he still needed more information. "I have a few more questions, Professor. Hopefully, you guys can answer them without violating whatever DOD or DHS confidentiality agreement is keeping your lips tied."

Kleezebee smirked, but didn't seem upset. "Go ahead. I'll answer what I can."

"So Bruno's one of these replicas, right?"

"Yes. Absolutely."

"Okay, so where's the original Bruno? And what about Mary Stinger and the other people he impersonated? Are they walking around somewhere?"

"Excellent question. Some of Bruno's various identities were duplicated from the bodies of people who'd died. After someone dies, there's a forty-hour window in which we can duplicate them before complete DNA breakdown occurs."

"What about the ones who haven't died?"

"Sorry, that's part of an ongoing operation and classified."

Lucas exhaled and tucked in a lip, wondering if any more of his questions would be blocked. "How do you get access to their remains?"

"We own our own chain of mortuaries, which gives us priority access to the recently deceased."

Grim, Lucas thought, *but effective.*

He wondered where else Kleezebee might have replicas, besides General Alvarez's unit. "I understand why you have replicas inside the military, but what about in the government? And positioned throughout various industries too, I bet."

"Absolutely. Both. Though it can take years for one of our replicas to work its way up the chain of command in order to be in a position of influence. Tactically, we have to be very patient and plan far in advance, especially within the appointed branches of the government and the armed forces. It's much easier for our replicas to infiltrate the various intelligence agencies or corporations."

"How do you control the copy?" Lucas asked, thinking about Bruno's flying takedown of L a few minutes ago.

"During replication, we introduce new base coding sequences into his synthetic framework, which allows us to control him."

Lucas nodded. It sounded like Kleezebee had everything covered.

"Any more questions?" Kleezebee asked.

Both Lucas and Drew shook their heads.

"Then we've got work to do," Kleezebee said, walking out of the Med-Lab. Bruno, Lucas and Drew followed the professor into the video room.

"Status report?" Kleezebee asked his technicians.

"Looks like they're getting ready to drop a probe into the Korean energy field," the center tech reported.

"Put it on the center screen," Kleezebee told him.

"What's up?" Lucas asked.

"There's an energy dome near one of the U.S. military bases in South Korea," Kleezebee said, before asking the tech, "Can you tap into the telemetry?"

"You can do that?" Lucas asked.

"Yes, the probe's one of ours. One of our subsidiaries manufactures them for Uncle Sam."

Lucas was impressed by the breadth of surveillance technology at Kleezebee's disposal. His boss was far more than simply a professor turned real estate developer. Lucas figured there were a lot more layers of Kleezebee below the surface, just waiting to be revealed.

The wall of video screens was filled with live feeds from all over the world, one of which showed an aerial view of the energy field. An Air Force plane flew over the dome and dropped a cylindrical object from its cargo bay.

"Probe has entered the field, receiving data now," the tech said.

"So I was right. It can be penetrated through the crown," Lucas mumbled.

Bruno nodded, putting a hand on Lucas' shoulder.

"Well?" Kleezebee asked the tech.

"Reading an incredibly dense gravitational eddy at the center of the object. . . . Sensors report numerous subspace distortions around a condensed spatial pathway. . . . The vortex seems to be streaming differentially charged tachyon particles."

"Sounds like an unstable wormhole in an advanced state of decay," Drew said.

"A self-contained one, at that," Lucas added.

"Can you extrapolate the telemetry and identify where the micro-singularity leads?" Kleezebee asked.

"Applying a trans-vector algorithm. . . ." the tech said. "Sorry, sir, but I'm unable to determine its endpoint. There seems to be a strange phase shift within space-time. I can't get a lock."

"Have you heard of anything like this before, Professor?" Drew asked.

"No, this is something entirely new," Kleezebee said. He asked the tech, "Can you use the new sensors to give me an energy reading before it's crushed?"

"Six times 10^{31} terajoules."

Kleezebee turned to Drew. "That number sound familiar?"

"Yes—our experiment's energy spike. They must be related."

"Seems likely at this point."

"Probe has stopped transmitting, sir," the tech said.

"So let me get this straight. Our E-121 experiment spawned a bunch of artificial wormholes?" Lucas asked, dumbfounded by the revelation.

"Sir, the logs show the probe was scanned several times before it was destroyed by the anomaly," the tech reported.

"Source?" Kleezebee asked.

"It appears to have originated from the far side of the singularity," the tech answered.

"That means there's some level of intelligence on the other side," Lucas said.

Drew turned his wheelchair to face Kleezebee. "Can we communicate with them—if there is a 'them'—and tell them to stop? Maybe they don't know what kind of damage they're doing."

"I wish we could, but we don't have that kind of technology. Even if we did, I doubt it would make much difference. I don't think the energy fields are here by accident. There's clearly a specific agenda behind them," Kleezebee said, just as his cell phone began to ring. He stepped away to answer the call.

Lucas whispered in Drew's ear, "We could've used Kleezebee's sensors to trace the energy spike. I wonder how long they've had them?"

Drew shrugged. "I wonder what else don't we know? There's obviously a lot more to the professor than meets the eye."

"Now we know where he spends all his cash."

"Still, this took a load of capital to build, not to mention the ongoing costs to maintain," Drew said.

"He could have a benefactor, or he's in cahoots with good old Uncle Sam."

"Kleezebee accept help? Or money? Does that sound like the professor we know?"

"No, he likes to fly solo. Be the man in charge," Lucas said.

"Then he must've been at this for a while. Probably most of his life, wouldn't you say?"

Lucas nodded.

Kleezebee held his hand over the phone's receiver and told the tech, "Bring up Kunsan in Korea. Show me the airfield."

The tech changed the video feed for the center screen. It was now showing one of the Air Force base's runways where a black B-2 Spirit stealth bomber was taxiing along the tarmac. The sleek, triangle-shaped aircraft was turning into the wind and was almost ready for takeoff.

"Damn it, no!" Kleezebee shouted before continuing with his private phone conversation.

"Looks like they're going to attempt to collapse the energy field," the tech said.

"How?" Drew asked.

"By dropping in a Big Ivan."

"Are they nuts?" Drew shouted.

Bruno tapped Drew on the shoulder. "What's a Big Ivan?"

"It's a hundred-megaton thermonuclear bomb, the biggest ever made, by far. The Soviets were so scared of it they never actually tested it at full power."

"Actually, we estimate its yield to be closer to two hundred megatons," the tech said. "The Russians made a few enhancements to its tertiary to double its effective yield."

"Two hundred megatons?" Bruno asked.

"Yes, it's thirteen thousand times the destructive power of the warhead we dropped on Hiroshima, Japan," Drew replied.

"Holy shit," Lucas snapped.

Drew shook his head. "This has virtually no chance of working. It's simply not enough power and will probably make the situation worse. It's like throwing a stick of dynamite into a raging forest fire, hoping the relatively small explosion will snuff out the flames."

"Unfortunately, the President's science team seems to think it will. Dr. Kleezebee's been trying to talk them out of doing this," the tech said.

Drew replied, "The sudden influx of that amount of radiation in a small contained space will most likely cause a cascading reaction that could exponentially increase the dome's size and destructive power. There's no telling what might happen."

"Not to mention the lingering effects of nuclear radiation on our planet," Lucas added.

"Their scientists believe the radiation will be contained within the dome and processed through its vortex," the tech said, "potentially killing whoever is on the other side."

Drew shook his head adamantly.

"Why in God's name would they double it to two hundred megatons?" Bruno said.

"Pure desperation," Drew answered. "I'll bet their physicists ran the numbers and realized their solution was a pipe dream. To overload and destroy a self-sustaining energy vortex of this magnitude would take much more power than we could ever hope to generate. The military could simultaneously drop in every WMD on the planet, and the energy field would only laugh and keep on charging. It's simply not enough power to overload its energy matrix."

"Leave it to the military to try to blow up whatever they don't understand," Lucas added.

"Exactly. And it might end up killing us all," Drew replied.

"How's that?" Bruno asked.

"A two-hundred megaton blast could conceivably cause a tiny but permanent shift in the Earth's orbit around the sun. It's the very reason the Russians were afraid to test Big Ivan at full power. We're barely inside our sun's habitable zone as it is, and even the slightest change could cause us all to die a slow, frozen death."

"Or fry in a microwave oven," Lucas added.

When Kleezebee returned from his phone call, Drew told him, "Professor, we have to stop this."

"It's too late," Kleezebee said, pointing at the video screen. The B-2 bomber was already airborne. "What's the target?" he asked, looking at the tech.

"There's a swarm of energy fields on the ground in Seoul, South Korea. Geocode tracking reports the primary target is located at 37.1 degrees north and 127.3 degrees east. Looks like they're going after the largest dome."

"Distance to the target?"

"One hundred fifty miles and closing fast, sir."

"Show me the ground feed from Seoul."

A center monitor changed to show a cross-section view of downtown Seoul. In the foreground, an immense energy dome was eating its way through the center of the city. There were two additional energy fields to its left, though they were much smaller and farther away.

This was the first time Lucas had seen multiple energy fields on the ground at the same time. Each was a different size, carving up the city and leaving a network of destruction trails behind. It reminded him of the sandy underbelly of his first ant farm experiment.

Despite his brother's warnings to the contrary, Lucas could understand why the military was taking decisive action. The spread of energy fields had escalated faster than anyone had predicted, and the world was running out of time. Someone needed to act, and quickly.

"The one on the left is huge. It's got to be five miles wide," Lucas said, thinking about all the innocent people being killed across the globe. Guilt and remorse wanted to creep into his heart, but he kept them at bay, vowing to stay strong and stay focused. If there was a chance to make any of this right, he'd probably only get one shot at it. That meant keeping emotion out of the equation.

"It's the most powerful one we've seen so far," the tech replied. "It's been on the ground for almost fifteen minutes."

"Can you tighten up on the target? Make sure all digital multi-streams are active and being recorded," Kleezebee said.

The tech adjusted the feed and the camera zoomed in considerably closer. They had a front row seat to the detonation.

"Thirty seconds," the tech said. "The transport has entered stealth mode and is off radar."

Lucas wondered why the military chose to deliver Big Ivan from a stealth aircraft. It was unlikely the phenomenon had onboard radar, so why try to conceal its approach? He thought about it for a few seconds and concluded the aircraft's flight crew was just following standard deployment protocols. Most likely, they were required to use stealth mode when live nuclear weapons were being deployed.

"Pull up the aircraft's onboard feed," Kleezebee said.

Next to the center monitor, a high-resolution video feed from the underside of the bomber's fuselage appeared, providing a close-up view of the aircraft's target. From above, they could see the energy field chewing its way through the Korean city.

The bomber's camera showed the enormous tip of Big Ivan as it was dropped from the plane's cargo bay. Even though the bomb's aerodynamic casing was the size of a small bus, it quickly disappeared from view as gravity guided it toward the energy field at terminal velocity.

"Sir, the ordnance has been deployed and is approaching the target."

A few seconds after Big Ivan entered the dome, a blinding, powerful flash lit up the energy field from deep inside.

"Right on target," Bruno said.

Lucas looked at the other monitor to view the detonation from the ground level camera. He waited for signs of the detonation to extend beyond the dome's open crest, yet nothing appeared. The anomaly contained the blast, just as the government's scientists predicted.

So far, so good, Lucas thought. *Maybe the President's scientists were correct.*

The energy field started to oscillate in color and the dome began to grow. Its expansion was slow at first, then, after a few seconds, it picked up steam and grew quickly. The hairs on Lucas' arms stood straight up when the energy field suddenly quadrupled in size and turned a reddish-orange color.

"Yep. We were right. They just pissed it off," Kleezebee said.

Lucas assumed his boss was only speaking metaphorically and would never actually believe the energy field was some form of creature. Just then, the dome's perimeter wobbled for a few moments before splitting into two equal halves like a single-celled organism reproducing through mitosis. "Ah, that can't be good."

The twin domes started revolving around each other, cutting an even deeper and wider channel into the earth as they moved. The stealth bomber flew off into the distance as the energy fields continued their march across the Korean landscape, moving faster now.

"That should put an end to the Big Ivan idea," Drew said.

"And to Seoul," Lucas added, with emphasis.

"How will we know if Earth's orbit was changed?" Bruno asked.

"We'll have to run a few calculations," Drew answered.

"Or just wait for the weather patterns to change," Lucas said.

"Boss, what would you like us to do next?" Bruno asked.

"There's not much we can do right now," Kleezebee said. "Let's get some shuteye and start fresh in the morning."

19

Lucas and Drew rode the elevator down from Sublevel 2, where they found Kleezebee and Bruno standing together in the middle of the surveillance room. Lucas took the last sip of his soda and tossed the can in the trash bin next to the elevator.

"Food was pretty good, considering," Drew said.

"I thought the eggs were a little bland, but the bacon was just the way I like it—extra greasy."

"Mom didn't seem to like it much. She barely touched her food."

"I don't think she slept that well last night, being in a new place and all. I'm worried about her."

Drew's gaze sharpened. "So am I. We should take turns keeping an eye on her. It's what Dad would've wanted."

"Yeah, for sure. Did you bring the notebook?" Lucas asked.

"Of course. Got it right here in my backpack. You need it?"

"Yeah. I think we should show DL your QED equations," Lucas said as they walked up silently behind Kleezebee, who was in the middle of a conversation with Bruno.

"—by the time you get him outfitted, I'll have its location and the rest of the assets in place," Kleezebee said.

"What are the rules of engagement, boss?" Bruno asked.

"Stun only. There better not be any casualties this time."

"Count on it, sir."

Kleezebee flashed a glance at Lucas, but didn't say anything.

Lucas nodded hello. So did Drew.

Lucas turned his attention to the middle row of video screens, which showed activity at three locations he recognized. The first was his apartment complex, where military troops had surrounded the building. A squad of men was approaching the front entrance.

The second location was a lengthwise view of his mother's neighborhood. The camera was too far away to see much detail, but Lucas could see soldiers and Humvees lining the street.

The third screen contained a high-angle feed, possibly shot from the clock tower of the Student Union, showing a platoon of men guarding the open shaft leading down to NASA's underground facility. Two soldiers were standing next to the opening, prepping their climbing gear.

Kleezebee looked at Lucas. "It's General Alvarez. He's searching for you."

"Where? I don't see him," Lucas said, checking the three middle screens.

"He's outside your apartment," Kleezebee answered, turning to his tech. "Can you give me a close-up? I want to see who he's talking to."

The camera zoomed in on General Alvarez standing near the door to the manager's office, then panned to the right, showing a shorter man with two black eyes and a heavy gauze bandage taped over his nose.

"That guy's a mess," Lucas said.

"Must be the guard L overpowered in the desert," Kleezebee said, shooting a friendly glance at Lucas. "I didn't know you had it in you."

"Well, technically, neither did I," Lucas replied with a grin. "One never knows what one's copy is gonna do."

"Alvarez is never gonna stop. Not until you're dead," Bruno told Lucas. "In his mind, you killed his daughter."

Lucas agreed with Bruno. "So what's the plan, Professor?"

"I'm afraid we have no choice. We're going to have to kill you."

Lucas wasn't sure what to make of the remark. "You're just kidding, right?"

"I'm dead serious. You need to die a horrible, public death or else the general will never stop gunning for you. Follow me."

Kleezebee used the hidden access panel inside the fire extinguisher to open the secret entrance to the Med-Lab, where Trevor was working.

"Let's get started," Kleezebee told Trevor.

Trevor retrieved a bucket of BioTex from the shelf and poured it into the middle recess of one of the medical tables.

"Ah, I understand. You're going to duplicate me again," Lucas said.

"Precisely," Kleezebee said.

"But what happens when the body dissolves into BioTex? Won't Alvarez realize something fishy is going on?"

"You mean like what happened to D in the desert?"

"Yes. We don't want him getting suspicious. I'm guessing what happened to D's body wasn't part of the plan."

"No, it wasn't. When Alvarez came for your copies, we had no idea he'd incapacitate them. It's possible the drugs he used compromised the replicas' sugar level in some way," Kleezebee explained, looking at Bruno like he was waiting for an answer.

Bruno nodded. "The drugs may have caused D's bio-systems to switch into survival mode, to rally against the forced unconsciousness. It would explain the tremendous loss of energy reserves."

"Which is why he dissolved too quickly," Lucas said.

Kleezebee nodded. "Temperature and humidity can also affect dissolution time, which is normally several hours. This time we're not taking any chances by letting the general capture you. Instead, he's going to see you die, but we're not going to leave any forensic evidence behind. It's going to be more dramatic. And hopefully more effective."

"But just me? Not Drew, too?"

"From what our inside man told us a short while ago, they think L took off with D's body from the grave. Right now, Drew is dead in their minds and they're only looking for you. So I'd like to keep it that way. That means Drew doesn't leave this silo. Copy or otherwise," Kleezebee said in a commanding tone, looking at the men standing around him. "Understood?"

"Sure, Professor. Whatever you think," Lucas answered. So did the others.

Trevor reached above the medical table and lowered a retractable arm with a flat, four-pronged electronic probe attached to its end. A bundle of multi-colored wires connected the probe to the retractable arm's housing, which Lucas presumed was used for the programming download. Trevor checked the contents of a four-inch gray plastic tube attached to the side of the electronic probe. The plastic tube resembled a tube of caulk and had a funnel-shaped tip.

"What's that?" Lucas asked.

"It injects the BioTex with the activating enzyme."

Trevor inserted both the electronic probe and the plastic tube tip deep into the surface of the BioTex, then entered a series of commands into a handheld device. The area around the probe's submerged tips began to glow like an underwater diver's flashlight, only this one was orange. A minute later, Trevor removed the probe and allowed it to retract to the ceiling.

Kleezebee grabbed Lucas' right wrist and inserted his hand into the BioTex. Lucas held his breath when the viscous substance sent a warm sensation rippling across his skin. He could sense the synthetic being's presence as it smothered his hand and wrapped around his nervous fingers. It felt like a freshly mixed batch of pre-heated Play-Doh as it seeped into the crevasses between his fingers. The pliable material had tremendous strength, squeezing his hand tight and partially restricting the blood flow. The DNA transmission was in full swing.

Lucas wondered if parts of his consciousness were being harvested as well. If they were, would it somehow make him less of a human being?

While he waited for the process to complete, his mind drifted farther and farther away from the moment. He considered the spiritual implications of the BioTex technology. He was sure certain religious groups would argue that his rightful place in heaven might come into question if he allowed his soul to be transferred to another being. Others might argue that once his consciousness was downloaded, the synthetic copy should be considered a sentient being and eligible for salvation.

Even more compelling was the question of replica dissolution. What would happen if the replica's handlers ordered it to dissolve into an inert state and effectively lose its self-awareness?

Would that be considered suicide, or perhaps homicide?

Drew and Lucas had both been raised to be good Christians by their mother. Dorothy was a devout Catholic, but she never forced her religious beliefs onto the other members of the family. She allowed Lucas and Drew to find their own paths and decide for themselves. "Faith is a personal journey," she proclaimed. "Each of you must find your own path to God."

Unlike his brother, Lucas had trouble accepting most of the Church's doctrine, feeling as though ninety percent of the world's population had been tricked into donating their hard-earned money to something that could never be proven or quantified.

He believed their fear of mortality was masquerading as blind faith. He didn't begrudge anyone their personal beliefs, however. In truth, sometimes he found himself a little jealous of their convictions. He could see the comfort others found in their religion, but he couldn't bring himself to take the leap. It went against everything he believed in as a trained scientist.

Regardless of his own personal views, Lucas had difficulty resolving the conflicting religious and scientific questions raised by the BioTex technology. The more he thought about it, the more his mind fluttered.

He'd known a few people who'd taken classes called the "Philosophy of Science" and seen papers with titles like "The Ethical Implications of Cloning."

Up until now, he thought it was all a bunch of abstract nonsense and a waste of time. Now he wasn't so sure but decided it was best to leave the philosophical questions to people with more life experience. Hard science he could handle, but he certainly didn't feel qualified to form solid judgments on such slippery topics.

Once his memory and DNA were downloaded, the BioTex released his hand, snapping Lucas back to reality. He stepped away to observe the transformation process.

One by one, his features began to appear from within the synthetic ooze lying before him. It was as if he were watching a rendering of a 3D computer-generated model, except it was happening in real-world space.

Drew asked Kleezebee, "How long have you guys been developing the mimetic properties?"

"Longer than I care to admit. It's been a long, slow process but the results have been worth the effort."

"I should say so," Lucas said, slipping back into his thoughts again. No wonder the professor was never in his apartment. With everything on his plate, when did Kleezebee have time to sleep? Between his university duties, his real estate development operation, managing the silo, and developing all this cool new technology, Kleezebee must've been stretched pretty thin. It brought the meaning of multi-tasking to a whole new level.

Drew said, "I assume you're using nanotechnology to manipulate its synthetic framework. Some form of real-time genetic engineering. I'd love to know more about how this amazing material works."

"Perhaps when we have more time," Kleezebee replied, reviewing a batch of paperwork just brought into the room by a video technician.

* * *

Ten minutes later, the replica sat up on the medical table, turned its head, then spoke to Lucas using his own voice. "Hello, I'm Dr. Lucas Ramsay, pleased to meet you."

Lucas studied every millimeter of his twin's face, looking for imperfections in the replication process, but found none. Even his jagged scars and dimpled cheeks were duplicated perfectly. The replica smiled at him, sending an eerie tingle down Lucas' spine.

"Damn impressive, Professor. Nice work," he said to Kleezebee, wondering if this copy was more stable than the first. If not, then Bruno would have to tackle this one, too, and put it out of its misery. "Can I ask it some questions?"

"Sure, fire away. I'm sure L won't mind," Kleezebee said.

"Do you know you're a copy of me?" Lucas asked his twin.

"Sure do. I'm a BioTex duplicate of the single greatest mind on the planet!"

Drew guffawed, beaming a toothy smile. "Oh yeah, that's you, all right. My brother, the smartass."

Lucas ignored Drew's verbal jab. "What was our dad's favorite TV show?"

"*The X-Files*," his twin answered correctly. "Dad had a big crush on Scully, the redhead."

"What about Mom?"

"Mom never watched TV. She preferred to curl up with a good book and a bowl of homemade strawberry ice cream."

"Right again. But those were simple. Let's try something a bit harder," Lucas said, formulating a trick question. "How many girlfriends have you had and what were their names?"

"We've only had one real girlfriend. Her name was Jill and she was this smokin' hot blond who lived up the street. We were fourteen at the time and spent hours making out in her parents' basement. But she never let us past second base."

Lucas looked at Kleezebee and nodded.

Then his replica added, "However, we did lose our virginity to a forty-year-old librarian named Robyn. We did it on the floor of the library. The whole thing lasted about thirty seconds, though. She ran off crying to her car and we never saw her again. She quit her job the next day and never came—"

"Okay, that's enough. We get the idea," Lucas said, throwing his hands in the air.

At that moment he realized the replica had no real emotions, no shame and no common sense. Otherwise, he never would've revealed the embarrassing incident with the librarian, and he certainly wouldn't have admitted he was a two-pump chump. Especially in front of his boss. He wished he could go back in time and never ask that last question.

"Well?" Kleezebee asked. "Are you convinced?"

"Yes, L's memories are intact and accurate," Lucas answered, thinking about the replica's curious use of the pronoun "we" in his answers. He wondered if it was a conscious effort on the part of the duplicate, or if it was encoded as part of the fabrication process. Maybe it was some type of residual personality trait inherited from him? Too bad he hadn't taken a few psychology classes during his undergrad days; he might've been able to answer that question.

Lucas slid two steps backward when the replica jumped down from the table and stood uncomfortably close to him. "Listen, L," he said, holding out his hands in a stop position. "You might be a perfect copy of me, but I still need you to respect my personal space."

"Sorry about that, Dr. Ramsay," L replied, moving back two feet.

"Don't you need to go eat a box of candy bars or something to replenish the sugar supply?" Lucas quipped.

"Bruno, why don't you take L down to outfitting? I'll send the bio-updates down when they're ready," Kleezebee said.

20

Replica L followed Bruno into the armory on Sublevel 5, where three more soldiers, each one an exact copy of Bruno, were putting on equipment vests and checking their rifles. L felt like he'd just walked onto the set of Rod Serling's *Twilight Zone*. "How many of you are there?"

"Eleven in all," the main Bruno said like it was no big deal.

"How do you tell yourselves apart?"

"We can't, and neither can you. That's half the fun of it," Bruno2 said, stepping aside to allow the other two Bruno copies to leave the armory.

"I assume the real Bruno is walking around here somewhere?"

"Actually, he died a long time ago. He was one of DL's oldest friends and the professor's been replicating us ever since," Bruno1 said, handing L a set of combat fatigues and boots. "Here, put these on while I find a vest for you."

L let his street clothes dissolve and be replaced by his own skin, then slipped into the pants of the green camouflage uniform. He finished dressing and laced up the heavy black tactical boots. Bruno1 helped him into an equipment vest. It fit perfectly. Suddenly, L's stomach felt empty and he had an overwhelming craving for cotton candy, which was strange since he hated the sticky treat.

Bruno1 checked the sights of an assault rifle, then handed it to L, along with a metal clip of full ammunition. "Go ahead and load the weapon."

L flipped the magazine around, inspected its contents, then inserted the open end into the rifle's stock. The motions came naturally to him. He knew the original Lucas had never loaded a rifle in his life, but somehow he knew exactly what to do.

Curious, he thought. *Must be part of my mission-specific programming.* He forced the clip upward, hearing a ratcheted click. "Did I get it right?"

"Yes, perfect."

L pressed the release mechanism to discharge the clip, catching it in his other hand. He held up the open end. "Why do these bullets have crimped ends instead of a projectile?"

"Because they're blanks. We never use live ammunition unless we're left with no other choice."

"Won't this be a problem when we have to defend ourselves?"

"We're not authorized to engage until we're fired upon first, and when we do, we're not to harm anyone. Besides, we have other tools at our disposal."

"Can't we just miss them on purpose?" L asked, putting the rifle down on a storage container to his left.

"Even poorly aimed weapon fire can cause collateral damage," Bruno2 said, beating the other Bruno to the answer.

"Kleezebee expects the mission to be carried out to the letter, which means zero casualties," Bruno1 added. He handed L a semi-automatic M9 Beretta handgun and a magazine full of blanks.

"Cool, a nine-mil," L said.

Bruno1 reached for his beltline and pulled out his vibrating cell phone to answer it.

L rubbed the tips of his fingers over the 9MM's contoured grip and polished barrel, waiting for Bruno1 to finish his call. He aimed the gun at an empty spot on the wall and imagined what it would feel like to squeeze the trigger and feel the weapon's lethal recoil when the round left the barrel, traveling without thought to its target. He felt invincible with it in his hands, even if it was loaded with blanks.

He slid the gun into its holster and flexed his palm and fingers a few times, trying to loosen the soreness inflicted on the real Lucas by the

BioTex. He looked at both sides of his hand, wondering why his body was registering pain from something that happened to someone else— before he even existed. Had he formed some type of empathic relationship with his donor?

He thought about his recent birth, reliving the moments leading up to his creation. He remembered how nervous he was slipping his hand into the gooey substance, right before his viewpoint shifted from the real Lucas to his current self—the copy. He recalled his first thoughts as a replica, sitting up and introducing himself . . . to himself. His head was swimming with vivid childhood memories, all of which now seemed like artificial flashbacks inserted from someone else's life.

Despite what his logic was telling him, his memories and emotions were alive and felt absolutely real. Yet he knew he was the copy, making the entire experience difficult to process.

During Man's evolution on Earth, he wondered if there was a single moment in time when an ape's pure instinct for survival evolved into self-awareness, thereby classifying the mammal as a sentient being. Was it an instantaneous change in perspective, or did Man's primordial emotions slowly develop and adapt over time?

And what about the peripheral, non-essential emotions, like laughter and humility? Did they suddenly manifest or did they have to be cultivated and learned through complex social interactions with other evolved primates?

Maybe it was simply a random convergence of factors that developed out of necessity, or possibly it was nothing more than the inevitable result of an ever-advancing intelligence.

Whatever the case, he remembered from his first semester Biology class that certain biological traits would persist over time, passing from one generation to another when survival was involved. And those that didn't involve basic instincts, including the fight or flight response, would eventually wane and become secondary, sometimes disappearing all together.

He wondered how those genetic tendencies would evolve now that he was a copy of the original. Would his race of BioTex replicas develop their own evolutionary chain of improvements? Or would they stay the same from one incarnation to the next? And how would his existence affect the rest of the universe, now that he was in it?

When he was the real Lucas, he'd studied every facet of Einstein's Theory of Relativity, pondering the complexities of time fluidity and the twisted paradox of Cause and Effect. Temporal Mechanics would cause a mental meltdown for most graduate students, but like his younger brother, he welcomed its complexities. He knew he wasn't caught in a time loop, but his current reality was distorted and seemed to be governed by a close cousin to Cause and Effect.

His twin consciousness transcended the limits of a single life and a single perspective, leaving him as both the real Lucas and the replica, but not both simultaneously. He was the true embodiment of the quantum paradox: he was both the wave and the particle. Much like Schrödinger's cat, the feline who was both alive and dead at the same time, he was a stateless contradiction, living somewhere between the worlds of theory and fact. Perhaps it was more accurate to say he was living somewhere between human and alien. Either way, his existence was difficult to quantify.

Then he realized, as a synthetic being, he had no real family and no home. His life had been rebooted, bringing him back to where it all started. Once again, he was an orphan whose passions were imprisoned between the margins of fortitude and heartache.

L snapped out of his thoughts when he heard Bruno1 speak into his cell phone and say, "Yes, send them down to the armory."

L felt a cramp in the middle knuckle of his right hand, which soon spread to the rest of his fingers. His hand turned a scarlet color as it slowly wilted like a water-starved tulip. "Hey Bruno, I need a little help here."

"Check your pockets," Bruno1 told him. "They're stocked with candy bars and other sugar rations. You need to eat one of them now." Bruno1 looked at L's hand. "And I do mean right now."

L inventoried the contents of his pockets and found a five-inch caramel-covered chocolate bar. He tore its plain white wrapper open and consumed the snack in only three bites. Within seconds, a wild rush of energy surged throughout his body, invigorating him. "Wow, talk about intense," L said, watching his malformed hand and fingers spring back to life in human form.

"I take it you were feeling rather hungry just before the deformation began?" Bruno1 asked, not waiting for an answer. "Hunger is precursor to reversion and means your sugar reserves are low. If you want to avoid a public spectacle, you should refuel immediately once hunger starts. It's better to stay on top of your sugar intake, though, and make sure you top-off every chance you get."

"Seems rather impractical," L said, pulling out a stale golden sponge cake from the right front pocket of the vest, "to have us stop in the middle of whatever we are doing to wolf down a five-year-old Twinkie." L tapped the Twinkie against the metal rifle rack, emitting a loud **CLANG**.

"New replicas take time to build up adequate fuel reserves. In the beginning, you only have a short window to refuel—just a few minutes."

"That's not much time to find sugar. Will it increase?"

"Yes, once your synthetic engine adjusts to your new human metabolism. It's like breaking in a new car, or bringing doses of medication up to a steady state. You need more at the beginning, but eventually, your body will give you more advance notice when reserves are low."

L raised his eyebrows while looking at Bruno1's rotund waistline.

"I know what you're thinking," the man said, rubbing his belly. "I have a lot invested in my rather stout figure and must be able to go for days without a pit stop. But don't forget, my size is simply an internal volume adjustment, nothing more. I can choose any programmed identity, like skinny little Mary, for example. My external shape has nothing to do with how much onboard fuel I'm carrying."

"It's more about building up glucose reserves," Bruno2 said. "Your artificial nanocells need the stored energy to maintain their volatile memory. Without it, they'll suffer a cascade failure and revert to pure BioTex."

"You mean I'll collapse into a puddle of red goo?"

"More or less, yes."

"Wouldn't it make more sense for us to wear a device that acted like a fuel gauge?" L asked. "With all your advanced technology, I have to believe there's something better than waiting for your stomach to growl, then running to the fridge to scarf down a dozen Ding Dongs."

Bruno1 opened one of the corrugated storage boxes stacked in front of the rifle rack and pulled out a pentagon-shaped digital watch. "You mean something like this?"

Bruno2 pointed to the watch on his right wrist, which was partially camouflaged by his forearm tattoos. "We all wear them. They also function as a communication device, a proximity sensor, and a bunch of other cool stuff. We'll teach you about the rest, if and when it becomes necessary."

"I always wondered about that thing," L said, drawing on the memories of his Authentic. He took one of the watches from Bruno1 and latched it around his wrist. "How does this it work? Is there a hidden speaker and microphone somewhere?"

"No, it uses a non-linear, neuro-electrical connection. As long as you're wearing the device, communications will be delivered through your nervous system and directly into your inner ear. No one else will hear it. To transmit, press the face of the watch and speak normally."

"Does everyone hear what I'm saying? Won't that be confusing if we're all talking at the same time?"

"They're wirelessly networked through a central comm system, which uses artificial intelligence to monitor and deliver communications automatically. So only the intended will hear your comms."

"Like a smart voice router," L said. "Aren't you afraid someone will steal them and reverse engineer the technology?"

"Not possible. They've been encoded with biosensors, allowing them to only be used by our kind. If it loses physical contact with a BioTex replica, the advanced technology inside the watch self-destructs. To a human, it would appear to be just an ordinary watch."

"So, basically, don't take it off your wrist or it fries," L said.

"Correct, unless you turn off the self-destruct mechanism first."

Before L could ask about the self-destruct mechanism, a balding, pot-bellied male technician in a lab coat walked into the room. He was carrying an enormous syringe, big enough to scare an elephant.

"They're here to install tactical programming," Bruno1 said.

"Okay, but where are you going to stick that thing?" L asked, worrying about his backside. "It looks like Schwarzenegger's forearm."

"In your left ear canal," the tech reported. "That's where your direct neural interface device is located."

L pushed the tech away from him. Synthetic copy or not, the injection sounded painful. "Are you kidding me? My ear? Don't get near me with that thing. Bruno, is he serious?"

"Yes. It's fine. We do it all the time."

"You just need to deactivate your pain receptors," the tech said, holding up the probe for insertion.

"Am I supposed to know how to do that? Bruno, help me out here."

"Close your eyes, tilt your head back, and concentrate on your ear's cellular structure," Bruno1 replied. "You have the ability to control your shape, which means you can morph any part of your body into gelatinous form. It'll allow you to receive the encoder probe without pain."

"Like this," Bruno2 said, tilting his head back. The side of his head began to lose its shape and consistency, turning a scarlet color. He inserted most of his left hand into the shimmering glob, then withdrew it a second later. "See? No pain," he said, while his ear and the side of his head returned to human form. "Pretty slick, huh?"

L was still skeptical but decided to try to give it a shot. He closed his eyes, tilted his head back, and concentrated on his left ear canal. He thought he might be getting the hang of it when he felt a watery sensation inside his left ear canal, but then his right eye drooped down across his cheek. His vision went askew, and he knew he was in trouble.

"Dude, your eye," Bruno2 said.

"Oops, my bad," L said, covering the deformity with his right hand. He quickly adjusted his concentration, making his eye return to its normal shape and location. "Whew, that's better. This is gonna take some practice."

"You'll get the hang of it. Go ahead. Try it again," Bruno1 said. "Only this time, try not to think of anything but your left ear."

L took a deep breath, then exhaled a rush of wind across the roof of his mouth. He mumbled quietly, "Don't think about your groin. . . . You don't need its contents melting down your leg. . . . Concentrate on your ear canal. . . . You can do this."

L continued his efforts and eventually succeeded in converting his left ear to the native BioTex. He was able to hold the semi-liquid state long enough for the technician to insert the probe and complete the fifteen-second programming update.

"Okay, you're good to go," the balding tech said.

"Glad that's over with. It's harder to do than it looks," L said, feeling his ear return to normal shape. Without thinking, he inserted the tip of his index finger and began to rub the inside of his left ear, making the moisture squeak. He removed his finger and checked it for earwax, realizing his new ability would make removing the water from his ears much easier after his daily shower. Things were looking up, he mused.

"Gentlemen, it's time to deploy. We have a mission to complete," Bruno1 told the group in a commanding voice.

L stuffed four extra ammunition clips inside his vest pockets. "You can never have enough ammo, even if they're only blanks."

"You're catching on quick, Doc," Bruno1 said.

"Oh yeah, That's right. I'm a doctor," L said, remembering the day his Authentic earned his PhD.

"See, there are perks to being synthetic. It's not all sugar and goo."

L grinned. "This is gonna be fun."

"Lock and load," Bruno2 replied.

Bruno1 escorted L and Bruno2 up to the ground floor, where Bruno3 and Bruno4 were waiting in front of the silo's entrance. Two lumbering tanker trucks with gleaming chrome pipes along their sides and one dark, unmarked sedan with tinted windows pulled up in front of the group.

* * *

Drew leaned back in his wheelchair to watch the array of video monitors in the surveillance room. The screens were filled with energy fields wreaking havoc across London, Moscow, Las Vegas, and New York City. Densely populated neighborhoods, and even entire cities, were being razed without mercy.

He'd seen enough. "Lucas, we can't just sit here while thousands of people are being murdered in their homes."

"I agree. But what can *we* do?"

Drew furrowed his brow, pretending not to know the answer to the question he was about to ask. "Remind me again, how big was the energy spike in our lab?"

"Six times 10^{31} terajoules, but I'm sure you remember that."

Drew's concentration drifted from his brother. He stared straight ahead at nothing in particular, while the tip of his tongue pushed at his lips, protruding out of the corner of his mouth. His head bobbed like it was ready to join the crowd on a dance floor.

"Hey, I know that look," Lucas said. "Come on, spill it."

"Assuming we could generate enough energy, and then somehow channel it into the dome's vortex, do you think it would be sufficient to destabilize the wormhole?"

"In theory, yes, it might work. But the energy requirement would be huge."

"What would be your estimate?"

"At a minimum, we'd have to match the energy field's total output."

"Which is six times 10^{31} terajoules, same as the E-121 energy spike, right?"

"Of course, but where are you going with this?"

"I've been thinking about taking the Big Ivan idea to the next level," Drew said, opening the red-and-blue theory notebook from his knapsack. "Remember those equations I saw the two NASA techs working on when we followed Mary to the conference room?"

"Vaguely. I think you said they had something to do with controlling virtual protons in a quantized field?"

"Exactly," Drew answered, pointing to a set of equations on page fifteen, with the letters QED written above them.

"Quantum Electrodynamics?"

"Do you remember the tremors in our lab right before E-121 vanished?"

"Sure, but I don't see the connection."

"What if NASA was running a vacuum energy test at the same time we were running our experiment? It might have caused some type of subspace linkage between the two, amplifying both."

"A QED amplification conduit," Lucas mumbled, thinking it through. A few seconds later, he nodded when the facts crystallized in his brain. He smiled. "You might be on to something."

"Let's hope so, 'cause I can't stand watching *that* anymore," he said, pointing at the video feeds. Everywhere he looked, the screens were filled with death and destruction, from all across the planet.

"You and me both," Lucas said, showing a furrowed brow.

"I'm pretty sure my theory is sound, but the problem will be the power requirements. Do you think it would work? Combining ours with NASA's?"

"It's possible. But we should run this by DL. He'll know for sure."

Drew followed Lucas to Kleezebee's location across the room.

"Excuse me, Dr. Kleezebee, but Drew has an idea you need to hear," Lucas said.

Kleezebee looked up from the paperwork he was poring over, bringing his eyes to Drew. "Okay, shoot. What's up, sport?"

"When we were on NASA's Sublevel Twenty, I saw something in one of the labs. Two techs were standing in front of a grease board working on a set of equations. I could only see part of their work, but I'm almost positive it had something to do with Quantum Foam."

"What's Quantum Foam?" Bruno asked.

"It's a subatomic storm of creation and destruction that takes place constantly inside empty space," Drew replied.

"Wait a minute. If it has a storm in it, how can it be empty?" the guard asked.

"The laws of QED say that *on average* the vacuum of space is empty. Which means there are other times when empty space isn't empty. It all depends on when you happen to look at, or sample, the empty space. The storm happens so fast, sometimes you see it and other times you don't."

Bruno shrugged and muttered, "Ummm..." Obviously, the information confounded him.

Drew tried to dumb it down a little. "Think of it like the percolating foam on top of a bubble bath, except it takes place at a subatomic level. The storm is always churning away, creating particles of matter and anti-matter, which instantly destroy each other and give off energy. Now imagine you're in the same bathroom, but it's dark, and all you have is a strobe light that's flashing slowly. If you happen to open your eyes at the same moment the light is on, you'll see the foam creating and destroying virtual particles. If you look when the light is off, you won't see it, even though the foam's still there, doing its thing."

Bruno stood there with a puzzled look.

Drew continued, "The way it works is empty space borrows energy from the future to create one particle of positive mass and one particle of negative mass. When these two particles meet, they annihilate each other and release tremendous amounts of energy. This, in effect, pays back the borrowed energy to the future. This constant creation/destruction cycle is what we call Quantum Foam."

"Okay, I think I'm starting to get it," Bruno said, rubbing the top of his glistening skull.

Lucas added, "It's like on *Star Trek*, when there's a breach in the engine room's anti-matter chamber. When matter and anti-matter meet, they instantly destroy each other and everything around them. We think this is where all the excess interstellar radiation comes from."

"Ah yes, Gene's show," Bruno replied, smiling at Kleezebee.

"And why is all of this relevant to the situation at hand?" Kleezebee asked Drew.

"The night E-121 vanished from the core, we felt powerful underground tremors. If NASA was running a Quantum Foam experiment at the exact same moment when we fired up our E-121 experiment at full power, then maybe—"

"The zero-point energy produced by their experiment was drawn into yours."

"Like interstellar light being sucked into a black hole," Bruno said with an upturned corner of his mouth.

Kleezebee continued, moving his eyes from Drew to Lucas, "You think NASA's experiment caused the energy spike. A quantum amplification wave of sorts."

"Yes, sir, we do," Lucas said. "And that's not all. Go ahead and tell him, Drew."

"Professor, I don't think it's purely coincidence these domes are using the same amount of energy as the energy spike. I think they're related in some fashion. We might be able to use the energy produced by NASA's experiment to overload a dome's power matrix and collapse it."

"How?"

"Not sure. I haven't figured that part out, yet. I'll need a better look at those equations and crunch some more numbers."

"If I can get you back down there, do you think you can show me where you saw those equations?"

"Not a problem. I have the location memorized."

"How are we going to get past the soldiers?" Lucas asked.

"By killing two birds with one stone," Kleezebee said, putting a hand on the shoulder of one of the video techs. "Where's the squad right now?"

"Ten miles out, sir," the man reported.

"Good. Then we still have time. Get them on the horn for me."

21

Even though the city streets were mostly abandoned, Bruno waited for the green arrow to appear on the traffic signal before turning left onto 22nd Street from Kolb Road. Now only five miles east of campus, he was driving the lead car of their three-vehicle convoy in the right-most lane, keeping under the posted speed limit. L was to his right, staring out the passenger's window, while two more Bruno copies were directing the lumbering tanker trucks behind him.

Bruno's handheld, ten-watt Motorola radio squelched from inside the middle console, startling him for a moment. "Rabbit, this is Base, do you read?"

Bruno dug for the two-way radio, taking his eyes off the road.

"Hey, watch out," L said, snapping out of his trance.

One of tanker trucks blew its horn three times when Bruno's black four-door sedan drifted to the right, nearly hitting the curb. Bruno swerved the car to the left, just missing a newspaper dispenser chained to a light pole. His heart was pumping full steam when he rolled down his window and gave the other Bruno copies a courtesy wave. He picked up the radio and pressed the talk switch. "This is Rabbit. I read you loud and clear, over."

"There's been a change in plans," Kleezebee said. "I need you to deploy to checkpoint Alpha. You've got forty-seven minutes."

"Roger that. Proceeding to Checkpoint Alpha," Bruno replied, adjusting the angle of the camera mounted to the dash. It was disguised as a portable GPS unit. "How's the video feed, sir?"

"We're receiving you five by five. Is L ready for this?"

"I think so," Bruno replied, looking at L.

"Excellent. Make sure you're not captured."

"Will do, Chief," Bruno said before hearing Kleezebee's sign-off.

"Are we going to make it there in time?" L asked.

"Yes, if I can keep this thing off the sidewalk."

"So we're really going to do this?"

Bruno nodded. "We don't have a choice. DL's counting on us."

Bruno pressed the transmit button on his radio. "Chase One and Two, this is Rabbit. Did you guys copy that? We're redeploying to Checkpoint Alpha. You guys continue on with your original mission."

"Understood," one of the Bruno copies reported.

"Ten-four," the other said.

Bruno looked into his rearview mirror as they drove through the next intersection. The tankers behind him slowed down, then turned left, per their instructions. "Good luck, guys," he said.

* * *

"What's their ETA?" Lucas asked one of the silo's video surveillance techs, keeping his eyes on the video monitor just below the center screen. It was streaming live from the camera mounted on Bruno's dashboard.

"Approaching the checkpoint now," the tech said.

"Are the tankers in position?" Kleezebee asked.

"Yes, sir, location confirmed."

"Go ahead. Call the press."

The video screen flickered twice as Bruno's sedan inched forward toward Checkpoint Alpha, which controlled access to the campus from 6th Street. The checkpoint was comprised of two semi-circles of sandbags piled four feet high, manned by two National Guardsmen each. A red and white-colored barricade stretched from one set of sandbags to the other, blocking the street. A Humvee with a roof-mounted machine gun was parked behind the post, in case anyone tried to breech the checkpoint.

The wide-angle camera was aimed straight ahead, out over the hood. One of the checkpoint guards disappeared from view as he walked up to the driver's window. Both the miniature U.S. flag mounted on the left side of the hood and the two-star command flag on the right were flapping in the breeze.

"Here we go," Kleezebee said.

"Too bad we don't have audio," Drew said.

"If Bruno does his job, we shouldn't need it. The guards will surely recognize his passenger, then take action."

A few seconds later, the screen showed Bruno's vehicle backing away from the checkpoint at high speed, providing an underside view of the lower concourse to the university's 58,000-seat stadium to the right. Smoke from its spinning tires hung in the air as the vehicle spun ninety degrees counterclockwise, then accelerated west along 6th Street.

"ETA to the tunnel?" Kleezebee asked.

"Four minutes."

Lucas checked the video feed monitoring the open stairwell shaft above NASA's bunker and the one in front of his apartment complex. The soldiers guarding both locations took off running, scrambling away from their posts. "Excellent. The chase is on."

"What about my mom's house?" Drew asked.

The tech changed one of the other monitors to show Dorothy's neighborhood. The soldiers were no longer positioned along her street.

"Wow, better than we hoped. Looks like they *all* got the message," Lucas said.

"What's the lead separation?" Kleezebee asked his man.

"Two minutes, sir."

"That's too close. Notify the tankers and show me the tunnel feed."

The center screen switched to a lengthwise view of a two-lane road. The camera was mounted deep inside a tunnel whose surface had been desecrated by a blanket of brightly colored graffiti. Two military tankers were sitting at the far end of the tunnel, just outside the entrance, parked on opposite sides of the street. Clouds of white and blue smoke were puffing out of their tailpipes.

"Can you zoom in?" Drew asked. "I can't see Bruno's car."

"He'll arrive in a moment," the tech answered, not changing the camera's focus.

"ETA to the flash point?" Kleezebee asked.

"Twenty-seven minutes, sir."

"Cutting it a little close, don't you think?" Lucas asked his boss.

"Unless something unexpected happens, we should be fine. Are the big rigs in place?"

"Ready and waiting, sir," the tech answered.

* * *

"There are the tankers. Looks like we're a go," Bruno told L, checking the sedan's jittery rearview mirror. The swarm of vehicles chasing him was growing larger in the reflection.

"Dude, the access ramp is coming up fast," L said, tightening his seatbelt before gripping the top of the dashboard with both hands.

Bruno waved to his brethren as the sedan blurred past the waiting tankers. He eased off on the gas pedal, preparing for a sharp left turn once they cleared the thousand-foot tunnel.

"I sure hope this works," L said.

"It should; there's no other way onto the Interstate from here. They have to come this way."

Bruno's mirror showed the tankers pulling their front bumpers together, blocking his view of the oncoming procession. Bruno changed lanes and flipped on his left turn signal.

"A blinker? Really? Now?" L asked.

"Sorry, old habit," Bruno said after a short chuckle. He turned off the blinker and peeked again into his rearview mirror. All he could see were the tankers blocking the tunnel entrance.

As his sedan turned left and approached the incline to the freeway, Bruno looked to his left. The two Bruno replicas were standing together just inside the tunnel's entrance, on his side of the tanker trucks.

"Thanks for the help, guys," he told them on the radio.

"Good luck and Godspeed," one of the Bruno copies replied.

* * *

"How many Bruno copies are there?" Lucas asked Kleezebee when the video feed showed two of them standing together just inside the tunnel entrance.

"Eleven in all."

"Couldn't afford an even dozen?" Lucas joked.

The video tech laughed. Kleezebee sneered at him.

"Sir, the sedan's made it onto the freeway and is headed south," the tech said.

"Give Bruno Two the go ahead."

The screen showed one of the Bruno replicas attaching a tan-colored object to the rear section of both tanker trucks.

"C-4?" Lucas asked his boss.

"Something like that."

"I know you want to delay the soldiers, but won't that take out the tunnel completely?"

"It shouldn't. We only partially filled the tankers. But if it does, there's always the news helicopter," Kleezebee said, pointing to the upper right screen. A circling aerial view showed the tankers facing each other outside the tunnel's entrance.

"Oh, so that's why you had them call the press," Lucas replied, nodding to applaud Kleezebee's strategy. "Smart."

"I try," Kleezebee grunted.

Lucas looked at the tunnel feed just in time to see the two Brunos crowd together, then vanish from sight. The tankers exploded into a billowing cloud of smoke and fire.

"Where'd they go?" Lucas asked, not trusting what his eyes had just seen.

"Nowhere, they're still right there," the tech replied. "Well, sort of."

"Are they using some kind of personal cloaking device?"

Kleezebee shook his head. "It wouldn't have protected them when the trucks exploded."

"Then what happened, Professor?"

"They slipped into an inter-dimensional rift in subspace."

"They did what?"

Kleezebee motioned for one of his video techs to join him. The professor grabbed hold of the tech's forearm, just above the man's watch, then held the arm close to Lucas' face.

"I've seen Bruno wearing that same watch," Lucas said.

"Well, it does a lot more than just tell time," Kleezebee said. "It contains a subspace rift regulator that the wearer can use to hide inside a subspace flap. That's where the two Brunos are right now, waiting for the area to clear. They're perfectly safe."

"Unreal," Lucas smirked. "What else don't we know?"

Kleezebee didn't respond.

Lucas wasn't surprised. He fiddled with the orange buttons around the perimeter of the tech's device. "Can you show me how this thing works?"

Kleezebee nodded to the tech before returning his eyes to the video screens.

The tech put his watch hand on Lucas' shoulder, then pressed a combination of buttons on the device with his other hand.

A moment later, Lucas was standing in a dark space, wishing he'd brought a winter coat and flashlight with him. The only thing he could see was the glow of the tech's watch to his left. He extended his hands and tried to walk forward, but couldn't move. He felt like he was trapped inside a locked refrigerator with the light off. "Why is it pitch black in here?"

"There's no light source in subspace," the tech said with a patronizingly superior attitude.

Lucas felt like an idiot for asking such a stupid question. Of course there was no light in subspace. Stars only existed in normal space. "Right. I get it. We're in subspace. But where exactly?"

"We're inside a subspace bubble that's straddling the interconnecting membrane between two parallel universes. It's like an envelope wedged into a doorjamb."

"Which explains why we can't move. We must be in some kind of force field that's protecting us from the intense gravimetric forces inside the linkage."

"Correct."

"If the two Bruno copies are hiding in one of these right now, how will they know when it's safe to return to normal space?"

"Our watches contain a proximity sensor," the tech said, holding the timepiece in front of Lucas' eyes. He pressed a pair of buttons simultaneously, illuminating a wire frame representation of the surveillance room on the watch face. Two red blips were in the center, with a single red dot to the left.

"I take it we're the two in the middle, and the other one is Dr. Kleezebee?"

"Yes, and the diagonal row shows my co-workers, sitting at their stations."

Lucas thought about calling out to Drew as a joke, but decided against it. The tech didn't appear to have much of a sense of humor. "Can you take us back now?"

The tech pressed a few more buttons on the device, instantly returning them to normal space.

"Enjoy the trip?" Kleezebee asked.

"That was pretty cool, I have to admit," Lucas replied, feeling a tad woozy. He rubbed his hands together to get the blood flowing again.

"What was it like?" Drew asked.

"Dark and cold. I felt like a shrink-wrapped sausage in there."

"Did it hurt?"

"Nope," Lucas replied, flexing his fingers as if he were playing the piano. "You should give it a try, little brother."

"No, thanks, I'll pass. I like regular space just fine."

"Did you guys develop this technology?" Lucas asked the professor.

"We did." Kleezebee nodded. "Besides BioTex, it's one of our most useful inventions."

"That's an understatement. James Bond would've had a field day with that thing. So when do I get one?"

"These watches have sensors that only allow our kind to initiate a subspace rift," the tech replied.

"So you're a replica, too?"

"As a matter of fact, I am. But that's not—"

"Gentlemen, we don't have time for this," Kleezebee said, pointing up at the screens.

The news helicopter was tracking Bruno's sedan from the air. The military chase vehicles, led by the Humvee with the mounted machine gun from the checkpoint, had cleared a path through the tanker explosion and entered the tunnel. They were turning left onto the access ramp leading up to the freeway.

"What's the separation?" Kleezebee asked.

"Ten miles. Do you want to deploy the semis?"

"Let's wait and see. We may not need them."

* * *

Bruno whizzed past a pair of eighteen-wheelers parked on the freeway's shoulder. "Can you see Alvarez back there?"

L climbed into the back seat and looked out the rear window. "No, the only thing I see is a helicopter following us. I think it's one of Channel 13's."

"Good, then we probably won't need the semis to slow them down," Bruno replied, raising the handheld radio to his mouth.

"Base, this is Rabbit. Do you read?"

The radio squelched. "Rabbit, this is Base. We read you loud and clear."

"I'm five miles from the primary flash point, awaiting final instructions."

"Increase speed to seventy-seven miles per hour and maintain course."

"Acknowledged . . . setting cruise control to seven-seven."

"So, that's it? We just drive straight ahead?"

"What'd you expect?"

"I thought I'd at least get to fire my weapon before we die," L said, holding the rifle in a firing position out of the right rear window.

"But they're only blanks."

"I know, but still, it would've been a blast to shoot it."

"Go ahead, let 'er rip."

"Seriously?"

"Sure, why not? Just don't unload the entire clip. It's going to be loud."

* * *

On the video feed, Lucas saw a long, slender black cylinder poke out of the sedan's right rear window. "What's that? In the window?" he asked Kleezebee's tech.

"Looks like a gun barrel . . . and someone's shooting it."

"Is there any way to adjust the camera so we can see what they're shooting at?" Lucas asked the tech.

"I tried, but the servos aren't responding."

"It's probably nothing," Kleezebee said. "The chase vehicles are out of range and there's nothing else on the road, other than our big rigs."

Lucas thought for a moment, then realized what was happening. "I must be blowing off a few rounds," Lucas said, smiling proudly.

"Sounds about right," Drew said in a matter-of-fact way.

Lucas scowled at his brother. "Like you'd do any different. No red-blooded American male in Arizona would ever pass up a chance like that."

Drew shrugged. "Hey, whatever floats your boat."

"One minute, thirty seconds, sir," the tech said.

"Show me the horse track in Green Valley," Kleezebee said.

The upper left screen changed to show a wide-angle, landscape view of the northern edge of Green Valley. A sprawling mountain range cut across the upper section of the screen. The rugged brown ridges and valleys were dotted with jagged rock formations. The mountains faded to black in the far distance, serving as a backdrop for a towering cement plant in the foreground.

In between the cement plant and the track's parking lot was flat, open desert. The desolate landscape was dotted with half-wilted bushes and saguaro cacti. Winter wasn't a beautiful season in the desert, turning the greens pale and dry. The right edge of the screen was filled with a sea of orange-tiled roofs, packed together like war protesters storming the White House gates. The line of houses clearly marked where nature met civilization.

"Is that the best angle you have?" Kleezebee asked.

The tech nodded.

The bottom of the screen contained a section of the track's lower grandstands. "Look at all the paper," Lucas said, seeing thousands of tiny strips of white paper littering the track's infield and seats.

A short minute later, Lucas asked, "Where should we see it?"

"Just on the other side of the cement plant," the tech answered, "along the freeway's access road."

Right on cue, a bright flash filled the racetrack security feed, just beyond the cement factory. Moments later, the flash dissolved, leaving behind an energy dome exactly where the tech had predicted.

"Nice work," Kleezebee said, patting the tech on the back. "Looks like our team planted just the right amount of bait."

Lucas wasn't sure what they were talking about but decided to wait until later to ask, when Kleezebee wasn't as busy.

The news helicopter circled around, pointing its high altitude camera at the massive dome, which was now moving away from the cement plant, traveling south. It engulfed all six lanes of the Interstate. Bruno's dark sedan slid sideways, careening out of control. It left a trail of smoke and skid marks before its inertia carried it into the northern edge of the energy field.

The helicopter flew over the dome, allowing the camera to capture Bruno's sedan whipping around. The sedan was shredded into chunks of metal, glass, rubber and plastic car debris and sucked through the vortex.

"And then there were ten," Lucas mumbled, thinking of his security friend.

The helicopter swung around to show Alvarez's convoy approaching at high speed from the north, while the energy field continued its southerly trek toward the Green Valley retirement community.

"Do you think they bought it?" Drew asked.

"We'll know soon enough," Kleezebee said.

22

"Are you two ready for a road trip?" Kleezebee asked Lucas and Drew.

"More than ready, Professor," Drew answered, sliding the theory notebook into the zippered pouch of his knapsack. "But we need to check on Mom before we leave."

"I thought you might want to do that," he said to Drew. "Inform the security team we'll be up in ten. Make sure they bring the climbing gear," he told all the techs.

Lucas turned and asked Kleezebee, "Have you figured out how we're going to get past the soldiers guarding the hole down to the QED lab?"

Kleezebee stared at the video screens for a few seconds, then turned to face his lead tech. "Twins ought to do it."

The tech picked up one of the three phones sitting on his console desk. "Who do you want me to send?"

"Seven and Eight. But make it clear I want them to use stunners only."

"Got it, boss," the tech replied with the phone's receiver plastered against his right ear.

"Twins?" Lucas asked.

Kleezebee smiled. "A pair of young, beautiful women should be hard to resist, wouldn't you agree?"

Lucas figured Kleezebee was going to use the twins as some form of distraction, but he wasn't sure how. Kleezebee's matter-of-fact tone gave him the impression that the professor expected him to put the pieces together on his own, and he certainly didn't want to disappoint his boss. "Great idea, Professor. Using twins sounds perfect."

Kleezebee opened a yellow travel bag sitting on an unoccupied section of the video control desk. "Did you remember the boosters?" Kleezebee asked the tech.

"Yes, sir. They're in there."

"Excellent." Kleezebee flung the tote bag over his shoulder. "We should pick up some bottled water on the way up."

* * *

Forty-five minutes later, Lucas got out of the Humvee and followed behind Kleezebee as the man inched his way along the outside of the Math Building toward its southwest corner. Kleezebee gave his crutches to Lucas, then pressed his back against the red-bricked wall of the structure. He peeked carefully around the corner. Ten seconds later, he turned and whispered to Lucas, "Seven and Eight are pulling up now. Let's hope this works."

Lucas looked back at Drew, who was sitting in the rear passenger seat of the truck they'd used to travel to campus from the silo. One of Kleezebee's armed security guards was standing near the Humvee's bumper-mounted winch, looking directly at Lucas. He was starting to lose track of who was authentic and who was a replica, with multiple copies of nearly everyone in Kleezebee's crew running around. Lucas was fairly certain the guard was a replica, but couldn't be sure. The silo's senior lab tech—who definitely was a replica, because he'd introduced himself as one—was sitting in the driver's seat with his hands wrapped around the steering wheel. Lucas gave his brother and the other two men a thumbs-up signal.

Lucas crouched behind the professor and leaned slowly to his left. He could see four soldiers in combat uniforms only a few hundred feet away from him. They were clustered together just to the left of the open shaft leading down to the underground NASA bunker. One of the soldiers was doing all the talking. He paused for a moment, and then suddenly the entire squad erupted into a collective laugh.

Figures, Lucas thought. Leave it to the military to waste resources guarding an open pit, especially when the rest of campus and most of Tucson had been deserted. If he were in charge, he would've boarded up the hole and called it a day.

A blue mini-van with a heavily tinted rear window squealed around the corner and approached the soldiers from the west. Country music blared from its wide open side windows, and two blond-haired women sat in the front seat. The vehicle swerved across the center stripe and came to a skidding stop with the front wheels on the sidewalk about fifty feet from the soldiers' position. Lucas could see strands of blond locks flapping across the girls' faces as the stiff, southerly breeze riffled through the van.

The two girls—exact copies of Kleezebee's beautiful assistant, Mary Stinger—stumbled out of the van, laughing and whooping. They wore faded blue jean cutoff shorts and skin-tight white tops that accentuated their identical figures. A moment later, they leaned against the hood of the van and giggled loudly, passing a bottle of alcohol between them.

Kleezebee winked at Lucas. "Wild Turkey. Bruno's favorite."

The four soldiers, now standing side-by-side and facing the girls, looked like they'd been struck dumb. None of them moved or said anything. They stood there like horny statues, staring at the twins with their mouths drooling.

Lucas realized Kleezebee was right. A pair of twins would be a major distraction—especially a pair of hot, drunk twins dressed like Hooter's girls. The squad of testosterone-charged soldiers didn't stand a chance.

"At least I'm not the only one to fall for that one," Lucas mumbled under his breath, thinking about Bruno's sexy alter ego who he'd been lusting after during his stint on Kleezebee's team.

The driver, Mary1, leaned her butt against the driver's door and waved at the soldiers. "Heya, boys," she called out. "You guys wanna party?"

All four soldiers remained silent, puffing their chests out and smiling.

Mary1 remained by the vehicle while Mary2 walked erratically toward the men, swinging her hips almost as wildly as her arms. Halfway into her journey, her ankle rolled over and she fell to the ground, laughing like a drunk college coed.

All of the soldiers slung their rifles and left their guard position, sprinting to her rescue. They encircled the girl, showering her with attention.

"Works every time," Kleezebee whispered to Lucas. "Damsel in distress."

"Sexy ones at that," Lucas added.

While the men were focused on her sister, Mary1 reached into the driver's seat, pulled out a stunner, then snuck up to the solders caring for Mary2. She fired the weapon several times, striking each of the men in succession, sending them limp to the ground. One of the blasts hit Mary2, but she seemed unaffected. Lucas figured BioTex replicas were immune to electrocution, probably due to their latex substructure.

Mary1 turned back to face Kleezebee and let out a shrieking whistle with two fingers inserted into the corners of her mouth.

"There's our cue," Kleezebee said, grabbing his crutches from Lucas. "Why don't you go see if Seven and Eight need any help getting the soldiers into the van? Then we'll head down below and see what's what."

Lucas watched the drunken killer twins morph from a pair of Marys into a pair of Brunos. He knew they were just BioTex replicas, but he was still sad to see them go.

Hot was hot—synthetic or not.

* * *

Fifteen minutes later, Lucas unclipped the rigging harness from his chest, after being lowered by rope into the open pit that used to be NASA's elevator shaft. The shaft was musty and dark, already starting to smell like mold. He heard the drip-drip-drip of water echoing from below, and hoped a sewage line hadn't broken somewhere. He didn't like the idea of trudging through raw wastewater.

Billy Ray, the lab tech who'd preceded him into the shaft, took hold of the harness and rope after Lucas slid out of the gear.

Lucas looked up from Sublevel 18 and through a swirling column of dust particles. He gave Kleezebee a thumbs-up signal. "All clear," he shouted at the professor. Soon he heard the motorized grind of the bumper-mounted electric winch hoisting the gear back to the surface.

Now it was Drew's turn. First, his folded wheelchair came down the shaft, followed by Drew, who was carrying the professor's crutches and yellow travel bag. Lucas gave Kleezebee's items to Billy Ray, then helped Drew into the wheelchair.

After the harness made the steady climb back to the surface, Kleezebee slipped on the gear next and started his descent. Lucas decided to take a step back to allow more room for the professor to land, but his heel caught the edge of a cement chunk behind him. He grabbed onto Drew's shoulder to keep from falling backward into the debris.

"Shit, that was close," Lucas said, flexing his ankle to check its condition. "They could've done a better job with the cleanup down here." He felt fortunate, though, not to have injured himself more seriously. It was slightly tender, but the pain was manageable.

He still needed to carry Drew down the stairs to the 20th Sublevel, which would be impossible with any kind of serious ankle injury. His legs were still recovering from carrying Drew up those same stairs, and the last thing he needed was a bum ankle—or any other physical problem, for that matter. With the hospitals evacuated, he wouldn't be able to run to the emergency room for medical attention.

Everything in the world had changed thanks to the energy domes wreaking havoc across the planet. At least that was the situation for now,

LINKAGE   299

assuming he and Drew would be able to set things right with a little
assistance from the professor and his team.

"How's your leg doing?" Lucas asked Drew after seeing a
bloodstain on the stairway. He assumed the redness was from the gash in
Drew's thigh—the injury he'd received while sliding down the debris
pile during their escape.

"I don't know. Can't feel a thing."

"That's good. I guess," Lucas said. "But we need to clean and
redress your bandage when we get back to the silo. Now that the
hospitals are closed, we can't take the chance it gets infected."

Drew nodded and wrinkled his nose, but didn't respond.

Lucas unclipped Kleezebee's safety harness once the professor's
feet were firmly planted on the stairwell's landing. Drew handed the
crutches to Kleezebee, which the professor promptly handed to Lucas.
"You'll need to carry these down for me."

Lucas groaned silently, realizing he and Billy Ray were the only
able-bodied men present. They'd have to do all the heavy work from
here on out, meaning he needed to prepare himself and suck it up. His
friends needed his help, and so did the rest of the world.

"Sure, Professor, not a problem," he said, holding the crutches
aside while Drew climbed on his back, piggyback-style. Drew had the
knapsack strapped to his back, which contained several bottles of water,
plus the theory notebook and a smattering of writing supplies.

Kleezebee picked up his yellow tote bag and put his arms
through the two straps, hoisting it across his back. At least Lucas didn't
have to carry the sack, too. Any more weight and he'd never make it
down in once piece.

When Billy Ray started down the stairs empty-handed, Lucas
said, "Dude, can you help me out here?" Lucas pointed to Drew's
wheelchair, which was leaning against the cement wall.

"Oops, sorry about that," Billy Ray answered. "My mind's
focused elsewhere."

"No problem."

Lucas stood still and waited for Kleezebee to head down first, holding onto the handrail as he hobbled his way down each step. Unless the professor was in better shape than he looked, Lucas knew the journey was going to be slow and painful for everyone, and he was right—it took just short of an hour to reach the landing on Sublevel 20.

Kleezebee unhitched the yellow bag and sat down on the bottom step when they arrived at their destination.

Lucas's lower back was screaming for a break, so he leaned the crutches against the wall and bent down to let Drew slide off. Drew sat on the step next to the professor. Billy Ray unfolded the wheelchair and helped him into the seat.

"Where's that water?" Lucas asked.

Drew opened his backpack and gave him a bottle.

Lucas twisted off the plastic cap and chugged it down, barely stopping to swallow. "Hand me another," he said, tossing the empty bottle into the corner. The water was lukewarm, but he didn't care. All that mattered was it contained something wet and soothing. He took his time with the second bottle, savoring every sip, while sweat continued to trickle from his scalp and down his neck. A few minutes later, the bottle was almost empty.

"You about ready?" Kleezebee asked after standing up and sliding the crutches under his armpits.

Lucas tipped the bottom of the bottle above his head to drain the last few drops into his mouth. He tapped the end of the bottle twice, then answered, "Yep, I'm good."

"Lead the way," Kleezebee told Drew.

"It's the fifth door on the right," Drew said, rolling his wheelchair forward. Kleezebee followed him, but without his yellow bag, which was still sitting on the floor. Lucas assumed the professor had left it behind on purpose, perhaps because Kleezebee was pissed at him for making everyone wait while he enjoyed his water break.

Lucas slung the bag over his shoulder and followed behind the rest of the group. He kept turning around to check behind him, feeling like he was forgetting something, but he couldn't figure out what. He figured it must have been his imagination; it had already been a long day, and he was getting tired.

The professor's bag weighed about five pounds and was heavier at one end, making it awkward to carry. As Lucas walked, something inside the bag, possibly metal, clanked with each step. He was even more impressed with Kleezebee's strength and agility for having carried the tote bag down the stairs, broken ankle and all.

Drew counted out the lab doors they passed. "Three . . . four . . . five. This is it—the QED lab."

Drew pulled at the closed lab door, but it didn't open. There was a security keypad next to the door with a horizontal card slot along the top of it.

Kleezebee stepped in front of Drew, then took the tote bag from Lucas. He opened it and removed a handheld electronic device with a credit-card sized keycard tethered to it by a ribbon-style communication cable. He inserted the card into the slot and began entering commands into the device. The professor tried multiple times to breach the door's security system, but his device wasn't working.

Eventually, Lucas grew impatient with Kleezebee's futile efforts. "Do you mind if I give it try, Professor?"

Kleezebee held out the device in one hand, but Lucas didn't take it from him. "No, thanks, I have a better idea. I need you to step back."

Kleezebee moved out of the way, allowing Lucas to take a running leap with his feet aimed at the door just to the left of its handle. His heels made contact, bending the metal frame inward slightly, but the door remained shut. When he hit the floor, he landed on his right hip, sending shooting pains from his waistline down to his ankles.

He gasped from the pain. "Fuck, that hurt," he said, squirming on the ground.

Billy Ray extended his hand to Lucas. "Need a hand, Dr. Ramsay?" he said in a thick Southern drawl.

Lucas gripped the tech's hand, allowing the man to pull him up off the floor.

"Maybe we should try it together?" Billy Ray asked.

"Good idea," Lucas said with discomfort in his voice. He rubbed his hand over his sore hip before taking two steps back from the door. "Go on three?"

"Sure. You count it out."

Lucas counted to three and they coordinated the assault on the door. A section of the metal doorframe broke loose and flew across the lab as the door flung open with a loud metallic screech, smashing its handle into the wall on the far side.

"Sometimes, brute force is only way to fly," Lucas said with pride, walking into the QED lab with a fading limp.

Three free-standing grease boards were stacked along the right wall. Their clear surfaces were covered in mathematical equations written in both red and blue marker ink.

"Are those the equations you saw?" Kleezebee asked Drew.

"Yes," Drew said, pushing his wheelchair toward them.

"Looks like they're out of sequence," Lucas said, bringing the mobile boards together end to end. He stood back to garner a better view of the mathematics.

"I think you should put the last one first and then swap the middle one to the end," Drew said.

"Yeah, now I'm thinking," Lucas said with a smirk on his lips, rearranging the boards as his brother suggested.

"Definitely some form of energy extraction from subspace," Drew said.

"They appear to be incomplete," Kleezebee said, looking around the room.

"Not only that, their cascade variants are all wrong," Drew said, shaking his head. "I'm surprised this worked at all."

"Just more of our hard-earned tax dollars being flushed down the toilet," Kleezebee said.

"They should've hired us to do it. We're probably a shitload cheaper than these guys," Lucas said.

"And you would've gotten it done right," Kleezebee said, smiling at Drew. The professor put his free hand on Drew's shoulder. "What do you think, sport? Between the two of us, we should be able to finish these equations."

"It might take a while to fix their work, but it's doable," Drew said, pulling out a yellow pad and pencil from his backpack.

Kleezebee told Lucas and Billy Ray, "Why don't you two look around to see if there's any paperwork or notes lying around? Maybe there's something that'll shed some light on the missing calculations."

Lucas and Billy Ray began searching the lab, starting with the tallest storage cabinets built into the wall to the right of the entrance door. Lucas opened the double doors and found five shelves crammed full of manila file folders. Each folder had a date written on its index tab. The files were sorted in chronological order, starting five years ago.

He peeked inside a few of them, but only found hand-scribbled notes on legal-sized sheets of paper. He didn't see any calculations. He tried to read the notes, but the penmanship was horrible.

"Shit, I thought my writing was bad. This guy must have been an ER doc in a former life." He checked a dozen more folders but still didn't find any calculations. He moved on to the next cabinet, sifting through the disorganized stack of equipment stored in the next cabinet, when he heard footsteps coming from outside the lab's open door.

"Shhhh," he told Billy Ray, who was humming an old country tune. Lucas pointed at his right ear, then at the open door. Billy Ray nodded.

Lucas was a good twenty feet from Kleezebee and Drew, who were working together in front of the grease boards. Kleezebee was closest to him, standing to Drew's left, sucking on one of his unlit cigars. Lucas used a short, low-pitched whistle to get their attention. Kleezebee turned first, then Drew. Lucas pointed at the door then held up a finger to his lips. Both men nodded.

Lucas initially thought the footsteps might belong to Kleezebee's security guard on the surface, but dismissed the idea when he heard a faint ratcheting noise—the unmistakable sound of someone cocking a gun. Then he heard the jiggle of door handles, each rattle separated by a couple of footsteps.

The sounds were getting progressively closer, making Lucas realize the person in the hall was still a few doors away. He figured he had enough time to close and lock the lab door before the stranger arrived, so he inched the entrance door closed, trying not to make a sound. Before it closed, he turned the handle to retract the latch, hoping it would quietly slide back into place when he released pressure on the mechanism. He was able to silently close the door and let go of the handle, but the door latch wouldn't engage because of the damage caused during the break-in.

Lucas backed away from the door and crouched down with his back against the storage cabinet. He opened the left cabinet door for additional cover and leaned in, using one eye to peer through the gap in the doorjamb. Next to the lab door was a fire extinguisher, which he intended to use as a blunt-force weapon once the stranger entered the room and had moved past him. He just needed to time his attack properly.

Part of him was amazed at how comfortable he was with the idea of bashing someone's brains in with a fire extinguisher. Until recently, violence wasn't a big part of his life. Now it seemed like violence was waiting for him around every turn. He pushed those thoughts aside and prepared to spring into action.

Billy Ray wrapped his callused fingers around Lucas' left bicep, and then suddenly, the two of them were in a cocoon of darkness—a damn subspace rift.

Shit, Lucas thought, *I can't help Drew while I'm stuck in here.*

"What the hell? Take me back!" Lucas yelled into the darkness. "My brother—"

"Not until it's safe to return. I have my orders," Billy Ray said.

"I don't care if it's safe or not. Take me back."

"Sorry, not going to happen. Not 'til it's safe."

"And when will that be?"

"When my proximity sensor tells us the coast is clear," Billy Ray answered, holding his glowing watch face out in front of Lucas where he could see it. The device contained a wire frame floor plan of the QED Lab with a pair of red blips in the top left corner and two more blips in the middle. A slow-moving single dot was approaching from the right.

"Look, there's only one guy. It'll be easy for the two of us to take him out," Lucas said, pointing to the moving blip.

"I told you before, not until the area is clear."

"We have to help them," Lucas said. "Give me that thing." He tried to tear the watch from Billy Ray's wrist, but failed.

"I'm the only one who can operate it," Billy Ray said, keeping the watch out of Lucas' reach. "If you take this off me, the subspace rift will collapse and kill us both."

* * *

Kleezebee looked around for his yellow bag and saw it sitting on the floor next to the wall, too far away to be of any use. When the lab door opened, Randol Larson from the Advisory Committee walked in with a revolver pointed at him. Kleezebee, still leaning on crutches, raised his hands partway above his head—any higher and he'd fall over.

Drew quickly followed suit.

"You really should've stationed more than one guard by your winch," Larson said, pointing the gun initially at Kleezebee's chest, then at Drew. He curled his upper lip in an arrogant sneer, showing his teeth like an angry dog. "I was told you were dead."

Drew shrugged, pushing his hands even higher over his head.

"What do you want, Larson?" Kleezebee asked.

"Where's the other one?"

"Who?"

"Don't try to play me. Unlike my idiot brother-in-law, I didn't buy that whole campus escape to Green Valley, not for one goddamn second. I'm sure you used the explosion as a diversion, switching cars in the tunnel." Larson pointed the gun back at Kleezebee. "Tell me where he is, or so help me God, I'll put a bullet in you."

"He's not here," Drew replied before Kleezebee could stop him from answering.

"Bullshit."

"I'm telling you the truth."

"I doubt it. From what I've heard, you two never go anywhere alone."

"Go ahead and search if you like; you'll never find him," Drew said.

"We'll see about that," Larson said, pulling out his cell phone.

"You won't get a signal down here," Kleezebee said.

"Then I'll just call Rafael from the surface. I'm sure it won't take his men long to find Lucas," Larson said, jerking the gun toward the door. "Let's go."

Kleezebee followed Drew out the door, with Larson trailing behind.

* * *

"Okay, it's safe to return," Billy Ray said, pressing a series of orange buttons on his watch.

A split second later the two of them were back in the QED lab, standing beside the open cabinet door. Lucas motioned for Billy Ray to follow him to the lab door, where he leaned around the corner to spy down the hallway.

Drew and Kleezebee were about thirty feet away, with their backs to him. Kleezebee limped slowly along on his crutches, and Drew rolled next to him in his wheelchair. They were followed by a slender man with blond hair who was holding a gun and waving it around as he walked, acting as if he wanted his captives to move faster.

Kleezebee, with his injury, was forcing the group to move slowly and it didn't appear the gunman was too happy about it. When they turned the corner at the end of the hall, Lucas recognized the gunman.

"Larson!" he whispered. "How the hell—?" He turned to Billy Ray and said, "We have to rescue them."

"How?"

"We'll have to improvise," Lucas replied, unhooking the three-foot-long fire extinguisher from the wall.

"Sorry, but I'm not trained for this," Billy Ray said, touching the buttons on his watch. The tech slipped back into the subspace rift.

"Are you kidding me?" Lucas said in a whisper to the heavens, as if the tech could somehow hear him. "Damn it, Billy Ray, I really need your help." He waited a few seconds, but the man never returned. He couldn't wait any longer. It was time to get moving before he lost track of his friends.

Lucas balanced the fire extinguisher on his right hip as he jogged down the hallway. Once he caught up to the gunman escorting his brother and Kleezebee, he slowed his pace and crept along the walls to keep out of sight until he was ready to strike.

He wondered what Larson's plan was once they reached the stairwell. There was no way Drew was going to be able to climb the stairs by himself. Did Larson expect Kleezebee to carry him? Or was Larson going to? It didn't make sense, but then again, maybe Larson hadn't thought it all the way through.

The opportunity Lucas was waiting for presented itself when he was only ten feet behind Larson. As the trio neared the seating lounge next to the mangled elevator, Lucas spotted a long, decorative planter wall that ended at a four-foot-wide cement column ahead on the right. If he could get to the other side of the column undetected, he might be able to get the drop on Larson.

While Larson was moving slowly behind his captives and focused on them, Lucas snuck around to the right, bent over and crept behind the half-wall, moving quickly to the far side of the cement pillar. He visualized Larson's speed and angle down the hallway, calculating the timing of his next move. He chose to wait for a three count, then stepped out and swung the fire extinguisher as hard as he could.

The canister caught the right side of Larson's head, making a loud metal clanking sound. The attorney was sent flying across the hallway and so was the gun he was holding. It jettisoned out of Larson's hand, landing several feet away from him. Luckily for everyone, it didn't fire.

"Take that, you asshole," Lucas hissed in controlled anger, standing over Larson's motionless body.

"Damn it, Lucas, I didn't want anyone hurt," Kleezebee yelled.

"Sorry, Professor, but I couldn't just let him haul you away to God-knows-where." Lucas put the dented fire extinguisher on the ground. "I had to do something."

"Yes, I understand. But you didn't have to do this. I had the situation under control."

"Not from what I could tell," Lucas replied, wondering what his boss meant. "It looked like you were being led away at gunpoint. Am I missing something here?"

Just then, Bruno and two other men came running out of the stairwell door. Bruno stopped short and took stock of the scene before him.

"What happened?" Bruno asked.

"You're late," Kleezebee said. "I needed you here thirty seconds ago."

"Sorry, boss. We came as quickly as we could."

"How the hell did Larson get past your guy on the surface?" Lucas asked.

"He used to be a Marine, remember? I'm sure it wasn't difficult for him to take our man out," Kleezebee said, kneeling down next to

Larson. "This is all my fault. Damn it, I should've had more men guarding the elevator shaft."

Lucas looked at Bruno and the other two security guards and suddenly understood what Kleezebee meant when he said he had it under control. "Oh, I see. You knew Bruno was watching and would bring reinforcements the minute Larson showed up and took your guy out on the surface."

"Yes, that's why I was walking slow. To buy time until he and his men got here. We had a long climb to the surface ahead of us and there would've been ample time for Bruno's team to get into position and take control of the situation," Kleezebee said, touching the tips of his fingers to Larson's neck. "He's still alive. Barely. We need to get him to medical right away. Where's Billy Ray?"

"He's hiding in a rift," Lucas answered. "He ducked out right after Larson took you down the hall."

"Bruno, see if can you raise him."

Bruno pressed a few buttons on his watch, "Billy Ray, come in. Do you read me?" Bruno motioned to his two guards to fan out and check the area.

Lucas walked over and picked up Larson's gun.

Bruno spoke into his watch again. "DL needs you down here on the double. We're by the elevator." A second later, Bruno turned to Kleezebee. "He's on his way, boss."

"When he gets here, you and he take Larson back to the silo and get him to sick bay. Leave your other two men down here as tactical support while we handle the problem from this end. But I want at least three posted up top." Kleezebee pulled out a slightly used handkerchief from his back pocket and handed it to Bruno. "No more surprises."

"Already done, Chief."

"Do you think that's wise? Larson knows we're alive," Lucas said, wondering why Kleezebee felt compelled to show compassion to a man who, if given another chance, would sell them out in a heartbeat. "I don't understand why you want to help him. He's the prick who shut down our experiment. And he wants Drew and me dead, remember?"

"You're right, he's a prick. I can't stand him, either, but it's not a sufficient reason to leave him down here to die. And what he wanted doesn't matter, now. We have him under control."

Billy Ray arrived in a full sprint from down the hall. He and Bruno each grabbed an end of Larson and carried him into the stairway on their way to the surface.

"So what's the plan, Professor?" Drew asked.

"First, you and I need to finish those equations. Then we need to find the equipment NASA used to cause the power surge."

"I have an idea where their equipment might be," Drew said.

"Okay, explain."

Drew sat up slightly in his chair. "We felt the ground shake in our E-121 lab every now and then, which we assumed was NASA running one of their experiments. It's not much of a leap to figure they were testing a massive power source. I'd bet it's somewhere close to our corner of the building."

"We've got twenty floors to cover. Where do you suggest we start looking?" Lucas asked.

"Right here, on this floor. It's the most logical place, since it's where they were working on the equations."

"Agreed," Kleezebee said. "We start with this floor and work our way up if need be. Sweep and clear, one floor at a time. We'll find it."

"If I remember correctly, our lab should be directly above the far end of this hallway, down by the conference room," Drew said.

"Lucas, you take one of Bruno's men and search that section of the floor and report back anything you find. Drew and I will return to the QED lab to complete the equations."

"Aye-aye, Captain." Lucas slid Larson's gun inside the waistline of his pants. Ten feet down the hallway, he turned around, looking past the guard who'd joined him and back at his brother. "Uh, what exactly are we looking for?"

"A Quantum Foam Generator," Drew said. "It's probably huge, like a power plant or reactor. There should also be high-tech equipment connected to it, like in our lab. You'll know it when you see it."

"Got it," Lucas said, jogging down the hallway, sidestepping the debris littering the corridors.

* * *

An hour later, Lucas and his armed escort kicked open another lab door and walked inside the dark room. The first dozen labs they'd checked weren't what they were looking for—most of them were either empty, or appeared to be some sort of animal testing facility with empty cages and medical equipment and tables. Maybe lucky number thirteen would prove to be different.

Lucas found the light switch and turned it on. "Yahtzee!" he said, seeing the immense lab. The interior looked promising. It was clearly a high-tech laboratory. Four banks of computer and other electronic equipment stood to his left. There was an enormous test chamber straight in front of him. It was made of a black metallic alloy that seemed to absorb the rays from the overhead lights and stretched all the way up to the ceiling. It had to be at least sixty feet tall.

He ran to the viewing window and looked inside. "That's got to be it," he said, hoping the guard standing by the entrance could hear him.

Inside the chamber he saw a three-story, silver-colored reactor, with four high-voltage Tesla transformer coils surrounding it. The swirling electrical coils were taller than the reactor and shaped like giant mushroom stools. To his right was a grease board with half-erased equations written in red and blue marker ink. He assumed it was the missing board from the QED lab.

He sprinted out of the lab and ran full steam back to the QED lab with his bodyguard chasing him.

"Drew! Professor! We found it," he said, stumbling through the doorway when the toe of his sneaker caught the corner of the doorjamb. He was out of breath, gasping for air.

"Great timing," Kleezebee said. "We just finished the equations. What does the generator look like?"

"The thing is huge. It has to be at least ten times the size of our E-121 reactor, and it's surrounded by giant resonator coils. I think even you would be impressed."

"Let's go check it out," Drew said with excitement.

Minutes later, the three of them were just outside the generator's test chamber, looking through the viewing window.

"Whoa, it's enormous," Drew said.

"I told you," Lucas replied.

"What do you think it cost to build?"

"A lot more than they gave us to build our reactor, that's for sure."

"I'll bet it can crank out a few terajoules," Drew said, smiling. "Do you think it'll work, Professor?"

Kleezebee nodded slowly. "With the new equations, we just might be able to stabilize the reactor long enough to generate the power stream we need. But we'll need to make sure your E-121 experiment is calibrated properly."

"Uh, that's going to be a little difficult since the science lab's been completely destroyed, Professor," Lucas said. "And we certainly don't have another eighteen months to build a new reactor."

"You won't need to."

"What do you mean?"

"We've been working on something not all that different from your E-121 reactor. We should be able to use it to run your experiment."

"Not all that different?" Lucas asked, wondering why Kleezebee chose those specific words. "What do you mean?"

"Actually, it's a near duplicate," Kleezebee said. "You know the old saying . . . Why have the government pay for one, when you can have them foot the bill for two, at twice the price?"

More lies and secrets, Lucas thought, trying to wrap his head around the revelation. He understood the rationale behind overstating project costs to obtain excess grant money, but he was concerned why Kleezebee thought it necessary to have a duplicate reactor built and never tell him or Drew. Didn't he trust them? Was there something wrong with their design? Or was it that Kleezebee thought he needed a backup, just in case the first reactor crashed? It certainly wasn't needed for Kleezebee's BioTex, nor was it needed to power their ultra-cool communicator watches.

Then again, perhaps the duplicate reactor existed solely for profit. It wasn't a total stretch to think Kleezebee's men could've been sponging off Lucas and Drew's hard work, pilfering their revolutionary ideas to line the professor's pockets. He didn't want to believe it, but it was possible. At this point, he couldn't discount any explanation, not after all he'd learned recently about his boss.

"Where is this *near duplicate*?" Lucas asked.

"On the seventh floor of the silo," Kleezebee replied without hesitation.

"What about Trevor's control system?" Drew asked Lucas.

"Shouldn't be an issue," Lucas answered. "I have his source code backed up to my cloud storage space. All we need is a cluster of Linux servers and we should be able to recompile and run it."

"But aren't this room and the silo too far apart for the arc to take place?" Drew asked.

"Actually, we're close enough if you consider the vastness of space," Kleezebee said. "Relative to the size of the universe, they're virtually right on top of each other."

"Hmm. I never thought of it that way," Drew replied. "What do you think, brother?"

Lucas heard his brother say something, but he really wasn't listening. He was still trying to figure out why Kleezebee needed a second reactor. Not knowing was eating away at his gut like a swarm of maggots devouring a corpse. He couldn't stop obsessing about it. He had to know. "Sorry, but I have a question, Professor. Why did you need to build a copy of our reactor?"

"Sorry, classified."

"Wow, really? That's how you want to spin this?"

The professor didn't answer. He only blinked and stared.

Lucas continued, "You really think government classifications matter now, Professor? With all those energy domes destroying the world? Come on, Drew and I are about as far *in the loop* as it gets right now, wouldn't you say? I think we've earned the right to know."

Kleezebee hesitated for a moment before answering, "You're right, but knowing the whole truth might be a little hard to accept. Are you sure you're ready to hear what I have to say? It'll change your perspective on everything—and I mean everything. Including what you thought you knew about me and your friends and colleagues on our team."

Lucas looked at Drew with a rapid heartbeat thumping away in his chest. His brother nodded at him. Lucas turned his eyes to his boss. "We're sure. Why the second reactor, Professor?"

"Okay then . . . we're using it to power a trans-galactic communication system."

"A what?" Lucas said, scrunching his face until it hurt. That was the last thing he'd expected to hear. The professor must be putting him on.

"It's the power source for our subspace transmitter."

Lucas held out his hands, shaking his head slowly. "A trans-galactic communication system? Seriously?"

"Yes. I'm dead serious."

"Okay then, who are you using it to communicate with, exactly? Little green men from some distant planet or galaxy?"

"No. I can assure you, no little green men."

"Then who?"

"My people. Well, our people, actually. We need it to contact them and let them know where we are. We're ready to go home."

"Home? Where?"

The professor's face went blank and his lips fell silent, as if he were trying to find the courage to tell someone their parents had just died in a fiery plane crash.

"Quit stalling, Professor. Tell us," Lucas snapped.

"Well, my young friend, it's a long story."

"We're listening."

Kleezebee cleared his throat and sucked in a deep breath before he spoke. "I'm not who you think I am. Nor are any of my people. In a rudimentary sense, our past is your future."

"What?"

"Our journey to Earth started four hundred years from now, in another time and place. One that's far away from here in both the literal and virtual sense. Let me explain . . ."

23
April 25, 2411

Kleezebee turned off the digi-pad containing the final draft of his 1200-page historical manuscript titled *"Pathological Absurdity: An Historical Profile of Twentieth Century Politics."* He'd just put the finishing touches on the yearlong project and was ready to transmit it through subspace to his copyeditor Dorrie, back home on Earth. It would be the second hyper-novel he'd published in as many years. He hoped his new exposition would be better received by the critics than the first.

He leaned back in his easy chair, rubbed his eyes, and then stretched out his arms until he heard the bones in his elbows pop. It was almost time for his duty shift to begin on the bridge, but he felt lethargic and stiff from sitting and reading for so long. He knew he needed to get into the sonic shower to wake himself up, but decided to remain in his chair a few more minutes to enjoy the spectacular view of the galaxy streaming by his quarters at faster-than-light speed. He'd earned the extra break; it had been a grueling six months in deep space. His eyes went into a million-mile stare as the stars sped by in long streaks—a sky full of shooting stars, he thought—a child's dream.

He propped his feet up on the leather ottoman with his hands behind his head, then called out to the computer, "Stella? Music, please."

"Specify source and volume," the computer responded.

"Why break with tradition? Let's go with Paradise Theatre, track three. Volume ten, as usual."

"One moment, Captain."

He closed his eyes and sang along to the lyrics when the cabin's audio system kicked in at full volume. The classic rock ballad dwarfed the hum of the ship's Quantum Pulse Drive engines, and the deck plating pulsated beneath his fleet-issued boots.

"Too Much Time on My Hands" was his all-time favorite Styx song, something he liked to play before every duty shift to energize his mind, body, and soul. His fingers tapped along to the thunderous beat as his mind slipped away to bask in the mood-altering rhythm.

Just a few more minutes, he thought—he didn't want to leave his sanctuary. Historical writing and his classic rock music were his escapes.

Kleezebee's handpicked science crew had just finished an intensive study of a stellar nursery near the fleet's two outposts in the Neethian System. They were a shade over two hundred light years from home on his newly commissioned starship, the USS *Trinity.* The ship was performing admirably, despite a few glitches with its revolutionary Quantum Pulse Drive engines, and the occasional problem with the gravity plating on the lower three decks.

Despite the minor setbacks, it had been a fruitful mission thus far, highlighted by the discovery of a scarlet-colored substance germinating in one of the nebula's molecular clouds. His team of astrobiologists was still analyzing the gelatinous material, but its bio-mimetic properties were promising. He intended to send a full report to Fleet Operations once they'd run a few more tests to complete their analysis.

"Stella, music off," he shouted to his empty cabin. "What's the exact time?"

"Seven oh seven a.m.," the synthesized female voice reported. "Captain, I just received an encrypted communiqué from Admiral Jenkins with Fleet Ops. Would like me to play it?"

"Yes, pipe it through," Kleezebee said, moving to his work desk. He sat down and moved a digital picture frame out of the way. He kissed his index finger, then touched it to his wife's lips, which activated the living 3D holo-cell he'd recorded a year earlier.

Caroline and their five-year-old son Brett were standing in front of a short brick wall along the north rim of Grand Canyon, both smiling and waving at the camera. The spectacular landscape stretched to the horizon, reaching out to infinity and beyond. The jagged rocks of the canyon were covered in a wild array of purples, reds and oranges, igniting a wash of profound memories in his head.

Few people appreciated how vibrant the desert could appear, especially when the sun was low on the horizon, showering the national monument with long, brilliant rays of color. It was a glorious day with his family in the stunning surroundings, one he hoped to repeat soon.

He sighed, wishing he could hug his son and kiss his wife. It had been six months since he'd taken command of the *Trinity*, and each day since they embarked on this scientific mission seemed to tick by even more slowly than the previous.

He'd met his wife while waiting outside the chancellor's office during his final year at the New York Science Academy. A whirlwind romance ensued the following day, culminating in their marriage six months later, after he'd earned advanced degrees in both physics and engineering. That same summer, he was recruited by Fleet Operations and rose to the rank of captain in record time—only six years.

Captain Kleezebee waved his hand over a rectangular niche in the center of his desk, activating three twelve-inch, silver-colored cylinders that rose up out of the recess in a triangular formation. Once fully extended, the multi-spectral emitters powered on, displaying a full-color, 3D representation of an elderly man's head and shoulders, wearing a red fleet uniform with five silver stars on the collar.

Admiral Jenkins reminded him of his father: olive-skinned, dark eyes, short in stature, plump, and neatly groomed, with a bulging nose too large for his face. Jenkins always spoke in a deliberate manner, enunciating every word completely, just as his late father had. And this recorded communication was no different.

"Hello, DL, I hope this message finds you well. I'm pleased to see from your last mission report that you and your newly commissioned crew are meshing well. I look forward to reading your final analysis of the Hawthorne Nebula, which I expect will be riveting. Also, congratulations on receiving Fleet approval to build the first rift-slipping prototype. It's truly exciting technology, which has everyone here in Fleet Operations acting like school kids before summer break. Keep us apprised as you run the first field test."

Kleezebee adjusted his backside in the seat as the Admiral's message continued playing.

"I'd rather not have to disrupt your study of the cosmos, but we have a critical situation brewing. Long-range telemetry from the colony on Neethian-3 has detected sudden activity along the Krellian border. Fleet intelligence believes the Krellians may be massing for an all-out invasion. *Trinity* is the closest ship to that sector, so we'll need you to change course to investigate and report back what you learn."

Kleezebee gulped, while waiting for the rest of the briefing to be delivered. He wasn't a seasoned battle commander, and if they encountered the Krellian Empire directly, he was sure he'd lose some of his crew.

Jenkins continued. "Your orders are not to engage unless given no other choice. It's been twenty-nine years since our last encounter with this ruthless species, so we have to assume they've beefed up their capabilities since then. Your ship's limited armaments would be no match, which is why we're sending the battle cruiser *Challenger* to assist. However, she's three days away, so learn what you can until then, but keep a safe distance on our side of the neutral zone until she arrives. Good luck and Godspeed. Jenkins out."

Kleezebee deactivated the vid-screen, then sat back in his chair to contemplate his next move while staring at the photo on his desk. His loving family seemed farther away than they had just minutes before. He held them in his mind for a few moments longer, then let them go. It was time to put sentimentality aside and get to work.

The fate of the galaxy was now at stake, with his ship and inexperienced crew leading the charge. It wasn't going to be easy, not when facing a predatory species like the Krellians. Hands down, they were most deadly foe the Earth had ever encountered.

* * *

First officer Bruno Benner waited anxiously in the command chair on the bridge of the science vessel *Trinity*. Captain Kleezebee was on his way from his quarters and was due to arrive any second. He wasn't sure what to make of the first-time Captain, or the ship's crew for that matter. Bruno had seen his share of missions during his twenty-year career thus far. Many of them had been filled with wondrous discoveries, as well as bloody, senseless deaths.

Deep space was an unforgiving place for the uninitiated, and many of his crewmembers were just that. But there was little he could do about it, except work his ass off to train the crew and maintain discipline at all times.

His job was simple—keep the ship running smoothly and carry out the Captain's orders to the letter, both of which he'd excelled at thus far in his career. A career that would soon wind down, once he made the decision to transition to civilian life. He'd been thinking long and hard about it for a few months now, feeling his love for the vastness of space starting to wane. Eventually something would trigger his decision to retire, but he didn't know what that trigger might be.

His eyes focused on the rush of movement heading his way from the other side of the bridge.

"Here's this week's duty roster, Commander Benner," a striking female bridge officer said, handing Bruno a six-inch Digi-stick, which resembled a 20th century glow stick, only black, with a pull-tab on the side. Lieutenant Nellis was over six feet tall, with an athlete's body and long blonde hair held back in a tight bun. High cheekbones framed a small, turned-up nose and piercing blue eyes, making her look more like a runway model than a first-year officer on a ship assigned to exploring the far reaches of the Milky Way Galaxy.

"Thank you, Lieutenant," Bruno said, sitting back in the captain's chair on Deck 1, glancing for a moment to admire the graceful lines of his beautiful underling.

He knew Nellis would never be interested in him, even if it weren't against regulations. He was an average-looking guy with little in the way of conversation skills or a sense of humor. Plus he was twenty years her senior—not exactly the recipe for a whirlwind romance. But he could dream, though, as he planned to start work on improving his courting skills, if time permitted down the road.

A man can only be alone for so long in the universe, he decided, feeling a stab of pain hit his heart. Eventually a man must turn his attention to something more profound and more important than space exploration and duty assignments.

That's when it hit him—at that exact moment—right there in the Captain's chair. He wanted a family of his own, meaning this would be his last fleet assignment. Then he'd file for retirement and begin the grueling search for a wife before his biological clock ran out of steam.

He knew time would soon ravage his mind and his body, meaning he needed to find that special someone who would have his back no matter what the future brought his way. Someone who could put up with his endless flaws and help him learn to be an attentive father and a better man.

Bruno exhaled, feeling relieved. He finally had a plan for his future and his legacy. Now he just needed to find the time and the proper words to explain it all to his captain, and then to Fleet Operations.

"Is there something wrong, sir?" Nellis asked, snapping Bruno out of his thoughts.

"No, Lieutenant. Just got lost in my thoughts for a second," Bruno answered her, using the pull-tab on the Digi-stick to slide out a wafer-thin screen. The transparent display lit up to show him the digital roster. Everything was in order. Everything but his social life, that is.

"Excellent work, as usual, Nellis. Log this into the ship's computer. Make sure all department heads are notified," he said, closing the Digi-stick and giving it back to her.

She nodded and walked back to her duty station to his right, then she straightened her posture, standing at attention when the jump pad's arrival tone played its customary four-note tune.

"Captain on the bridge," she announced to the bridge crew.

Kleezebee stepped off the jump pad next to the science officer's duty station, wearing his red and white captain's uniform with four brass pips on the collar.

Bruno and the rest of the bridge officers snapped to attention, waiting for Kleezebee to assume command.

"At ease, everyone," Kleezebee said.

Bruno stepped aside, allowing Kleezebee to sit in the captain's chair.

"Set course to one-eleven mark three, maximum speed," Kleezebee said.

"Sir, that'll take us directly into Krellian space, across the DMZ," Bruno replied.

"You have your orders, Commander."

Bruno turned to the helmsman. "Mr. Heller, come about, set course to one-eleven mark three, best speed."

The helmsman ran his hands over the navigation console like a concert pianist playing a Bach concerto. "Course laid in, sir."

"Time to the border, Mr. Heller?" Kleezebee asked.

"Eleven minutes, sir."

"Shields up. Charge all weapons."

Two minutes later, the communications officer said, "Captain, I'm picking up a long-range distress call on one of the lower EM bands."

"Source, Mr. Blake?"

"It's coming from Colony Three-Five-Nine on Neethian-3."

"Alter course, maintain speed," Kleezebee said.

Just then, something rocked the ship, sending everyone lunging to the port side. Two of the bridge officers and their chairs toppled to the floor, while sparks flew from one of the unmanned duty stations behind the captain's chair. The tactical alert siren sounded.

"Captain, we were just hit by the leading edge of an intense gravimetric shockwave," Nellis reported.

"What's the source of the wave?" Bruno asked her.

"Colony Three-Five-Nine, sir."

"Ship status?" Kleezebee asked.

"Minor hull breach on decks eleven and twelve—contained— shields holding," Nellis replied. "We've also lost gravity plating in Cargo Bay Four."

"Dispatch repair crews," Bruno ordered.

"Minor injuries on Deck Twelve, but engineering reports all systems operational," Nellis said, before she entered additional commands into her console. "Shields at ninety-two percent."

"Maintain course and speed. Sound general quarters. All decks," Kleezebee said.

"Yes, sir," she said, glancing at Bruno for a second.

* * *

Ten minutes later, Helmsman Heller turned in his chair, making eye contact with Bruno. "Entering Neethian System, Commander."

Bruno turned his focus to the Captain. "Orders, sir?"

"Slow to sub-light," Kleezebee said.

"The origin of the shockwave is Neethian-6, an L-class planet. We're in visual range," Nellis said as the whine of the ship's engines changed their pitch, indicating sub-light speed had been achieved.

"On screen and magnify," the captain said, standing from his command chair.

The bridge's twenty-foot viewscreen showed floating hunks of rock and rubble loosely assembled in a spherical shape. Other than a few dozen pinpoints of starlight scattered across the background, nothing else was in view.

"It appears the debris cloud is all that's left of the planet. Sensors are picking up substantial amounts of charged ididium-236 radiation, suggesting a massive detonation," Nellis reported.

"Didn't we just fire up a refinery on Neethian-6?" Bruno asked Nellis.

"Yes, two months ago. The engineers finally developed a method to safely extract the volatile ididium deposits," she replied.

"Someone must have lit a match," Heller said from the helm.

"This is going to severely cripple our E-121 production," Bruno said.

"Captain, I'm detecting a series of subspace distortions in and around the debris field. They appear to be localized fractures in space-time and they're drifting in space like icebergs," Nellis reported.

"Sir, if one of them comes in contact with the engine core, it will cause a breach in containment," Bruno said.

"Plot a course around them, Mr. Heller," Kleezebee said.

"Acknowledged. Adjusting course to compensate."

"Sir, should I launch a micro-probe into one of the fractures to investigate?" Nellis asked.

"There isn't time. Best speed to Neethian-3," Kleezebee said. "Bring the forward plasma cannons online."

Within seconds, the main viewer showed a blue-and-white planet growing larger as they got closer.

"Approaching Neethian-3, sir," Heller said.

"Standard orbit, Mr. Heller."

"Captain, I'm not picking up any other vessels in the area," Nellis reported.

"Cancel tactical alert, but keep the shields up," Kleezebee commanded. "Open a channel."

"Open, sir," Communications Officer Blake replied.

"Colony Three-Five-Nine, this is Captain Kleezebee of the science vessel *Trinity*. We received your distress call and are standing by in orbit to assist."

The bridge crew waited for a response, but none came.

Kleezebee repeated his hail a second time. Once again, there was no response from the colony.

"Bio-signs?" Kleezebee asked Nellis, taking a seat in his chair.

"Scanning, sir . . . none detected."

"Scan the surface for trace signatures."

"No plant or animal life . . . no vegetation . . . no structures detected anywhere on the planet."

"Could our sensors be malfunctioning?"

"Running a Level One diagnostic," she said, hesitating before she spoke again. "Sensors are working perfectly."

"What about atmospheric interference?"

She shook her head.

"Perhaps we should send a landing party to investigate?" Bruno asked.

"Surface conditions?" Kleezebee asked Nellis.

"Radiation and temperature are within acceptable levels. The atmosphere is . . . breathable."

"Assemble a team," Kleezebee told Bruno, nodding sharply.

Bruno hurried to the jump pad. "Lieutenant Nellis, you're with me. Mr. Blake, have Dr. McKnight and a security detail meet us in Jump Bay Two."

Bruno stopped in Outfitting on his way to the jump bay, changing out of his uniform and into his desert fatigues. He was looking forward to the *Trinity*'s first official away mission, something a science vessel rarely had the opportunity to do.

* * *

Bruno transported down to Colony Three-Five-Nine with six other members of the crew, and found himself standing in the middle of a vast, barren wasteland. It was perfectly flat and stretched off to the horizon.

His eyes scanned the area, but all he could see was a deep, charcoal black color in every direction. The planet's surface was completely devoid of features, as if it had been flattened and then scorched by a blowtorch of unimaginable size.

The four security officers fanned out and stood guard around the landing site, with their backs to Bruno, Dr. McKnight, and Lt. Nellis.

"Are we in the right place?" the elderly Dr. McKnight asked, repositioning his medical satchel over his right shoulder.

"We're standing in what should be the center of a thriving settlement," Nellis said.

"Not anymore," the doc said.

"I thought the colony was surrounded by a mountain range," Bruno said to Nellis.

"It was," she answered. "I'm not sure what happened here."

"Well then, there goes the curb appeal," McKnight said with a smirk on his face.

Bruno knelt down and scooped up a handful of the black soot covering the entire area. He rubbed the powdery substance between his fingers. "What is this stuff?"

Nellis tested a sample with her handheld M-Spec scanner. "I'm not detecting any organic or chemical compounds whatsoever. It's as if this powder isn't there."

Bruno raised his fingers to his nose and took a whiff. "How is that possible?"

"Unknown, sir," she replied, putting a sample of the material into a travel container.

"Scan the area for life signs," Bruno told her before blowing the powder off his finger tips.

She adjusted her scanner's settings, then held the device up while slowly turning in a circle. "Other than the seven of us, I'm not detecting anything organic within a two-hundred kilometer radius."

"Nothing?" McKnight asked.

She shook her head. "Affirmative. I'm not reading any plant or animal life."

"What about chemical signatures?" Bruno asked.

"None, sir."

"Could something natural have caused this?"

"Unlikely. There would be some form of trace evidence."

"Then it must be some type of attack."

"It's possible; however, I'm not detecting any residual power signatures or elevated radiation."

"Is it those damn bugs?" McKnight asked Bruno, eyes wide. "We're practically in their backyard."

"If it is the Krellians, they've got some new type of weapon we haven't seen before. Something capable of leveling entire planets, topography and all."

"I knew I should've packed more than a gallon of Extermin8," McKnight said.

"We should report this to the captain," Nellis said.

Bruno nodded, activating the communications device on his wrist. "Bruno to *Trinity*."

"Go ahead," Kleezebee replied from the bridge.

"Sir, there's no sign of the colony. It's just—gone, and I mean completely. So are the residents."

"What do you mean, gone?"

"I mean everything has been obliterated, like it was never here in the first place. Even the mountain ranges have been leveled."

"Did you run scans for life signs?"

"Yes, sir. However, they came up empty. There's absolutely nothing organic within a two-hundred kilometer radius, including plant and animal life. All we see is some type of black film covering the entire surface. We suspect it might be some new type of Krellian attack, though we can't detect any residual energy signature. If this is some type of weapon, it's something completely new, sir."

Bruno waited, but Kleezebee didn't answer.

"Sir? Did you receive my last transmission?" he asked, waiting again for his commander to respond.

Fifteen seconds later, Kleezebee answered. However, this time his voice was charged with energy. "Collect your team and return to the ship. On the double."

"Aye, sir. On our way."

* * *

After transporting back to the ship, Bruno changed back into his uniform before returning to his post on the bridge. When he stepped off the jump pad, he wished he'd arrived a minute sooner. He didn't know what he'd just walked into, but whatever it was, it had everyone on edge.

"Shields at maximum. Weapons hot," Nellis reported.

"Stay alert, people," Kleezebee said, looking over his shoulder at Bruno. Kleezebee's eyes were dark and intense, telling Bruno to man his position at the tactical station.

"Mr. Blake, send a data burst to Fleet with today's mission log," Kleezebee said.

"Aye, Captain."

"I'm picking up a buildup in tachyon particles, two hundred thousand meters off the port bow," Nellis reported.

"On viewer."

The screen changed to show a patch of stars oscillating as if they were being viewed through the bottom of a glass boat. Moments later, the same area of space began to change, fading in an enormous hive ship, at least a thousand times the size of the *Trinity*. It looked like a giant honeycomb with hundreds of identical octagon cells, each roughly the size of the *Trinity*. A web of yellow energy connected the eight sides of each green-colored cell with its neighbor.

"Sir, that's a Krellian destroyer, and she's on an intercept course," Nellis said.

"Hail them," Kleezebee said.

"No response, sir," Blake said a few seconds later.

The Krellian ship began to split apart, splintering into dozens of smaller cell groupings. Each cell group moved away from the others, working themselves into flanking positions around the *Trinity*.

"Captain, someone's tapped into our main computer . . . they're accessing our data core," Nellis said.

"Can you shut them out?"

"Attempting to isolate the core and encrypt the network interface—" Nellis said, working her controls feverously. "Got it!"

"How much did they get?"

"A hundred percent of the medical and historical databases, but it looks like we stopped them before they downloaded our tactical and scientific data banks."

"They're charging weapons!" Bruno reported, activating the tactical alert siren from his console.

"Which one?" Kleezebee asked.

"All of them, sir."

"Evasive maneuvers!"

The enemy ships opened fire, sending a barrage of blue energy bursts streaming at the port side of Trinity's bow. The ship rocked hard to starboard when they made impact.

"Minor damage on Deck Twelve. Shields down to sixty-two percent," Nellis said. "Looks like they're targeting engineering."

"Return fire, full spread."

The forward battery of plasma cannons discharged, sending a torrent of energy pulses at the advancing enemy ships, striking several of them center mass.

"Multiple hits," Bruno said.

"Minor fluctuation in their power grids, but no detectable damage, sir," Nellis said.

The Krellian swarm fired a second volley, hammering the *Trinity* with even more force than before. Blake's communication console erupted into fire, searing his left hand and wrist. He screamed in pain.

"Medical team to the bridge," Kleezebee shouted.

"Sick bay's not responding, sir," Nellis replied a few moments later.

Several more salvos hit the ship, each time jolting the ship farther off course.

"Shields down to twenty-seven percent. Bulkheads buckling on Deck Twelve, Section Four," Nellis reported.

"Re-modulate shields, continuing firing all batteries," Kleezebee said. "Attack pattern omega."

Bruno fired the forward and port cannons. "Direct hits, sir."

"Enemy shields still at full power," Nellis said.

The ship's communication system came on. "Engineering to the captain. We're close to losing containment down here. The reactor's nearing critical."

"Captain, we have no choice but to withdraw," Bruno said. "We can't take any more of this pounding."

The ship was hit two more times. Kleezebee sat motionless in his command chair, his eyes pinched and aimed at the deck plating.

"Captain!" Bruno shouted, trying to get his boss to act.

"Mr. Heller, hard to starboard," Kleezebee said after bringing his eyes to bear. "Lieutenant Nellis, activate the rift generator."

"But sir, it hasn't been fully tested," she replied.

"We don't have a choice. Energize it now, while we still have sufficient power. Set destination coordinates for Earth."

"Aye, sir," Nellis replied, furiously entering commands into her station's console. "Projector stream charged and online."

"Coordinates set for sector zero-zero-zero," Heller said.

A vertical energy rift began to form directly in front of the ship, resembling a crumpled white envelope being opened lengthwise in space. It grew wider and longer with each passing second, letting in bright beams of light from the other side of the rift.

"Take us in," Kleezebee shouted, just as the Krellians hit them with another onslaught. The bridge crew stumbled to the right, like crab fishermen battling a rising swell in the Bering Sea off the coast of Alaska.

"Hull breach on Deck Seven, venting atmosphere," Nellis said.

"Entering rift," Heller reported.

The *Trinity* was walloped again.

"Shields are down," Nellis said.

"Maintain course and speed," Kleezebee said.

"Captain, we've been boarded," Nellis said.

"Location?"

"Deck Twelve, Engineering."

"They must be after our E-121 supply," Bruno replied. "Dispatch security teams."

The Krellians fired again, missing the ship, but bombarding the rift's event horizon with blue energy.

"Their weapons are overloading the rift. It's destabilizing," Nellis said, right before an electrical discharge arced across the bridge between the active duty stations, knocking her, Blake, and the helmsman to the deck.

The bolt continued through Kleezebee's torso and pierced Bruno's neck, completing its circuit by connecting to the power supply installed under the base of the jump pad.

A moment later, Bruno's eyes went dark, just as he watched Kleezebee's body fall limp in the captain's chair.

24

Kleezebee woke up slumped over in the captain's chair. Water poured through a rupture in the bulkhead above the bridge, splashing the right side of his face. His lungs tried to gather in a deep breath of air, but a mouthful of salt water entered his mouth instead. He spit it out in a fit of coughing, ridding his tongue of the salty taste.

A salmon-sized fish came through the crack in the ceiling, smacking his cheek before glancing off his thigh and sliding across the deck plating. It came to rest in a pool of ocean water near the communication officer's station, flapping its fins.

The only equipment active on the bridge was the emergency lighting system, casting a dull yellow pall over everything. All the control stations appeared to be offline, including the main viewer, which was hanging off the wall, slanting to the left. He could no longer feel the juddering pulse drive engines through the floor, meaning they were offline and the ship was now running on battery reserves.

Bruno was nearby, but moving sluggishly on the deck plate. The rest of the bridge crew lay motionless near their duty stations.

"Take it slow," Kleezebee said, helping Bruno to his feet.

"Do you think we made it home, Skipper?"

"We'll soon find out."

Nellis was to Kleezebee's right, on the other side of Bruno, lying on her back with her legs twisted to one side. He could see her chest expanding and contracting, so he knew she was still alive.

"See if you can revive the lieutenant," Kleezebee told Bruno.

Bruno nodded and went to Nellis.

Kleezebee sidestepped his way around debris to the other side of bridge, where he found Officer Blake lying on his left side with his feet submerged in the water accumulating around his station. He slid Blake's body away from the rising water level, then checked his vitals. The young man's pulse was accelerated, possibly due to the burn injuries sustained earlier. He shook his communications officer, then rapped him on the cheek. Blake finally let out a low groan, and then opened his eyes.

"Easy does it, Chuck; you took a pretty good jolt. How do you feel?"

"The pain's manageable, sir. I'll be all right," Blake replied, holding up his burned arm. Kleezebee helped him up. "Orders, sir?" the man asked in a weaker than normal voice.

"Sound the emergency evacuation alarm. We need to get everyone off the ship before we're completely under water," Kleezebee said. "Dispatch medical teams to help the injured."

"Aye, Captain," Blake replied.

The general alarm sounded, with Stella's computer voice telling the crew to abandon ship.

Heller was face-down with his head and shoulders lying under a toppled station chair. Kleezebee uncovered his helmsman and rolled him over on his back, only to find Heller's face badly disfigured from the electrical burns. "Dave, can you hear me?"

There was no response. He checked Heller's vitals: no pulse, no respiration. So far medical teams had been unresponsive to hails, probably busy else elsewhere he figured. He needed to do something and quick, leaving him with only one choice—old school CPR. He tilted Heller's head back, pinched his nose and covered the officer's mouth with his own. He blew twice into Heller's mouth, but his chest didn't expand. His hands went to Heller's sternum, rapidly pushing down thirty times in succession, before blowing air into Heller's mouth again.

"Bruno, I need Dr. McKnight here now. Dave's non-responsive," Kleezebee said, continuing resuscitation on Heller.

"I'll go find him," Nellis said after Bruno had revived her. She ran past the powerless jump pad, opened the emergency hatch, and climbed down the exit ladder to Deck Two.

"Is there anything I can do?" Blake asked, favoring his badly burned arm.

"Both of you, grab what you can and get to the escape pods. I'll meet you on the surface," Kleezebee said, continuing CPR on Heller.

"Captain, I should remain here with you," Bruno replied.

"No, you need to go. That's an order, Commander. Make sure Chuck and the rest of the crew get off the ship safely."

Bruno nodded, helping Blake to one of three escape pods along the rear wall of the bridge. He pressed a red, flush-mounted switch on the wall to the right of the pod, raising its hatch. Blake took a seat and Bruno strapped him in.

The egg-shaped pod was just big enough to accommodate two adult passengers and had a seven-day supply of battery power, air, vegetarian ration packs, and water. Each pod was equipped with an on-board navigation system, short-range communications, two EVA spacesuits and a portable toilet that the crew affectionately called a *bumper-dumper*. There were no weapons.

Bruno turned around, unlocked the cabinet below his weapons station, and retrieved all three stun guns plus the four extra energy cells.

"These might come in handy," he said, handing the energy weapons to the injured Blake. He hurried over to the science station, opened a sliding panel door, and pulled out the removable data drive before returning to the pod. He handed the data core to Blake. "Keep this safe. As soon as I close the hatch, press the green button to eject the pod."

"What about you?" Blake asked, looking at the open seat next to him.

"I'll take the next one," Bruno said. "When you reach the surface, use the nav-system to locate the nearest shoreline."

"Then what?"

"Use the pod's thruster assembly as a boat motor. Just be sure to sample the atmosphere before popping the hatch."

"How will I find the others?"

"Hone in on the emergency beacons. They activate automatically as soon as a pod is launched. Now go," Bruno said, lowering the hatch until it latched into place. Moments later, he heard the pod eject.

"I thought I told you to evacuate with the rest of the crew," Kleezebee said, dragging Heller's body away from the rising water.

"I know, sir, but you're going to need my help with Heller."

"Did someone call a doctor?" McKnight asked, climbing out of the emergency hatch, carrying a med-kit.

"Good to see you made it, Doc," Bruno said.

"Damn, I should've brought my swim trunks," McKnight said on his way to Kleezebee, high-stepping through the water filling up the left side of the bridge. "What do we have here?"

"He was hit by an energy discharge from his station. I've been administering CPR, but he's been unresponsive for about five minutes."

McKnight held up his flashing medical scanner, passing it over Heller's chest and head several times. "I'm not detecting any brain activity and his lungs have been thermalized," he said, pulling the device away.

"Wait, you have to do something," Kleezebee said, grabbing the Doc by the elbow.

McKnight's shook his head, his voice filling with sorrow. "I'm sorry, sir. But I'm afraid there's nothing more we can do for him. He's gone, Captain."

Kleezebee squeezed Heller's hand gently, then bent down close to his ear. "Goodbye, cousin," he whispered, thinking of all the times they'd played Ultimate Rummy together in his quarters. "And just so you know, I never once let you win a hand."

"Captain, we're running out of time," Bruno said, seeing the water level rising dangerously close to their position.

"Where's Lieutenant Nellis?" Kleezebee asked.

"She's helping evacuate the crew on the lower levels," McKnight said. "We're taking on water all over the ship."

"All right, then, to the escape pods. Let's hope the bugs in engineering can't swim."

* * *

Kleezebee felt the bottom of the escape pod scrape along the floor of the shoreline, right before the capsule leaned forward and came to a dead stop. He opened the hatch, and felt blistering rays of sunshine on his face and a stiff breeze in his face. A hand appeared through the open hatch from the outside.

"Good to see you, Captain," Bruno said, helping him out of the pod.

Kleezebee found himself standing on a rocky beach in the middle of a makeshift camp. Stacked up around the site were corrugated containers, dozens of ration packs and water containers, two bumper-dumpers, one quart-sized glass container filled with the gooey nebula substance, and a portable communication unit. "How many made it out safely?"

Bruno's face went dark. "Twenty-four."

"Only twenty-four?" he asked, his heart feeling a stabbing pain.

"Yes, sir. Sorry, sir."

The news hit Kleezebee hard. Seventy-five souls went down with his ship. On his watch. He swallowed hard and turned away from Bruno. He looked back at the ocean, past the fourteen empty pods pushed up on shore, hoping to see additional capsules bobbing their way across the whitecaps. There were none. He took a moment to collect his thoughts, then asked, "Any sign of the Krellians?"

Bruno shook his head. "None at all. I don't see how they could've survived the swim from that deep in the ocean."

"Have you determined our location?" Kleezebee asked, looking at the moon low on the horizon. Its crescent shape was still visible despite the abundant sunshine filling the sky. He wiped off the sweat dripping from his brow.

"It looks like we made it home," Bruno said, handing him an empty, rusty tin can of Maxwell House coffee, though the label was in Spanish. "There's more trash like this along the beach."

Kleezebee was surrounded by Lt. Nellis, Chuck Blake, and Dr. McKnight, plus seven security team members, two astrobiologists, one geneticist, two ensigns, two nurses, one chef, the barber, two machinists, and one engineer—Lt. Roddenberry, whose nickname was E-Rod—a brilliant man he'd known since his first year at the Science Academy. In all, six females and eighteen males had made it out alive.

"Are we picking up any radio chatter?" Kleezebee asked Bruno.

"Nothing on standard Fleet frequencies. But we're receiving several broadcasts on the lower AM band. Most are in Spanish, but we did find a faint signal in English."

"Let's hear it."

Bruno played the broadcast on the portable comm unit.

". . . more following today's top stories. *Casino Royale*'s premiere makes a splash with Sean Connery at the helm. *Surveyor 3* successfully lands on the moon after historic three-day trek. Violent war protests break out in San Francisco over recent U.S. bombings in Haiphong. The Beatles sign a contract to stay together for ten more years. Two thousand Red Sox fans burned alive when gas main erupts and levels Fenway Park."

"That's enough, turn it off."

"What do you think, Skipper? You're the history buff."

"You're right, we're on Earth. April, sixty-seven by the sounds of it. I'd say we're probably in Mexico, given the excessive heat and the Spanish broadcasts."

"*Nineteen* sixty-seven? As in the past?"

"Yes, it appears so."

"How?"

"Perhaps when the Krellians fired on the rift's event horizon, their weapons somehow ruptured the fabric of subspace, sending us back in time," Nellis answered.

"But I thought time travel wasn't possible," Bruno said.

"It's not. It's simply a myth started by a few over-imaginative science fiction authors of the twentieth century. Einstein was proven wrong in twenty-one eighty-seven when E-121 was first discovered and we used it to power our engines close to light speeds. Time does not slow down when you approach light speed, it simply shudders, like a three-legged table in an earthquake. What has already transpired cannot be undone."

"But the radio broadcast?" Nellis asked.

"It may be a fake," Bruno said.

"Or we're not on Earth," Nellis added. "We might be picking up an ancient radio signal that has traveled from Earth, arriving here four hundred years later. However, that would also mean someone went to all the trouble to fake the rubbish along the beach, too. That seems unlikely."

"What do you think, Skip?" Bruno asked Kleezebee.

The captain bent down and picked up a crumpled sheet of heavy-bond paper buried in the loose sand. He wiped off the paper and read its contents aloud. "Playboy . . . February, nineteen sixty-seven . . . Kim Farber . . . Playmate of the Month." He tossed the paper aside. "I don't know how, but I'm pretty damn sure we're on Earth. But a couple of things concern me . . . David Niven was the star of *Casino Royale*, not Sean Connery, and I don't remember reading about a deadly gas explosion at Fenway Park in nineteen sixty-seven."

"Orders, sir?" Nellis asked.

Kleezebee didn't respond. He couldn't stop thinking about the 3D holo-cell of his wife and son at the Grand Canyon, now buried deep at the bottom of the ocean. Half a mile down, and a lifetime away.

"Captain?" Nellis asked again.

Kleezebee snapped out of his trance. "Let's set up camp for the night and see if any more survivors make their way here. We've got about an hour or so before sunset, so let's get to it. We'll head inland in the morning to find the nearest city."

"Aye, sir," several members of the crew said in unison, before walking away.

Kleezebee grabbed one of the security team members by the elbow. "Lieutenant, establish a secure perimeter at fifty meters, and rotate your guards in three-hour shifts. Pull in some of the other men if you need to fill shifts."

"Roger that," the lieutenant replied.

"E-Rod, do you have a moment?" Kleezebee asked his longtime friend, looking to the rear of the crowd.

The engineer stepped forward.

Kleezebee put his right arm across the back of Roddenberry's shoulders. "Eugene, I need you to scuttle the pods before we leave tomorrow, so make sure you've cannibalized whatever you can from them tonight. We'll also need the emergency beacons deactivated. We don't want any unfriendlies salvaging our equipment."

"You got it, DL."

* * *

Just after sunrise the following morning, Kleezebee woke up to the sound of a donkey braying in the distance. He rolled over in the sand, sat up, and looked inland. A short Hispanic man wearing a wide-brimmed straw hat, a dirty long-sleeved shirt, and gray slacks was leading a pack mule down the dirt path to their base camp. His dark brown face was almost as weathered as his prehistoric leather sandals, looking as though he'd spent every moment of his life under a heat lamp.

"*Hola muchachos,*" the man shouted in a friendly voice, grinning from ear to ear. His dark eyes beamed with youthful mischief, despite his obvious age.

Kleezebee sprang to his feet and rushed over to the visitor. Kleezebee's security detail was only a few steps behind him. The captain stopped a few feet away from the man when a waft of body odor hit his senses. The Spanish-speaking man smelled as if he hadn't bathed in weeks. "Do you speak English?"

"*Sí, señor.* I speak very much *Engleesh.*"

"Can you tell me where we are?"

"You are on a beach, *mi amigo.*"

Kleezebee tried not to laugh, but couldn't stop himself. "Not what I meant. Is there a city nearby?"

"*Sí.* Very much close." The man held out his hand and shook it, palm up. "For five dollars American, I will take you."

One of Kleezebee's soldiers pressed the barrel of his stunner pistol to the Mexican's temple. "How about you just tell us where it is?"

The man pointed inland to the north. "Chicxulub. Two kilometers."

"Thank you," Kleezebee said, pulling the guard's hand down and away from the visitor's head. "What's your name?"

"Jose Cesar Enrique Humberto Ramirez," the man answered, pulling out a colorful Mexican blanket and a necklace from one of his donkey's packs. "You need blanket? Only two dollars."

"No, thanks."

"I like you, Gringo, how about one dollar?" the peddler asked, pressing the blanket close to Kleezebee's face. It smelled of donkey and sweat. Kleezebee turned his head, pushing it away.

"What about necklace? It was *mi esposa's.* Real turquoise. Good deal. Only one dollar."

"No, but I'd be interested in your donkey and packs. We'll need them for our long trip home. How much?"

"For you, *mi amigo,* I make you good deal. One hundred dollars," Jose said. "I give you blanket and necklace. No charge."

Again, the soldier put the stunner to Jose's head.

"How about ten dollars," Jose said without hesitation, his eyebrows raised and face filled with nervousness.

"We don't have any money. How about a trade?"

Jose pointed at the soldier's weapon. "*Sí, señor.* The pistola?"

"No. Not the pistol. Pick something else. We have food, water, and supplies."

"I very much like the watch," he said, staring at Bruno's wrist.

"Deal," Kleezebee said, not hesitating. He motioned for Bruno to give up his watch. Bruno took it off and gave it to Jose.

Jose slipped his hand through the twist wristband. "*Gracias, señor. Muy bueno.*" He stood silent for at least a minute, playing with the buttons around its perimeter.

"You should probably be on your way now," Kleezebee said, ushering the man gently with his hand.

Jose smiled, took off his straw hat, bowed quickly, then turned around and walked back down the path, leaving his mule, trinkets, and packs behind.

Kleezebee waited for the man to disappear over the shallow rise just beyond the end of beach, then went and sat next to Bruno and E-Rod near the campfire, rubbing his hands above the flames. "We're going to need cash if we plan on surviving in this time period."

E-Rod flicked a coal over with a stick. He pushed it to the middle of the crackling fire. "I suppose a rescue is impossible."

Kleezebee shook his head. "Nobody knows where we are—or when we are, for that matter. No, I'm afraid we're stuck here for a while, until we can figure out a way home."

"Orders, Skipper?" Bruno asked.

"You, E-Rod, and I will walk into town to see if we can barter for transportation or additional mules. It's a long way home to the U.S."

The donkey let out several snot-filled brays just behind Kleezebee. The animal nudged him in the back of the neck, twice, with its soggy nose. "Anybody know what we're supposed to feed this thing?"

Bruno laughed. "I don't think the ration bars are going to cut it, boss."

25

"Wow, it must have been hard, not seeing your family for such a long time," Drew said without a hint of disbelief after Kleezebee's whopper of a story.

"Are you kidding me?" Lucas said to Drew, wondering why his brother wasn't reacting to what they'd just heard.

"What?" Drew replied with a surprised look on his face.

"You believe all that shit?"

"Sure, why not?"

"I know you're skeptical, but what I just told you is the truth," Kleezebee said.

"Sorry, Professor, but it's a little hard to swallow."

"Trust me, it's all true. Every word of it. Why would I make up something like that?"

Lucas shook his head and shrugged. "So now what? Are we supposed to call you Captain Kleezebee?"

"No, I'm still the same old professor you've always known. Nothing's changed except now you know where I'm from."

Lucas didn't respond. How could he? Everything he thought he knew about his mentor was complete fiction. His perception of reality had been shaken to its very core and he needed a few minutes to reassess the situation. It was nearly incomprehensible that his bearded, low-key, flannel-wearing advisor was really a starship captain from the future.

Then there was the whole E-Rod thing, suggesting the famous mastermind behind the *Star Trek* franchise, Gene Roddenberry, didn't just invent the mythology of the popular show, he'd actually lived it. It was where he got all the ideas—from Kleezebee's future.

Lucas took a few seconds to run through it again in his mind, then gave in to the insanity of it all. The whole story was so preposterous, it must be true. What else could it be, other than the truth?

"So what happened after the trip into Chicxulub?" Drew asked.

"We made our way across the Mexican desert and entered the United States. Fortunately, for us, crossing the U.S. border in Nogales was much easier back then, and we were able to get our people and supplies into the country without too much hassle. We entered southern Arizona, found jobs in Tucson, and settled into our new lives. It took a while, but eventually everyone accepted the fact we weren't going home anytime soon."

"I can imagine," Drew said, nodding.

Kleezebee continued. "Some of them paired off and started new families, while others married women from this version of Earth. I still held out hope we'd someday return home, so I never remarried. Instead, I enrolled in the University of Arizona and earned my doctorates in short order, then got a job in the physics department. I worked my way up from there. We've been trying to find a way home ever since."

"Since you're obviously on Earth in the past, I take it you eventually decided time travel was possible?" Drew asked.

"Actually, just the opposite. It took us awhile to prove it scientifically, but we're definitely not from your future, or ours."

"What?" Drew asked. "I don't understand."

"When we were hurled through the rift, we were sent to a parallel universe, to an alternate version of Earth. Given everything we now know, it's the only conclusion that explains why some of your historical facts are different than ours. It's clear we don't share the same past, so by extension, we can't be part of your same future."

Lucas couldn't believe what he was hearing. "Inter-dimensional travel? Really? So basically you're talking about the exact same theory I proposed in my thesis. The same theory that everyone blasted to hell across the Internet."

"Yes. That's why you needed to run your paper by me first."

"How the hell was I supposed to know that, when you keep us in the dark—about everything?"

"What paper?" Drew asked, looking at Kleezebee and then at Lucas.

Lucas hesitated for a moment, then decided to come clean with his brother. "A couple of weeks ago, I emailed my equations for opening a rift in space to *Astrophysics Today*. I was hoping to get published and generate some cash for Mom's medical bills. But it totally backfired. That asshole editor, Dr. Green, ripped me a new one on his blog. That's the real reason Larson shut us down, isn't it, Professor?"

Kleezebee nodded. "Mostly."

Lucas thought about the facts, lining them up in his head. He locked eyes again with his brother. "So basically, if I hadn't sent my paper to Green, Larson wouldn't have shut us down, forcing us to run the experiment a second time. And we all know what happened after that. So it all boils down to this . . . If I hadn't clicked that stupid send button, the end of the world never would've happened. A single email—that's all it took. Seriously, it boggles the mind when you think about the chain reaction it caused."

"You couldn't have known what would happen, Lucas. It's not your fault," Drew said in his sympathetic voice.

"Yes, it is. All this death and destruction is on my hands. I killed all these people. No two ways about it."

Drew stared at Lucas, but didn't say a thing.

"What's done is done. So let it go," Kleezebee said. "History is what it is. You can't change it. Like your brother said, you couldn't have known. Besides, NASA is also at fault here. So am I. We're all culpable in our own way. So let's move on, shall we?"

Lucas agreed and appreciated the support from the professor and his brother, though he was still upset—mostly with himself.

Drew turned to Kleezebee. "How did you prove it, Professor? The alternate universe part."

"Matter in each universe vibrates with its own specific subatomic frequency, meaning your universe and ours vibrate differently. Eventually, we were able to use that fact to rule out time travel and determine what actually happened to us."

Neither Drew nor Lucas said anything.

"Do you remember what I taught you in my Quantum Mechanics course? That the laws of physics can vary from one universe to the next?"

Drew and Lucas both nodded.

"The same is true for the flow of time. It can vary as well. In your universe, time flows at a rate slower than ours. When we crossed over, we entered your history and did so at a point that was four hundred years behind ours. That means we're re-living your version of Earth's history."

"I see. So it wasn't time travel. It was a time differential, due to the fact that time advances faster in your home universe than ours," Drew said in a matter-of-fact way. "Interesting. I never would've considered that."

"Wow, this story just keeps getting better and better," Lucas replied with a full-on smirk.

Kleezebee put his hands on Lucas' shoulders, squeezed gently, and then said in a soft, gentle tone, "Look, Lucas. I know you're upset, but you need to listen to me carefully. Right now it doesn't matter where I'm from, or how I got here, or that you sent your thesis to Green. We can't change the past. All you need to be concerned with is what do we do next to stop the Krellians before they destroy this planet and all of humanity."

Lucas nodded. He didn't want to admit it, but Kleezebee was right. Billions of lives were at stake, including his mother's, and they still had a job to do.

"So, that's how you knew what real estate to buy and when. You used your knowledge of Earth's history for profit," Drew said. "The parts of history that didn't change from one universe to another."

"To some extent, yes. We also earned substantial royalties from several technology patents we own. We pooled our money and purchased old missile silos from the U.S. government to serve as our network of underground bases."

"How many do you have, Professor?"

"Thirty-seven. All but two of them have working jump pads, which is how we move our staff and supplies around the world."

"Can you tell us who will win the next five Stanley Cups? I could place some bets and be a billionaire before I'm thirty," Lucas replied sarcastically.

Kleezebee quickly shook his head. "Sorry. There's no guarantee history will unfold exactly the same on your version of Earth. The very nature of the multiverse stipulates that there must be differences, some subtle, some not. For example, in our universe, Arnold Schwarzenegger became governor of California, and Ronald Reagan became President. Also, our Michael Jackson never went through gender reassignment surgery to become Belle Mae Watson, the country music singer."

"What happened to the real Bruno?" Drew asked.

Kleezebee choked up for a moment. "He died of prostate cancer in 2001. We used our BioTex to keep his memory and his spirit alive."

"Why is all this happening now?" Lucas asked. "It can't be simply because of me, right?"

"Two reasons. First, the U.S. Navy was finally able to recover the E-121 modules for us from our ship. We had to wait for Earth's technology to catch up before our ship's power core could be salvaged from the deep-sea trench. Once they had it, our replicas inside the Navy had it redirected into our hands."

"And the second reason?"

"You brought the Krellians here by changing the specs on your E-121 experiment."

"The Krellians are behind the energy fields?"

Kleezebee nodded. "We think so. When you changed the experiment, NASA's energy spike sent the E-121 canister to our home universe, which the bugs must've intercepted and traced back to your dimension and time. We assume they've been looking for us ever since we disappeared through the rift."

"Why would the bugs care where you went?"

"They want our BioTex, assuming they were able to decipher the data they downloaded from *Trinity's* data core. It would give them a huge tactical advantage in the war."

"Of course, that's assuming the war's still going on after all these years," Drew added.

"Trust me, it is. As long as there's advanced technology to be had, they'll never stop trying to acquire it."

"Unbelievable," Lucas said, looking at the ground, shaking his head. "We're in the middle of an intergalactic war."

"Actually, it's more like a trans-dimensional war," Drew replied. "I take it the gooey stuff from the nebula was the BioTex."

"An early version of it. We studied the sample and eventually learned how to synthesize a limited supply from alpha material we saved from our ship. If the Krellians get their hands on it, it would make them unstoppable. They'd be able to increase their numbers geometrically through endless cloning. They might even capture and replicate some of our own high-ranking officials, to infiltrate our leadership and uncover the location of our colonies. Multiple worlds and trillions of lives are at stake."

"Why didn't you tell us this before, Professor?" Drew asked.

"We operate on a strict need-to-know basis for obvious reasons. Plus, we weren't absolutely sure the Krellian Empire was behind these attacks until recently, when we started putting all the pieces together. Remember when I told you in your apartment that I'd seen the black powder once before, a long time ago?"

Lucas nodded.

"It was on Colony Three-Five-Nine after the attack, but we didn't know why it was there or what had created it. We'd never seen the energy fields, either. When the domes left behind the same residue on campus, we began to suspect the Krellians were behind the attacks. It wasn't until you uncovered the source of the energy spike that we understood how our enemy found us here."

"Basically, we phoned them and told them where you were," Drew said.

Kleezebee nodded. "When we later analyzed the pattern of the domes, we realized they were tracking us, appearing in places our replicas had been."

"Shit, that's how you knew where the Green Valley energy dome would appear. You used BioTex to lure it there," Lucas said.

"Yes."

"Can we stop 'em?" Lucas asked. "The bugs, I mean."

"Possibly, but it won't be easy. They're a warrior race of sadistic, malevolent creatures that can't be reasoned with, bargained with, or dissuaded from their mission. Their singular goal is to scavenge entire worlds, consuming their resources, their technology, and their inhabitants."

"They're cannibals?"

"No, they don't eat their own, but they do think of all other species as a food source."

Lucas remembered the pyramids of human remains left behind by the energy fields each time they disappeared. "If they eat other species, why are their domes leaving behind the pyramid of remains when they retract to their dimension?"

"We believe it has to do with your Earth's most virulent contagions, like NVL and Striallis. It's likely the Krellians detected them in the bodies of those they returned. It's probably the reason your planet has not been consumed en masse thus far. Your *flavor* has upset their palate, and your technology is of little interest to them. They are here mainly for my people and our technology."

"So your version of Earth was able to avoid these viruses?"

"Yes, those two we did. But we had to deal with a few you avoided, like H1N1 and AIDS. Trust me, it's been no picnic in our universe, either."

"What do the Krellians look like?" Drew asked.

"They're nine-foot-tall crustacean-like arthropods. They have a hard outer shell that acts like armor, but they're bipedal and walk upright. The closest analogy on Earth would be a fusion of a giant beetle and a crawfish. They have a powerful set of front claws, long, suction tentacles, a tail with a serrated-edge stinger, and they drool uncontrollably. Their appearance is revolting to say the least. And the smell—"

"Next, you're going to tell us they have acid for blood, like in the movie *Aliens*," Lucas said.

Kleezebee laughed.

Lucas wasn't trying to be funny.

"No, but they're ruthless predators who'll fight to the death to achieve their goals. They simply will not stop until every advanced civilization in every universe has been consumed, and its technology acquired."

"If you leave our planet, will they stop their attacks?" Drew asked.

"That would be a logical assumption."

"Okay then, how would they know when you're off-world?"

"In order to track us, their energy fields must have some sort of remote sensors that can detect our specific bimolecular signatures. From what we've been able to gather, they aren't very accurate, particularly during the daylight hours. We assume that's why their domes employ a systematic farming pattern to cover an entire area once they've detected us."

"Most of the time?" Lucas asked.

"It all has to do with the number of active domes in the area. When there are three or more, we believe they use a hidden signal to network their sensors together, to perform multi-point triangulation. We try not to remain out in the open and stationary for too long, especially at night. Our replicas are even more vulnerable since their BioTex signature is easier to detect among this Earth's inhabitants."

"When my replica was sucked up on I-19, didn't the bugs get their hands—I mean claws—on some of your BioTex?" Lucas said.

"Correct, but they don't have the activating enzyme. Despite their supremacy, they're not a very technically astute species. They're able to use third-party technology, but advanced physics and reverse engineering are not their forte."

"Then it should be relatively easy to outsmart them."

"One would think so, but they're very cunning and can sense deception. We've tried to outmaneuver them numerous times over the course of our conflict, with limited success. It's been quite humbling for the humans in my time-stream. The Krellians learn quickly, almost instinctually."

"They're going to find the enzyme, aren't they?" Drew asked.

"It's only a matter of time. So far, they've been thinking two-dimensionally, only consuming surface resources. But eventually, they'll expand their efforts to underground locations. Fortunately, we do have some time to work with."

"Well maybe *you* do, but *our* planet is being consumed one square mile at a time!" Lucas snorted.

"Do you have a plan?" Drew asked.

"I'm hoping we can use the Quantum Foam Generator to provide the supplemental power we need to contact our home world. Once they know where we are, they should be able to open a rift to us in this universe so we can return."

"Why do you have to contact them first? Can't you just open a rift from our side to get home? I have to assume you know the quantum signature of your home universe," Lucas said.

"We do, but they probably have safeguards in place to stop unscheduled travelers from entering their space. Then there's the problem of time advancing differently in both universes. They'll need to open the bridge from their side."

"Makes sense," Drew replied, nodding.

"Huh?" Lucas said, suspecting that Drew was full of shit.

"Think of time as flowing like the mighty Mississippi River," Drew told him. "Their universe is in the future, or upstream, and ours is downstream, in the past. When trying to swim across the strong current, it's only possible to hit your mark if you start your swim from the upstream side. The same thing is true with a trans-dimensional bridge. They'll have to open it from their side."

This was one of those times when Drew was three steps ahead of Lucas. He wasn't sure how Drew knew the answer, but the explanation did help him understand the concept. He looked at his boss. "So what do we do next?"

"You two get back to the silo and begin preparations. This time, be sure to follow my specs to the letter. I'll stay here and get the generator running. When I'm ready, I'll call you."

"Call us?" Lucas asked, worrying he didn't have the strength for yet another trek up the stairs with Drew on his back.

Kleezebee opened his equipment bag and, after sifting through its contents, pulled out a pair of Motorola handheld radios.

"Use this to stay in contact," Kleezebee said, handing one of the two-way transmitters to Lucas.

"What's the range?"

"Fifty-two miles. More than adequate. Stay on channel forty-four," Kleezebee said, digging into his bag again.

"Will it work down here?"

The professor pulled out two silver devices with a red toggle switch on the side. Each was the size of a cigarette pack with a stubby black antenna sticking out of the top.

"Place these signal boosters in the stairwell. One at the top and one at the bottom. They're battery-powered and will take care of the problem."

"Excellent," Lucas replied with admiration for his mentor's ability to foresee needs and plan accordingly.

Drew unfolded his handwritten calculations and gave them to Kleezebee. "Here. You'll need these, Professor."

26

It took a while to carry Drew back up the stairs and get him to the silo, where they rode the underground facility's elevator down to the 7th floor. They found Bruno waiting for them with a steaming cup of coffee in his right hand. Lucas expected Bruno to be chowing down a few caramel-covered treats, not drinking a cup of Joe. If Kleezebee hadn't told him about Bruno's death in 2001, Lucas might've thought this man was the real Bruno, not just another replica. The fresh coffee stain on his shirt would've been a dead giveaway.

"Welcome back, gentlemen," Bruno said in his usual jovial voice.

"Good to be back. How's Mom doing?" Lucas asked, worrying everyone had forgotten about her. He envisioned her lying on the floor in the bathroom for hours, crying out in pain. He thought it might be a good idea to get her one of those emergency necklaces advertised on late-night TV, the kind with the push-button radio transmitter built in so she could call for help. Assuming of course, the planet survived and he wasn't prosecuted for mass murder.

"Great. She's upstairs in her quarters. We just had lunch together."

"I need to go spend some time with her," Lucas said to Drew. "After I help you and DL save the world, of course. I gotta do something to atone for my sins. On multiple fronts."

Drew nodded. "Me, too."

Lucas looked down the hallway in both directions. "Where's the reactor?"

"Just two doors down on the left. Follow me," Bruno said.

Lucas held the radio he was carrying up to his mouth, then pressed the switch on the side of it. "Dr. Kleezebee, can you hear me? This is Lucas."

The radio squawked. "Read you loud and clear."

"We're here in the silo. Bruno's taking us to the reactor."

"Excellent. I've entered the new equations for NASA's reactor, and we should be ready to begin the power-up sequence within the hour. Call me when you're ready."

"Ten-four," Lucas said.

"You're supposed to say *over* when you finish a sentence," Drew said.

"I really don't think DL cares," Lucas said, clipping the radio to his belt. He wanted to say something else with a little heat in it, but chose not to with Bruno within earshot.

Bruno held the door to the reactor room open; Lucas and Drew went through to the inside.

"Yeah, it's a near duplicate all right," Lucas said, looking at the reactor sitting in the middle of the room. However, unlike in their lab, it wasn't in its own sealed chamber with a twin-door air-lock system. But it did appear to have most of the same components—the ring of electromagnets, the cold neutron beam, and all the coolant pipes, power cables, and other equipment. To the right was Kleezebee's version of the Primary Control station, with its twin consoles, video screens, and control instruments in between.

"There's the E-121," Drew said, pointing at two familiar looking metal containers in the corner. A three-ring binder was sitting on top of them.

"I'm assuming the containment receptacles are around here somewhere, too?" Lucas asked.

Bruno nodded. "In the bottom container. But DL had us pre-load the reactor with one of the E-121 spheres. You should be all set."

"Awesome," Drew replied, rolling over to the containers. He opened the binder sitting on top. "Here's the procedure manual."

"Where's the computer equipment? I need to recompile Trevor's code," asked Lucas.

"Our Linux servers are on the first floor, in the data center. Trevor's up there now, prepping the servers."

"How'd he know to do that?" Lucas asked.

"You installed the signal boosters, didn't you?"

Lucas thought about it for a second. "Oh, DL called ahead," he said, nodding as if he should've known the answer. Kleezebee must've used a channel other than forty-four since he didn't remember hearing anything on his radio.

"All Trevor needs is your user name and password to download the code from your cloud storage space," Bruno said with a hint of impatience in his voice.

"My user name is *DRLREMC2* and the password is *CATSRULE3X*. Do you need the IP address?"

Bruno wrote on a slip a paper before answering. "Trevor already knows your stuff's on Bitwise Server Group Twelve."

Lucas figured Trevor must've been looking over his shoulder when he accessed his storage space from the lab. It wasn't a big deal. The source code was his anyway. "Actually, it's Server Group Eleven. They moved me to a different cloud last week. His stuff's in a folder called Gigantor, with an upper case G."

"Got it," Bruno said, scribbling one more time on the paper before walking to the door. "I'll get this to him right away."

Lucas waited for Bruno to leave the room before speaking to Drew. "How do you think Kleezebee's inter-dimensional beacon works?"

"They're probably going to open a micro-rift to their home universe, and then send a compressed data stream through it."

"ET phone home," Lucas wisecracked.

Drew laughed. "I'd bet it's an S-O-S that's encoded with our coordinates within the multiverse."

"I wonder how long it will take 'em to respond?"

LINKAGE** 357

"The real question is where? I don't think they'll send a communiqué back. They're most likely going to open a portal from their side."

"Probably down here where it's secure and out of sight."

Both of them looked at each other, before staring at the open section of the floor right behind the Primary Control Station.

"You don't think?" Lucas asked.

Drew smiled. "We'll know soon enough."

Five minutes later, Bruno returned. He looked at his watch. 'Trevor says he'll be ready in three minutes."

"That was quick. Damn, those must be some lightning-fast servers," Lucas said.

"You ready to get started?" Drew asked, flipping through the procedure manual.

"Let's light the fires and kick the tires, Big Daddy," Lucas quipped with a military inflection in his voice.

* * *

Forty-five minutes later, they had completed the startup procedures and the reactor was humming along.

"Man, I love that sound," Lucas said. "So what's next?"

"There's a new page of instructions added onto the back," Drew replied, handing the binder to Lucas.

Lucas looked them over. "Seems simple enough. Let's get 'er done."

Drew entered the new command sequences into his console, while Lucas followed up by adjusting a few of the riser panel's instruments. It only took another minute to complete.

"That should do it. All we need to do now is wait for DL to call," Lucas said.

"Let's hope he got NASA's reactor working," Bruno said.

"Yeah, otherwise, we're all fucked," Lucas said, leaning back in his chair.

"What's the word on Larson?" Drew asked Bruno.

"Last I heard, he was in surgery, but he's expected to pull through."

"That's a damn shame," Lucas replied. "You do realize the first thing he is going to do is call the general and tell him we're alive."

Bruno nodded. "Yes, assuming his memory's intact and he's able to speak. You cracked his skull pretty hard. There could be permanent damage."

"Imagine that, a self-serving attorney who can't think or speak."

"Just goes to show you, there is a God in Heaven," Drew added.

Bruno walked out of the room without saying anything.

"I hope we didn't offend him," Drew said.

"I don't see how," Lucas replied. Then he smiled when a new string of thoughts entered his mind. "Maybe he had one too many spicy burritos today? You may have to loan him your extra can of air freshener."

Drew laughed.

"So what's your take on this whole Kleezebee-from-outer-space thing?" Lucas asked, trying to stop his own laughter.

"It's pretty wild stuff. But when you look at everything we know about him, it all fits."

"It certainly explains all his toys . . . and his cash."

"He does seem to always be two steps ahead of everyone else."

"Well, I'd be, too, if I knew the future."

"There's no guarantee his past and our future are always going to be the same. Not when we're from two different universes."

"Yeah, I know. It's not always a slam-dunk."

"It's probably a good thing he's smarter than everyone else."

"Everyone, except maybe you," Lucas replied.

Drew looked a little embarrassed when he smiled.

The radio activated with Kleezebee's voice. "You guys ready?"

Lucas depressed the transmit button on the radio. "Yes, sir. We're powered up and ready to proceed."

"On my mark, wait precisely ten seconds, and then engage your neutron beam."

"Roger that," Lucas replied in his most military-like voice.

Once Kleezebee gave his mark, Lucas and Drew waited exactly ten seconds, then proceeded with their experiment, firing the neutron beam right on cue. Both Lucas and Drew reviewed the chamber's video feed to verify the E-121 canister had vanished.

"Looks like it worked," Lucas told Kleezebee over the radio. "E-121 is on its way."

Their radio squelched with Kleezebee's next communication. "Excellent work. Go ahead and power down. I'll meet you in the surveillance room in one hour."

"Ten-four," Lucas responded, before turning down his radio.

"DL can't be serious," Drew said. "How's he going to climb up those stairs on crutches and still get here in an hour?"

"The guards up top must be helping him up the stairs."

Drew nodded. "So what do you think DL stands for?"

Lucas shrugged. "Your guess is as good as mine. Next time we're alone with Bruno, let's ask him. He probably knows."

Drew looked at the door behind them. "Let's go check on Mom while we have some time. I'm sure she could use the company."

"Good idea. Let's stop at the mess hall on the way. I'm starving."

* * *

Ninety minutes later, Lucas and Drew were chatting in the silo's surveillance room with Kleezebee, Bruno, and several video technicians after eating and then checking in on Dorothy. Two armed guards had just joined them, taking positions on either side of the elevator doors. Energy domes were still terrorizing the planet, filling the video screens with scenes of destruction and mayhem.

"This had better work; we're running out of time," Lucas said, haunted by the activity on the screens. Even though Drew and Kleezebee wanted him to let the guilt go, he couldn't. It was staring him in the face and he knew it would follow him for the rest of his life.

"How long will it take for your people to answer, Professor?" Drew asked.

"It all depends on their ability to decrypt my message and follow the instructions I sent them."

"What did you tell 'em?" Lucas asked.

"I gave them the exact spatial coordinates of this room, as well as my equations."

"Equations?"

"To open the bridge from their side. When we were marooned on Earth, we had only just begun to explore the possibilities of the new rift-slipping technology. I continued to refine the equations here, but we have no way to know if our people back home have done so as well. The equations I sent will ensure they have what they need to make this happen."

"Assuming they won't need some time to build the equipment they need to open the rift. You might be stuck here for a while longer."

"Certainly a possibility."

"Maybe they've spent the past fifty years perfecting the technology on their own and building the hardware."

"If that's true, all they needed to know was that we're still alive, and our location in the multiverse."

* * *

Four hours later, Lucas was leaning back in his chair, watching the video screens, when he nodded off for a second. His nose snorted once, waking him up. He looked around to see if anyone noticed. Everyone seemed to be focused on other things and nobody was looking at him.

He stood up and walked briskly around the room, swinging his arms to get the blood flowing. He needed caffeine. "I'm going to run down to the mess hall and grab a soda. Drew, you want one?"

Drew nodded.

"Anyone else? Coffee? Soda? Bagel?" Lucas asked.

Both Bruno and Kleezebee declined.

The video techs ignored him.

As he walked to the elevator, his shadow suddenly appeared ahead of him and started jiggling along the back wall, jumping from one place to another with no predictable pattern. At the same time, Lucas noticed the look in the guards' eyes changed, as if something had caught their attention. The men leaned to the side and looked past him as he approached the elevator.

Lucas turned around to see what they were looking at and saw a flickering bright light near the center of the room. It resembled a tiny lightning storm, maybe six inches wide, and it was expanding gradually.

"Guys!" Lucas yelled, pointing at the phenomenon. Kleezebee and Bruno turned to face him, as did Drew, whose eyes seemed to grow to the size of ping-pong balls.

The security guards ran past Lucas with their weapons drawn.

Kleezebee scrambled around from the far side of the light and held out his arms. "Stand down," he told his guards. "They're our friends."

The security guards lowered their guns and moved to the right of Kleezebee, who was now standing on crutches a few feet in front of the light. Bruno slipped between the guards and Kleezebee, while the video techs got up from their stations and waited to the far right of the security guards. They all seemed eager to greet their long-lost brethren.

Lucas moved to the left of Kleezebee and put his hand on his mentor's shoulder as a gesture of solidarity.

Kleezebee looked at him and smiled.

Lucas nodded as Drew rolled in next to him, on his left.

The portal, now six feet in diameter, seemed to stabilize as its oscillating light rays slowed their pace. A trio of green laser beams appeared from the rift's center, spreading out horizontally across the elevator doors.

"Don't be alarmed, they're just following safety protocols and scanning the area," Kleezebee said.

The beams danced independently around the room, like spotlights piercing the night sky above a Hollywood movie premiere. Their pattern seemed random, moving quickly in multiple directions, until every inch of the surveillance room had been mapped. Then they vanished.

"Here we go," Bruno said with excitement in his words.

Fifteen seconds later, murky silhouettes of three tiny figures began to take shape at the center of the portal, as if they'd just stepped into view at the far end of a giant funnel.

The figures moved forward, toward the portal's event horizon, slowly growing in size. The figures thickened and solidified with each passing second. Even though they were no longer hazy shadows, Lucas still couldn't make out much in the way of detail. Their heads were larger than he expected, perhaps because they were wearing spacesuits or helmets of some kind, and it looked like they were carrying something in their hands.

Lucas looked at Kleezebee and then Bruno. Both men seemed to be mesmerized with anticipation, each smiling like a groom-to-be, enjoying his last night of freedom at a local strip club. Lucas was proud to be sharing this moment with his friends, who had toiled for decades to reach this epic milestone.

It was too bad History hadn't been invited to this reunion. If it had, Lucas' name would've been forever etched into the annals of time for something positive and historic, never to be forgotten. But he knew that wouldn't be his future. His would be one of shame and persecution for being the asshole who brought the Krellians and their energy domes to Earth in the first place.

Lucas turned off the self-pity party in his head and turned his focus to his mentor. He wondered what Kleezebee was thinking right now. He couldn't imagine what it was like for the professor to be without his wife and son all these years, dreaming of them and longing to hold them close again.

Would they be waiting for him on the other side with loving smiles and open arms?

What if they weren't? What if Caroline was dead or had remarried?

Would getting his people home be enough for Kleezebee, or would it tear his guts out, leaving him a shell of a man?

Drew was sitting next to Lucas' hip in his wheelchair, looking like a kid waiting for a hot fudge sundae to be delivered, completely oblivious to the complexities of Kleezebee's homecoming. Drew was a glass-half-full kind of person, always looking on the bright side, always expecting things to work out.

He admired his little brother for having that type of blind faith in the unexpected, but he wasn't wired that way. Lucas dealt with life's twisted sense of humor by planning for the worst and hoping for the best. It might seem like an overly simple concept to some, but it allowed him to sleep at night. Especially now, with all the blood on his hands. Fate had a funny way of finding him, often with harsh results.

Lucas looked back at the portal just in time to see the visitors stepping through to his universe. He gasped and his chest tightened forcefully when he realized what had just came through wasn't human. He wanted to run for cover, but his feet wouldn't move.

In an instant, his brain recorded what his eyes were seeing: three nine-foot tall creatures had arrived, each with a pair of giant claw-like appendages extended out in front. Their bodies were burnt orange in color and made of stacked layers of donut-shaped modules—like exposed vertebrae—held together by thin connecting tissue or bone. Their heads were stretched back horizontally into an elongated sphere, with two sets of glowing, compound eyes along the front. Mucus dripped from the creatures' mouths, sliming down to the floor as the aliens moved. A collection of tentacles hung down from the rear of their exoskeletons like dreadlocks, maybe twenty feet long, with a pulsating orifice on each end. Stinger-like tails thrashed about behind the creatures, with barbs or serrated edges along the pointed tips.

Two of the creatures advanced forward, standing in front of the third like a football team's offensive line moving to the line of scrimmage to block access to the quarterback. The first two aliens were carrying grappling devices mounted to their claws.

Before the two security guards could get off a shot, the aliens fired, impaling the men with the jagged hooks. Almost immediately, the creatures retracted their weapons, ripping the men apart from the inside. Blood and guts splattered everywhere.

The third alien raced forward, using the back of its mighty claw to knock Bruno, Kleezebee, and Lucas across the room in one swing. Lucas landed upside down with his back against the wall, knocking the wind out of him. He was dazed, gasping for air, but alive. Bruno landed on top of Kleezebee, just to Lucas' right. Neither of his colleagues was moving.

The aliens' tentacles snaked quickly along the floor and began siphoning the human remains through the pliable opening on the ends. When some of the bigger hunks were ingested, the tentacles bulged like a boa constrictor swallowing a rabbit for supper.

Lucas tried to stand, wanting to protect Drew, who was sitting helpless in his wheelchair, but his legs wouldn't cooperate. The alien was much quicker than Lucas could've predicted. It snatched Drew from his wheelchair and wrapped him inside a web of tentacles before carrying him back to the portal. Drew was hanging horizontally against the creature's side, looking back at Lucas, with his leather pouch hanging free outside his shirt. Lucas cried out for Drew just as the creature disappeared through the rift with his brother in tow.

Two of the techs picked up the security guards' handguns and fired at the two remaining creatures. The invaders raised their claws to protect their heads while the techs fired a continuous volley into what Lucas guessed were their torsos. A gooey orange substance gushed from their bodies each time a bullet hit its mark. The creatures backed up single file toward the rift, with their tentacles continuing to suck up the last few chunks of the guards.

The creature nearest to the techs took the brunt of the weapons' fire, while the other one slipped through the portal. The remaining creature appeared to be succumbing to its wounds as it stumbled sideways into the portal's event horizon. The rift closed around it, chopping off one of its claws and legs. It flopped to the floor.

Lucas was bent over, holding his abdomen, when the elevator doors opened and a four-man security team rushed into the room, followed by two medics Lucas recognized from the infirmary. He figured one of the video techs must have called for reinforcements. The security team dashed to surround the quivering alien, leaving behind boot prints in human blood.

One of the medics, a woman, ran up to Lucas, "Are you injured?" Lucas nodded. "Where does it hurt?" she asked.

"Everywhere," Lucas grunted with diminished breath. He felt like he'd been hit by a cement truck. "I think they just knocked the wind out of me."

The female medic helped him off the floor and then raised his hands over his head. "Try to relax. Take slow, deep breaths."

Lucas' breathing slowly returned to normal. "Better," he said, nodding. His whole body ached. "I'll be all right. Go help my friends," Lucas told her, pointing at Kleezebee and Bruno.

While the medic was tending to his friends, Lucas staggered over to the portal's last position, pushing his way through the guards surrounding the wounded creature. The alien was convulsing, spurting jets of orange blood from its severed limbs and bullet wounds. Its claw, stinger, and tentacles were not moving, no longer a threat.

"Where's my brother?" Lucas asked the creature, ignoring its putrid smell. There was no response. He kicked the creature in the head, crushing one of its four eyes. "Answer me!" he screamed at it before one of the guards pulled him away from the marauder.

"I doubt it understands you," the guard said.

"Those *things* took my brother!" Lucas said, trying to squirm free from the guard's arm lock. "I have to get him back!"

"Look at it," the guard said, turning Lucas' body toward the creature. The convulsions had stopped, and its eyes had started to dim. "It's almost dead. It's never going to tell you anything."

Reality set in, sending a torrent of emotions washing over Lucas. His mind and body went numb. He dropped to his knees with his mouth open and his eyes full of tears. He sobbed into his hands as his heart screamed in silence for his brother.

* * *

Several minutes later, Lucas felt a sudden calm come over the room. He wiped off his cheeks and nose, and then looked up. The guards were helping the medical team remove the alien's carcass from the surveillance room. Both Kleezebee and Bruno were alive and receiving treatment from the female medic who'd helped him earlier. Lucas stepped around the pool of orange blood and walked up to Kleezebee. "We have to go after Drew."

"I wish we could, but there's no way to find him. Even if we knew where he was, we can't open the rift from this side."

"We can't just sit here. There has to be something we can do."

"Trust me, he'll be all right. They won't hurt him."

"How the hell could you possibly know that?"

"Because the Krellians didn't send through a battalion of warriors to kill us all. It was only a small surgical strike. They're going to want to trade."

"For what?"

"The BioTex."

"But why Drew? Why not me or you? We were much closer to it."

Kleezebee looked at Lucas with an apologetic look on his face. The man's expression changed and so did his eyes. He looked like he was about to throw up.

Lucas could sense another revelation was about to erupt from his mentor's lips. "I know that look," he snapped, feeling a rising swell of trepidation mounting in his chest. "There's something else you haven't told me. What is it? Tell me, damn it! What the hell is going on?"

"I know why they took Drew and not the rest of us."

Lucas flared his eyes at the man, sticking out his chin in anger.

"Because Drew is my son," Kleezebee said with obvious heartbreak fueling his words.

Lucas' brain went into a spin. "What?"

Kleezebee ushered Lucas to a chair sitting in front of the video control station. "Have a seat and let me explain."

Lucas sat down in the chair with his arms folded across his chest. Every cell in his body was filled with anger and disbelief.

Kleezebee took a seat across from him. "Remember when I told you earlier that after we crashed, my crew began to pair off and start new families?"

"Yeah."

"Well, I couldn't bring myself to choose a new woman. I loved my wife too much, and I still held out hope we'd get home. But eventually, after twenty years of futility, even I began to doubt our chances of getting home. I gave in to the realization we might be marooned on your planet for a long time, quite possibly for generations. I was lonely and decided I needed a son, someone to carry on my legacy and continue the work, but I was too old and too busy to raise a child, and I certainly didn't want a new wife."

Lucas was starting to suspect Kleezebee had knocked up Drew's mom. "Jesus Christ, Professor. What did you do?"

"I had our geneticist open a fertility clinic."

Lucas hesitated for a moment, thinking about the professor's last statement. "I'm guessing it was the same one that Drew's bio-mom chose."

"Yes. We needed a woman with no family, a compatible genetic makeup, and who possessed superior intelligence. Lauren Falconio fit the bill. After she selected her donor sperm, we hijacked her pregnancy and inseminated her with my sperm. I'm not proud of what we did, but if we hadn't, Drew wouldn't be here today."

It took a minute for the words to sink in before Lucas was able to speak again. "How did the aliens know Drew was your son?"

"When they scanned the room, they must've checked our genetic markers and determined he was my offspring."

"What about me?" Lucas asked, wondering what earth-shattering revelation was next. "Am I one of your 'offspring,' too?"

Kleezebee shook his head. "No, you're not. Only Drew."

"How can I believe anything you say at this point?"

"Well, believe what you want, but it's true."

Part of Lucas was disappointed that Kleezebee wasn't his father, too, but the rest of him felt a deep sense of regret and he wasn't sure why. Then his mind put a spotlight on his childhood, helping him remember some key moments from his early life. That's when it hit him. That's when he realized how he felt about his adoptive father—pride.

He was proud of the unaccomplished man who'd taken him and Drew in, even if he never amounted to much in the grand scheme of things. John was a man of deep conviction and unwavering honesty, something Kleezebee lacked from head to toe. But at the same time, Lucas was angry at the world for not recognizing his father's genius when he'd released his amazing pest control invention.

Dishonest, manipulative men like Kleezebee got all the breaks, he decided, leaving genuine souls like his father to flounder in obscurity. Just like everything else in life, it wasn't fair and he'd just about had it with everyone and their secret agendas.

Lucas brought his eyes up. "So my being part of this . . . is what, an accident?"

"Hardly. After we had your intelligence tested, we arranged for the two of you to be roommates in the orphanage. I had hoped you two would bond."

Lucas figured Drew was going to be pissed when he learned that Kleezebee, his bio-dad, knew his whereabouts the entire time, but chose to leave him in the orphanage to fend for himself. The video screen in the back of his mind suddenly played a movie of Drew crying himself to sleep night after night in the orphanage, which wouldn't have been necessary if Kleezebee had stepped up and taken responsibility for his progeny.

Maybe Kleezebee wasn't confident in his skills as a single parent, or perhaps his wife Caroline took care of all the child-rearing, leaving Kleezebee to focus solely on work. Whatever the reason, Lucas had just lost more respect for Kleezebee. Not as an accomplished scientist, but as a man and father.

"Do the right thing" was something his adoptive father always preached to him. And now Lucas understood what John was trying to teach him. *"It's not what you make of yourself in the world that matters, it's how you carry yourself. Respect is a reputation well earned and it takes a lifetime of dedication to accomplish."*

"What about our adoption?" Lucas asked. "Did you arrange that, too?"

"We may have helped nudge it along a bit."

"So you've orchestrated everything since day one."

Kleezebee nodded. "We needed to keep close tabs on you. And Drew."

"And the free rent?"

"I would've done that regardless. And you should probably know Trevor isn't just your lab assistant; he's also your bodyguard."

"That makes sense, in retrospect." Lucas said. "Why didn't you tell Drew he was your son?"

"Simple, really—he has a family. A good one. Telling him I'm his biological father would only muddy the situation."

"But he *has* a right to know."

"You may be right, but I'd prefer you not tell him, or your mother. It could destroy your family, and I'm sure you don't want that."

Lucas wasn't sure if he agreed with Kleezebee's reasoning but nodded anyway. Regardless of what Kleezebee thought or expected of him, Drew was his primary responsibility. If he later decided to tell Drew the truth, he would. Kleezebee would just have to deal with it. *Fuck him*, he decided.

Lucas started thinking about his biological parents and the humiliating stories he was told about their criminal pasts. He'd always secretly hoped their backgrounds were a fabrication of lies, but never expected it to be a possibility—until now. "Was my bio-mom really a drug addict?"

"Yes, and your biological father died in prison. That all happened before we placed you with Drew."

So much for ridding himself of some emotional baggage. He'd never be that lucky. "What about Drew's bio-mom? Is she really dead?"

Kleezebee nodded in a strange manner, acting as if he wasn't telling the whole truth.

"Oh my God, you didn't run her car off the road, did you?"

"No, it was a tragic accident. We had nothing to do with it."

"Well, what is it, then?"

"The photograph Drew carries around his neck isn't hers. It's a picture of one of my crew, someone who died a long time ago."

"What? Why would you give him a fake photo?"

"We didn't have a good photo of Lauren to use."

"Then why'd you even bother?"

"We needed something he'd carry with him at all times. There's a tracking device and audio transmitter hidden inside the photo's backing paper."

Lucas' head spun when those words landed on his ears. Did he just hear the professor correctly? Had Kleezebee been eavesdropping on them all their lives? Lucas was certain somewhere along the way, a few embarrassing or slanderous conversations must've taken place between him and Drew that Kleezebee never should've heard. "Was the audio on all the time?"

"No. Not all the time."

Lucas wasn't sure he believed him. "But you always seemed to know when we needed help."

Kleezebee nodded. "I kept tabs."

Lucas was still pissed, but now wasn't the time to dwell on the transmitter and the privacy issues. He decided to save that debate for later, and focus for now on saving his brother. That was when an idea popped into his head. "Can we use the tracking device in the pouch to find Drew?"

"If we could get close enough, yes. But it won't work across dimensions. For now, we have wait for the Krellians to contact us and arrange an exchange."

Not much of a plan, Lucas thought. He expected something more out of Kleezebee—the man who was a former starship captain and supposed to be the master planner. He'd hoped for a more direct response to the Krellian threat. "Can't we just overpower them the next time the portal opens?"

"And do what? Send in a handful of men? If they're opening the portal from one of their hive ships, we'd be outnumbered a hundred thousand to one. It'll just get everyone killed, Drew included. No, we're going to wait to see what they want, and then formulate a rescue plan. Right now, the best course of action is to step back and think rationally. They may look like simple overgrown bugs, but they're very cunning and formidable."

Bruno tapped Kleezebee on the shoulder. "Boss, we really need to start preparing for the exchange."

Kleezebee acknowledged Bruno's request, then turned to Lucas. "Are we good?"

They were far from good, Lucas thought, but he wasn't going to push too hard against Kleezebee, at least not while Drew was being held captive by the Krellians. His main responsibility was to save Drew and protect his mom. And to do that, he needed Kleezebee. For the time being.

"Well?" Kleezebee asked.

"Yeah." Lucas nodded, though he didn't want to. "We're good."

27

An hour later, Lucas was standing next to Trevor and Bruno in the video room, listening to Kleezebee give instructions to a gathering of armed guards. Three of the ten men were Bruno copies. "When the rift opens again, I want you to spread out and flank the opening just in case they decide to attack. It'll be harder for them to select their targets if we're not all grouped together. Did you bring the stunners?"

"Yes, sir," one of the men replied, opening a black duffle bag. He pulled out weapons and distributed them to his squad. He also gave a stunner to Trevor.

"Can I get one of those?" Lucas asked, hoping to join the fight. Even though he didn't have any formal training, he figured he could aim and shoot an energy-based weapon much easier than a regular handgun. How hard could it be?

Kleezebee nodded, taking a stunner from the guard handing them out and giving it to Lucas. He put the tip of his finger on the switch sitting on top of the gun. "Set your weapons to stun level two, which is right here. I doubt level one will be sufficient to incapacitate their sentinels."

When Kleezebee clicked the switch, Lucas could see the gun's green power meter increasing from halfway to full. As it did, the indicator showed the weapon's energy bank increasing to maximum, giving off a short-lived hum that increased in pitch. Everyone else standing nearby followed suit, filling the room with a symphony of harmonic sounds.

Kleezebee told his techs. "I want all our sensors and recording equipment trained on the portal to see if we can trace it back to their location. We may not get another chance, so let's get it right the first time."

* * *

Another hour crawled by before the Krellians finally made their appearance. Their arrival started with the portal opening with a flicker of light, in the same manner and location as before, sending the security team into action. The guards fanned out and took position ten feet in front of the expanding rift with their backs only a few feet from the elevator doors.

Kleezebee hobbled around on crutches behind the gauntlet of men. Lucas joined him. It was the most defensible position in case they needed to make a quick retreat into the elevator. Trevor and the original Bruno copy were standing to the left, just in front of the hidden entrance to the med-lab. Both of them were armed with stunner weapons.

A single Krellian warrior stepped through the rift carrying a naked human female out in front like a protective shield. The redheaded young woman's eyes were closed and her limp body was covered in blood and bruises. The lower section of her right leg was shredded as if it had been torn off at the shin, then cauterized by an intense heat source.

The creature swung her from side to side as it stepped forward, furnishing Lucas with a clear view of her back. He almost puked. The alien had impaled the center of her spine with one of its tentacles; wearing her like a ten-cent hand puppet. Blood was dripping from around the insertion point.

Her eyes opened halfway and focused on Lucas while she reached out slowly with one trembling hand.

"Kill me, please," she said in a weak, thready voice.

Her face was creased in pain, sending a stab of anguish into Lucas' heart. He wanted to help her by putting her out of her misery, but he couldn't. Drew's life was at stake, and he knew taking action would probably kill him. He needed to make a choice—a tough choice—one that would surely haunt him forever. He broke eye contact with her and looked away.

When he brought his eyes back, her wilted body quivered, then fully energized as she began to speak in a low-pitched, monotone voice. It sounded as though two bellowing male voices were speaking in unison.

"WE HAVE CRIPPLE. GIVE US SUBSTANCE OR CRIPPLE DIES. UGLY SPECIES DIES. BLUE PLANET DIES. WE RETURN IN ONE REVOLUTION. GIVE US SUBSTANCE AND WE GIVE CRIPPLE."

After the short speech, the creature stepped backward into the rift, managing to get one of its legs across the event horizon before Bruno did what Lucas couldn't bring himself to do—take action. The security chief fired his stunner, blasting the alien on the right side, which sent an energy discharge traveling across its body and down its tentacles. The female interpreter fell from the tentacle's grip just as the alien disappeared through the rift. The portal closed an instant later, leaving her lying on the floor in the silo, crying.

Everyone except Lucas rushed forward to help, kneeling down next to her. He stood alone, embarrassed by his earlier cowardice. How could he face her now? What would he say?

She started crying in a feeble voice from the center of the crowd of Good Samaritans surrounding her, blocking Lucas' view of her eyes.

"Let's get her to the infirmary," Kleezebee commanded with his back to Lucas.

Trevor stood up. So did Bruno with the woman draped across his arms. The giant Swede removed his white tunic and lay it over her naked body, restoring some of her humanity. Lucas stood aside as Bruno rushed her to the elevator. Her head and lone remaining foot were hanging below his arms, flaccid and calm.

Lucas could now see her face, but mercifully, her eyes were closed. He prayed she couldn't feel the pain from the injuries across her frail-looking body. Bruno stepped into the elevator and was quickly followed in by Trevor. The doors closed in a swoosh a few moments later.

Kleezebee slid his crutches forward, bumping into Lucas' left elbow. "We'll take the next elevator."

"We?"

"You and I need to debrief her. Maybe she knows where they're holding Drew."

"Shouldn't we let them treat her first? She didn't look so good."

"That's precisely why we must talk to her *now*. What if she dies or lapses into a coma? If she can provide some intel, we're going to need it. Twenty-four hours isn't much time to mount a rescue plan."

* * *

Lucas was standing in the infirmary along the back wall between Kleezebee and Bruno. They were still waiting to speak to the unconscious woman, who was being treated by a male physician and three nurses. Trevor had returned to the Med-Lab at Kleezebee's behest.

"I'll be right back," Lucas said to Kleezebee, before wandering over to the isolation ward's viewing window. He couldn't help himself; he needed to check again. He wiped off the glass, using his right index finger as a squeegee to clear a patch of frost blocking his view. The creature's body was right where it was supposed to be, lying on the table farthest from the window, and it wasn't moving. He checked, but found nothing slithering down from the table or hiding in the corner of the room.

He'd seen it happen too many times in the movies where the alien's body wasn't actually dead, only to suddenly spring back to life and catch the unsuspecting heroes by surprise, usually while they were enjoying a premature victory celebration.

Lucas returned to his colleagues and nodded once. "It's all good. Still dead."

"Can we really afford to just keep waiting, boss?" Bruno asked Kleezebee with a curious look on his face.

Kleezebee looked at him, then at his watch, then at the medical team. He sighed and shook his head several times. "No, the wait ends now," he said, lifting his chin and hobbling closer to the medical team. "Doc, give her something to wake her up." It was the third time Kleezebee had made the demand.

"Look, I told you before, Professor, she's not strong enough. Giving her a stimulant now might kill her."

"We can't wait any longer. My son's life is at stake," Kleezebee replied in a sharp voice.

"No, I'm not going to take the risk."

Kleezebee grabbed the doc by the collar, pulling the man close to his face. "Give me the damn syringe and I'll inject her myself." Kleezebee let go of the doctor, shoving him back a step in the process.

"Okay. Okay," the doc replied, handing Kleezebee a syringe loaded with a stimulant. The man backed away with his hands out to his sides. "But you're responsible if she dies."

One of the nurses used an alcohol swab to sterilize the woman's neck. While the alcohol dried, Kleezebee held up the syringe, removed the needle guard, then tapped the needle gently while squeezing the plunger until a drop of liquid appeared on the tip. It was as if the professor had done it a thousand times before. He aimed the needle at her neck, inserted it, then pressed the plunger to shoot the load of stimulant into her system. He handed the empty syringe to the nurse assisting him.

"Should only take a few seconds," the nurse said, looking at the doctor, then back at Kleezebee.

The fingers on the injured woman's left hand twitched, then her head turned toward the center. Moments later, she opened her eyes and looked directly at Kleezebee, who was leaning over her like a mother hawk ready to feed her young. He spoke softly to her, "What's your name?"

"Alicia," the woman answered in barely more than a whisper. "Where am I?"

"You're in a hospital. My name's Dr. Kleezebee."

"DL Kleezebee?" she replied, her words a little more coherent than before.

"Ah . . . Yes. You know who I am?"

"No, but my handler did. I could hear it thinking about you. They've been searching the galaxy for you."

Kleezebee lifted one eyebrow and tilted his head as if he were moderately surprised. Perhaps it was more of a look of pride, knowing he was important enough for his enemy to dedicate years of their lives in pursuit of him.

"Was anyone else with you?" Lucas asked, leaning in to catch her attention.

She hesitated, showing a look that indicated she was deep in thought, searching for something in her memories. Just then, the machinery monitoring her vital signs reacted like an angry child, throwing a barrage of chirps and beeps across the room.

Her eyes turned sharp, looking at Kleezebee. "Julie Ann!" she screamed, trying to sit up. She thrashed her arms at Kleezebee, hitting him several times in the face. Kleezebee wrestled with her, trying to deflect the attack. Two nurses jumped in, grabbing her shoulders, and pulled her back down to the bed.

Kleezebee stepped back and stumbled on his crutches when she started kicking her legs at everyone around the bed.

Lucas gasped when her mangled stump of a leg whacked him in the thigh, narrowly missing his groin.

The nurses struggled with her arms but managed to restrain her long enough for Lucas and Kleezebee to lash her down using the leather straps sewn around the bed frame.

"Let me go," she cried out, pulling at the arm straps keeping her subdued. "I have to find my sister. Where is she?"

"We need you to calm down," Kleezebee answered sharply, holding her right hand with both of his. "Your sister isn't here. You're the only one we rescued."

The doctor slid in next to Kleezebee, replacing one of the nurses.

She turned her head toward the edge of the pillow and started crying with anger. A minute later, she stopped suddenly, as if something important just caught her attention. She opened her eyes, looked back at Kleezebee, and asked, "Where am I?"

"In a hospital."

"No, not that. What planet am I on?"

"Earth."

"No, no, no," she said, looking around frantically, like she was afraid for her life.

"Yes, Earth."

"Oh God. Please, no."

"Everything's going to be okay, Alicia."

"But it's occupied territory," she replied with panic in her voice. "They'll be coming for us. We have to get out of here."

Kleezebee smiled softly at her, rubbing the back of her hand with his thumbs. "No, child. We're on a different Earth. You're perfectly safe here. Trust me."

"Julie Ann," she said in a sad voice, trailing off in volume as she lay her head back on the pillow. She stared silently at the ceiling with a blank expression on her face.

"Can you tell me what happened to you?" Kleezebee asked her.

She brought her eyes back to the professor. "My sister and I were walking back to our village when those creatures appeared out of nowhere. They took us prisoner."

"The Krellians?"

"Yeah, sentinels armed with shredder hooks, but we didn't know who they were at first. We'd only heard stories about them."

"Then what happened?"

"They took us up to their ship and delivered us to one of their leaders, who stripped off our clothes."

Alicia then lifted and twisted her torso, revealing a raised scar on her right shoulder, carved into her skin in two sections. The bottom was an infinity symbol and the top was a pair of broken lines, like wiggly sevens, only split at the midpoint. "They made one of the older women do this to me with a hot knife. She was crying as hard as I was. I know she didn't want to brand me, but she didn't have a choice."

"How long ago was this?" Kleezebee asked.

"I'm not sure. A couple of months, maybe."

"Is that the last time you saw your sister?"

Alicia nodded. "She and I were split up right after. I haven't seen her since."

"Did they do this to your sister, too?" Lucas asked, watching her eyes turn sad again when his question landed on her ears. He thought the girl was going to start crying again, but she didn't. It was clear Alicia was fighting her emotions, but somehow she held it together and didn't break down again.

"For some reason, no, they didn't. I think she may have been traded to one of the other factions . . . or worse."

"Other factions?"

"There are dozens of them. Some get along peacefully but some fight over territory and feeding grounds. I think it's why they brand us. Like cattle."

"Where was your village?"

"On Colony Twelve."

Lucas looked at Kleezebee to see if the professor knew the name of the colony. His blank expression indicated he didn't.

She added, "I found out later they'd already invaded Earth, which is why no one warned us they were coming."

Lucas tugged at Kleezebee's shirt sleeve, then nodded for the professor to follow him away from the bed. Both of them moved to the corner of the room, where they huddled together to have a chat.

"What if Earth was already occupied territory when our E-121 module arrived?" Lucas asked in a low voice, not wanting the girl to hear what they were talking about. She was already emotionally unstable and he didn't want to make the situation worse.

Kleezebee's eyes indicated he was deep in thought. Then he nodded with pinched eyebrows. "If that's true, then our enemy intercepted it. Not our people. It would explain their sudden appearance here."

"And their possession of the rift opening technology," Lucas added.

The professor nodded, hobbling back to the bed.

Lucas followed, knowing his actions caused this innocent girl to suffer unimaginable pain when the bugs impaled her spine in order to communicate. His list of victims was growing by the minute, making his insides ache even more. They'd better come up with a plan to get Drew back, and soon, then figure out a way to end all this suffering across the universe. His shoulders couldn't support the weight of any more guilt.

"Was anyone else on the ship with you?" the professor asked the girl.

"Yes. A lot of us. All women."

"No men?"

She started crying again. "They eat them. We could hear their screams."

Lucas' face went numb as those words sank in.

"Some of the men killed themselves so they wouldn't be eaten," she said through more tears. "The Krellians . . . they like to eat their food alive."

Lucas' mind went into frenzy mode, worrying for Drew. He tapped the professor on the arm and waited for Kleezebee to look at him before he spoke. "I thought you said Drew would be safe?"

Kleezebee shook his head quickly without saying anything, then shot a disapproving look back.

Lucas understood the gesture. The professor wanted him to shut the hell up. It wasn't easy, not with the flashes of blood and guts filling his thoughts, but he held his tongue. For now.

"Why only the men?" Kleezebee asked, turning back to the girl.

"They keep the women as breeders," Alicia answered, tears streaming down her face.

"Breeders?" Lucas snapped, feeling the knot in the pit of his stomach swell. He wanted to scream and punch something, thinking of what the bugs might be doing to his brother.

Alicia's voice cracked as she tried to catch her breath between the waves of emotion and tears pouring out of her. "They keep us pregnant . . . so we can . . . provide them with more food. They prefer live children. Oh my God, it's so awful to watch. I can't stand it when they come for the newborns."

Lucas clenched his jaw as he stared at the edge of the bed, wondering how God, if he existed, could allow such barbaric creatures to exist in the universe. His mind spun with a terrifying vision of Drew lying on a table as the main course of a meal, while a swarm of Krellians pulled at his arms and legs, tearing them off at the joints as if they were eating a live chicken.

"If there are no men, how do they keep you pregnant?" Bruno asked from behind Kleezebee. His voice was soft and tender, but Lucas still couldn't believe the callousness of his friend's question.

Alicia answered anyway, pushing the words out through her obvious grief. "They farm semen from them before they're—" she said, stopping mid-sentence. "Those of us who can't bear children are used as translators or nannies, or we're thrown into the feeding pit with the men."

Lucas figured that's what she meant earlier when she talked about her sister's fate and used the words "or worse."

"Alicia, I know how hard this is to talk about, but we need everything if we're going to help you and your sister. Do you think you can answer a few more questions for us?" Kleezebee asked.

She nodded, wiping the tears from her cheeks. "I'll try."

"Can you tell me what happened to your leg?"

The girl gulped as her eyes filled with more despair. She took a few deep breaths before answering. "Sometimes they run low on food and the sentinels decide to ration us. But it doesn't always sit well with the others. Sometimes one of them will sneak into our cell after dark and drag us to different room, away from the others. That's what happened to me and another girl one night. We both tried to get away, but the creature kept hitting us with its claw. Then it started on her. Every time I close my eyes, I can still see the girl's face, screaming at me to help her. She couldn't have been more than fifteen. I was so scared I couldn't move, so I just sat there in the corner and covered my ears so I didn't have to listen to the sound of her bones crunching." She closed her eyes while drawing in a series of quick, shallow breaths before she spoke again. "Oh my God—the blood—it was everywhere."

Lucas couldn't imagine what this young girl had been through— nor did he really want to. But he couldn't ignore her. Her plight infuriated him. It was more than any human should ever have to endure. His empathy for her galvanized his resolve. His brother was in the hands of these heinous creatures and hearing Alicia's story fueled his internal drive to save Drew at all costs.

She let out another round of tears before looking up at Kleezebee. "When it finished with her, it came after me. I wished I was already dead. I almost passed out when it started on my leg, but one of their sentinels showed up to stop it, then it took me to another chamber where it burned my leg to stop the bleeding. A few minutes later, I was moved to a room filled with some fancy equipment, where my handler put its tentacle in my back."

The room fell into an emotional silence. Everyone's eyes were focused on the girl, as was their compassion, Lucas assumed. He imagined the collective hearts of Kleezebee and the rest of his crew were now beating with the force of a thunderous herd. His was; why should theirs be any different?

Kleezebee unstrapped Alicia from his side of the bed. Lucas did the same on the other side, wondering what else he could do to help this girl.

Alicia sniffed a few times as her tears slowed, using her forearm to wipe her nose. Lucas spun and found a box of tissues behind him and gave it to her. She blew her nose and thanked him.

Kleezebee asked her, "When you were connected to the creature, do you remember what you said to us?"

"Yeah, I think I remember most of it."

"Do you know if my brother is still alive?" Lucas asked.

She nodded, then reached over and touched his hand. Despite all she'd been through and all the pain she was in, she still had compassion for Lucas' situation.

His heart reached out to her. He admired her strength and courage. If she could handle captivity, he knew Drew could handle it, too. "Are they going to give him back if we hand over the BioTex?"

"No. They're planning to invade as soon as you turn over the stuff they want. They're never going to pass up such a rich feeding ground. You have to get everyone out of here."

Lucas looked at Kleezebee and then at Bruno, hoping for some indication of what to do next.

Bruno seemed distracted, standing a few feet away, touching his finger to his ear. A few moments later, he touched his watch, and said, "10-4," before walking up to the professor and tapping him on the shoulder.

Kleezebee turned, allowing Bruno to whisper something in his ear. When Bruno was finished, the professor smiled and said, "Excellent. You know what to do."

Bruno nodded, then quickly left the infirmary.

"What's going on?" Lucas asked, figuring the only course of action was to storm the rift when the creatures reappeared. Maybe his earlier suggestion to attack wasn't so idiotic after all.

Kleezebee didn't respond. Instead, he asked Alicia, "If we can get you back on their ship, do you think you'd be able to show us where they're holding my son?"

"No way. I'm never going back. I'll kill myself first."

"What about your sister? She could still be on the ship," Lucas said, hoping to change her mind. It was a lot to ask of the girl, but they really didn't have a choice at this point.

She sighed, then sat quietly, gently shaking her head while staring off into space. She might've been considering his request, or resigning herself to the fact that Julie Ann was long gone.

"Can you at least draw us a map?" Lucas asked, wondering if the girl's connection to the sentinel's thoughts had provided her with access to the ship's layout.

She looked at him for a few seconds, then answered, "Yeah, I think so."

Lucas smiled, then ran to the medical table and picked up a red pen and clipboard. He turned the medical paperwork over to check the backside of the paper—it was blank.

He hustled back to the bed and gave her the pen and paper. "Here, draw on this."

28

Lucas handed Alicia's map to Kleezebee, then followed the professor back to the elevator and rode with him down to the surveillance room, where they met up with Bruno and Trevor.

"Sir, we confirmed the data and their ship's spatial coordinates," Bruno reported, handing a report to Kleezebee.

Kleezebee looked over the paperwork for a minute, then replied, "Nice work, gentlemen." He gave the report back to Bruno, who passed it to Trevor.

"What's going on, Professor?" Lucas asked.

"Our scans of the rift provided us with new data. Looks like I was wrong."

"About what?"

"It might be possible to open the rift from this side."

"So we *are* going after Drew?"

Kleezebee nodded. "But we'll need a plan to deal with their army."

Bruno stepped forward and stood at attention. "My team and I are ready to go. Just give the order, sir."

"Count me in, too," Lucas said, patting Bruno on the back. "Trust me, we'll get Drew back."

"You realize this is probably a suicide mission, for all of you."

"Then so be it," Lucas replied. "I'd rather die trying to save my brother than just sit here waiting to be eaten by those *things*. Hell, give us some frag grenades, and we'll take out as many of those ugly bastards as we can."

"Look, I want to get Drew back just as much as you do, but let's not go off half-cocked. We need to step back and think this through," Kleezebee said, walking away with his hand stroking his gray beard.

Lucas moved to intercept his boss, but Bruno latched onto his elbow and said, "Give him a few minutes."

The colorful tattoos on Bruno's forearms danced as his powerful grip held Lucas in place. When Bruno flexed his left arm in just the right way, the artwork connected with a fresh memory in Lucas' head. He suddenly realized the drawings weren't just random artistry. They were imprecise and aging a bit, but he recognized the misshapen head, long stinger tail, and pair of claws.

He shot Bruno an inquisitive look, pointing at the man's tats. "Hey, I just realized something. Your ink—they're supposed to represent the bugs, aren't they?"

Bruno nodded, his face turning sour. "I wear them as a reminder of what stranded us here. So we'd never forget what we're up against."

"Shit, and all this time I thought they were a loose representation of scorpions, or something along those lines," Lucas said, studying the renderings more carefully. His eyes observed something new about the creature's physical appearance—its segmented body. His mind churned through several ideas until one of them bubbled to the surface. It involved his dad's failed pest control device.

Lucas turned to his boss, barely able to contain his sudden excitement. "Dr. Kleezebee, is it all right if I make a quick trip home to Phoenix? There's something there I need to get."

The professor whirled around and looked at Lucas as if he were sizing him up for something. "What is it?"

"An invention my old man was working on before he died. If my mom hasn't tossed it away, it just might help us breech the Krellians' stronghold."

He shook his head, tightening his scowl. "I don't think splitting up is a wise idea right now. The safest place for all of us is right here. We need to stick together."

"Please, sir. For Drew's sake and ours. I think—no, check that—I know my dad's tech can help us."

Kleezebee didn't respond, so Lucas continued his plea. "Please, sir, I need you to trust me on this. It won't take long for me to run up to Phoenix and grab what I need. I'll be back before you even miss me. But I really need to do this. Right now, I'm completely useless around here and I need to do something to help get Drew back and stop all the senseless deaths. Please, I beg you, Professor. Let me go and do this."

Kleezebee hesitated, then looked at his watch. "Fine, but you're not going alone. Bruno will escort you."

Lucas locked eyes with Bruno. "Okay, but I'm driving this time."

"I don't think that'll be necessary," Kleezebee said, turning to his lead tech. "Is the jump station still viable at the hockey arena?"

The man typed into his computer, then reported, "Confirmed, sir. The pad's still online and operational."

"What about ground transportation once you arrive?" Kleezebee asked Bruno.

"Our van should still be parked in the underground garage."

"All right then, you go with Lucas. But make it quick."

* * *

Ninety minutes later, Lucas and Bruno returned from their trip to Phoenix. Lucas put a torn, dirty cardboard box on the floor in front of Kleezebee, then blew a cloud of dust off the top. He'd found it in a corner of his dad's workshop next to a pile of old clothes ready for donation to Goodwill.

"So what do you have for me?" Kleezebee asked.

"My dad's best invention," Lucas said with a proud grin on his face. He unfolded the box and pulled out a black device the size of a cigarette pack, which was attached to a two-inch-square power transformer. He untangled the six-foot electrical cord before handing it to Kleezebee. "Dad called it a sonic pad."

Kleezebee tested the device's retractable legs before wiping the dirt off the ring of sensors lined up across its middle, directly below the miniature antenna protruding from its top. He gave the unit to Bruno.

Lucas pulled out another item lying in the bottom of the box—a notebook containing his dad's handwritten notes. He opened the journal, fanning the pages to demonstrate its contents before giving it to Kleezebee. "Dad's handwriting is worse than a doctor's, but I can translate it if you need me to."

"What's this thing do?" Bruno asked, holding the sonic pad away from his body as if it were an explosive.

"It's for pest control. And it works awesome." Lucas thought about mentioning the device's one minor flaw, but decided against it. He didn't see how the liquefaction of a dog's brain had any relevance to their current situation. At least the device wasn't harmful to humans.

"Pests?" Bruno asked.

"Dad networked a series of these around our yard to kill scorpions. If one of them crawled inside the perimeter, the motion sensors triangulated its location, sending a finely tuned blend of infrasonic and ultrasonic sound waves at the creature. The blast was powerful enough to shatter the bug's segmented body. They'd explode like popcorn."

Kleezebee was busy skimming through the journal and remained silent.

"My dad hated scorpions. They were always wandering inside the house at night and after Mom stepped on her third one, he decided we needed to do something else. The commercial pesticides he sprayed were slow to work, if at all."

"Damn ingenious," Kleezebee said, pointing at one particular page in the notebook. "The pad emits an inaudible set of specifically calibrated sonic pulses to attack the creature's nervous system."

"Do you think we can adapt it?" Lucas asked his boss.

"For what?" Bruno replied.

"For the Krellians," Lucas answered.

Kleezebee let out a thin smile from the corner of his mouth. "This just might work. But we'll need to crank up the juice considerably."

"I was thinking we could use E-121 for the additional power," Lucas said.

The professor gave him a proud look. "Excellent idea. We can use it to power all of them."

Bruno gave the device in his hands to Lucas, then looked inside the box. "Ah, boss. Looks like there's only one."

"Right now there is," Kleezebee said in a matter-of-fact way, still scanning the information in the notebook.

Lucas knew where the professor was going with this. "You're gonna use the BioTex to duplicate more of them, right?"

"Yes. We'll need to arm each member of the rescue team with one of the modified sonic pads. We certainly don't have enough ammo to take out a hive ship full of sentinels."

Lucas smiled, feeling damn good about himself. "I figured you could use the BioTex for inanimate objects, too."

"Yes, we can. Though Trevor will need to modify the replication code a bit. Granted, it's not a very efficient use of our technology, but given our limited options, we really don't have much of a choice."

"Do we have time to make 'em all?" Lucas asked, wondering how long it would take Trevor to make the changes.

"We're good," Kleezebee said, opening the Med-Lab's hidden door and walking inside. Lucas followed him to where Trevor was standing and working.

"Rig a power source based on E-121 and make as many copies of this as you can," Kleezebee told Trevor. "I need it weaponized by morning."

"*Ja,* will do," the Swedish giant responded, taking the device from the professor.

* * *

The following day Lucas was heading to the video room to meet up with Kleezebee and his staff after food run along the way.

The Krellians were due to reappear in sixty-two minutes for the exchange, but first he stopped at the mess hall on the way to fill up on caffeine—he'd battled a serious case of insomnia through the night, leaving him exhausted. He couldn't get Drew out of his mind. He kept seeing his little brother sitting in a corner of a Krellian holding cell, surrounded by the blood and guts of hundreds of men, all of whom had been eaten right before his eyes.

The Jolt cola he grabbed in the cafeteria did the trick and energized his body, but it still didn't change the way he felt on the inside. When he looked back over the events of the past few days, it all seemed surreal. He felt like he was in some low-budget sci-fi movie, one filled with endless twists and turns, almost too absurd for anyone to believe. Yet it was real and happening to him, and to his family.

If he and his brother somehow survived this mess, he promised himself to write a novel about their experiences. Even if no one ever read their story, he felt it was important to chronicle the events and to pay homage to those who'd suffered and died.

He'd spent several hours of the previous evening consoling his mother after explaining what had happened to Drew. It wasn't easy to confess his sins and his failures to her, but he managed to get through it. He took great care to relay the tragic events with a positive spin, but despite his optimism, Dorothy took the news of Drew's abduction extremely hard.

"Promise me you'll get him back. I don't care what it takes, you get it done. You hear me?" she said while hugging him tight the previous night. He could still hear the words ringing in his ears, stinging like acid rain on the edges of his heart.

Ever since Lucas met his brother in the orphanage, he'd been Drew's protector. It was his singular, most important job. His life wasn't about E-121 experiments, thesis papers, or fame and fortune. It was about Drew and the rest of his family. That was all that really mattered in the world—family. He knew it and accepted it, especially after he'd promised his dying father he'd always watch over Drew and keep him safe.

Yet when the Krellians came through the rift and snatched Drew, he froze like a total coward, showing his true colors. There was no denying it. He was a miserable failure as a man, as a son, and as a brother. His mom didn't come right out and say it, but he knew she was very disappointed in him. He worried that if he failed to get Drew back, she'd never forgive him. And seeing the disappointment in her eyes was something he couldn't live with, not on top of everything else.

After stopping at the mess hall for his caffeine fix, Lucas decided to take another detour to the armory before heading to the surveillance room. He went inside, planning to stock up on a few items he might need. He never bothered to get approval from Kleezebee to carry heavy today, mainly because he was gonna do it regardless of what his boss said, but also because this wasn't the professor's decision. It was his. He was going to do his job and get Drew back, or die trying. End of story. He was tired of being a coward and wasn't going to let anyone or anything stop him. Not the professor, not Bruno, and certainly not the Krellians.

A traditional handgun would be too loud for a stealthy assault, so he decided to grab two of Kleezebee's stunners, instead. He strapped one of them to his ankle and slipped the other one inside the back of his trousers. He put on one of the Kevlar vests lying in a stack to his right, concealing it with his shirt.

He went outside and stood tall in hallway, taking in a few deep breaths to steel himself. He was ready. Ready for whatever the universe had in store for him. There were only two possible endings to the story, and he was ready for whichever one fate threw at him today.

* * *

When Lucas stepped out of the elevator and walked into the video room, he found Kleezebee and Trevor fitting Bruno with a jet-black vest. Five feet away from them was a four-wheeled sled with a stack of five-gallon containers filled to the brim with scarlet-colored liquid.

The vest contained a series of bulging pockets with a set of electrical wires hop-scotching between them. All the vest needed was a few dozen sticks of dynamite and Bruno would've looked like a suicide bomber ready to take out a shopping mall.

Bruno's street clothes bulged from under the vest—white polo shirt, dark slacks, and brown loafers. The polo shirt fit his sagging gut much better than his uniform top did, except it highlighted his baseball-sized bellybutton recess. The only part of Bruno's outfit Lucas recognized was the pentagon-shaped watch. Overall, Bruno actually looked good in casual attire.

"What do ya think?" Kleezebee asked Lucas, leaning forward on his crutches to tug at the open belt clip hanging from the front of Bruno's vest. "Trevor did a hell of a job integrating your father's device."

"Yeah, no doubt," Lucas said, beaming a prideful smile. "Looks a little snug, though, don't you think?"

"It's not bad," Bruno said, clipping the belt to close the vest around his midsection.

There was a second vest lying on the table next to Trevor. Since it was much too small to fit Trevor or Kleezebee, Lucas assumed the vest was for him. Either that, or it was for one of the skinny security officers to wear. He assumed they only had time to make two vests, not the dozen Kleezebee ordered.

"We're calling it a Sonic Disrupter," Kleezebee said.

Lucas picked up the second vest to inspect it. He was surprised to see six of his father's sonic pads installed around the outside of the garment, each one nestled inside its own pocket. "Nice work. Dad would be proud."

"Trevor constructed it out of interwoven layers of Kevlar, plus he added a few layers of graphene nano-fibers for added strength. Should be able to withstand one hell of a beating."

Lucas continued his inspection and found electrical wires running from each sonic pad to a common pouch sewn inside the back of the vest. Lucas tore open the pouch's Velcro closure.

"That's the E-121 power unit," Kleezebee said, holding up a push-button activator switch. "All you need to do is press this button to set off the pulse."

Lucas didn't see any wires connecting the switch to the vest. "Wireless?"

Kleezebee nodded.

Bruno walked around the room with the vest wrapped around his chest, though not in a normal upright posture. He was leaning slightly backward. "I don't know. It's a tad back-heavy because of the E-121 module."

"We could add a counterweight to the front, if you'd like," Kleezebee replied.

"Nah, if you make it any heavier, I'll be too slow to react. I think I just need to get used to it."

"Why are you using multiple emitters in one vest?" Lucas asked the professor.

"We tested it on the alien corpse and found we needed to use multiple combinations of infrasonic and ultrasonic waves. Otherwise, it had little effect. It took a bit of engineering for Trevor to make the adjustments needed so we could load the vest with the properly tuned emitters."

"You should've seen the horrible mess when that thing finally popped," Bruno added, looking satisfied.

Lucas laughed, imagining what the explosion looked like.

"It took longer to tweak your father's technology than we expected, so we only had time to make the two vests," Kleezebee said.

"I take it the other one is for me?" Lucas asked.

"Yeah, go ahead and put it on," Kleezebee said, testing the trigger on the activation switch. "If something goes wrong during the exchange, I want you and the security team to do whatever is needed to bring Drew home."

"So you *are* gonna let me help?"

"Of course. Besides, I know there's not a chance in hell you'll sit back and let us handle this without you."

"You got that right," Lucas answered, flaring his eyebrows. "Will I get a gun?"

"Not without the proper training first. You need to let the tactical team enter first and secure the area before you go in. Understood?"

"Sure, professor. Whatever you need," he answered, checking to make sure the stunner was still tucked deep inside the back of his waistband. It was. He wondered why they weren't going in ahead of schedule, in a pre-emptive assault. "But why wait until the exchange? Don't we have the element of surprise on our side?"

"Yes, we do. But they might just return him without a fight."

"You don't really believe that, do you? After what Alicia said?"

"Well, she was rather emotional and could've been misinterpreting things. The smart move here is to try a diplomatic solution first. An all-out assault is our last resort."

"Once we have him back, what then?" Bruno asked.

"We'll cross that bridge when we come to it. For now, let's try to rescue Drew and not get us all killed in the process."

"You got it," Bruno said, nodding once.

Kleezebee turned to face his techs and said, "Once we're back, be sure to close the rift immediately."

"Yes, sir."

Lucas slid on the Sonic Disrupter Vest, but initially had trouble buckling the belt. He didn't say anything about the snug fit, fearing they might discover the protective vest hiding under his shirt and the stunner tucked in his pants. He figured two layers of protection couldn't hurt, as long as he could breathe properly. He finally got the belt clipped and waited for Kleezebee's orders, which came moments later when he addressed everyone in the room.

"As a gesture of good faith, Bruno and I will step through with a small amount of BioTex. I suspect they'll want to test its authenticity. Once they do, I'll demand they return Drew before we conclude the exchange."

"What if they refuse?" Lucas asked.

"Then it's Plan B and your team. Until then, I need you to stand down and monitor the exchange," Kleezebee answered before looking at Trevor. "Remember, don't bring the rest of the material until I call for you."

Trevor nodded.

Kleezebee held up a pair of pendant necklaces. "The techs have built a one-way video/audio transmitter into these pendants. They should allow you to see what's going on during the exchange." He pointed to a pair of unmanned video screens, just to the right of his lead technician. "We'll pipe the signals through to those monitors."

"Will they be powerful enough to carry the signal back here, across dimensions?" Lucas asked.

Kleezebee didn't answer. Instead, he looked at his lead tech.

The tech nodded. "Won't be a problem, sir. We've programmed the transmitters to scan the rift and match its energy signature. We should be able to piggyback the carrier wave. Should have plenty of signal strength."

"Assuming the bugs leave the rift open the entire time," Lucas added.

"True," the tech answered.

29

Twenty-two minutes later, the Krellians opened the rift in the same location as before. It started as a pinpoint before growing to full size, sending flashes of light rippling across the walls.

The aliens had put out the welcome mat right on schedule, adding a sliver of optimism to counterbalance Lucas' growing anxiety. Unlike his colleagues, Lucas refused to pin all his hope on Kleezebee's approach. The professor's rescue plan was founded on a set of optimistic assumptions, most of which Lucas considered unreliable.

Plus, since everything Lucas was involved in lately had turned to shit, why should today's plan be any different? *Expect the worst and hope for the best* was the only motto that seemed to work for him.

If he *was* going to die today, he intended to go out on his feet, fighting like a wildcat—a University of Arizona Wildcat. He sucked at all things sports-related, so joining a paramilitary team on an inter-dimensional bug hunt would have to make up for it. He let out a guarded smile, more out of pride than from high expectations, while he adjusted the hidden stunner's position inside the back of his pants.

The elevator bell sounded, delivering seven additional security team members, who scampered out of the lift while carrying stunners and traditional 9MM handguns. They spread out in formation to take flanking positions in front of the portal with their weapons drawn.

Kleezebee slipped the transmitter necklace over his head, then moved in front of the rift on crutches, where he waited for Bruno to join him. Bruno, who was already wearing his copy of the necklace, bent down to snatch a one-gallon jug of deactivated BioTex. He carried the container in his arms, walking with heavy feet to Kleezebee's location. Other than Bruno's Sonic Disruptor vest, neither man was armed.

Lucas joined Trevor at the remote monitoring station near the front of the room. He watched the screen while his boss and friend entered the trans-dimensional portal and stepped into their home universe. The portal's surveillance system functioned perfectly, allowing them to see and hear everything. Lucas raised his left hand, then knuckle-bumped the elderly video tech sitting to his left. "Great job," he told him emphatically.

He was sure the tech already knew who he was, but he wanted to know the tech's name. His right hand went out for a shake. "My name's Lucas Ramsay, by the way."

"Claude Vandersteen. Pleased to meet you," the old guy said, shaking his hand in earnest.

The monitor in front of Lucas contained the video transmission from Kleezebee's pendant. Bruno's feed was streaming live on the other monitor to his right, directly in front of Trevor.

Kleezebee and Bruno were standing inside a sparsely-lit room with angled eight-foot long wall segments, which glistened like algae-green sheet metal. Based on Kleezebee's earlier description of Krellian ship design, Lucas assumed the shape of the room was octagonal.

Three Krellian sentinels were standing with their backs against the visible wall segments, aiming their grappling hook weapons at Kleezebee. Lucas wondered why their warriors didn't carry more powerful energy-based weapons, like phase pistols or pulse rifles. Granted, the grappling hooks were deadly and reusable, but their range was limited. Then the answer hit him when he realized their enormous claws would make it impossible for them to pull the trigger on a more conventional weapon.

"Makes you wonder how they operate their ship controls with those enormous claws," Claude said.

"Yeah, it must be tough for them to wipe, too," Lucas replied.

Trevor laughed, sending a patch of spittle from his mouth as he snorted and doubled over in his chair.

Lucas took a moment to relish the big man's chuckle. It was the first time he remembered hearing the Swede bust a gut about anything, making Trevor seem more human than before. Perhaps the stress of the situation had finally gotten to his massive friend.

The elevator doors behind them opened again, delivering another seven-member squad of men to the surveillance room. This time two of the reinforcements were Bruno copies. They joined the other men already standing guard in front of the still-open rift.

When Kleezebee turned to his left, the video pendant showed a human female approaching his position. She was stark naked, in her twenties, and full-figured. The other monitor showed Bruno turning to greet her, too.

"Looks like the women aren't allowed to wear clothes, ever," Lucas said, watching the amber-haired woman carry some type of hooded garment draped across her arms, possibly a robe. The rust-colored clothing was much too small to fit the creatures. The woman gave the robe to Kleezebee in exchange for his crutches.

"Oh shit," Lucas said, seeing the professor unbutton his shirt. "What if they make Bruno change, too? They'll take the activator switch away."

"Then he won't be able to activate the vest," Claude replied, typing on his wireless keyboard, then using the touch screen to swipe through a few control screens. "But not to worry, I can remotely trigger the vest if Bruno can't, as long as the rift remains open."

"Then let's hope it stays open," Lucas replied as a new window appeared on the tech's computer screen with a title bar that said **REMOTE ARMING SEQUENCE**. Below the title was a red outlined button labeled **FIRE**.

Lucas wondered if he'd be the one to press the kill switch. If so, he needed to know more about the control system the technician was using. "What about my vest? Can they both be set off?"

"The system can activate them at the same time, but you must activate the secondary transmission channel like this," the tech said, pointing at the monitor. He swiped twice and pulled the contents of the display down, showing an underlying page of six buttons—each with text underneath. One of them was labeled DUAL ACTIVATION in red lettering. Lucas studied the screen, memorizing how the tech navigated to it as well as the location of the activation button.

The tech entered more commands into the keyboard before using his hand to touch and swipe back to the original Remote Arming Sequence screen. A partially filled computer graphic, like a meter, was now showing in the corner. It read **OUTPUT LEVEL**.

"Vest's power level?" Lucas asked, wondering why it wasn't clearly labeled like the others.

Claude nodded and said, "Sure is."

The meter showed it was set very low and Lucas didn't understand why. "Shouldn't we be using full power?"

"No. We don't want to take the chance of overloading the disruptor pads, so I've set the power level to ten percent."

"Is it enough to kill 'em?"

"Absolutely, many times over. The vest's E-121 power supply is much more powerful than we really need. When we tested it on the alien corpse, we were successful using only a five percent nominal yield. Ten percent should be more than enough to kill anything in that room."

While Kleezebee changed his clothes, his body kept swaying and so did the pendant. The video feed jostled and blurred as it bounced around his chest. After Kleezebee bent down to slide off what Lucas assumed was his underpants, the professor's hidden camera held still long enough for Lucas to catch a glimpse of the naked woman standing in front of him. She was still holding the pair of crutches. Kleezebee put on the robe and lashed it around his waist. His video feed went black.

"Come on, DL, pull it out," Lucas coaxed him, needing to see what was happening.

The video screen's image returned to normal when Kleezebee adjusted the pendant's position so it hung outside the robe.

"Good thing you used a pendant cam instead of a button cam," Lucas said, watching the streaming footage sway back and forth repeatedly until the pendant came to rest.

Both Bruno and Kleezebee faced the woman as she scooped up the professor's clothes and walked away, giving Lucas a clear view of her shoulder tattoo. It was the same hand-carved branding mark Alicia showed them earlier in the infirmary. Moments later, she returned with another robe, giving it to Bruno.

"I hope it's a double XL," he wisecracked.

"Let's see what she does with the vest," Claude said after a short chuckle.

Kleezebee kept his pendant trained on Bruno as he removed his pants. "God, I hope we don't have to see him without his—"

"Too late," Claude replied as Bruno removed his boxers.

Kleezebee's camera feed turned away from Bruno, providing a panoramic view of the octagon-shaped room. The wall segment to the professor's right had an arched passageway that led into another chamber. Flaming torches were burning on either side of the opening, making the room look medieval.

"Not exactly high-tech," Lucas said.

When Kleezebee turned back, Bruno was dressed in the robe with his pendant hanging outside the garment. The woman was picking up Bruno's clothes.

"Since his clothes aren't dissolving into BioTex, I assume they're real?" Lucas asked.

"*Ja*, real clothes," Trevor said, breaking his silence. "Vest not fit on uniform."

The woman put Bruno's vest on top of the clothes, and carried them through the passageway, out of sight.

"Is that going to be a problem?" Lucas asked Claude.

"It depends on where she takes it," Claude answered as the woman walked back into the room empty-handed. "She couldn't have gone far, so we should be okay."

Four gray-haired men, all at least sixty years old, entered the exchange room wearing white ceremonial garb. Based on their dress and mannerisms, Lucas assumed they were diplomats from Kleezebee's planet. At least not all the men had been eaten, giving him renewed hope that his brother might be returned in one piece. "Looks like a geriatric toga party," he mumbled, trying to relieve some of his own stress with a little more humor.

The old men stood in pairs, facing the entrance. Two ultra-slender naked females—no more than eighteen years old—carried in an eight-foot-long banquet table and put it between the two pairs of men.

"You don't think its dinner time, do you?" Lucas asked his colleagues, worrying his brother might be the entrée. Trevor looked more concerned than the tech, but neither of them answered.

A Krellian sentinel entered the room with a human female impaled on the end of one of its tentacles. Four more aliens followed in behind it, then moved to surround Kleezebee and Bruno.

"Here we go," Claude said.

The sentinel used the female translator to say, "SHOW US."

Bruno placed the one-gallon container of BioTex on the table and slid it close to the Krellian puppeteer. The elder statesmen closest to the creature removed the container's lid, allowing the sentinel to slip one of its remaining tentacles into the goop.

"It must be siphoning a sample," Claude said.

"*Ja*, to test it," Trevor added.

The creature withdrew its tentacle and began to speak on its own, bypassing the woman translator. Its language sounded like a computer modem on steroids as it whined and squealed at a feverous pitch. Lucas figured the alien was reporting its findings to the others, or perhaps to its superiors. There was no telling who or what might have been monitoring the proceedings.

Thirty seconds went by before the sentinel stopped its communication and then turned to face the other aliens in the room. Its chest plate lit up like the Las Vegas Strip with an array of lights buried deep inside its exoskeleton. The chest plate gave off a dull hum as the lights flashed in an irregular pattern. Lucas could see the faint outline of organs and other tissue inside the towering beast.

Bruno turned his body to show some of the other aliens whose chest plates were flashing in a similar fashion. Lucas assumed the Krellians were communicating with each other over some form of biological network. He thought the other bugs were receiving data from the sentinel, or perhaps all of them were receiving orders from a remote location.

A few seconds later, the sentinel stuck its tentacle back into the female hand puppet. The creature raised her high into the air and squealed, as if it were celebrating. The other aliens joined in the festivities with their own rendition of the noise.

It reminded Lucas of a Native American war cry that preceded an all-out assault. "I've got a bad feeling about this."

The Krellian sentinel used the female translator to speak to Kleezebee. "SECOND SUBSTANCE MISSING."

"I want to see my son first!" the professor shot back.

One of the other warriors approached Kleezebee, opened its right claw, and held it open just inches from Kleezebee's jugular.

Lucas looked at Claude, but the tech's hand never moved. Lucas reached out with his left arm to position the tip of his finger a quarter inch from the touch screen's **FIRE** button.

Claude grabbed Lucas' wrist, pulling it back. "Not yet. They could simply be posturing, testing for weakness. Let's see what happens."

"You can kill me if you want," Kleezebee told the bugs, "but we're not giving you the activator enzyme until you bring me my son."

The sentinel tilted its head, then squealed as if Kleezebee's demand pissed it off. "HOLD POSITION," the creature answered through its female translator.

Both Bruno and Kleezebee turned their bodies toward the wall opening. Moments later, an alien soldier armed with a grappling hook device in one of its claws appeared with Drew wrapped inside its tentacles, carrying him like a loaf of bread on its side. It raised its empty claw, then opened and snapped it shut several times, only a foot in front of Drew's neck.

"Oh my God, Drew!" Lucas said, his heart ready to explode.

"Release him and let him return to Earth," Kleezebee demanded. "Then I'll hand over the remaining material."

"GIVE US MATERIAL OR CRIPPLE DIES," the sentinel replied, as its chest plate flashed and hummed.

Lucas looked at Claude. "We have to do something, now!"

The tech didn't answer, his eyes glued to the video feeds.

"Okay. Okay. Just don't hurt him," Kleezebee shouted, as he turned slowly back toward the portal. The change in view showed two sentinels standing guard in front of the portal's opening. The professor's voice changed as he used a controlled, softer tone. "Claude, go ahead and send Trevor through."

Claude finally turned his attention to Lucas. "You need to calm down and stop overreacting. We have this covered." He gave Trevor a hand wave, telling him it was time to step through.

Trevor stood up from his chair, grabbed hold of the flatbed cart, and rolled the stack of canisters toward the rift.

Kleezebee turned forward to face the creature in charge. "Okay, I did as you asked. The material is on its way. Give me my son."

The sentinel let out a short squeal and its chest flashed twice. The alien holding its claw around Kleezebee's neck backed away to make room for the other creature to deliver Drew to Kleezebee. Bruno moved next to Kleezebee and stood behind Drew, who was now sitting on the deck.

Lucas watched Trevor step into the portal and disappear with the balance of the ransom material—the activator enzyme. Lucas took his eyes from Trevor and looked back at Claude's video feeds, but now both of them were dark and offline, even though the rift was still open.

Claude was now pounding away at the keyboard in obvious panic.

"What the hell just happened? I thought you had this covered?" Lucas screamed at him.

Claude didn't answer, his hands working quickly across the array of equipment.

Get them back!" Lucas said, shaking the man's shoulder, hoping to get a response.

"I can't. The feeds were shut down at the source," Claude said, stopping his work and sitting back in the chair.

"Why?"

"I have no idea," he said, throwing up his hands.

"You have to do something!"

Claude didn't budge, sitting there looking shell-shocked.

Lucas couldn't believe what was happening, or this man's incompetence. He decided it was time to take action. He stood up and tore off his Disruptor Vest, then tossed it into the portal, sending it to the exchange room on the other side.

He went back to the console station and used both arms to push Claude out of the way, sending the tech flying out of his chair. Lucas quickly changed screens and armed the dual transmitter system the way Claude showed him earlier, then swiped back to the power screen and raised the energy level to a hundred percent.

"Ten percent, my ass," he yelled at Claude while his finger pressed the FIRE button on the screen.

Lucas grabbed the stunner from the back of his waistband and pulled open the Velcro strap holding the other stunner against his ankle. He ran for the portal with both guns in hand.

On the way, he motioned for Bruno's guards to follow him to the Krellian ship. Lucas yelled a commando scream as he jumped into the rift like Rambo breeching a terrorist encampment.

30

When Lucas arrived on the other side of the rift, his feet slipped out from under him, sending him crashing onto the floor. He knew he needed to roll out of the way, and did, as fourteen of Bruno's security detail stormed through the portal behind him. They, too, slipped on the floor, one after another, sending them sliding past Lucas on their butts.

"Welcome to the party, pal," Lucas told the last guard to arrive.

The exchange room looked like a biological bomb had detonated: the walls were covered in a flood of orange blood, as runny chunks of the Krellian tissue oozed down from the ceiling, dripping into piles on the deck plating. It reminded him of Dexter's putrid-smelling kill room, minus the plastic.

When he stood up and walked to the banquet table, gravity tugged at the seat of his blood-soaked pants. He found the geriatric men squatting on the floor, cowering in the fetal position. The naked female translator was still alive, but lying on her side with a stubby piece of tentacle hanging from her spine. Her face and body were covered in orange tissue and she was sobbing into her hands.

Bruno's security detail deployed to cover the corridor outside the wall opening. Lucas lowered his weapons and searched the room for his brother, but couldn't find him. Kleezebee and Bruno were missing, too.

He found his disruptor vest lying next to the female translator. He looked down at it, expecting it to be smoldering. It wasn't. He hand-checked the condition of the wires and sonic pads; they hadn't overloaded as Claude had feared.

"Too bad Dad's not here to see this," he said. His father's invention was a resounding success. Well, after a little of Kleezebee's tweaking and Lucas' decision to use full power.

"Let's fan out, search the ship," one of the commandos yelled. Lucas assumed he was the leader. The name on the man's uniform ID'd him as Harkins.

"I'll join you," Lucas said, following them into the hall.

"Team leaders, I want three teams of four men. Sergeant Nash, you and Phillips remain here and guard the portal."

"Yes, sir," Nash replied.

The security teams scurried off, each taking a different hallway. Lucas decided to follow the group containing the commander. They went to the right and so did he.

The Krellian ship was divided into a labyrinth of short, angled hallways lined with flaming torches. Lucas expected the passageways to be filled with smoke, but they weren't—they were only filled with the runny splatter of orange blood and tissue.

Each shiny green corridor looked identical, making it tough for Lucas to maintain his bearings. He felt like he was running through a carnival funhouse, trying to navigate a maze of endless mirrors. Even if he rescued his brother from the bugs, he wasn't sure he could find his way back to the exchange room.

The end of each corridor had an octagon-shaped hatch that forked into two adjoining hallways. Harkins made only right turns, which Lucas assumed was the most efficient method for searching the seemingly endless network of passageways.

Lucas kept expecting to be ambushed by a Krellian welcoming party as they turned each corner, but all they saw was orange blood and tissue on the floors and walls—seemingly everywhere. It appeared the range of the disruptor vest was far greater than they hoped. Or maybe his decision to max out its power did the trick. Or both.

Either way, it didn't matter: the ultrasonic blast took out the Krellians with extreme prejudice.

Eventually they came across a twenty-foot-wide nook on the right. Access to the room was blocked by a lattice of black riveted metal bars, stamped flat instead of round. Beyond the door was a hay-like substance covering the floor. Interspersed with the hay were random patches of black and brown spots.

Just then, movement caught his eye from the back-left corner. He could see a group of human women bunched together—all of them naked.

About half of the females—two of whom were clearly under sixteen—had fully extended bellies. His mind flashed a single word that Alicia had said earlier, after they'd rescued her from the clutches of the sentinel warrior. *Breeders.*

Shit. That's right. She said the Krellians used the females as breeders in order to further their food supply of humans. His heart sank, realizing the pregnant girls were nearing full term, ready to give birth any day.

A second later, an awful odor found its way into his nose. He realized it was coming from the hay. It reeked of urine and excrement, making Lucas want to puke. Somehow he managed to hold the vomit back even though the smell was a hundred times worse than the chemical smell in Griffith's chem-lab back home.

"Let's go, men. Kleezebee's not in there," Harkins said, turning his head and shoulders to continue down the hall.

"Hey, wait a minute! We can't just leave them here," Lucas said.

"We're not here for them."

"But they're human. We have to get them out."

Harkins moved closer to Lucas, shuffling through his men. "Look, we don't have time for this."

Lucas raised his stunner and fired it at the ceiling. "Make the time, goddammit."

Harkins leaned in close and sneered at Lucas.

One of his men—the shortest of the group—said, "He's right, boss. We can't leave them here." Three more of his team stepped forward and said the same thing.

"No, we can't," Lucas added, waiting for the commander to respond.

Harkins bit his lower lip and shook his head. A few seconds later, Harkins told Lucas, "Fine, but they're *your* problem."

Lucas nodded without hesitation, knowing the delay could mean he might never see his brother again. But he had no choice; it was the right thing to do. Earlier, when Alicia first appeared through the rift, he failed to act when she held out her hand and pleaded for his help. He wasn't about to make the same mistake twice. He couldn't leave the women there to die.

Harkins told one of his men, "Hand me a brick."

Harkins took the C-4 from the man and broke it into three smaller blocks before attaching them to the inside of the door's hinges. He inserted a detonator into the center of each block, then said, "Stand clear."

One everyone was a safe distance away, Harkins detonated the explosives. The power of the blast sent the bars clanking across the hallway in a cloud of acrid smoke. "Let's move it," Harkins said, "they probably heard that and are on their way with reinforcements."

Lucas ran inside the cage, leading the way. "Ladies, you need to come with us."

None of the two dozen women budged from the back wall. He held out his right hand, trying to appear friendly and spoke again, this time using a much louder voice. "It's okay; we're here to help you. But you need to come with us right now."

A soft voice called out from the left, "Lucas? Is that you?"

"Yes. It's me," he said, stunned. He brought his eyes around to search for the source. The throng of women parted, allowing one of the smaller women in the back to work her way forward.

Lucas couldn't believe his eyes when he saw a dark-haired beauty that he recognized. She stepped forward and smiled, even though streams of tears were covering her face. "Abby? . . . How the hell?"

She flew into his arms and cried hysterically.

He held her tight, feeling the hand-carved alien tattoo etched into her shoulder. "It's okay, you're safe now."

Lucas ran it all through his head in a flash and came to the realization that the theater flash must've been some type of sampler probe, not a destructive energy dome like he first thought. It must've snatched her up, along with the rest of the students standing completely inside its perimeter. Jasmine had been cut in half because she was straddling the edge of the field, but not Abby.

Abby leaned away slightly, looking up at him with her fear-stricken eyes. "They've got Drew."

"I know. That's why we're here. Do you know where he is?"

"No," she said, shaking her head and sniffing. "I only saw him once, when they carried him past our cell."

"We have to leave, now!" Harkins yelled.

Lucas broke free from her embrace and led her out of the confinement cell. Abby stood half-crouched among the men in the hallway, with her arms and hands trying to cover her privates. Lucas removed his shirt and gave it to her to wear. The other women joined them in the corridor, flocking around him, thanking him for saving them.

"Do you remember the way back to the exchange room?" Harkins asked Lucas.

"No clue. I lost my bearings."

"I can take him, sir," the shortest man in the team said.

Harkins didn't respond right away. Instead, he turned slightly and spoke into his communicator watch. "Harkins here." A few seconds later, his eyes grew wide and his voice was charged with excitement as he spoke. "Where? . . . Okay then, secure the area."

Harkins stepped in front of the group and spoke in a command voice, making eye contact with several members of his team. "Let's get everyone back to the portal."

"What's wrong?" Lucas asked, keeping Abby close.

"We have a situation," he said, returning his attention to his team. "Let's go, men. Double time it."

* * *

After rushing through a maze of hallways, the group finally turned the last corner on their way back to the rally point, escorting the girls they'd rescued from the Krellian holding cell.

Lucas could see a group of soldiers standing guard outside the exchange room. He wasn't sure what "situation" had caused Harkins to order the fall back, but the pain in his chest was telling him it wasn't good. He feared something horrible had happened to Drew. Or Kleezebee. Or Bruno. Or Trevor. Maybe all four. Or perhaps another alien hive ship was closing in on their position.

Abby kept a tight grip on Lucas as he held her back, letting four members of the tactical squad go through the door first. A few seconds later, the other girls were ushered inside by the remaining solders. All seemed quiet, so Lucas thought it was safe to bring Abby forward. He did, keeping his arm wrapped around her as they turned left and went through the door.

The second his eyes focused on the inside of the exchange room, two things happened simultaneously: his heart lit up with a massive rush of joy, and Abby screamed, "Drew!"

There he was. Safe and unharmed, standing with the help of Trevor's powerful arm, next to Kleezebee and three members of the rescue team. His little brother's smile was full and infectious, and aimed squarely at him.

Abby ran to Drew, as did Lucas, passing a small collection of girls who were standing together.

Abby planted a passionate kiss on Drew's lips.

Lucas slowed his approach, waiting for his brother to finish the smooch and come up for air. When he did, Lucas asked him, "Are you okay?"

"I'm hungry and exhausted, but other than that, I'm fine," Drew replied with Abby's arms wrapped around his neck.

"Where the hell did you guys go?" Lucas asked Bruno.

The guard held out his watch. "We never left. We knew they'd attack, so we ducked into subspace."

"Shit, I ran right past you."

Kleezebee lifted one of his shoes, letting the orange blood and tissue drip from his heel. "You detonated the vest, didn't you?" he asked Lucas.

Lucas nodded. "Yep. Both of them. And I cranked 'em up to full power."

Harkins added, "I think it took out the entire ship, sir. We encountered no hostiles—anywhere."

Kleezebee's eyes darted about the room, obviously thinking the facts over. "The supercharged disrupter signal must've been transmitted across their bio-comm network, destroying them all." He patted Lucas on the back. "Nice work."

"Thanks, Professor. But it was just dumb luck. I really wasn't thinking clearly. I just knew I had to do something once the video feeds went dark."

"I'm sure it was more than just luck," Kleezebee said.

"I'd say more like instinct," Bruno said, sending a congratulatory nod at Lucas. "Well done, Dr. Lucas."

"Orders, sir?" Harkins asked Kleezebee.

"Search the rest of the ship. There are probably more humans on board."

"Yes, sir."

"What about the energy domes? Any change now that the creatures are all dead?" Drew asked.

"I suspect we've seen the last of the energy fields," Kleezebee said, nodding. "Assuming this ship was controlling them."

Lucas turned to his little brother and smiled. "How about that? Dad's invention might've just saved Earth!"

"Too bad we can't tell anyone," Drew replied.

"Can we go home now?" Abby asked in a soft, meek voice.

Kleezebee cocked his head in Bruno's direction. "Escort them, please."

Lucas whispered into Drew's ear, "When we get home, there's something I need to tell you about your biological father."

Drew looked confused for a moment, then nodded.

Bruno helped Drew and Abby through the rift.

Lucas stayed behind. "So, Professor, what are you going to do with your new ship?"

"I'm going to take my people home, assuming we can figure out how to fly this thing."

Lucas looked around at the blood and guts covering the walls. "It's gonna need a fresh coat of paint and a ton of disinfectant." He sniffed the air. "A little Febreze wouldn't hurt, either."

Kleezebee laughed.

31

Lucas returned to the silo through the portal and found Drew sitting in his wheelchair. Abby was sitting in an office chair next to him, still wearing Lucas' shirt. He wondered if Kleezebee intended to find her some real clothes.

Lucas checked the video screens but didn't see any active energy fields. In fact, half the screens were switched off and the room was abuzz with talk of the crisis on Earth finally being over.

They'd done it—as a group and as individuals, they'd saved the world. He felt like an enormous weight had been lifted from his shoulders. There was no way to ever make up for the people who were already dead, but at least no more were going to die because of him.

Atonement comes in small doses, he decided.

"You said you had something to tell me?" Drew asked him.

Lucas looked to make sure Kleezebee wasn't nearby. The professor was across the room, standing next to Bruno and talking with the white-robed elders from his home world. If he kept his voice down, the professor shouldn't hear him.

"You know how you always thought your bio-mom was impregnated by anonymous sperm?" Lucas said, keeping his voice calm and steady.

"Yeah."

"Well, as it turns out, it wasn't so anonymous after all."

"What do you mean?"

Lucas pointed in Kleezebee's direction; he was still in deep conversation with Bruno and the elders.

"Bruno?" Drew asked.

"No, not him . . . Kleezebee."

Drew stared at Kleezebee for what seemed like a full minute, then said, "No, I don't believe you."

"Well, believe it. It's true. He owns the fertility clinic your mother used."

Drew shook his head vigorously. "Nah, you're putting me on again, aren't you? Kleezebee would never do that."

"Trust me, it's true. Hey, look on the bright side. At least he didn't do it the old-fashioned way."

The look on Drew's face went from friendly disbelief to one of bewilderment. Then it changed again, this time showing anger and concern.

Lucas tried to stop Drew when he rolled his chair toward Kleezebee. Drew fought off Lucas' grip, sped across the room, and nearly smashed into the back of Kleezebee's leg. He tugged on his mentor's sleeve.

"Excuse me, Professor, but I need to ask you something."

Kleezebee whirled around. "Sure, what is it?"

Lucas saw Drew take in a deep breath before he spoke, like he was about to dive underwater for a long swim. "Lucas told me you're my real father. Is this true?"

Kleezebee glared at Lucas, looking more than pissed.

Lucas shrugged. "Sorry, Professor. He had a right to know."

Kleezebee turned to Drew and his face went soft. "Yes, it's true. I'm your biological father."

Drew leaned back in his chair, wrinkling his nose and flaring his eyes. "Why didn't you tell me?"

Kleezebee took a moment before he answered. "You already had a family, and I didn't want to butt in. I knew you were healthy and happy, and that's all that mattered to me. Besides, I got to see you almost every day. That was enough for an old man like me."

Drew's face turned a deep shade of red, then he looked at Lucas as if he were searching for guidance. Lucas wanted to help but didn't say anything. Drew needed to handle this on his own.

Drew turned back to Kleezebee and wrapped his arms around Kleezebee's legs, nearly knocking the man off his crutches.

Lucas could see Kleezebee fighting back tears, trying to maintain his self-control. The professor pried Drew's arms loose, then bent down and hugged him back.

When the family reunion was finished, Lucas went to Drew and the professor, realizing they hadn't brought the four-wheeled cart back from the Krellian ship. "Dr. Kleezebee, didn't we forget something? What about all the canisters?"

Bruno laughed. "They were filled with spoiled milk from the mess hall. Only the first canister I carried was real."

"So let me get this straight. Trevor wasn't transporting the enzyme?"

"No. I would never do that," Kleezebee said. "Not even for my own son. I figured they wouldn't check them, too. Not after sampling the first container that Bruno brought with him."

"Wow," Lucas said, thinking about how his boss had gambled with Drew's life, and done so based on a paper thin assumption. But it worked out in the end and he was thankful.

Kleezebee leaned on one crutch and put his free hand on Lucas' shoulder. "I hope you realize that you two, with help from your father's marvelous invention, saved billions of lives in both dimensions. All of the Ramsay men are transdimensional heroes. Congratulations!"

"Too bad we can never tell anyone," Bruno said in a matter-of-fact way. "But regardless, props to both of you. And your old man."

Drew replied with pure joy, "We have to tell Mom that Dad's invention saved the world!"

"Oh yeah, she'll love to hear that," Lucas said, realizing that atonement wasn't the only thing that came in small doses. So did vindication, though only his family and Kleezebee's crew would ever know about it. But at least it was something. Dorothy had supported John's endeavors all those years, even during the lean financial times. He couldn't remember one time when she wavered, despite constant second-guessing by her friends, her co-workers, and even her estranged father-in-law, Roy.

Lucas wondered if Grandpa Roy would ever man up and apologize for his pigheadedness. The grumpy old man would have to change his perspective once he learned his only son wasn't a dismal failure after all, wouldn't he?

"It's a shame the government will never know what we've done for them. They still think we're mass murders," Drew said.

Bruno replied, "The minute Larson recovers from surgery, the first thing he'll do is contact General Alvarez and tell him you're still alive. I doubt we can fool them again."

"He's never going to stop looking for us, is he? Even now? After this?" Lucas asked.

Bruno shook his head. "No, I'm afraid not."

Lucas asked Kleezebee, "I don't suppose you'll help us clear our family's good name? Not for me, but for Drew and my parents."

"Sorry, can't do it. Going public would require exposing our technology and our existence on your world. But what I can do is offer you sanctuary on our world. You'll be treated as heroes and live in peace."

Lucas didn't answer. He needed a moment to think.

Kleezebee continued. "Look, I know you think this is all your fault. But like I said before, it's not. NASA and I are the reason all of this happened. Not you. In the end, you had nothing to do with this. What happened in the E-121 lab was an accident, a horribly tragic accident that you couldn't have seen coming. Not when I kept you in the dark all these years. That was the wrong approach, and for that, I apologize. So right now, I need you to forgive yourself. You've done enough to atone for what happened."

"I'd like to, Professor, but every time I close my eyes, the dead haunt me. I'll don't think I will ever rid myself of the guilt, no matter what you say. And to be honest, I'm not sure I really want to."

"I understand. You're an honorable young man, Lucas. But you need to try because this simply wasn't your fault. The best course of action right now is for you to come with us to our universe. We've done all we can do here. The planet will heal eventually. It's time to go, Lucas."

Lucas let his eyes fall to the floor, feeling a feral mix of emotions spinning inside. Their lab was gone and all that was left on this Earth was a mountain of unpaid medical bills and an even bigger pile of public scorn headed his way. He had no future and neither did his family.

Plus, there were a slew of people who wanted his head on the end of a stick. Those same people would probably blame Drew as well, and possibly even his mother. There was no way he'd ever let that happen, no matter how guilty he was or wasn't—his family didn't deserve that. No, they needed to go to Kleezebee's universe. That much was clear. But at the same time, he knew Drew would never go without him.

Lucas locked eyes with his boss. "All right, I'll go. But I'm not doing this for me. I'm doing it for Drew."

"What about Mom? And Abby?" Drew asked.

"They're welcome, too. So are you," Kleezebee said, turning to Bruno. "You should probably go get Dorothy and bring her down."

Bruno spun on his heels and headed for the elevator.

"What about Grandpa Roy?" Drew asked Lucas.

"What about him?"

"I know you've been secretly emailing him."

"Only recently. But trust me, he'd never come. His military career is all he cares about."

"Don't you think we should ask him? After all, he's family."

"No. Mom would never allow it. He blew his chance with that brawl at Thanksgiving."

For the next half hour, Kleezebee took charge of the introductions between his crew and the diplomats from his home world. Then the elevator's bell chimed and Dorothy walked out of the lift with Bruno holding on to her right elbow. She was grinning from ear to ear, obviously ecstatic to see both of her boys were safe.

Lucas tugged on Drew's shirtsleeve to direct his attention away from Abby. He whispered, "Mom's here."

Dorothy came over to them, then hugged Drew and kissed him softly on the cheek. "I thought I'd never see you again." She hugged Lucas, too. "Oh, I'm so happy both of my boys are home safe and sound. I prayed all night for your safe return. Thank the Lord almighty."

Dorothy stared at Abby, who was sitting next to Drew, holding his hand. She was still wearing only Lucas' shirt, which left most of her legs and upper thighs exposed.

"Mom, this is my . . . ah . . . girlfriend, Abby," Drew replied with a look of pure fright in his eyes. "We just rescued her from the Krellian ship."

"Are you all right, dear?" Dorothy asked her.

Abby nodded and then stared off into space. She wrapped her arms around Drew with her right cheek pressed flat against his chest.

"She'll be okay, Mom. She just needs a little time to recover."

Lucas walked over to Kleezebee and asked, "How long do we have before we need to leave, Professor? I'm sure my mom will want to grab a few things." He figured Kleezebee would need at least several days to recall his people and gather up their advanced technology, since he probably wouldn't want to leave anything behind that might cause a shift in the balance of power on Earth.

"It'll take twenty-four hours to evacuate our people and equipment. You have until then."

Wow, only twenty-four hours? Lucas thought, realizing Kleezebee must've had exit plans on deck for years. "Okay, we'll be packed and ready."

"Just keep it light."

"Sure thing, Professor."

* * *

The following morning, Lucas and Drew returned to the video surveillance room with their mother and Abby. Bruno and his security team had provided protection while they returned home the night before and collected a few personal mementos, including clothes and the family photo albums. When they stepped off the elevator, they saw two groups of personnel and equipment walking through the portal to Kleezebee's home universe. The rest of the room was nearly empty.

"Are you ready to go?" Kleezebee asked.

"Yes, sir, we are," Lucas replied, helping his mother toward the rift.

Drew and Abby were a few steps behind. Bruno was carrying two suitcases filled with their keepsakes.

"What about Trevor?" Lucas asked.

"He went through an hour ago with our entire inventory of BioTex," Kleezebee said.

Lucas held onto his mother's arm as they stepped into the rift. A few seconds later, they were through and standing on the other side, where they met up with Trevor and several of the elderly diplomats they'd rescued the day before.

Now it was Drew's turn to step through.

Lucas spun around and waited, seeing a faint shadow appear near the portal's midpoint. It started as a fuzzy mass, then grew in size. After it solidified, Bruno stepped through with the pair of suitcases.

"I thought Drew was next?" Lucas asked Bruno.

"Don't worry. DL is sending him through right behind me."

"What does DL stand for, anyway?"

The round man laughed, looking at Dorothy then back at Lucas. "If I tell you, you can't let him know you heard it from me. He'll have my head."

"Don't worry, my lips are sealed. Come on; tell me, what does it mean?"

"Drockmorton Leslie."

Lucas broke into hysterical laughter. "Really? Drockmorton? No wonder he goes by DL. I would, too." Lucas let his smile and his amusement linger as he focused his attention back on the rift.

"How much longer?" Dorothy asked.

"Shouldn't be long now, Mom."

The rift shimmered a few times, then a pair of faint shadows appeared. Lucas could see the outline of a person in a wheelchair and a figure standing next to it—Drew and Abby. They were holding hands.

"Here they come," he told his mother.

Just then, the portal flickered twice like a TV set on the fritz, then the rift suddenly collapsed. Lucas watched the vision of Drew and Abby fade to a pinpoint and disappear while they were still inside the conduit.

"Oh my God!" Bruno shouted.

Dorothy gasped, squeezing Lucas' arm in a viselike grip.

"What the hell just happened?" Lucas screamed at Bruno, burning his gaze into the man. "Where's my brother?"

TO BE CONTINUED
In Book 2, Incursion (available now)

We hope you enjoyed *Linkage*, the first book in the Narrows of Time Series. The story continues in the next two books, *Incursion* and *Reversion,* both of which are available for purchase now.

BOOKS BY JAY J. FALCONER

Frozen World Series
Silo: Summer's End
Silo: Hope's Return
Silo: Nomad's Revenge

American Prepper Series
Lethal Rain Book 1
Lethal Rain Book 2
Lethal Rain Book 3 (Coming Soon)
(previously published as *REDFALL*)

Mission Critical Series
Bunker: Born to Fight
Bunker: Dogs of War
Bunker: Code of Honor
Bunker: Lock and Load
Bunker: Zero Hour

Narrows of Time Series
Linkage
Incursion
Reversion

Time Jumper Series
Shadow Games
Shadow Prey
Shadow Justice
(previously published as *GLASSFORD GIRL*)

ABOUT THE AUTHOR

Jay J. Falconer is an award-winning screenwriter and USA Today Bestselling author whose books have hit #1 on Amazon in Action & Adventure, Military Sci-Fi, Post-Apocalyptic, Dystopian, Terrorism Thrillers, Technothrillers, Military Thrillers, Young Adult, and Men's Adventure fiction. He lives in the high mountains of northern Arizona where the brisk, clean air and stunning views inspire his day.

You can find more information about this author and his books at www.JayFalconer.com.

Awards and Accolades:
2020 USA Today Bestselling Book: Origins of Honor
2018 Winner: Best Sci-Fi Screenplay, Los Angeles Film Awards
2018 Winner: Best Feature Screenplay, New York Film Awards
2018 Winner: Best Screenplay, Skyline Indie Film Festival
2018 Winner: Best Feature Screenplay, Top Indie Film Awards
2018 Winner: Best Feature Screenplay, Festigious International Film Festival - Los Angeles
2018 Winner: Best Sci-Fi Screenplay, Filmmatic Screenplay Awards
2018 Finalist: Best Screenplay, Action on Film Awards in Las Vegas
2018 Third Place: First Time Screenwriters Competition, Barcelona International Film Festival
2019 Bronze Medal: Best Feature Script, Global Independent Film Awards
2017 Gold Medalist: Best YA Action Book, Readers' Favorite International Book Awards
2016 Gold Medalist: Best Dystopia Book, Readers' Favorite International Book Awards
Amazon Kindle Scout Winning Author

Printed in Great Britain
by Amazon

11524936R00241